Titles by Christine Blevins

MIDWIFE OF THE BLUE RIDGE
THE TORY WIDOW
THE TURNING OF ANNE MERRICK

THE

Turning of Anne Merrick

Christine Blevins

BERKLEY BOOKS, NEW YORK

THE BERKLEY PUBLISHING GROUP
Published by the Penguin Group
Penguin Group (USA) Inc.
375 Hudson Street, New York, New York 10014, USA

Penguin Group (Canada), 90 Eglinton Avenue East, Suite 700, Toronto, Ontario M4P 2Y3, Canada
(a division of Pearson Penguin Canada Inc.) • Penguin Books Ltd., 80 Strand, London WC2R 0RL,
England • Penguin Group Ireland, 25 St. Stephen's Green, Dublin 2, Ireland (a division of Penguin
Books Ltd.) • Penguin Group (Australia), 250 Camberwell Road, Camberwell, Victoria 3124, Australia
(a division of Pearson Australia Group Pty. Ltd.) • Penguin Books India Pvt. Ltd., 11 Community
Centre, Panchsheel Park, New Delhi—110 017, India • Penguin Group (NZ), 67 Apollo Drive,
Rosedale, Auckland 0632, New Zealand (a division of Pearson New Zealand Ltd.) • Penguin Books
(South Africa) (Pty.) Ltd., 24 Sturdee Avenue, Rosebank, Johannesburg 2196, South Africa

Penguin Books Ltd., Registered Offices: 80 Strand, London WC2R 0RL, England

This book is an original publication of The Berkley Publishing Group.

PUBLISHING HISTORY
Berkley trade paperback edition / February 2012

Library of Congress Cataloging-in-Publication Data

Blevins, Christine.
The turning of Anne Merrick / Christine Blevins. — Berkley trade pbk. ed.
p.   cm.
Sequel to: Tory widow.
ISBN 978-0-425-23679-6
1. United States—History-Revolution, 1775–1783—Fiction.   2. Widows—Fiction.   I. Title.
PS3602.L478T87 2012   2011019252
813'.6—dc22

PRINTED IN THE UNITED STATES OF AMERICA

10   9   8   7   6   5   4   3   2   1

ALWAYS LEARNING   PEARSON

To my sister, Natalie,
childhood nights, and stories whispered under the covers

❧ PROLOGUE ❧

In the distance, the resound of ax iron biting into wood echoed up from the valley floor, adding ringing harmony to the morning song of a nearby thrush. Legs crossed tailor-style and fingers interlaced as if in prayer, Jack Hampton sat stock-still in the shade cast by a thicket of roundleaf gooseberry—his dark brows knit in concentration. Puffing out a breath, he released his hands with grand flourish, scattering eight buttons onto the dark green wool of the blanket spread between himself and his friend Titus.

"Three brown, five light!" Titus Gilmore did not bother to conceal his glee as he whispered the tally.

"*Bugger and blast!*" Jack issued the jaw-clenched curse, flicking a pair of dried beans from his meager pile into the veritable mountain of beans Titus had already collected.

With a grin akin to an undertaker's at a hanging, Titus scooped up the gaming pieces. He had sliced the buttons from a deer's horn, smoothing and shaping them to belly a bit and bevel at the edges. No more than an inch in diameter, one side of each ivory-colored disk had been stained with an umber pigment that matched the deep brown hue of his skin. With a casual toss, the former slave let the buttons fly from his cupped hand to land with the lighter sides all facing upward.

"*Pah!* You lucky bastard!" Jack eyed the results and swept his few remaining beans toward Titus. "Take them—take them all! I swear to Christ, I don't know why I bother playing this stupid game. There's no skill to it—naught but luck—dumb and pure."

"Passes the time, though, don't it?" Titus sifted his bean winnings into a small drawstring sack, judging the weight of it on his palm. "I gauge that's another dollar at least—making for a total of five dollars owed to me by one Mr. Jack Hampton."

"Aw, now, Titus"—Jack wagged a finger—"it's but three I owe."

"No. It's five. Three dollars lost at buttons and beans, and two lost at darts back in Stillwater."

Smacking the heel of his palm to his forehead, Jack muttered, "Darts."

A sudden spate of drumming coming up from the road snapped Jack and Titus to attention.

"The call to assemble!" Titus scooped up his buttons.

"Get your glass!" On hands and knees, Jack crept forward to peer through the bramble while Titus scrambled to fish a brass-cased spyglass from his buckskin pouch. Keeping within the cover of the brush, the men lay close to the edge of the ridge, propped on elbows, the nutbrown cloth of their shirts masking their presence from enemy eyes below.

Sliding the telescoping spyglass to full open, Titus aimed the lens to the south and fixed focus. "The road's been cleared."

"That can't be . . ." Jack tucked a strand of jet-black hair behind his ear, squinting to see through the hazy morning mist. "We dropped those big pines into an awful tangle . . ."

"And those big Germans have gone and cleared the tangle away—see for yourself." Titus passed the spyglass to Jack.

"Goddamn those cabbage-eaters!" Jack peered through the lens. "I thought that bit of ax work would cost them at least half a day."

"And the Redcoat vanguard is beginning to form . . . Do you see?" Titus pointed to a growing company of mounted cavalry.

Jack nodded. "They're getting ready to move, alright."

The pair inched forward as far as they dared, and watched as General Burgoyne's formidable eight-thousand-man army coalesced into a colorful double column snaking through the wooded valley.

The red-coated infantry companies followed the vanguard, marching in the lead to the trill and thump of fife and drum, their polished musket barrels aglint in the morning light. The Redcoats were followed by close-ordered ranks of blue- and green-jacketed Hessian grenadiers and Jäger riflemen. After the Germans came a large contingent of Loyalist militia, wearing mismatched clothes and carrying sundry weapons. The militiamen were followed by a cadre of Canadian hatchetmen. Many beaded-and-befeathered Seneca and Mohawk warriors marched along with their British ally, and even more Algonquian braves from the far-western frontier had joined in the fight against the hated, land-hungry Americans.

"Here comes the baggage train," Titus said. "Keep your eyes peeled for Mrs. Anne and Sally—we don't want to miss any signals."

A huge gaggle of camp followers came tagging along with a long train of carts and wagons overloaded with the supplies required to maintain Burgoyne's multitude in the wilderness. While officers' ladies were allowed to ride, the wives and children of the common soldier traveled on foot along with the herd of profit-seeking sutlers, peddlers, and prostitutes. So intent on monitoring this raucous and disordered passage, Jack did not notice the sound of oh-so-careful footfalls creeping up from behind.

A circle of cool iron pressed into his neck, the touch of it accompanied by the distinct double clack of a flintlock being pulled back to full cock. Jack did not move a muscle. Out of the corner of his eye, he could see Titus, stiff and wary, with a rifle barrel pressed into the spongy black hair at the base of his skull as well. After waiting what

seemed an eternity, a deep, ominous voice at the end of the gun intoned, "Your Yan-kee tongues echo across the valley."

Jack rolled over, swatting the Indian's gun aside. "Goddamn you,
Neddy!"

Neddy Sharontakawas, the younger of their two grinning Oneida
scouts, settled the strap of his weapon over his shoulder. "Did we
cause you t' mess your breeches there, Jack?"

Titus pulled up to a sit and gestured with the dagger he'd managed
to slip from the sheath at his belt, admonishing the elder Indian scout.
"I'd expect you t' know better than to sneak up on a man like that,
Isaac."

"I expect a man to have some sense . . ." Isaac extended a hand and
helped Titus up to his feet, his grin turned to a sneer. ". . . Four eyes
lookin' to forward and none to back—makes no sense at all."

Captain Isaac Onenshontie earned his rank fighting with Braddock's army in the Seven Years' War, and he bore his veteran status in
proud display. His Iroquoian surname, meaning "flying arm," was bestowed to honor his prowess with the war club dangling from his belt.
The cluster of eagle and owl feathers attached to the tuft of hair at the
top of Isaac's otherwise plucked pate denoted high-distinction among
his warrior brethren, and the series of blue-black arrowheads tattooed
from shoulder to shoulder, spanning the breadth of his chest, were a
testament to battles fought and enemies vanquished. Under this seasoned war chief's tutelage, Jack and Titus were learning the ways of
woodland survival and warfare, and they were both ready to accede
to the inherent wisdom found in Isaac's rough lesson.

Isaac gave still-seated Jack a nudge with a moccasin-shod foot. "We
saw your woman."

Neddy sent the turkey feathers bunched on the crown of his cap to
quivering with a vigorous nod. "And she's wearin' stripes today."

"Then we'd better get going." Jack scrambled to his feet and took
up his rifle.

To mask their party's number from British scouts, Jack and Titus
literally followed in the footsteps of their Oneida guides, treading
along a steep deer path that switchbacked down to a bend in the road.

They took a stand a little more than ten yards from the road. Crouched behind the moss- and fungus-covered mass of a fallen conifer, they watched the parade of British teamsters pass, urging sullen oxen with snapping birch switches. Though burdened with heavy pack baskets, and often with little ones cradled in knotted shawls at their hips, the soldiers' wives all seemed happy to be on the move, keeping the pace while chattering and herding their children. Jack kept watch until Burgoyne's prodigious baggage column dwindled to a handful of stragglers. Just when he figured he'd somehow missed seeing Anne, she and Sally rounded the bend, pushing a two-wheeled barrow piled high with their goods along the bumpety corduroy road.

"She's very pretty, your woman," Neddy whispered.

Annie was smiling beneath her broad-brimmed straw hat, and she was made even more beautiful by the dappled light filtering through the leaves. Peering from behind the pile of deadfall, Jack knew Anne's smiles were meant for him, and he was surprised how intensely he missed being with her after only a few days apart. It was all he could do to keep himself from running out to catch her up in his arms. He smiled, remembering he had felt the same way the very first time he ever laid eyes on Anne Merrick.

May 20th, 1766—the day we learned Parliament repealed the Stamp Act . . .

He was but a printer's apprentice back then, running the streets of New York City, passing out the broadsides proclaiming the news. *The pages were still damp and fresh off the presses, and how the church bells rang and rang . . .*

Happy, cheering New Yorkers were thronging into the streets to celebrate the good news. Jack ran up Broad Way, and handed the last of his sheets to a grumpy old Tory standing on the steps of St. Paul's, a pretty but woebegone young woman at his side.

I thought she was his daughter . . .

The girl stood forlorn in the midst of such joy and happiness, and Jack could not help but swing her up into his arms. Her sudden smile was so beautiful, he kissed her full on the mouth, and ran off to join his mates on the Commons. A brief moment on a banner day—a moment and a kiss he never forgot.

Almost ten years went by before he saw the girl again. Following a rumor, Jack and a mob of fellow Sons of Liberty paid a call on Merrick's print shop, and he recognized the Widow Merrick as the girl he'd kissed, and learned the old man he mistook for her father had, in fact, been her husband.

Poor thing. Bride to a groom three times her age . . . The thought of Anne married to the likes of Peter Merrick made Jack wince. He began to worry the dark stubble on his jaw as he watched Anne and Sally pushing their barrow along the road, skirts belling in the breeze. *Striped skirts* . . .

On one hand, the use of this most urgent signal for their very first exchange of information was a strong portent for the success of this new mission for General Washington. On the other hand, success at the business of gathering intelligence ensured it would be some time before he would hold Anne Merrick safe in his arms.

Jack held tight to the sight of Anne as she passed by—the to-and-fro of her chestnut braid marking the sway of her hips like a pendulum on a longcase clock. He watched her figure grow small, and smaller yet, until she disappeared around the next curve in the road.

The scouting party waited with quiet patience until all vestiges of female chatter and rumbling wagon wheels were borne away on the breeze. On a wordless signal, Neddy and Titus ran in the direction opposite the parade, toward the abandoned British camp. Jack and Captain Isaac moved with more careful purpose, flanking the road, eyes scouring from forest floor to tree limbs for any telltale sign.

At the sound of Ned's call mimicking that of a turkey, Jack and Isaac broke into a full-on gallop. On the straightaway, they could see Neddy off to the left, waving them in and pointing the muzzle end of his rifle up to a small scrap of blue ribbon tied to the low-hanging branch of a sycamore. At the base of the mottled tree trunk, Titus was busy burrowing like a squirrel through the loose duff.

Isaac took a lookout position near the roadbed, and Jack joined Titus digging around the tree. Neddy snatched the ribbon from the branch and tied it to the colorful clutch of feathers and silver charms dangling from his riflestock.

"Here 'tis!" Titus unearthed a corked, blue-glass bottle and tossed it over to Jack.

Jack pulled the stopper on the familiar bottle, breathing in the trace lavender scent as he shook out a paper tube. No bigger than his little finger, the tightly wound paper was tied with a thread. He pulled the scroll open and studied the writing on the narrow page, very pleased that their maiden transmission was progressing just as planned.

"Among the Redcoats but two days, and the girls have already reaped results—have a look . . ." Jack showed the missive to Titus. "A very *long* recipe."

Curious, Neddy came to peer over Jack's shoulder. "A recipe?"

"Mm-hmm . . . a recipe." Jack smiled, running a knowing fingertip between the wide-spaced lines of neatly penned instructions describing exactly how to prepare and bake a peach cobbler.

Neddy fell stern. "Your woman oughtn't wear the stripes to pass a recipe, Jack."

"Don't fret so, Neddy," Titus said with a grin. "I guarantee there's more writ on that slip of paper than what meets the eye."

"Secret writing . . ." Jack explained. ". . . Made to appear by the heat of a flame. I'll show you once we—"

"*Stah!*" Isaac cocked his head like a deer being stalked, motionless but for the feathers fluttering at his topknot. "Listen!"

After a moment's concentration, they could all discern the sound first detected by Isaac's sharp ears—a thudding canter of ironshod hooves on wood.

"Dragoons!" Titus jumped to his feet.

Jack stuffed both message and bottle into his pouch, and swung his rifle down from his shoulder. With weapons cocked, Neddy and Isaac took the point. Jack and Titus fell in behind, and the foursome melted back into the trees.

Part One

SARATOGA

With Loyalty, Liberty let us entwine,
Our blood shall for both, flow as free as our wine.
Let us set an example, what all men should be,
And a toast give the world,
Here's to those who dare to be free.
Hearts of oak we are still;
For we're sons of those men
Who always are ready—
Steady, boys, steady—
To fight for their freedom again and again.

<small>HEARTS OF OAK, Author Unknown</small>

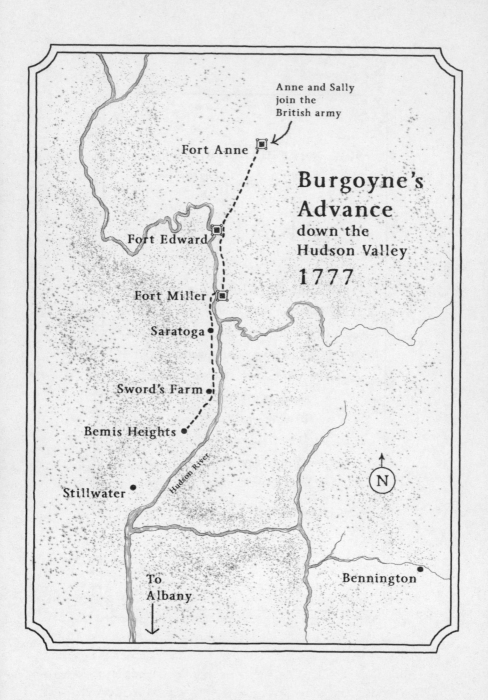

Anne and Sally join the British army

Fort Anne

Burgoyne's Advance down the Hudson Valley **1777**

Fort Edward

Fort Miller

Saratoga

Sword's Farm

Bemis Heights

Hudson River

Stillwater

N

To Albany

Bennington

✤ ONE ✤

Those who expect to reap the blessings of Freedom, must, like men, undergo the fatigue of supporting it.

THOMAS PAINE, *The American Crisis*

ON CAMPAIGN WITH THE BRITISH ARMY

"I wonder what has gone awry—" Anne Merrick collected her skirts, planted a mud-caked shoe on one barrow wheel, and hoisted herself up by a foot and a half. "Perhaps a wagon has thrown a wheel . . ."

"I dinna think so . . ." Sally Tucker drew the brim of her straw hat forward to shade her eyes, noting the sun pulsing in its zenith. "A cart with a bad wheel is easily pushed to the side. This column has not budged in some time."

Anne stepped up to improve her view, scaling the cargo piled high in their barrow.

Sally encouraged the precarious perch by taking hold of her mistress's apron strings. "Steady now, Annie . . ."

After establishing a foothold on the surface provided by their bundled tent, Anne fished a spyglass from her pocket, snapped it to full open, and scanned along the congested roadway all the way to the bend. Other than the lazy swish of bovine and equine tails chasing swarms of black flies, and the here-and-there tendrils of tobacco smoke twisting up from the wagoneers' clay pipes, Anne could detect no commotion. The forward movement of British might on the march had once again been brought to a complete standstill.

"What d'ye see?" Sally asked.

"Absolutely nothing."

The man driving the cart ahead twisted around in his seat and shouted, "Don't put yourself to such a bother, missus. I'd wager pounds to pence those damned rebels have bedeviled our progress with mischief of some sort. Before you know it, the drummer boys will come along, beating the call to make camp."

"You're most probably correct, Mr. Noonan." Anne hopped down from the cart. "Did you hear that, Sal? More rebel mischief, no doubt."

Soon enough, a pair of drummers wearing bearskin caps and green wool coats marched toward them along the shoulder of the road. Confirming Mr. Noonan's prediction, they beat the call to halt on roped drums marked with the Crown's insignia and the number twenty-four—the advance guard—the 24th Regiment of Foot.

"Hoy, lads!" Sally shouted. "What news?"

"Rebels!" one boy shouted, without missing a beat. "Dammed up the stream and flooded the road."

"No little thing, either," the other boy added, marching by. "A terrible mess—a right carfuffle up there."

The drum call touched off a frenzy of activity, and the ordered file became a noisy, confused jumble as teamsters whistled, whipped, and wrestled their beasts to claim a campsite alongside the road General Burgoyne's artificers had engineered through the wilderness. Anne and Sally joined the confusion, pushing and pulling their overladen barrow off the rutted road, coursing a path through the pasty muck churned up by hoof and wheel, aiming for a place upwind of where the teamsters were gathering their fly-plagued oxen into herds.

"Phew!" Sally's freckled face scrinched in disgust. "The smell of this camp rivals that o' the tanning pits on Queen Street, na?"

Anne drew out the lavender-infused hankie she kept tucked at her shoulder, and pressed it to her nose. "I say we find a spot on higher ground today—out of the mud and among the trees where the air is wholesome and cool."

"Oooooh . . ." Sally cast a wary city-girl eye up at the dark grove of hardwoods. "I dinna think tha's a wise course. All manner of heathens, beasts, and wee deevilocks are creepin' about in those woods. Best we just cluster in here amongst th' wagoneers and camp women."

"Deevilocks! Pish!" Anne mocked Sally's brogue. She grabbed the barrow handle and steered toward the trees. "Do you want to know what we'll find in those woods? Shade and fresh air, that's what . . . and if it storms again, those big trees will help to shelter us from the wind and rain."

"Och, but yer a willful woman." Sally ran to catch up to her mistress and help push their barrow up the slope.

Once beyond the tree line, they found many others of the same mind, validating Anne's logic. A sutler had set up a grogshop in the shade, and a company of German artillerymen were pitching their tents nearby on forested sites carpeted with fern.

Though Anne and Sally were simply attired in muslinet shifts, front-laced bodices, and summer-weight skirts, wrangling their heavy barrow up the slope proved hot work on a sultry day. Once they chose a level site beneath the canopy of broad-leaved trees, straw hats were swept back to dangle by ribbons and skirt hems were tucked into waistbands at each hip. Soon garters were loosened, and stockings were rolled into circular sausages and jammed into kicked-off shoes.

After sweeping a spot beneath a sugar maple clear of deadfall and stones, they unfurled their tent, drawing out the four corners, and orienting the door flaps to face the road. Anne pulled a strapped bundle of short poles from the barrow.

"This is much better than that first campsite we chose at the very base of a slope, don't you think, Sal?"

"What a pair of featherheads we were!" Sally said with a giggle. "An ill-wrought wobbledy mess, that tent was . . . on a rainy night, no less. That tempest was as fierce as a West India hurricane."

"I thought for certain we'd be whisked away." Anne laughed, recalling their unfortunate maiden campsite. Once the storm had let up, they claimed one of the camp kitchen fires and, soggy and sleep-deprived, commenced to baking. With a dozen bannocks and a crock of berry jam, Sally was able to entice a trio of Scots grenadiers into schooling them in the art of pitching a proper tent.

The short poles were joined with tin sleeves to form three long poles. Anne dove under the canvas, slipping the ridgepole into the canvas channel sewn into the ridge of their wedge tent. The two poles equipped with iron pins at the ends were used to prop the ridgepole at fore and aft. Once raised, Sally circumnavigated the tent and used the blunt end of her hatchet to pound iron stakes through peg loops interspersed around the base, pulling the canvas taut and pinning it to the ground. When finished, she stepped back with hatchet resting on shoulder and one hand on her hip, admiring the trim lines of their shelter.

"Perfect, na?"

"Not quite . . ." Anne poked her head out through the door flaps and pointed to the neighboring German soldiers, who were busy digging the narrow trenches around their tent meant to catch and divert rainfall.

"Fegs!" Sally's shoulders slumped. "I thought we might forgo th' trenching today. After all, there's nary a cloud in the sky . . ."

"It has rained practically every night. A little work now will save us from having a torrent running through our tent later."

While Sally trudged off to borrow digging tools, Anne dragged their cots from the barrow. The ingenious oak frames scissored open to support a narrow canvas sling that was surprisingly comfortable. She recalled that, back in Peekskill, when they were outfitting themselves to infiltrate the British encampment as peddlers, Jack disapproved of the purchase.

"Field beds are awful cumbersome cargo, Annie."

"A waste of funds," her brother, David, insisted. "True peddlers make do with a piece of oilcloth for ground cover and straw-filled mats for beds."

Straw-filled mats indeed! Anne took great pleasure dressing each cot with a goose-down pillow and a striped blanket, so glad she had turned a deaf ear to their admonishments. Though the portable beds were unwieldy to transport, a dry berth suspended above the hard, wet ground made camping tolerable.

Accustomed to city life and thick brick walls, Anne had a difficult time finding sleep as it was, with naught but a thin sheath of canvas betwixt her and all manner of nocturnal creatures throwing up a din to raise the dead on most nights. She could not imagine having to lie down among the creeping crawlers—the mere thought of it drew her shoulders into a cringe.

Sally returned with a pair of square-bladed spades on lend from the Germans. After carving a drainage channel around the perimeter of the tent, the women took a moment to admire their handiwork.

"Abroad a little more than a fortnight," Anne said, "and we've become quite expert in settling our camp."

"Och, aye," Sally agreed. "A sight better than most British army men, and as good as them pernicky kraut eaters."

"I expect David and Jack should be proud of us."

Sally sighed, her features suddenly soft. "O, but I've a fist-sized hole in my heart for my David. I miss him so . . ."

"I know . . ." Anne leaned a shoulder to rest against the maple. "I'm missing Jack as well, but we must . . ."

An odd buzz caused them both to startle. Taking a step back from the tree, Anne eyed the upper branches for a beehive or a hornet nest, when her gaze was pulled downward by an ominous slither across the top of her bare foot.

Inches from where she stood, a large snake drew into a tight coil—the stacked buttons on the end of his tail buzzing in fury as it settled into a crook where the tree root curved up to the trunk. Gray, and marked with chevrons of darker gray, the rattler's coloration blended perfectly with the bark of the sugar maple. So well disguised, in fact, if not for the rattle, Anne would have had a difficult time spotting the reptile. With unblinking, riveting eyes and its black ribbon tongue whipping in and out from between a nasty pair of fangs, the snake raised its head in challenge—poised to spring.

Anne's eyes flashed up to meet Sally's, and in complete unison they let out a pitched shriek loud enough to raise the very demons from hell. Sally swung her spade in a scything motion, catching the upright viper, and sending it into a writhing sprawl. Anne ran up and brought her spade down in an arcing swipe, like that of an executioner, severing the snake's head in one thumping blow.

Panting, with hearts a-race, they stood over the twitching snake parts with fists clenched to their weapons, ready to strike again as if the snake were capable of reuniting head to body. When the viper's death throes subsided, Anne relaxed her stance, and stepped in, about to give the motionless reptile a wary poke with her spade, when someone shouted.

"STOP!"

Anne turned to see their screams had drawn a small crowd of Hessians, Redcoats, and sutlers from the neighboring campsites.

"Take care, madam!" A British officer stepped forward, holding out a warning hand. "That rattler is yet a dangerous thing. Leave this to my friend Ohaweio—he is adept at handling these situations." The officer was accompanied by a befeathered Indian wearing a matching red coat with green facings over his bare chest and leather leggings.

Sucking in a breath, Anne nodded, and handed her spade to the Indian. Sally dropped her shovel to scurry over and clutch Anne by the arm.

The Indian carefully scooped up the beheaded snake. Ohaweio held the rattler up for all to see; it was almost five feet long and as thick as Anne's forearm. Draped over the spade, the decapitated snake began to squirm and dance. The tail once again rattled a warning, and the bleeding end—so recently occupied by a head—jerked about, to and fro, as if to strike. Of a sudden, Ohaweio tossed the snake carcass to the side, scattering a group of German soldiers with more than a few girlish cries of dismay.

The Indian considered the reaction with a wry smile before squatting down beside the severed head. He said something in his native tongue, and Anne was taken aback by the English officer's nodding understanding, and his ability to translate.

"Ohaweio praises your kill, ladies, but warns, if you continue to hunt rattlers, you must understand that venomous snakes are at their most dangerous just after the kill."

"Continue t' hunt rattlers?" Sally sputtered. "Are you mad?"

"Not mad"—the officer smiled—"only sensible to the notion that your first rattlesnake encounter will most likely not be your last in this wilderness. Ohaweio advises caution when dealing with these creatures, alive or dead."

To demonstrate this, the Indian poked the lifeless snake head with a stout twig, and the viper instantly reanimated, hissing and tasting the air with its forked tongue. To everyone's amazement, further agitation with the twig caused the severed snake head to lurch with jaws snapping, burying its fangs into the twig. Anne, Sally, and the crowd scuttled back a step, uttering a harmonic, *"Ooooooh!"*

Ohaweio began digging a narrow but deep hole, still lecturing, and the officer continued to translate. "My friend says this type of rattler delivers a particularly deadly venom with its bite, but it is generally shy of humankind, and rarely attacks. Ohaweio suggests next time, best use cautious reason and leave the creature be—the snake will most likely wriggle away without causing any harm."

"Reason!" Anne let out a laugh. "I can assure you, sir, in this instance we acted on instinct and sheer terror. Sally and I are by habit city dwellers, and quite stupid to living in the wild."

Ohaweio swept the snake head into the hole with the spade and covered it with more than a foot of tamped-down earth. The Indian pointed and laughed when, for good measure, Sally went over and hopped up and down on the spot.

"There is no doubt you and your friend have saved us from a deadly situation." Swiping a sweat-drenched strand of chestnut hair from her brow, Anne noted the knotted silver braid adorning the officer's shoulder, the sash at his waist, and the ornate hanger sword at his side. "Please convey our sincerest thanks to Mr. Ohaweio, Captain . . . ?"

The officer bowed with a sweep of his feathered hat. "Captain Geoffrey Pepperell, of His Majesty's Twenty-fourth Regiment of Foot."

"How do you do, Captain Pepperell?" Anne dipped a shallow

curtsy. "Mrs. Anne Merrick, the camp's purveyor of writing materials, and my servant, Miss Sally Tucker."

Pepperell acknowledged them each with a nod. "I must say I am most impressed, Mrs. Merrick—a purveyor *and* an accomplished snake killer—Mr. Merrick is one lucky fellow."

"Hmmph!" Sally puffed. "Dead as a doornail, tha's what ol' Merrick is."

"A widow?" The corners of Pepperell's mouth twitched up for the briefest instant before correcting to a more compassionate frown with brows knit in proper concern.

Anne put her skirt to rights, working her hems free from her waistband, and she exchanged a look with Sally. Tall and lean, with skin tanned as tawny as his Iroquois companion, this Redcoat captain was the highest-ranking officer they had yet to engage in prolonged conversation, and a member of Brigadier General Simon Fraser's Advance Guard to boot. "Widowed five years now . . ." she said, drawing her hat onto her head. "Hence the need to peddle my own wares, and kill my own snakes."

"A trying time for you, no doubt." The Captain slipped his hat under his arm and struck a casual pose, when the Indian stepped forward. Spewing a long string of unintelligible syllables, Ohaweio brandished the decapitated snake torso in his fist, sending Anne and Sally skittering back in a yelp.

"Fear not, ladies," the Captain assured with a laugh. "Ohaweio simply wonders if you intend to eat your snake."

Sally's blue eyes went agog. "Eat it? *Feich!*"

Pepperell flashed a charming grin. "Snake meat is quite a delicacy, considered by many a welcome change from salt meat."

Sally puckered her face and shivered. "I'd sooner eat my weight in cow patties than nibble on the meanest morsel of tha' poisonous viper . . ."

"Captain Pepperell." Anne stepped forward. "Please tell Mr. Ohaweio he is more than welcome to the snake. I would like to offer you something in thanks as well . . . perhaps a cup of tea? We've a fine bohea on hand, and Sally could have a pot brewed in no time."

"I wish, Mrs. Merrick, I could join you, but as I was en route to a meet with my command when diverted by your distress, I really must be on my way." Geoffrey Pepperell fit his hat on his head. "Perhaps I might be allowed to impose upon your tea supply another time?"

"I assure you, sir"—Anne smiled—"it will by no means be an imposition."

"A pleasure to make your acquaintance, Mrs. Merrick." The Captain waved a gallant salute. "Till we meet again."

The women stood side by side watching Pepperell and Ohaweio weave a path through the trees. "It's a wonder how he babbles on in that outlandish heathen tongue, na?" Sally noted. "A spruce fellow, though—cuts a fine figure wi' a fancy feather in his cap and all . . ."

"Quite a handsome man . . ." Anne added, her eyes yet on the Captain. "Pleasing to the ear and to the eye."

"Oh, it's clear yiv caught his eye, as well," Sally said, with a waggle of her brow. "But best not let Jack know how charming and handsome your quarry is. Ye remember how he was the last time ye worked yer wiles on a Redcoat."

Sally's mention of Jack caused Anne to turn from the sight of the handsome Captain, and in a voice sharper than intended, she said, "That was before Jack knew I was working for the cause."

"Still, I worry." Sally placed a hand on Anne's shoulder.

Anne jerked away. "Don't waste your worry. This Pepperell is a very likely source for us. Jack would know, as *you* should know, the only interest any British soldier holds for me is in the intelligence I might glean from him to aid our cause. Becoming one with the enemy is how you and I soldier, Sally." Marching over to the barrow, Anne tugged a pair of tin pails free. "Let's get a fire going. I'm going to fetch some water for a wash."

"Aye, Annie—make yourself pleasant, and I'll commence baking," Sally said. "Time for us t' go a-soldiering."

Face washed, hair combed, and outfitted in a spotless apron, Anne Merrick marched up the road. The peddler's case she wore suspended by straps on her back like a soldier's knapsack bounced in time to her step and the cheerful tune she whistled.

This day is bright with possibility.

The business of gathering intelligence was an art—a complex combination of happenstance, intuition, and reason. It was an art, Anne found, she had a talent for.

When the British Army invaded New York City the summer before, the world was turned upside down, and Anne adjusted her coffeehouse business to cater to the Redcoat occupiers, doing as she must in order to survive the occupation.

Under the sign of the Crown and Quill, she learned the true value of keeping mind open, eyes sharp, and ears ready. She and Sally moved from table to table serving tea and scones to their very British clientele. They gathered empty mugs and plates along with earfuls on Redcoat military strategy and policy, sweeping up intelligence regarding troop movements and munitions shipments like so many crumbs into a dustpan.

To make the information useful to the rebel cause, Anne connected with an old friend of Jack's who ran a tailor shop on Queen Street. She and Sally were at once enmeshed in the tailor's spy ring, collecting valuable intelligence for the flailing Continental Army Command.

Under martial law, Anne was compelled to quarter British soldiers in the rooms she and Sally kept above the Crown and Quill. Seizing the imposition as an opportunity to expand their operation, the women set to beguiling the enemy officers housed under their roof. Not only did Anne gull Captain Edward Blankenship into divulging military secrets; Edward escorted her into the social echelon of the British High Command—where she was able to winnow even more vital information from the heedless prattle around punch bowls, gaming tables, and dance floors.

The peddler's case on her back seemed suddenly heavy, and Anne stopped for a moment, to shift its weight and catch a breath.

Poor Edward! A decent man used most cruelly . . .

Try as she might, she could not dispel the memory of him—lying on the floor of her shop wreathed in red-black blood—killed by a lead ball fired point-blank to his head by her own hand.

Blankenship was a casualty of war, Anne told herself for the hundredth time. She should not—could not—regret pulling the trigger. That one shot rescued Jack from Edward's expert blade and certain death. That one shot also safeguarded her dearest friends from the hangman's noose.

That shot saved my life.

Anne put a kick in her step, and set her mind to the business at hand. Defeating the British and driving them from America's shores would put an end to such casualties, for all.

Upon rounding the bend, she slowed her pace. Twenty yards ahead, the road disappeared in a swirl of murky water that had washed over the banks of a parallel running stream. A huge maple tree—its trunk at least four feet in diameter—lay across the stream. Large slabs of limestone and mounds of loose scree had been tumbled from the adjacent hillside to collect around the maple in a solid, water-diverting mass. Due to the recent rains the stream was flowing strong and high, and the rebel dam was perfectly situated to create an impasse on the road Burgoyne's engineers had carved between the foothills of the Adirondacks.

The air was filled with the ring of sharp iron on wood and punctuated by the crash of falling timber as axmen harvested the lumber from the adjacent woodland to bridge over the flood-damaged road. In a mix of English and German, officers strode about shouting orders at the soldiers standing waist deep in the stream, prying up stones, and shoveling up buckets of gravel. The debris was passed from hand to hand in a human chain snaking out onto dry land.

Straining on ropes lashed to the maple tree trunk, at least a dozen soldiers struggled with slippery footing trying to dislodge the dam. Others scrambled with hatchets and axes, hacking away at the tangle of branches and limbs.

A right carfuffle indeed! Duly impressed by rebel ingenuity, Anne veered from the road to the nearby encampment. She selected a tree stump near a marquee tent as an inconspicuous place to set up shop

and observe enemy operations under the guise of purveying her
wares. Slipping the shoulder straps, she set her case near the stump.
Cleverly wrought with brass fittings, the box opened like a clamshell
to lie flat in display, each half fitted with suitably sized cubbyholes
fully stocked with her wares.

Anne straightened the jostled contents to make a more attractive
display. The supplies for letter writing and record keeping were in
high demand, and she did a fair business among the Redcoats. She carried a good stock of quill pens, ink, and pencils—both graphite and
lead. Sundries like sealing wax, wafers, and the small sacks of ground
soapstone for dusting freshly inked pages sold tolerably well. When
all was said and done, individual sheets of writing bond and the
pocket-sized notebooks she and Sally stitched into leather covers were
top among her best sellers.

Anne removed a pair of placards strapped to her case, and set out
her sign. Hinged at one end to stand like an easel, fancy gilt block letters on a black ground proclaimed her business:

MERRICK'S FINE PAPER,
PENCILS, PENS, INKS,
AND SUNDRY GOODS

On the alternate face, she advertised her letter-writing service in
her best cursive script:

*for Letters Scribed
in a Fair Round Hand
apply to
Mrs. Merrick, stationer*

Anne took a seat on the tree stump. Adjusting her hat brim to
shade her eyes from the sun, she crossed her ankles and surveyed the
area.

*A cat's paw in this revolution, I am . . . and who knows what chestnuts
might be scratched up from the ashes today . . .*

Oh, she had not thought twice when her brother David, aide-de-camp in General Washington's command, asked her to infiltrate Burgoyne's camp. Operating under the same guise of staid Tory widow that had served the cause so well in New York, she and Sally were able to roam the British encampment freely, gathering information to pass along to Jack and Titus for delivery to the beleaguered Continental Army of the North.

Anne pursued her vocation with an egalitarian awareness, for gossiping with the camp laundresses at the washtubs could prove more fruitful than a conversation with the high-ranking officer whose linen was being scrubbed. And the gossip so readily gathered from sutlers providing rum and ale to the Redcoats could be as telling as any battle map.

At the very onset of their venture, this awareness reaped instant results. While waiting in a long queue to present her peddler's permit to the camp quartermaster for approval, Anne had noticed a young couple bidding each other farewell. She pointed to the pair and used the euphemism often applied to American girls who had succumbed to the charms of a Redcoat soldier.

"See there, Sal . . . Another poor girl struck with a bad case of scarlet fever."

"A soldier's farewell is aye bittersweet." Sally nodded, no doubt recalling her recent parting with David.

"Strange . . ." Anne's brow knotted. "We've both taken him for a soldier, yet he's not in uniform, is he?"

Touched by the tender kiss the pair exchanged, sentiment did not blind Anne to the soldier's bearing, ill-concealed by the yeoman's smock shirt and broad-brimmed hat. A moment later, she gave Sally a confirming nudge to the ribs when the lovers were parted by an officer ordering the young man to be on his way, to which he responded with an "Aye, sir!" and a snappy military salute.

Anne and Sally scurried over to comfort the tearful girl with the offer of a clean hankie and a commiserating, *"There, now, lass . . ."* In no time at all, the girl revealed her beau's true calling as special courier for General Burgoyne to General Howe, and—most important—

she divulged the location of the secret missive he carried in the false bottom of his canteen.

Between the lines of an innocuous recipe for peach cobbler, Anne conveyed these details written in an invisible ink she concocted with water and salt of hartshorn. The next morning, she and Sally donned their striped skirts and tied a scrap of blue ribbon to a low-hanging branch of a sycamore tree.

An auspicious beginning . . . If Jack and Titus had indeed found the message, and captured the courier, then they had intercepted an urgent message en route from General John Burgoyne to General Sir William Howe, the Commander-in-Chief of British forces in North America—information that could prove vital in achieving a battlefield victory the American forces so badly needed.

Palms pressed together like a penitent in supplication, Anne could not help but think on the less than happy consequences of her pursuit. If Jack and Titus had indeed captured Burgoyne's courier, then the young man she'd last seen tenderly kissing his lass farewell was most certainly hung for a spy—led straight to the gallows by the careless words of the woman who loved him so dear.

It was a tragedy very real and horrible to Anne, and the thought of it brought about a familiar wrench in her heart as the image of her son, Jemmy, bounded unbidden into her mind's eye—the boy she'd lost to smallpox five years before. The son she loved and missed with all her heart. Anne took in a deep breath.

At least that girl will never know she was responsible for the death of her beloved.

Be they Tory or Patriot, a steep toll was exacted on all who were unlucky enough to be arrested as spies. Anne had witnessed a spy's hanging on the Commons just days after New York City fell to the British. She massaged the sun-warmed skin curving up from her shoulder to her ear, recollecting the stoic patriot's single-minded clarity as he faced ignoble death, his last words a testament to his true purpose.

I only regret that I have but one life to give my country. Anne thought on those words whenever she found herself dwelling on the tragic by-blows of her pursuit or pondering over the variety of "what-ifs" and "maybes."

Anne gave her head a shake. *Deep thinking—a perilous pastime for soldiers at war.*

And she *was* a soldier. Like the brave patriot she'd seen stand the gallows, Anne endeavored to keep the ideals of the cause she fought for at the forefront of her brain, pushing the heavy consequences down into the depths of her heart.

"How much for a quill, miss?"

Anne glanced up. A bone-thin subaltern stood before her, juggling a heavy stack of ledgers under one arm while digging for coin in the pocket of his baggy breeches. Taking note of the number twenty-one embossed on the pewter buttons of his jacket, she answered, "Merrick's quills are but a tuppence for one of the King's finest fusiliers."

"Tuppence!"

Anne held a goose feather up for his inspection, demonstrating the resilience of the nib with her thumb. "A quality point, this. You'll find my quills properly trimmed and tempered to last."

"Here you have it . . ." The ensign dropped a two-penny piece in her cupped hand and took the quill. "The adjutant is yowling at me to get the company books in order."

Giving a nod to the turmoil on the road, Anne said, "Make good use of the time. Looks like our lads will be at least another day fixing this mess."

"Why the General chose this godforsaken route is beyond my ken." The young man shrugged. "The rebels are a constant irritant, and every day we delay is yet another day for them to wreak further havoc."

"Chin up, ensign. You are among the King's finest fighting men," Anne said. "I was in New York town, and I saw firsthand the stuff these jelly-boned rebels are made of. What a ragtag, misbegotten lot they are! When met on the battlefield, they will be easily routed. Never fear."

Anne's bombast earned her a soul-shrinking glare from the young officer. "I am *not* afraid, miss, but the rebels have proven they are no-body's fool," he said, tapping a finger to the ledgers under his arm.

"They understand how an army travels on its stomach, and how every delay serves to dwindle our meager provisions. These marauders move in our advance, burning crops and carrying off every bit of livestock, making it nigh on impossible for us to find forage. I fully expect the entire army will be moved to half rations soon."

The gloom-and-doom subaltern scuttled off to his bookwork, and Anne penciled the sale into her ledger. It was encouraging to hear the rebel tactics were having an effect on British supply lines, sensibilities, and stomachs. A soldier's daily ration of flour, salt meat, and dried peas was barely enough to keep a man in fighting fit—a move to half rations could only compound the many trials Burgoyne's army was already bearing.

"Mrs. Merrick!"

Looking up, she smiled, and waved to Captain Pepperell in the company of another officer striding her way. Rising to her feet, she greeted the men. "Welcome to my emporium—such that it is."

The officers whisked hats from heads, and Geoffrey Pepperell threw an arm around his friend's shoulder. "Allow me to present my comrade-in-arms and all-around good fellow, Lieutenant Gordon Lennox." Anne dipped a slight curtsy to the Captain's ruddy-faced companion, and Pepperell continued the introductions. "And this, Lennox, is Mrs. Anne Merrick—Purveyor of Fine Stationery and Snake Vanquisher Extraordinaire."

"The Rattlesnake Widow?" Lennox cocked his head in a nod and snapped a salute. "A pleasure indeed, madam! Geoff has regaled me with the tale of your kill."

"My kill!"

"As you can see, Mrs. Merrick," Pepperell added, "your fame precedes you."

"I would rather find fame in a manner that did not include a poisonous viper slithering over my foot, thank you very much." Anne's smile came with ease. She found herself liking this Geoffrey Pepperell. Unlike many of the stodgy martinets populating the officer corps with their off-putting aristocratic affectations, he was possessed of a rascal's charm combined with a sincerity that appealed—much like her Jack.

"This is fortuitous, finding you here on my doorstep!" Geoffrey took her by the hand. "I was only just on my way to seek you out—wasn't I, Gordie?"

"Coming to claim the promised cup of tea?" Anne asked.

"Coming to invite you to dine at the General's table tonight."

Anne pulled back her hand, and laced her fingers just beneath her breastbone, taking a moment to rein in her elation. "I don't know . . . The presence of a woman at a table of fighting men can only serve to scotch the wheel of conversation—"

Lennox interrupted. "Other women will be in attendance, Mrs. Merrick—my wife, Lucy, among them . . ."

"I will not take no for an answer," Geoff said. "As one of the providers of the feast, it is only fitting you should partake."

Anne's brows shot up. "A provider of the feast?"

"Rattlesnake soup!" Pepperell said. "Promise you'll come . . ."

Anne laughed. "I don't see how I can refuse."

"Wonderful! I'll come to escort you to the General's camp at sundown." Pepperell slapped Lennox on the back. "Away to the kitchen, Gordie, to see to our soup."

"The General's table . . ." Anne settled hands on hips, watching the pair march away. "Now, that is quite a chestnut!"

Sally threw back the painted canvas they had drawn over their barrow to protect the content from inclement weather, and Anne stood by, chewing her thumbnail.

"I really don't recall packing it, Sal . . ."

"Well, I *do*." Sally delved down to the very bottom of the barrow. "Hold on, now . . . Here 'tis!" She squirmed a misshapen, muslin-wrapped, twine-bound bundle from beneath the tarp, and tossed it over.

"Huzzah!" Anne peeled away the wrapping to unfurl her best day dress. As she held the gown at arm's length, her brows merged in dismay.

The garment was made of quality fabric—yards of imported

indiennes printed with a happy pattern of forget-me-nots twining over a cream-colored ground—but the dress was terribly crushed and wrinkled. Limp with damp, the Mechlenburg lace edging the sweeping neckline and embellishing the three-quarter sleeves drooped in a sad display.

"Dinna fash, Annie." Sally jerked her thumb to the plumes of smoke rising up east of the road. "The washwomen have their pots on the boil and their irons on the fire. A bit of starch and a good pressing will put your frock to rights."

Anne threw the dress over her shoulder and pulled forth the mending basket from the barrow. "We've plenty of blue ribbon. I can make some rosettes to dress my hair."

Sally tossed a hairbrush and a pair of iron curling tongs into the basket. "We can put a few curls in as well. Ye'll be the prettiest lady at the table."

They ran down to cross the road, and headed toward the stream where the camp laundresses took advantage of the easy access to water and a sunny day to catch up on the never-ending wash. Anne and Sally zigzagged through yards of clothesline stretched from tree to tree, hung with dozens of shirts pinned up to dry.

"Would ye just look at the amount of linen they have flaffin' on the breeze!" Sally noted. "The campwives are th' true workhorses of any army."

They burst through the maze of wet clothing onto a small clearing flanking the stream. Abuzz with industry and redolent with the clean steam of lye soap, this laundry-on-a-wilderness campaign was an enterprise to be admired.

Sally shouted, "Ahoy, Bab!" and waved to a tall woman agitating one of two great iron cauldrons on the boil.

Swiping face to forearm, the red-faced woman stepped back from her task and waved. "Ho there, lass!"

A half dozen women were working the laundry pots, their skirts immodestly kilted up above their knees to protect the fabric from being scorched or—worse—catching fire. Armed with a long, flat-paddle battledore, Bab agitated the boiling wash water and fished clean linen from the huge pot onto a sheet spread on the ground. Once cool, a pair of women twisted the sopping linen into ropes, wringing out the excess soapy water before moving it into a simmering copper tub filled with a rinse of starch and bluing. More stirring, another wringing, and the clothes were hung to dry.

While their mothers toiled, small boys and girls made a game of gathering and stacking piles of deadfall to fuel the fires beneath the pots. Bigger boys helped to tote buckets of water from the stream. Young girls flitted between the clotheslines, pinning up the wet laundry and gathering the dry for ironing.

"Bab! We've come t' ye in dire emergency," Sally explained. "My mistress is invited to dine among the quality at the General's table this very evening, and we find her finest frock in this sorry state."

"The General's table, ye say!" Barbara Pennybrig leaned in on her battledore, clever eyes shifting from the dress Sally held out for inspection to settle on Anne. "Caught the fancy of an officer, have ye?"

"That she has," Sally boasted. "A winning fellow, aye? A captain in Fraser's Twenty-fourth."

"So," the washwoman met Anne's eye and asked, "are ye aimin' t' become this captain's ammunition wife?"

"Ammunition wife?"

"Aye. His bed companion for the duration."

"Ochone, Mrs. Pennybrig, mind yer wicked tongue!" Sally bristled. "Mrs. Merrick is nothing if not a chaste and proper widow."

"I mean no offense, Mrs. Merrick, but I've belonged to this army for five and twenty years, and I surely ken the way of it—I do. A proper young widow ought be very wary of this captain." Bab dipped her battledore into the cauldron and pulled forth a sopping mound of linen. "A chaste young widow ought consider that this captain may have mischief on his mind."

Anne said, "You misunderstand. This man is an officer and a gentleman . . ."

"This is no rough-necked regular we're speaking of." Sally's brow crinkled with worry.

"An officer *and* a gentleman, you say." Bab slapped the steaming clothes onto the sheet. "I tell you true when I say it is no uncommon a thing for our gentlemen officers t' charm and woo a woman simply to fulfill the comforts once provided by the proper wife left behind. A widow might save herself a heartbreak by heeding my advice, aye . . ."

"I appreciate your concern, Mrs. Pennybrig," Anne said, "but I aim only to accompany the gentleman to dinner. I have no plan or desire to be any man's wife—standard or 'ammunition.'"

"Oho, Sally!" Bab laughed. "She's a smart one, yer mistress. Let's see t' her frock." The washwoman took the dress in hand and gauged the quality of the lace between thumb and forefinger. "Flemish, aye? Very fine, this. A dip in the starch and blue will bring it back to life." Producing a seam ripper from her pocket, Bab began to pick at the stitches, carefully removing the lace from the gown. "The dress could stand an all-over pressing as well . . ."

"At what charge?" Anne asked.

"Sally tells me yer a scribe—a lady what writes letters?"

"I am."

"And a lovely, schooled hand she has," Sally piped in.

"We might trade skills," Bab offered. "I've been wanting to have a letter scrieved to my Billy's sister, since he fell at Breed's Hill, but I haven't the silver for it."

"How sad," Anne said. "I had no idea Mr. Pennybrig was listed among the fallen."

"Ah no! Sergeant Pennybrig is hale and hearty as you or I. It was my first husband who fell at Breed's Hill—Bill Galey—the finest grenadier in His Majesty's Forty-seventh Foot. I followed Billy and the Forty-seventh for over twenty-three years." Though Bab's voice explained very matter-of-fact, Anne could see a sad softening in her eye. "Sergeant Pennybrig was kind enough to favor me with a convenient marriage when Bill died, so's I could continue on with the regiment."

"I'm so sorry . . ."

"Ahhh, yer sorrow's wasted on me, dearie. Many a campwife were left widows and shipped back to England as paupers due to Howe's misjudgment of the Yankees on that hill. Pennybrig's a good man with a big heart, and I'm lucky to have him." Bab draped the delicate lace pieces over one shoulder. "Come along. We'll take this dress to the Crisps for pressing, and then I'll see to the lace."

Anne and Sally almost ran to keep up with Bab Pennybrig's quick-step, sweeping through the maze of drying linen to the ironing station situated in the shade cast by a fragrant grove of spruce trees.

Three ironing tables—nothing more than wide planks covered with thick felt pads—were propped between barrels. Nearby, a small fire blazed, where flat irons of various shapes and sizes rested on a grate just above a layer of red-hot coals.

A heavyset woman in her middle years and three young women stood off to the side near a tub of water, passing a dipperful in agitated conversation. Anne was amused to see that Mrs. Crisp, the aptly named ironing woman, was conversely as soft and round as a dumpling. Though younger and considerably shapelier, the three Crisp girls all shared their mother's fair hair, blue eyes, and pretty features.

"Hey-ho, Emma!" Bab called.

Mrs. Crisp tossed the dipper into the tub and scurried forward, all a-swither. "Have you heard the awful news? Burgoyne's savages have turned wild agin' us!"

"What on earth are you talking about?"

"Scalping and . . . and murder!" Emma began to sob into her apron, her shoulders heaving. "Woe befall all bloody savages! My poor girls! Oh, what's a body to do? What's a body to do?"

"You must take hold, Emma." Bab pulled a tin flask from her pocket. "Have a tot of rum and pull yourself thegither."

Apple-cheeked Mrs. Crisp emerged sniffling from her apron to take a long, healthy draught from Bab's flask.

"That's better, aye?"

Emma blinked and nodded, helping herself to another drink before passing the flask back. The girls edged in, gathering around their mother. The eldest was no more than eighteen years—and the younger two were perhaps fifteen or sixteen, and alike enough for Anne to consider that they were probably twins.

Bab settled an arm around her friend's shoulders. "Now that wits have been collected, tell us exactly what it is yiv heard, and who ye heard it from."

Emma drew a deep breath, and began. "My lad Will—the one Pennybrig took into the regiment as a drummer? He just fetched over the news. A local lass engaged to marry one of Burgoyne's officers was seized by the General's savages on a rampage, shot dead, and most horribly scalped."

The eldest daughter added, "Her name was Jane MacCrea—a real beauty, Will says—with lovely red hair. She was on the way to marry her man—an officer here with the Loyalist brigade."

One of the twins added to the lurid detail. "The drunken Indians came whooping into camp today, ye ken how they do, with those bloody scalps swingin' from their belts . . ."

The eldest Crisp girl reclaimed control of the camp gossip. "Jane's beau at once recognized his beloved's red tresses, and he demanded the General avenge her death, and hang the murderer with all haste . . ."

"As he well ought," Bab said with a nod.

Emma Crisp closed the tale. "But the Indians not only refused to give up their man; they threatened to leave the camp. Will says Johnnie Burgoyne, afeart of losing his Indian cohort, has capitulated in favor of the redskin murderers, who continue t' roam free amongst us as we speak!"

"Good al' meggins!" Bab's flask reappeared, her head wagging in disgust. "Indians! Set me on edge the day they marched into our camp, they did. It's no wonder these Americans flock to the rebel standard when they are beset by such savagery employed by the Crown. I always said no good can come from loosing the heathens on English folk—no good at all."

"Barbara Pennybrig!" Emma chided. "If your Bill could hear you talk . . ."

"Ahh, my Bill harbored no love for the red man. We both bore witness to their horrors in Canada, fighting with Wolfe back in 'fifty-nine."

"But the Indians are our allies here," Anne said. "They fight *for* the Crown."

"Blether! The savages give a fig for the Crown! It's plunder and scalps they fight for—nothing more." Bab passed her flask on.

"They give me a bad case of the all-over fidgets, they do, hooching and heeching around their campfires after dark." Sally swallowed a scoof of rum. "I've caught several of the devils eyein' my hair with bad intent."

"Mind yer daughters, Mrs. Crisp," Bab warned. "For one thing is plain—loyal or rebel, the savages certainly seem t' covet the blond and ginger scalps."

Emma Crisp shivered, and the fair-haired Crisp girls huddled closer to their mother.

"Poor Jane MacCrea . . ." Anne took a sip from the flask. "Such mayhem was bound to occur once Burgoyne gave rum and stretch to his Indians."

"Yiv the right of it, Mrs. Merrick," Bab agreed. "Reckless Burgoyne is, feeding the redskins liquor and setting 'em loose on the settlements to slaughter and pillage at will—knowing full well the brutes can no more discern the difference between a Loyalist and a rebel than I can between an Ottawa and a Mohawk."

Emma asked, "What are we to do, if the Crown will not protect us?"

"Naught. For better or worse, we belong to this army and muckle good it does us trying to fathom the brain-workings of kings and generals." Bab pushed the gown into Emma's arms and regained possession of her flask. "Suds, starch, and hot irons—those are our concerns, ladies."

Sally wound the excess cording about her palm and issued a warning. "Brace yerself, now . . ."

Anne dug her heels into the earthen floor of their small tent. Knees locked, muscles clenched, she tried hard to present a counterforce as Sally gave her stay strings a series of good hard tugs. "I surely miss having my bedpost to cling to."

"There!" Deftly fastened in a reliable knot, Sally tucked the loose ends behind the leather-bound edge of the stays. She then tied an embroidered pouch around Anne's waist, settling it to hang over her left hip. "See t' filling yer pocket, and I'll ready my needle."

The women jockeyed for position in the narrow aisle between the two cots—Sally gathering her sewing things, and Anne rifling through the confusion for the necessaries to equip her pocket for the evening—a folding fan, a scent bottle, a clean handkerchief, and the token Jack had given her before the Redcoats came to invade and occupy New York. She never went anywhere without her token, and the General's table would be no exception.

Anne found the broken shard of cast iron amid the bits and bobs in her everyday pocket. No bigger than a walnut, the iron token weighed heavy in the palm of her hand. Jack wore its mate strung on a leather thong about his neck, and, when puzzled together, the two halves formed a whole—a small crown.

"For us—a token to remember the day by," Jack had said, when he pressed it into her hand the day the Declaration of Independence was first read aloud.

Rebellion and war ensured her days together with Jack had been memorable, but also few, far between, and never free of strife. Anne sighed, grasping the broken chunk of cast iron tight in her fist. Relishing the bite of rough metal digging into her skin, she whispered with conviction, "My heart belongs to you, Jack Hampton," before slipping it to sink down to the bottom of her pocket.

Sally glanced up from threading her needle. "What's th' matter, Annie?"

Anne shook her head, quick to swipe her sudden tears away with the hem of her shift. "This tent is worse than an Indian sweat lodge," she said, snatching up the fresh-pressed overdress, pushing her arms through the sleeve holes. "Best hurry and stitch me into my frock, afore I melt into a puddle."

"'Tis as hot and steamy as th' devil's nut bag, na? I can just feel my hair forming into a mad frizz."

While Sally joined the front edges of the bodice together with neat whipstitches, Anne fussed with the starch-stiffened lace that edged the scooped neckline. Grabbing a gauzy scarf from the jumble of garments strewn across the cot, she draped it over her shoulders, criss-crossing the ends to mask her exposed décolletage. "Sally—have you a pin in your cushion for this fichu?"

"Fichu? We'll have none of that . . ." Sally looked up and snatched the scarf away, letting it flutter to their feet. "Ye'll tempt more bears with that bit of honey, aye?"

"But where there is honey, bears come uninvited." Anne reached down to retrieve the discarded fichu.

Sally slapped her hand away. "Tha's th' point, in't it? Now just hold still—"

Anne tried not to fidget as Sally finished the seam, and just when the thread was knotted and snipped off, a masculine voice called, "Mrs. Merrick? Are you within?"

"It's him!" Anne whispered.

Sally poked her head between the door flaps and called, "Patience, Captain! My mistress will be with ye in a blink." Turning back, she pulled a rouge pot from her pocket and thumbed tint onto Anne's cheeks and lips. "Mr. Pepperell is very dashing in his regimentals, and yer th' very picture of lovely—a fine couple ye make."

Anne hissed, "He and I are *not* a couple."

"Ah, g'won, I meant nothing by it . . ." Sally whispered back. "I ken well where yer true heart lies—as do you, aye?"

Anne drew a deep breath. Puffing it out slow, she focused to relax the lines in her forehead and ease the tension in her neck, keeping her voice low. "I didn't mean to snap at you, Sal, but as much as I wish for us to achieve results, I so *dread* putting forth the requisite charade . . ."

Grasping Anne square by the shoulders, Sally leaned in a scant inch from her ear. "Neither of us enjoys being at th' beck and boo of these lobsterback scoundrels, but such are the quirks an' quillets of the battles we fight. As ye once said—there are many who bear far worse than we for the same cause."

Sally straightened one of the blue ribbon rosettes pinned into Anne's upswept curls, turned her friend toward the door flaps, and whispered, "Off wi' ye, now—bat yer eyelashes and flaunt yer bubbies—for Liberty and Country, aye?"

≈ TWO ≈

The success of the cause, the union of the people, and the means of supporting and securing both, are points which cannot be too much attended to.

THOMAS PAINE, *The American Crisis*

THE GENERAL'S TABLE

As twilight tipped into nightfall, Anne walked along with Geoffrey Pepperell from one end of the camp to the other. The cicada's pulse gave way to the chirp, croak, and buzz of cricket, toad, and katydid, and the moon had yet to show its face, making it difficult to traverse the uneven path. Anne held her skirts in both hands, picking her way carefully. "I had no idea the General's quarters were so far removed from the rest of the camp."

"Remote, but well worth the trek—Gentleman Johnny travels with an excellent larder, and his cook is studied in the French technique."

"Hold on . . ." Anne hopped and braced a hand to Geoffrey Pepperell's forearm, her foot extended out from beneath the hem of her gown. "It seems I've caught something in my shoe."

Before she could issue protest, the Captain was down on one knee, his warm fingers cradling her ankle. He slipped her shoe free and shook the hindrance into his palm. "An acorn." Pepperell tossed the nut over his shoulder, and held her shoe up for inspection. "This, madam, is as silly a shoe as I've ever seen on a military campaign."

Made of red brocade and decorated with rhinestone buckles, the silk pumps were the finest pair she owned. Anne braced a hand to the Captain's shoulder as she slipped her foot back into what was, admittedly, a silly shoe. Fingering the thick silver braid and fringe of Pepperell's epaulet, Anne said, "I notice you've also come figged out in your finest adornment."

"Touché!" Geoffrey Pepperell laughed, rising to a stand. From top to bottom, the dashing Captain was attired in his best—beginning with the lush ostrich plumes on his broad-brimmed hat, all the way down to the skintight white breeches tucked into polished cordovan boots. He carried an ivory-handled pistol tucked into a satin sash tied at his waist, along with a brass-hilted sword in his belt. A black silk cravat was tied loose at his throat, and the shirt beneath his red coat was ruffled at neck and cuffs.

Pepperell took Anne by the hand and pulled her along. "Look there—see?" He pointed toward the large tent coming into view. "Gentleman Johnny's marquee."

Amid the capricious blink of fireflies and stars popping onto the ever-darkening sky, Burgoyne's marquee tent beckoned. Framed by a silhouette of maple trees, the tent's oiled silk was illuminated from within, and it glowed as if fashioned from amber glass.

"How pret—!" The heel of Anne's shoe caught in soft earth, and she stumbled forward with arms flailing like a whirligig. Quick to react, Pepperell grabbed her, and kept her from pitching headlong into the dirt.

"Steady . . ." Hands lingering at her waist, his lips to her ear, he murmured, "I curse Negligence—why didn't I think to bring a light?"

Anne stepped away and began fiddling once again with her shoe, her voice a bit too loud. "And I curse Vanity, who bade me to don these ridiculous slippers. French heels after all the rain we've been having—what was I thinking?"

"I think you should lift your skirts—" Pepperell answered, a wicked twinkle in his eye. "At least until we cross over this muddy patch."

Like dipping a toe in bathwater, Anne hiked her hemline and

tested her footing before venturing forth. Feeling the boggy ground yield under light pressure, she pulled back as if scalded.

Pepperell took a few steps forward. "A quagmire. Your fancy slippers will not survive it. I must carry you over."

"Carry? Oh, no . . ." Anne spun around, but without a light, she could not figure an alternative route. "Such an imposition . . ."

"Come . . ." Arms wide, Geoffrey said, "I'm happy for any excuse to sweep a woman off her feet."

With awkward hesitation, Anne moved in and placed her arms about his neck. The Captain dipped down and swooped her up with ease. Cradling her like a babe, his right arm supporting her legs was lost in a froth of skirts and petticoats, and his left necessarily supported her back. The tips of his fingers pressed into flesh inches away from her breast, setting her heart a-race. Wriggling to shift into a less intimate hold, Anne found she only incited the Redcoat to tighten his grasp.

"Best not squirm, or we'll both go tumbling into the muck," Pepperell said. "Ready?"

No! Anne thought, but she nodded and said, "Yes."

Geoffrey moved forward slowly on the soft and slippery ground, his hanger sword thumping against his hip. It was a warm evening, and Anne could feel the heat of the man's body penetrating through the layers of linen and wool.

Jack would not like this, she thought, with an audible groan.

Pepperell paused. "Pardon?"

"Nothing . . . It's just . . ." She raised the timbre of her voice to mask the blatant pounding of her heart. "I'm—I'm so sorry my silly footwear is causing you to tote me about like a sack of turnips."

"Sack of turnips!" Without breaking stride, Pepperell gave her a little toss into the air. "You are no more than a bundle of feathers. I could carry you for miles."

Miles! Anne ached for the fan in her pocket. She was in the dark, in the woods, in the arms of a man—not Jack—and she was sweating.

Take a breath . . . not much farther . . . Anne focused on the glint of rhinestones rising and falling beyond the hemlines of her skirts as her feet bobbed up and down.

The Redcoat was not as tall or broad-shouldered as Jack, and he smelled different—not bad—just different. *Sandalwood.* That was the scent he wore.

Jack is soap, leather, and ink, and Geoffrey is . . . Anne stopped herself. *Jack would not like this.*

"Almost clear . . ." Pepperell murmured in her ear.

Anne looked up at his handsome face scant inches away, and even though his features were lost in the shadow of his broad-brimmed hat, she could somehow tell he was smiling, and she began to relax in his arms.

"And there you go—" Pepperell stopped and set her on her feet. "Silly slippers safe and sound."

"Such an imposition. Thank you, sir." Anne tugged at her stays, and smoothed her skirts. "Had I known, I might have . . ."

"Shhh!" Pepperell cocked his head. "Do you hear it?"

A faint melody hovered above the nighttime din.

Anne nodded. "A flute!"

Geoffrey hummed along for a bit before guessing, "Haydn, I think."

"Whatever it is, it sounds lovely . . ." Anne tugged the fan from her pocket and beat cool air onto her flushed face. "A respite from fife, drum, and the drone of those Scotch pipes."

They followed the melody to the area behind the marquee tent, where their fellow dinner companions mingled around a long table set in a clearing within a cathedral of tall maple trees. Off to the side, a quartet of mustachioed musicians dressed in Hessian green played a serenade on flute, hautboy, viola, and cello.

The fact that Gentleman Johnny did not stint when it came to his own comfort was common knowledge in the camp. Rumor claimed Burgoyne's personal baggage required no fewer than thirty-five carts equipped with special springs so as not to damage the delicate content he insisted on transporting along the rough and corduroy roads. Anne always assumed such camp talk to be gossip-fueled exaggeration, but she was struck dumb witnessing firsthand the level of elegance Burgoyne managed to drag into the wilderness.

It was as if she'd stepped into another world. The dining table sparkled under a scattering of glass lanterns suspended in the tree branches overhead. Ten place settings of the finest china, crystal stemware, and cutlery she'd ever seen were laid out on lustrous damask cloth. At the table's center, a silver bowl exploded with woodland blooms and was flanked by beeswax tapers burning in four-arm candelabra—the wavering candlelight dancing pretty among the maple leaves. Adding to the otherworld quality, plumes of scented smoke emanated from half a dozen cressets—the iron cages containing burning cedar knots situated just so around the perimeter, to keep mosquitoes and other pests away. After weeks of rough living under soggy canvas in the company of teamsters, sutlers, and camp followers, Anne could not help but be both enchanted and intimidated by the scene and the company.

"A moment, Captain." Anne stopped beneath the awning of the marquee to smooth her curls, fluff her skirts, and assess the quality of the waiting company.

The three ladies in attendance were dressed in shining satin and taffeta. Two of the five men wore the blue coats of the German dragoons. The other three wore British red. With the exception of Geoffrey Pepperell, and the pretty brunette smiling at Burgoyne's side, the men and women all wore their hair pomaded, powdered, and curled, as if dressed for presentation to the King himself.

Anne assumed the young woman with Gordon Lennox to be his wife, Lucy. The older officer speaking with Burgoyne was dressed in the uniform of the 24th Foot. This man was very familiar to Anne, though she could not place him in her memory. The presence of German officers came as a complete surprise. Fishing a handkerchief from her pocket, Anne blotted her brow and the back of her neck.

"I fear I'm underdressed . . ."

"Don't be silly. You are perfect."

"You're kind, Captain, but I'm neither blind nor stupid." Anne stuffed the hankie away and opened her fan to cool the flush from her cheeks. "Who is the brunette in blue?"

"Ah! That would be Fanny Loescher, the General's . . . companion."
Pepperell wagged his eyebrows. "They say she is part Huron."

Anne took heart in the fact that Burgoyne's paramour did not
bother to powder her black curls. "Miss Loescher is quite beautiful."

"The woman is no 'miss.'" Pepperell kept his voice low. "There is
a Mr. Loescher somewhere, but it seems he and the General have
come to a . . . a mutually beneficial arrangement for the duration."

"Really?" Anne arched her brows. "Would you say Mrs. Loescher
is the General's ammunition wife?"

Pepperell seemed disconcerted by the phrase. "Something of that
nature."

Anne pointed toward the two men in blue. "Are those Hessian
officers?"

"Brunswickers. The tall man is Colonel Friedrich Baum. The
portly fellow is his commander, General von Riedesel."

"And the tiny lady in yellow? The German general's mistress?"

"No, she is his true wife—the *Baroness* von Riedesel. A most dedicated woman, she follows the campaign with three children in tow—
her youngest yet a babe in arms."

Tall, and very distinguished in his full Redcoat regalia, General
Burgoyne noticed Geoffrey and Anne lingering on the outskirts and
waved them into the circle. "Young Pepperell! Come join us!"

All eyes turned and Geoffrey offered his arm. "Come along, Mrs.
Merrick, and I will make you known."

Fingers light on Pepperell's forearm, Anne swallowed back the
tightening in her throat and resisted a strong urge to hide behind the
unfurl of her fan. The quiet tone of this intimate party was a contrast
to the lavish military affairs she'd attended with Edward Blankenship
in New York, where it was easy to become inconspicuous in the hubbub. Here, with her plain hair and cotton dress, she was as flagrant as
a sparrow in a nest of cardinals.

"How do you do?" Anne smiled and nodded as one by one she was
presented to the company.

". . . my commander, Brigadier General Simon Fraser of the
Twenty-fourth Foot, Advance Corps," Geoffrey completed the round

of introductions. "And, last but not least, may I present Lieutenant General John Burgoyne, Commander of His Majesty's Canada Army."

"A pleasure," Anne murmured, dipping an abbreviated curtsy.

Simon Fraser stepped forward with a slight bow. "Your name and visage breed familiarity, Mrs. Merrick, but I canna fathom the how or why of it . . ."

His controlled Scottish burr combined with a close-in look at his features provoked an instant thud of recognition in her chest. This man had often frequented the Crown and Quill in New York, espousing a particular fondness for Sally's scones and peach jam.

Anne fluttered her fan, floundering for a response, when Pepperell offered, "Perhaps, sir, you've spied the lovely lady about the camp. Mrs. Merrick supplies the army with paper, ink, and quill, and her signboard proclaims 'Merrick's Stationery.'"

"Ink and quill . . ." Fraser repeated, eyeing her with a furrowed brow. "Aye . . . that must be it . . ."

"Take your seats, ladies and gentlemen!" Burgoyne ordered. "Dinner is served."

John Burgoyne claimed one end of the table, and Simon Fraser the other. Anne did not want to encourage any more recollections, especially one that might link her to the British officer she left dead on the floor of the Crown and Quill. She scurried to the chair on Burgoyne's right, as far as possible from the scrutiny of the 24th's commanding officer.

Fanny Loescher settled languid in a chair across the table from Anne and Geoffrey. Moving together as if fastened with buttons, the three German guests sat beside Mrs. Loescher. Once Lucy and Gordon Lennox took the remaining seats beside Geoffrey, the musicians struck up an energetic *allemande*, and four red-jacketed waiters capped with feathered turbans marched out from the marquee, each carrying a green bottle swathed in white cloth.

"Oh, dear Johnny! More champagne?" Fanny squealed and clapped her hands. "I swan! You *are* aiming to see me tipsy!" Set off by the pale blue satin of her gown, the woman's olive skin glowed in the candlelight, and her rouged lips parted in breathless anticipation as the orderlies reached in to fill the crystal flutes.

"An excellent vintage," Burgoyne assured his guests. "Mrs. Loescher and I sampled a glass while waiting for everyone to arrive."

"Now, tell the truth, Johnny." Fanny Loescher smiled and snapped open her fan. "You know very well we sampled more than one glass."

Anne and Lucy Lennox hid their smiles behind their fans. With a roll of her eyes, the Baroness von Riedesel did not bother to conceal her disdain for the General's paramour.

Burgoyne stood with glass raised. "I give you His Majesty, the King! God bless him!"

"The King!" The response came in a clatter of crystal, and everyone partook in a sip from his or her glass.

General von Riedesel rose and, in clipped, precise English, said, "To my patron, Charles, the Duke of Brunswick and Luneburg."

"The Duke!"

Colonel Baum popped up to his feet in a click of boot heels, his accent heavy. "To Braunschweig—ze home auf fightink men. *Prost!*"

"To Brunswick!"

Simon Fraser rose, his glass held high. "To Caledonia—the nursery of learning, and the birthplace of heroes."

"Caledonia!"

Geoffrey Pepperell leapt to his feet and put a diplomatic end to the nationalistic sparring. "A toast to honest men and pretty women of all nations!"

Anne raised her glass, and smiled. *To these United States.*

"Hear, hear!"

The waiters returned bearing the first service—rattlesnake soup ladled into shallow, wide-rimmed bowls. Each diner was served a miniature loaf of bread along with a dish of fresh-churned butter.

"Lennox and Pepperell have provided the soup course tonight," Burgoyne announced. "The wonderful bread is supplied by the courtesy of Baroness von Riedesel."

"Proper wheat loaves!" Lucy Lennox marveled.

"And it's still warm!" Anne tore her crusty roll in two. "What a special treat, Baroness."

"I am simply the intermediary," the young Baroness acknowledged. "A clever countrywoman of mine has contrived a portable oven from bricks she salvaged at Fort Anne. General Burgoyne supplied the flour and sponge. It is wonderful, no?"

Geoffrey and Gordon's rattlesnake soup proved to be more of a stew—chunks of tender snake meat in a brown broth thick with onion, carrot, beans, and potatoes. Other than the Baroness, who seemed to approach her bowl with the same trepidation Anne was feeling, everyone else seemed to relish the dish. Anne screwed up her courage and took a taste, surprised by the flavor. "It is *delicious* . . ." she assured the Baroness. "The taste of it puts me in mind of something . . ."

"Much like frogs' legs, I think," General Burgoyne offered.

"Exactly," Anne agreed, though she'd never in her life consumed a frog leg.

"Is it true, Mrs. Merrick," Lucy Lennox chirped between spoonfuls, "that you hunted down and killed this very snake with your own two hands?"

"I fear the tale is growing in the telling." Anne laughed. "There was no hunt. My maid and I simply reacted as anyone might when faced with sharing a campsite with a venomous pest."

"To enlighten the diners," Lennox piped in. "It should be noted that the 'pest' Mrs. Merrick faced was almost five feet in length and, in girth, the thickness of my forearm."

Geoffrey added, "My native scout claims it is one of the largest timber rattlers he's ever seen . . ." And with that preamble, he launched into an animated recounting of the adventure. ". . . and then Miss Sally Tucker replied," Pepperell concluded, putting on an exaggerated brogue, *"A'd sooner eat ma weight in coo patties, than nibble on th' meanest morsel of tha' poisonous viper . . ."*

Laughing along with the company, Simon Fraser clapped his hands together. "Now I recollect! You were the proprietress of the Crown and Quill, Mrs. Merrick, were you not?"

Anne forced a calm smile. *Careful.*

"The Crown and Quill, sir?" Geoffrey asked.

"A tea shop in New York town. A Scots lass by the name of Sally Tucker was at work there, producing the finest scones this side of the Hebrides . . ."

Undone by his recollection, Anne chose her words with care. "Sally is with me still, sir, baking her scones, bannock, and shortbread for the camp. She suffers no difficulty in selling her wares. I shall have her deliver a batch to you in the morning."

Fraser lifted his glass. "Grand!"

Geoffrey Pepperell shifted back in his chair. "So you own a tea shop in New York?"

"Actually, I own a printshop in New York." Anne's heart beat as fast and furious as the drum call to assemble. She took a slow sip of champagne and gathered her wits. Jack had advised it was best to keep to the truth as much as possible when put to any question—especially a question she'd rather not answer.

"You see, I come from a printing family—trained to set type and mix ink since I was a small girl. As is common in our trade, I was married off to a printer, bringing my skills to benefit his business. When Mr. Merrick died of the pox five years ago, I inherited Merrick's Press and Stationery."

"And the tea shop?" Pepperell persisted.

"The tea shop is merely an offshoot enterprise wrought by the rebellion. When the Sons of Liberty took control of the city, rebel mobs ran rampant and Loyalists were persecuted—some tarred and feathered. Those Loyalists who did not leave of their own accord were being run out of town. As Merrick's had always catered to a Loyal clientele, my shop was stormed by a mob who ruined my press and stole my types. I did not cotton to the notion of being forced to leave my wherewithal, so, digging in our heels, Sally and I took to selling coffee and scones in order to survive." Anne put on her best smile. "As you can imagine, we did not actually serve any tea until General Howe regained control of the city."

Lennox held his glass high. "To India tea and the restoration of civilization!"

Everyone laughed and touched glasses.

"I visited New York with Mr. Loescher this winter past." Fanny held her glass out and one of the waiters stepped forward to renew her supply. "It is a dirty, smelly place."

"The city has seen better days," Anne agreed.

Fraser said, "It's a wonder, Mrs. Merrick, that you survived to see Lord Howe's army regain control of the island. It must have been difficult for you during the rebel occupation."

Anne gave a little shrug. "As my girl Sally would say, needs must when the devil drives."

"We welcome you to our cadre, Mrs. Merrick," John Burgoyne said, "but I have to wonder what has compelled you to leave the safety of our British bastion in New York town and join this army on its journey?"

Anne looked the General straight in the eye. "I am bound for Albany, sir, to begin a new venture with my brother. At his suggestion, I took along my stock of wares and joined the army as a purveyor, and it is proving to be a safe and profitable means of transport for a widow alone."

Much to Anne's relief, her answer seemed to satisfy the General. He called for red wine to be served prior to the second service, and attention was diverted while bottles were uncorked and glasses filled.

"A new wine requires a new toast." Burgoyne rose to his feet once again. "May the enemies of Britain be destitute of beef and claret!"

"Hear, hear!"

General Fraser contemplated the red liquid in his glass. "Perhaps, Mrs. Merrick, you can refresh my memory. I seem to recall an incident—some recent tragedy at the Crown and Quill . . ."

Fluttering her fan at high speed, Anne could feel her face go red. "An awful, awful tragedy. It pains me so to even think on it . . ." Angling toward General Burgoyne, she put her wineglass to her nose, breathing deep.

Simon Fraser would not allow her to avoid the conversation. "An officer quartered in the rooms above the Crown and Quill set upon by rebel banditti, or some such, as I recall?"

"A truly horrible affair." Anne steadied her nerves with a good gulp of claret, giving herself a moment in which to spin a fairy tale for the persistent General Fraser. "Three officers were quartered in the rooms above my shop. We had all gone out for an evening of Faro and punch at Mrs. Loring's on Broad Way. Not feeling well, one of the officers returned home earlier than the rest of us. He must have surprised some miscreants who had broken into my shop, and he was brutally attacked with knife and pistol."

"Thieves?" the Baroness conjectured.

Anne nodded. "Or perhaps rebel spies searching for intelligence, as the officer in question was aide-de-camp to Howe. But I most suspect rebel fanatics bent on instilling terror among New York's Loyal citizenry. All rooms were ransacked, and the words 'Tory Take Care' were scrawled in blood on my floorboards." She forced a shudder. "You cannot imagine coming home to such a nightmare. Perhaps it was cowardly of me, but I took the dire warning to heart, and quit the city that very night."

"Far from cowardly . . ." Pepperell reached beneath the tablecloth, and rested his hand on Anne's knee. "I think you are one of the bravest women I've ever met."

Anne rescued the handkerchief from her pocket, dislodging Pepperell's hand from her knee in the process, and dabbed at an imaginary tear. "Oh, I don't know about brave . . ."

"You are certainly wise to seek sanctuary under your brother's roof," Fraser added. "Your continued loyalty to the Crown seems to have earned you the enmity of ruthless men."

"Spineless rogues, these rebels—" Burgoyne's tone filled with scorn. "Preying upon women."

Anne nodded. "It was foolish to think that I could survive the turmoil of war without the protection of a man."

"Not to worry, Mrs. Merrick." John Burgoyne reached over and gave her hand a brief squeeze. "You are traveling under my protection now, and I will see you safe to your brother's keeping in Albany."

"To Albany!" Pepperell proposed.

Anne raised her glass again in silent toast. *To Jane MacCrea, and all Americans who've suffered under British protection.*

Waiters bearing the second service emerged from the marquee to set groaning platters upon the table. Delicate poached trout fillets were garnished with a watercress salad dressed in sweet oil and vinegar. Thick slices carved from a charred saddle of venison swam in mushrooms and rich gravy. In the most fanciful presentation, a brood of roasted pigeons with beaked heads intact were glazed with maple syrup, stuffed with butternuts, and set inside a nest contrived of mashed sweet potatoes.

Lucy and Gordon Lennox took command of the dinner conversation, discussing the latest in theater, music, and literature, and no further mention was made of politics or rebellion. Every now and then, Geoffrey Pepperell leaned in to murmur in her ear about the food or drink. A misty fog floated in, hugging the trees, adding to the dreamlike quality of the evening. Sipping champagne from crystal, surrounded by cultured accents and the tink of silver on china, all overlaid with mellow notes played on cello and viola—if she closed her eyes, Anne could almost forget there even was a war.

Anne set her champagne glass to the side. *You are a soldier. This is the enemy.*

"Attention!" Fanny Loescher began tapping a spoon to her glass. "Attention, ladies . . . Shall we all go and pluck a rose?"

The women were each supplied with a lantern, and Fanny led the way into the woods, weaving to and fro along a fairly straight path, until, succumbing to the quantity of spirits imbibed, she fell backward into a thicket of fern. Lucy and Anne tugged Fanny to her feet.

"I swan, I'm about to burst! This is as likely a place as any to water the garden." Fanny proceeded to hitch up her skirts and squat.

Standing side by side, the Baroness, Lucy, and Anne turned their backs to Fanny, set lanterns on the ground, and extended their skirts outward, creating a curtain for modesty's sake. The young German baroness was the first to strike up the requisite small talk to disguise the shush of urine driving into the forest floor.

"It is worrisome, indeed, to see how lean the General's table has grown," she clucked. "Rattlesnake soup indeed!"

"The fare seemed very generous to me," Anne said. "Wine and yeast bread—fresh poultry, fish, and meat—this is quality far beyond standard rations."

"At Fort Anne we were regularly served eight courses with as many different wines, Mrs. Merrick," Lucy explained. "It is clear this overland trek is taking a toll on the General's larder."

"Mrs. Loescher is certainly a drain on his wine supply," the Baroness said, without even altering the volume of her voice.

"Your turn, Mrs. Lennox." Fanny took Lucy's place in line, holding out her skirts.

"The General seems less than his usual self tonight, Mrs. Loescher," the Baroness said. "Is he not feeling well?"

"He has his moods." Fanny heaved a sigh. "A courier arrived from Howe this afternoon, and Johnny's been out of sorts ever since. Very upset, he was, upon reading that letter . . ."

Anne tempered her eagerness at this revelation. "Bad news, was it?"

Fanny shrugged. "He didn't say, but it could not have been good news for all his huffing and puffing."

"It must have been a long letter . . ." Anne probed. "I would think men of such import would have much to say to one another . . ."

"Not long at all," Fanny said. "Written on the tiniest slip of paper folded into a hollow silver bullet—in case the courier needed to swallow it to keep the message from falling into enemy hands."

"Very clever," the Baroness said, "but can you imagine having to pass such a thing through your bowels?"

Lucy Lennox rejoined the line, and the Baroness stepped back to take her easement. Anne mined a new vein of conversation. "I suppose you ladies have heard the sad news of poor Jane MacCrae?"

Lucy nodded. "What a tragedy. Her beau went absolutely mad with grief . . ."

"Another reason for Johnny's foul mood—he was dealing with his Indians all morning long." Fanny hiccupped loud, pressing a hand to her stomach. "Pardon me! Too much rich food, I fear . . ."

"Too much champagne, Mrs. Loescher," came the Baroness's forthright response from behind the curtain of skirts.

"A great bulk of our Indian allies have deserted today over the Jane MacCrae affair," Lucy said. "Mr. Lennox is quite concerned."

"I said 'good riddance to bad rubbish' when I heard they left. Thieving and drinking rum is all Indians are ever good for." Fanny swayed in such an ever-growing orbit, she clutched Anne by the arm to keep from pitching forward. "But Johnny is terribly upset. He says we'll be needing every fighting man—redskin or white—to break the rebels' backs."

"It is plain to see why the General is troubled," Anne said, linking elbows with Fanny, "what with the rebels wreaking all manner of havoc, and his Indians gone wild. They say supplies are dwindling fast and there will be a move to half rations."

The Baroness stepped forward, and Anne stepped back to take her turn behind the curtain. Collecting her skirts into a bunch on her lap, she kept an ear on the conversation.

"Never fear, Mrs. Merrick; shortages will be temporary," the Baroness said, fanning open her skirts. "My husband tells me Colonel Baum will soon lead his regiment on a major foraging expedition. He is to seize rebel stores at a place called Bennington—provender, horses, and wagons—all is to be had there in great quantity."

"Colonel Baum." Fanny giggled, bumping Lucy with her hip. "He's a big, handsome fellow—"

Flustered, Lucy said, "Colonel Baum seems a most serious and disciplined commander, but I wonder, will one German regiment serve the purpose?"

The Baroness nodded. "Most certainly. Baum's dragoons are ranked among our finest warriors, and General Burgoyne is also assured that a good number of countryside Loyalists will also rise up and join the effort."

Anne was amazed. The simple business of "plucking a rose" provided more valuable information than any of the time she spent sitting right beside General Burgoyne at the dinner table. As the feminine contingent trooped back to the table, Anne began to compose in her head the message she would send to Jack, eager to get back to her tent and writing materials.

But the evening was far from over. Once the women resumed their seats, the waiters swooped in with the dessert course—gooseberry tartlets served with dollops of sweet cream surrounded by a colorful array of comfits and lozenges.

As the host, General Burgoyne initiated the evening's entertainment with a reading of a rather drab poem he had penned himself. Lucy and Gordon Lennox followed his lackluster recitation with a harmonic version of "Scarborough Fair" sung *a capella*. With a little urging from her husband, and using the viola as accompaniment, the Baroness sang an Italian aria in an angelic soprano.

"Brava!" General von Riedesel led, with fervor, the enthusiastic applause for his wife.

Burgoyne tapped his glass for attention. "I have it on good authority that General Fraser has prepared a bit of theater for us—"

Simon Fraser stood, drew his shoulders square, and cleared his throat. "From *Henry V*, by William Shakespeare:

> *If we are mark'd to die, we are enough*
> *To do our country loss; and if to live,*
> *The fewer men, the greater share of honour . . .*

Anne had never been to a real theater, but her family spent many an evening reading aloud the works of Shakespeare, which were prime among the volumes in her father's library. *Henry V* had never been among her favorite plays, as she preferred the comedies, but Simon Fraser's impassioned delivery combined with his slight Scottish burr lent an air of romance and dash to his performance.

> *From this day to the ending of the world,*
> *But we in it shall be remembered—*

We few, we happy few, we band of brothers;
For he to-day that sheds his blood with me
Shall be my brother; be he ne'er so vile,
This day shall gentle his condition;
And gentlemen in England now-a-bed
Shall think themselves accurs'd they were not here
And hold their manhoods cheap while any speaks
That fought with us upon Saint Crispin's day

After applauding Fraser's declamation with gusto, Anne reached into her pocket to clutch the little half-crown token she shared with Jack. How the world had changed, where she, too, was a soldier owning pride and kinship for her own "band of brothers," and the desperate cause for which they risked all.

"Bravo, General. *Bravo!*" the Baroness cheered. Mindful that Colonel Baum beside her, who, with his limited command of the English language, seemed close to nodding off, she added, "Mrs. Merrick, perhaps you can uplift the spirit of this gathering with a gay song or poem?"

Anne laughed, shaking her head in the negative. "I'm afraid my talents do not extend beyond setting down words in ink or lead type."

"Killing snakes," Geoffrey added, raising his glass of port in salute. "You are very good at killing snakes."

"I heard a clever riddle . . ." Fanny offered.

"A riddle!" Lucy Lennox clapped her hands. "Do tell, Mrs. Loescher. I so love riddles!"

Fanny Loescher stood to perform with black curls tousled from her fall into the fern, her rouged lips in a smear. Clutching the stem of her glass in a fist, she took one last gulp. Bracing a hand to the tabletop, she leaned forward, and the brown crests of her nipples peeked over the edge of her blue satin gown and her ample breasts readied to escape the confines of her dress at any moment.

"Now, listen carefully, and see if you can guess the answer." As if reciting a nursery rhyme to a child, Burgoyne's mistress launched into a singsong recitation—

My pretty friends, fain would I know,
What thing is it 'twill breed delight?
It strives to stand, but cannot go,
It feeds the mouth that cannot bite.

"Oh dear!" Lucy Lennox went wide-eyed. German brows shot up. Geoffrey Pepperell began to shake with stifled laughter, and Anne hid her blush behind her fan. Burgoyne issued a terse, *"Mrs. Loescher!"* but Fanny paid him no mind, and carried on with her riddle.

It is a pretty pricking thing,
A pleasing and a standing thing.
It was the truncheon Mars did use,
The bedward bit that maidens choose.

Fanny hiccupped, giggled, and winked. "Do any of you gentlemen *have* the answer? I know Johnny does . . . I'd wager Colonel Baum *has* the answer; don't you think, Baroness?"

A grim Baroness von Riedesel pushed back her chair. "The time has come for us to bid adieu, General . . ."

"On the contrary, Baroness, it is time for Mrs. Loescher to bid adieu to our party." Burgoyne took Fanny by the arm, but she jerked from his grasp, and scampered over to stand behind Simon Fraser.

"Does no one know the answer?" She giggled. "Here's another clue—

It is a friar with a bald head,
A staff to beat a cuckold dead.
It is a gun that shoots point-blank,
And hits between a maiden's flank.

"That is enough, Mrs. Loescher." Stern-lipped Burgoyne chased after Fanny as she skipped around the table, reciting the last verse to her riddle.

It has a head much like a mole's,
And yet it loves to creep in holes.
The fairest maid that e'er took life,
For love of this, became a wife.

Clapping two hands firm to Fanny's shoulders, John Burgoyne steered his drunken mistress toward the marquee tent. "Say good night, Mrs. Loescher."

"Cock!" Fanny shouted instead. "It's a man's cock!"

The abrupt departure of their host combined with the riddle's answer served as a match, igniting guffaws among the men and much fan flutter among the women. The dinner party drew to a hasty close as the guests parted ways in a murmur of "A pleasure" and "Till we meet again."

Pepperell borrowed a pierced tin lantern to light their way and, offering an elbow to Anne, said, "Best hold tight, at least until we reach the road."

"I will," she said, taking hold of his arm. "I'd hate to fall down à la Fanny Loescher plucking a rose . . . square on her hind end in the bracken with her skirts about her ears!"

"Skirts about her ears, you say? Hmmm . . . perhaps I ought think twice before ensuring your stability . . ."

The Captain's bold innuendo sparked a thrill Anne immediately tempered with innate female wariness. Over the course of the evening it was clear this officer was of a different stamp from those she'd manipulated in the past. Geoffrey Pepperell was not one for following standard protocol.

Very unlike prim and proper Edward Blankenship . . . but very much like Jack.

Anne drew her arm away, stopped in her tracks, and mustered up some widow-like sternness. "I never would have accepted your invitation to dinner had I known that I would encounter such ungentlemanly behavior. If I did not require the light you bear, I assure you, sir, I would part company with you this instant."

"Of course you are correct, and I apologize for overstepping the bounds." Very contrite, Geoffrey at once bowed and offered his hand. "I blame my lapse in manners on too much time spent in the company of rough men. I humbly beg pardon."

Being too dark to see his face with any clarity, Anne responded with a cool, "Pardon granted," and took his proffered hand with an uneasy sensibility that the man was not at all sincere in his apology.

Pepperell led the way with the door of the lantern open to offer the most light. Other than a muttered "Careful, now" and "Mind your step," the hand-in-hand pair reached the corduroy road in uncomfortable silence, where their quiet trek was instantly made friendlier by the scattered campfires flanking the road, and the here-and-there glow of wedge tents lit from within.

Anne pulled her hand free as they set forth on the road, but the Captain immediately reclaimed it. "A moonless night coupled with those silly slippers make for a treacherous path." He then launched into a long and amusing story of how he and Lennox had prepared the snake soup.

"Mind, Gordie Lennox is the finest of fellows, and my best friend, but he is no cook. I doubt he's ever boiled water for his own tea, so you can imagine, he near lost his breakfast watching Ohaweio skin the snake . . ."

The tension Anne carried in her shoulders slipped off, and she found herself laughing as Pepperell described his cooking adventure. "Lennox may be a disaster in the kitchen," Anne said, "but he and his wife sang a lovely duet this evening."

"Gordie is an asset to any drawing room," Pepperell acknowledged. "And the Baroness—she owns a voice suited for the finest opera house in London. Quite a surprise."

Anne nodded and added, "I enjoyed your commander's recitation. His selection from *Henry V* was most stirring."

Slipping his arm around Anne's waist, Pepperell's hand settled too comfortably above her hip. "I found Mrs. Loescher's riddle most stirring . . ." he leaned in and murmured into her ear. "My pretty friend, fain would I know, what thing is it 'twill breed delight?"

The warmth of his breath and timbre of his voice sent a confused tremble of pleasure and fear to course her spine. Anne spun free of his grasp, snatched the lantern from his hand, and ran off the road.

Pepperell was fast on her heels. "Wait!" he called. "Mrs. Merrick!"

Afraid she could no more control Geoffrey Pepperell's bold advances or her own reactions, Anne was driven to outpace the booted footfalls following close behind, weaving a quick path through a maze of tents, unhitched wagons, and hobbled draft animals. Ignoring his calls, she raced up toward the tree line until the flicker of firelight in the sky and the sound of manly voices joined in song pulled her to a halt.

Teamsters!

The hesitation was all Pepperell needed to catch up and begin an instant tug-of-war for control of the light.

"Leave me be!" Anne held tight, the wire bail cutting into the pads of her fingers. "I can make my own way . . ."

"You cannot," he said, wresting the lantern from her grip. "Be sensible. There are drunk and baseless men about."

"The pot calling the kettle black!"

"*Touché*, madam." Pepperell grew very serious. "Though I have given you ample cause to mistrust my intentions, you will only invite disaster by traveling alone through this camp after dark. Now, please— I insist upon seeing you safe to your door."

The teamsters began the chorus of a popular bawdy song, and Anne huffed a beleaguered sigh.

"I promise to behave . . ." The Captain thumbed the sign of the cross over his heart.

"On with you, then," she said, waving him along. "Light the way."

Veering to the right of the campfire revelers, they skirted around a cluster of cannon carriages and wagons laden with powder and shot. Careful to maintain an arm's length of space between them, Anne concentrated on following the soft rectangle of yellow light cast by the lantern he held aloft.

"Do you see that?" Pepperell waved the light toward the field of artillery, illuminating an eerie mist crawling between the carriage wheels. His voice dropped to a dramatic whisper. "They say the spirits of fallen gunners follow their cannon from battlefield to battlefield . . ."

"Save me from your ghost stories," Anne said. "I don't believe in spirits."

Pepperell stopped dead in his tracks, and his arm dropped like a tollgate—the back of his hand slapping Anne at the collarbone, sending her back a step.

Anne heaved a sigh. "I am neither amused nor frightened, Captain."

Grabbing her by the upper arm, Pepperell put a finger to his lips. "*Shhh . . . listen . . .*"

Layered atop the faded backdrop of the teamsters' boisterous song, Anne could hear a rhythmic clank of iron chains—*shink, shink, shink*—as if a gang of exhausted prisoners shackled in leg irons was trudging along.

Anne jerked away. "Naught but the wind . . ."

"There is no wind. Be very quiet now and follow me," he said, in a voice so low, Anne only just caught his command.

Taking the lead, Pepperell swept the lantern in a wide arc from left to right, and right to left. Anne followed a few paces behind as the ominous chorus grew in intensity with every step forward—the rattling chains joined by a creaking, like that of carriage wheels turning on ungreased axles. She scurried to close the space between herself and the Captain, taking hold of a fistful of his red jacket, gooseflesh rippling up her arms and across the back of her neck.

Pepperell quietly inched his sword free of its scabbard and handed the lantern to Anne, whispering, "Shutter it."

"Shutter our light?"

His voice went military and clipped. "Do as I say."

Anne snapped the tin door shut on the still-burning candle, and but for the pinpoints of light keeking out through the tiny punched openings, all was thrown into darkness. As her eyes adjusted, the pulsing rattle and creak were accompanied by a pitched moaning and throaty groaning.

Anne tugged at Pepperell's jacket. "Let's turn back."

He pulled the pistol from the sash tied about his waist, cocking back the hammer. The clack of his weapon signaled a sudden pause in the ghostly rhythm, and in the brief quiet moment, Anne could hear her heart pounding in her ears, and then the clank, creak, and moan just as suddenly renewed.

Pepperell leaned down and whispered, "When I give the word, aim the light and open the shutter. Understand?"

Anne nodded vigorously, pinching thumb and forefinger to the tab of tin serving as the lantern door latch.

Sword in his left hand, pistol in his right, Pepperell took three long strides toward the noise with Anne scurrying along, the tail of his jacket clutched in her fist. They came to a halt no more than three yards from a huge, dark mound silhouetted in the starlight and pulsating in time to the clank of iron links—*shink . . . shink . . . shink.*

With sword arm upraised, Pepperell barked, *"Now!"* and rushed forward.

Anne swung the lantern door open, shining a piercing beam on a woman bent over a wagon's tailgate—skirts thrown over her back—and the stunned grenadier at her rear, both of them squinting at the light.

Pepperell put the brakes on his charge.

The woman looked up with a tentative smile, and waggled her fingers. "Hey-ho, Cap'n!"

The grenadier grunted, "Douse th' bleedin' light."

Anne stood wide-eyed with lantern raised, a war drum thumping in her chest, transfixed by the sight of the copulating couple.

"Would ye douse the light there, dearie?" the woman asked, "so's a lass might enjoy her lad with a bit o' privacy, aye?"

"Oh—of . . . of course . . ." Anne sputtered, lowering the lantern.

Pepperell sheathed his weapons. "Apologies, soldier—I'm afraid I mistook you for rebel thieves." With a big grin and a wave of his hand he said, "Carry on!"

"Aye, sir!" The grenadier brought a knuckle to his forehead in a snappy salute, and at once set the harness chains to rattling and the wagon axles to creaking.

"Away with us." Geoffrey grabbed Anne by the hand and she let him lead her along, in quick strides, up a steep hillside. Slowing to a stroll upon reaching the tree line, Anne pulled free, and gave Pepperell a shove to the shoulder.

"Rebel thieves? I wish you'd voiced your concerns, sir."

Pepperell shook his head. "Really, I was expecting to find foraging raccoons. I was as surprised as you when we found . . . well . . . when we found a beast with two backs!"

Anne couldn't help but laugh at Geoffrey's genuine discomfiture in this odd situation. As much as he annoyed with his ardent pursuit, the man was quite charming. "Did you note the soldier's discipline?" she asked. "*In flagrante delicto* and yet the fellow did not fail to offer you a proper salute—a true guardian of the Empire!"

"And his partner! 'Would ye douse the light there, dearie?'" Pepperell mimicked in falsetto, throwing Anne into a peal of giggles.

"Please . . . stop . . ." Catching her breath, Anne wiped a tear from her eye. "I'll be waking the entire camp."

Geoffrey Pepperell took her by the hand. "My, but you are a lovely thing laughing . . ." Before Anne knew what he was about, the Redcoat captain drew her into a simple kiss.

Flustered, Anne tried to pull away, swiping the back of her hand to the warm imprint his lips left upon hers. "Captain Pepperell . . ."

"None of that . . ." He took her hand and pressed the palm to his heart. "We are fast friends now, having faced the dangers of the unknown together. I shall call you Anne, and you must call me Geoff."

His heart pulsed beneath her hand, and she caught her lips beginning to form his name. With a shake of her head, Anne tugged her hand free and marched away. "I shall do nothing of the sort."

Pepperell followed after. "We have not the time for these proprieties you crave, Anne."

"You, sir, are most presumptuous to call me by my familiar—we are barely acquainted." Anne pointed to her campsite. "I bid you good night."

The glow of canvas sanctuary beckoned and she picked up the pace to just short of running. Pepperell lost his hat racing after her.

Catching her by the arm, he twirled Anne into an embrace, the lantern he carried bouncing on her rear.

"I am a soldier at war, Anne. I know well enough how to seize the day . . ."

Locked in the circle of his arms, she looked direct into his eyes. Pushing two-handed against his chest, and in as stern a voice as she could call up, Anne said, "You are no gentleman, Captain Pepperell."

"You are correct in that . . ." He let the lantern drop and roll in a clatter, and laid claim to her lips.

Anne closed her eyes, and for a moment, she simply gave over to the pleasure of a man's touch—the rasp of stubble on her soft skin—chest muscles clenched beneath her palms—strong fingertips playing the groove of her spine . . .

"ANNIE MERRICK!!"

Levered back to her senses on the fulcrum of Sally's shocked cry, Anne broke off the kiss, and Pepperell released his hold. Like a winged spirit in a flurry of frizzled braids and muslinet, Sally flew out of the tent swinging a very bright, glass-cased lantern. She retrieved the hat Pepperell lost and tossed it to land at his feet. "Good night t' ye, Captain."

Anne fumbled through the folds of her gown for her pocket fan with downcast eyes, happy for the dark to conceal her face, which was ablaze with shame.

Pepperell picked his hat up by the crown and bowed with a feathery sweep of his arm. "Madam—I enjoyed your company immensely."

Fluttering her open fan at her breast, Anne managed a slight curtsy. "A lovely evening, Captain. Thank you."

"My pleasure." Pepperell fit hat to head, pulling the wide brim to a dashing angle. "Till we meet again, my darling, I will see you in my dreams." Touching two fingers to his lips, he threw a kiss and marched off.

Fists to hips, Sally watched Pepperell disappear into the darkness. "Gweeshtie! In't he a winsome devil!"

Without a word to Sally, Anne trudged into the tight quarters of their tent, wishing she could dive under a blanket, bury her face in her pillow, and hide in the oblivion of sleep. Instead, she fished nippers from the mending basket and began snipping away at the stitches at the front of her bodice. In silence, she shrugged out of the sleeves, pushing the gown into a circular puff in the narrow aisle between the two cots. Shoes, then garters and stockings, were added to the careless pile.

Sally stepped behind to undo the knot in Anne's stays, whipping the loose laces free of the eyelets. "So? How'd we rebels fare at th' General's table?"

Anne peeled off the stiff-boned article with a sigh and stretch of relief. "I'll tell you all tomorrow." She swung her peddler's case onto her cot. "It must be past midnight already and I've a long report to write—"

Sally tumbled the discarded clothes into a ball. "Ye harvested some fruit, then?"

"Mm-hmm." Anne sat down and opened her box. "A bumping crop—very ripe."

Sally sat down on her bed, opposite Anne. "It was plain to my eye tha' ye were successful at winning yer man's devotion . . ."

"He's *not* my man." Anne peeled a page of rose-colored foolscap from the short stack in the box, creased it long ways, and carefully ripped it in two. "You know, I really didn't mean to kiss him that way . . ." She glanced up and met Sally's eye for the first time. "I think perhaps I had too much to drink. Champagne, claret, Madeira—my glass was never empty."

"So ye drank overmuch an' gave yer Redcoat captain a peck." Sally reached over and slapped Anne on the knee. "What of it? Ye were on th' job."

"Oh, Sally!" Anne flung herself backward, throwing her arms over her face. "I'm no better than some dockside Betty."

"Come now, lass . . ." Sally pulled a jug of water out from under the bed. "Dinna be so hard on yerself. 'Twere naught but a brief kiss . . ."

"You don't understand." Anne bolted upright. "I think his kiss gave me pleasure."

Sally was quiet for a moment. She took a small beaker from the writing box and filled it to the mark with water. "Ours is a tricky business, Annie. 'Tis hard to keep a balance on this razor's edge we tread. But I believe 'tis one thing to gaze over the edge, an' quite another to fall. Ye needna fash—ye didna fall—tha kiss was but a wobble, is all." She leaned forward and picked a brown glass jar from the box and handed it to Anne.

Anne peeled back the beeswax cap on the jar of hartshorn salt. "A wobble, you think?"

"Aye . . . Given time, ye'll ken exact how t' wrap this lobsterback round yer wee finger, just as ye did th' other back at the Cup and Quill."

"I hope you're right . . ." Anne sifted a measure of hartshorn into the beaker Sally held. "It was easy to bend Edward to my will—he was a kind enough fellow, but there was no substance to him. Geoffrey is a man who knows what he wants and goes after it, much like Jack—strong-willed and dogged persistent."

"And there's why ye gave in t' his kiss, no doubt. He reminds ye of Jack. Ye see? Yer heart is ever true, even in its wobbling." Sally handed Anne the beaker, and stood to hang the lantern from a hook on the ridgepole just above their heads.

"Maybe that's it . . ." Anne stirred the liquid in the beaker until the powder dissolved, the silver teaspoon dinging a bright tune until the water showed crystal clear when held to the light.

"Yer writin' a report, so courtin' the Redcoat has already reaped results for our cause, and that suits our purpose here, aye? So quit yer bleatin' an' yer ditherin'—ye did well." Yawning, Sally slipped under her blanket, curling onto her side to hug her pillow. "Write it all down an' get some sleep."

Maybe Sally is right . . . With quill in hand, Anne bent her head to her work, first penning an innocuous recipe in black ink on the two long slips of paper. Switching quills to write with the invisible ink, she filled the spaces between the lines with all of the pertinent intelligence she'd learned that night.

With the hartshorn ink yet wet and visible, Anne reread the words she'd written. Geoffrey Pepperell was the key to valuable information that might save rebel lives, win battles, and help to end the war. She could not afford to risk alienating his affection, or losing his interest.

Waiting for the pages to dry, Anne plucked the pins from her hair, dropping each into a tin cup, as she tallied the sins she'd committed for the sake of her cause—lying, treason, counterfeiting, killing—*plink, plink, plink, plink.* Proving faithless to Jack Hampton was a crime she'd never considered—not until this night. *Plink.*

If only I could join ranks, and face the might of the King's Army head-on, how much simpler life would be.

She eyed the bottom of the second page wishing she could at least add a line to let Jack know how much she missed him—let him know that no matter what, it was only he who held the key to her heart. Anne dipped her pen into the invisible ink and wrote the words, "Message ENDS," between the last two lines of the recipe.

Without thinking, Anne moved her pen to the empty space right above the bottom edge of the page and drew with quick strokes. Blowing on the wet ink, she watched her little drawing disappear. When dry, she rolled the two sheets into a tight and tiny scroll, tied it off with a snippet of waxed thread, and dropped it into an empty scent bottle she stoppered with a cork. Holding the blue glass up to the light, she gave the bottle a little shake and smiled.

A secret message within a secret message . . .

Most likely Jack would never reveal the image—placed as it was at the bottom of the page—but for some reason just knowing her little drawing was there provided a great measure of contentment.

Anne closed the writing box and shoved it under the cot. She found her pocket in the tangle at the foot of the bed and, as was her habit, withdrew the half-crown token and placed it, along with her pistol, under her pillow.

Lying flat on her back, hands laced over belly, she stared wide-awake at the canvas overhead. A cooling breeze moved in through the door flaps, washing over her sweat-dampened shift. The wind-rippled canvas turned a liquid shade of gold in the lantern light, reminding Anne of champagne illuminated by the warm waver of beeswax candles.

Anne jumped to her feet and snuffed out the lantern. She fished the cast-iron piece from under her pillow, and clenched it tight, feeling the raw edge bite into her skin. With token in fist, and fist to heart, she lay back in the dark, focusing her memories on those few nights when Jack had shared her bed—calling up the feeling of his hard body pressed to her side . . . the weight of his leg thrown over hers . . . the caress of his hand heavy on the curve of her ribs . . .

With a groan, Anne squirmed and knocked knuckles to forehead, whispering, "What manner of woman am I?"

"One made of flesh and bone, just like any other," Sally's sleepy voice responded. "T' sleep, ye silly gomerel, for tomorrow's a new day, aye?"

⚓ THREE ⚓

You are fighting for what you can never obtain and we defending what we mean never to part with.

Thomas Paine, *The American Crisis*

On a Ridge, Facing East

"Hey-ho! Striped skirts today!" Titus passed the brass spyglass to Jack. "Have a look."

On a ridgetop overpeer, hidden in a thicket of furze, Jack lay on the flat of his belly beside Titus. Propped on elbows, the eyepiece of the scope to one eye, his other eye squashed asquint, he panned from left to right across the ordered procession of artillery, wagons, and people amassed on the road below.

"I don't see 'em . . ."

"Right there." Titus pointed. "Sally's in a white cap, and Mrs. Anne's wearing her straw hat with the blue ribbon."

Jack aimed his scope to follow the trajectory of Titus's arm and snorted. "You've just described practically every woman down there."

With the tip of his finger, Titus directed the lens end of the glass to the correct position. "Start at the head of the line, then count about a dozen wagons back."

Jack pushed back the brim of his hat and began counting. Just behind the eleventh wagon he found Anne and Sally at their barrow, waiting for their turn to cross the jury-rigged timber bridge the British had engineered to span the flooded road.

"Yep—there they are!" Even from a distance, the sight of the women always served as a dose of instant relief. Though fully dedicated and willing to risk his own life for the rebel cause, Jack was not at all comfortable that Anne and Sally bore the highest risk in their pursuit for enemy intelligence. Excited to see the women not only safe, but signaling a message, Jack gave Titus a rough shove. "The last time they both wore the stripes, we caught us a courier, remember?"

The women were ensnared in a massive standstill at the foot of the bridge, and he trained his scope on Anne. There seemed to be a slump about her shoulders, and Jack was concerned by the tired way she leaned on the handle of the barrow. The morning was closing in on noon, and from his position high up on the ridge, her face was lost in the shadow of her hat and he couldn't make out her features.

"The bloodybacks seem awful concerned about the quality of their bridge," Titus noted. "Very careful, they are, letting only one wagon cross at a time."

"Their column is moving slower than a toad in a tar bucket . . ." Jack swung his glass to the left and watched a single teamster, on foot, leading his oxen up and over the span. "Flooding the road was one of your most clever ideas, Titus. That hour's handiwork cost Burgoyne two days in time and rations."

Riding in from the opposite side, a Redcoat officer astride a chestnut mare came cantering over the bridge, the horse's gait drumming an echoing rhythm on the puncheon logs. Once across, the officer paused and rose up in his stirrups, the black ostrich plumes on his cavalier-style hat streaming grand in the morning breeze as he maneuvered his steed with skill around the periphery of the waiting crowd.

"Now, there's a fine hat for horseback!" Jack said. "Better-looking than those ugly leather helmets the dragoons sport."

"Let me see—" Titus took the glass and brought it to focus on the officer. "That *is* a fine hat . . . Hold on, now . . . He's having words with Mrs. Anne."

"Who is?"

"Captain Feather Hat . . ."

"Hand me back that peeper—"

Jack pulled focus to see the feathered officer had dismounted, cutting as fine a figure on foot as he had on horseback. With hat tucked under one arm, the man was intent in conversation with Anne, and it was clear to Jack that she was on familiar terms with the officer.

"The shitsack! I can see from here he ain't worth wrapping a finger around."

"C'mon, Jack . . ." Titus said. "The man's a captain in the King's Army, after all . . ."

"Exactly." Jack nodded. "Where any drooling idiot willing to part with a few guineas can buy himself a commission."

"I can see you're workin' yourself into a lather over naught," Titus said. "You best hand me the glass, brother."

Jack kept his eye to the spyglass, riveted to the unfolding scene like a hungry hawk soaring over an unknowing rabbit. He watched the officer pull a packet tied with a broad red ribbon from his breast pocket and offer it to Anne. At first demurring, then shaking her head, Anne cast a furtive glance over her shoulder as she accepted the item, almost as if she knew Jack was watching. Without taking his eye from the scope Jack announced, "He just gave Anne a present."

"Who did?"

"Captain Shitsack, that's who."

"What'd he give her?"

"I don't know—I can't see . . ." Jack inched forward, tugging on the end of the scope even though it was already fully extended. Smiling and nodding, Anne began to undo the wrapping and Sally huddled in, obscuring Jack's view. "Move your arse, Sal," he muttered.

Making a big show of being thrilled with the gift, Anne even spun around to show the item to the rotund wagoneer waiting his turn next in the queue.

"This is not good . . ." Jack said. "Not good at all. I don't like the look of him, Titus. He's got mischief on his mind—that's for certain. Look at him standing beside my Annie, grinning like the butcher's dog."

Titus tugged at Jack's sleeve. "Let's go. We need to fetch up the message the girls left for us."

Jack shrugged Titus off and kept his spyglass trained on the road, muttering, "Don't do it, Annie . . . Don't . . ." But Anne ignored his warning to pop up on tiptoes and give the officer a peck on the cheek. And just as Jack knew the Redcoat would, the Captain wrapped an arm around her waist and pulled her into a deeper kiss on the lips. Jerking the scope away as if his eye had been scalded, Jack emitted an audible and painful "Unghh."

"What happened?" Titus asked.

"She kissed him." Jack handed over the spyglass. "See for yourself."

Titus peered through the eyepiece for a moment, and handed it back. "You are such a foolhead! I'm sure the kiss you saw is but chalk and water on Mrs. Anne's part—pretense—she's acting as ordered, making connections among the officers to glean the information we need."

"Does she have to go 'ooh!' and 'ah!' and kiss him?"

"Don't you start . . ." Titus shook a finger. "This is neither the time or place for your kind of crazy. None of us are at play, Jack—you know what's at risk here—for Mrs. Anne most of all. Now pocket that damn spyglass and let's be on our way!"

Jack turned the scope back to the bridge. "I suppose he might be one of those namby-pamby Britishers who *pretends* to like women . . ."

Titus rolled onto his back, groaning, "By mighty! I swear, your brains have officially settled in your bollocks."

Jack watched the Redcoat hand off the horse's lead to Sally, and his feathered hat to Anne. Clutching the hat to her breast, she seemed to be also clinging to the man's every utterance with blissful wonder. Jaw tense, Jack could feel a ridge of mad hackles crawl up his spine. *You damn bloodyback bastard . . .*

The officer tossed his fancy coat up onto the barrow, rolled up the sleeves on his ruffled white shirt, and began shouting orders, taking control of the bottleneck at the foot of the bridge. Shouting and waving his arms to clear the path, he pushed Anne's barrow up the steep gravel slope to claim the head of the queue. Once given the go-ahead from the engineer on duty, the Captain pushed the barrow over the bridge with Anne strolling alongside, and Sally following behind leading the mare. Jack watched until they disappeared beyond sight.

"Enough." Snatching the scope from Jack, Titus collapsed the instrument to its shortest draw length, and screwed a battered brass cap onto the lens end. "You need to forget about the Redcoat captain and set your mind to our important business."

As if he'd just been woken from a deep sleep, Jack gave his head a vigorous shake. "You're right. Anne's at work, and so am I. Don't waste any worry over me, Titus."

Titus grinned and scooted out of the furze. "We've got to find that message—am I right?"

"As right as bean water, brother." As they scrambled up to their feet, Jack gave his friend's shirttail a tug. "Tell the truth, Titus—a man has to be some kind of a molly to wear a hat like that, don't you think?"

Jack followed behind Titus, rifle cocked and gripped in both hands—his every sense tuned to the woodland heartbeat as they traveled under the dense green canopy, switchbacking up to their hidden camp. The blue-glass bottle they'd unearthed at the base of a big maple tree had made its way down to the very bottom of his possibles pouch, adding an odd weight, and thumping a steady reminder with every footfall.

"I hope Neddy kept the fire going," Jack said. "I mean to put this message to a flame posthaste."

Titus glanced over his shoulder. "I'm hopin' Neddy's cooked up some grub."

"Hang on—" Jack pulled Titus by the shirttail to a stop as they neared the area of their camp. "We'd better give signal."

"Good thing you remembered," Titus said. "I forgot coming back from having a piss last night, and Isaac near slit my gullet. I never knew such jittery Injuns."

"Isaac and Ned are smart to be so careful—the wood is thick with

Burgoyne's savages." Jack cupped his hands to his mouth and gave the owl call he'd practiced, *"Ho-hoo . . . hoo . . . hooooh! Ho-hoo . . . hoo . . . hooooh!"*

"A natural turn you have for birdcalls, Jack. You've got the whoop owl exact!"

"I can do a fair turkey, like Ned, but my owl is better."

The pair turned off the barely discernable trace and navigated through thick brush and chest-high fern. Just as Jack caught a glimpse of the gray granite wall that sheltered their camp, a lead ball buzzed by—head high—thunking into a tree trunk, sending a spray of wood chips flying. Jack and Titus dropped to their stomachs.

"Goddamn it!" Jack called. "Hold your fire!"

"That you, Jack Hampton?"

"Shekóli!" Jack shouted the Oneida greeting Neddy had taught him. "It's only me and Titus."

"Come slow—hands where we can see 'em."

Jack and Titus scrambled up to their feet with hands raised over hatless heads, and walked forward into the clearing. The two Oneida guides came out from behind an outcrop, uncocking their weapons, and, without another word, took seats opposite each other on a pair of log benches positioned in a V near a fire ring. Isaac leaned in to stir a kettle of beans stewing over embers, and Neddy dropped dollops of sticky dough onto a flake of shale heating over hot coals.

"I don't see why you boys got all up in arms," Jack complained as he stomped back to fetch his hat and weapon. "I sent out a call . . ."

Isaac snorted. "We heard your stupid call."

"Owls never hoot before twilight, Jack," Neddy admonished. "A call like that at midday signals to all within earshot that you're a man . . ."

"A stupid man," Isaac added.

"Call like that," Neddy said, "can draw the enemy and get us all killed."

Jack looked at Titus. "I should've used the turkey call."

Titus slapped the dirt and duff from his clothes with his hat, his face a scowl. "Firing weapons can draw the enemy as well . . ."

Isaac shrugged. "Or scare 'em off."

Neddy flipped the corncakes sizzling in bear grease on his make-shift griddle. "You were gone a long time."

"We were gettin' ready to go and search for your scalped carcasses," said Isaac with a rare grin, "once we et." He dipped up a portion of beans with a tin cup, took a fresh-baked johnnycake from the hot stone, and settled back onto his seat.

"It's a comfort of a sort," Jack said, taking a seat beside Ned, "knowing you wouldn't leave us to the crows."

Ned scooped the baked cakes from the hot stone with a piece of birch bark. "Did the women leave a message today?"

"They did—" Titus plucked up a johnnycake, and sat beside Isaac, juggling the hot cornbread from hand to hand.

Jack rifled through his pouch and came up with the blue-glass bottle, waggling it in Neddy's face. "Light the candle, my friend, for it is time for a little magic."

Ned was quick to produce a stubby candle cemented into a tin holder by a pool of hardened wax. He lit the wick with a brand, and set it on the log bench. Jack shook the little scroll from the bottle, and unrolled the message.

"Two pages!" he cried, showing the first around. "A recipe for rattlesnake stew!"

Isaac nodded. "My woman makes a good snake stew . . ."

"As I recall, Isaac," Titus said, "your woman makes a good pemmican as well."

Taking the hint, the Indian brought out a sausage from the parfleche at his feet. He cut the length into four equal pieces, and handed one to each man. Isaac's pemmican was a perfect balance of dried venison, blueberries, and bear fat pounded and ground into a paste, then packed and sealed into deer intestines for transport.

Titus tore a bite from his portion. "A little of this pemmican goes a long way in smoothing the wrinkles from my belly."

Neddy sat beside Jack and watched with rapt attention as the first page was put close—but not too close—to the heat of the flame. As Jack moved the paper slowly from side to side, the empty spaces between the cursive lines of the recipe coalesced inch by inch into faint, brown-tinged block print:

HEARD IN CAMP AND AT DINNER
Rattlesnake Stew— Page 1
WITH BURGOYNE, FRASER, + OTHERS
Take a large rattlesnake—
COURIER FROM HOWE BROUGHT A
skin, gut, and wash it until clean;
MESSAGE HIDDEN INSIDE A SILVER BULLET
cut into pieces no longer than the
TO BE SWALLOWED IF CAPTURED
two joints on your finger.   ·
CONTENT WAS NOT REVEALED TO ME BUT
Set meat into a clean pot and put to them
GEN B MOST DISTURBED BY IT
a gallon of water. Season well with a
LOYAL MACCRAE GIRL SCALPED
handful of salt, a blade or two of mace,
AND KILLED BY GEN B'S INDIANS.
whole pepper black and white, a whole
AS GEN B PRESSES FOR JUSTICE
onion stuck with six or seven cloves,
INDIANS ANGER—DESERTING IN DROVES
a bundle of sweet herbs, and a nutmeg
THE MURDERER WALKS FREE—

"Goddamn! She's wheedled her way into having dinner with Burgoyne himself!" Jack leaned over the fire pit and handed the page to Titus. "I suspect the 'others' she mentions include a bastard of the feathered hat variety . . ."

Titus waved Jack back to his task. "Quit with your green-eyed yammering and see to the rest of the message."

Neddy worked at taking the curl out of the second page, pulling the narrow slip back and forth across his thigh. "What do you say, Jack? Maybe I can try to make the words appear . . ."

"Not this time, Ned." Jack took the paper from him and put it to the flame. "It has to be done just right—we can't risk scorching the message."

Titus reached across the fire and set the first page beside Jack. "So Burgoyne's Indians went and scalped a Loyalist woman—even the most loyal of Loyalists can't be too happy about that. Might turn a few to our side. The bit about the silver bullet is good to know, if we ever catch another courier, but I really don't see anything here that's stripe-skirt worthy."

Jack looked up from his work on the second page. "Where's Bennington?"

Titus shrugged. "Never heard of it."

"Two days' walk or one long day running from here . . ." Isaac said.

"A small village near Walloomsac River," added Ned. "The Continentals have gathered cattle and other provisions there."

"Listen to this—" Jack read the important lines aloud from page two of Anne's message:

Cover the pot and let all
REBEL DELAY TACTICS A SUCCESS
stew softly until the meat is tender,
REDCOAT MORALE SLIPPING
but not too much done.
PROVISIONS DWINDLING
Pick the meat out onto a dish.
A MOVE TO HALF RATIONS RUMORED.
Strain the pot liquor through a coarse sieve.
MASSIVE FORAGING EXPEDITION ORDERED
Return the meat; cut carrots into
ONE REGIMENT—BRUNSWICKER DRAGOONS
coins and add with peeled Irish potatoes.
ALONG WITH EXPECTED LOCAL LOYALIST MILITIA

Take a piece of butter as big as a walnut
BEING MUSTERED TO BENNINGTON
and roll in flour. Put into pot with
TO COMMANDEER HORSES,
one cupful each of catchup, and sack;
PROVENDER, AND MATÉRIEL
Stew till thick and smooth and send
MESSAGE ENDS.
to the table speckled with minced parsley.

Jack set the page aside. "A full regiment disengaging from the main army . . ."

"Plus Loyalist militia," Titus added. "That's a sizable force—at least six hundred soldiers, maybe more."

"There's the reason for the striped skirts." Jack struggled his bowl from his pouch and scooped up some beans. "Eat up, boys, and let's get a wiggle on it. Traveling by night, we can get this information to David by daybreak."

Titus and Jack at once began slurping their beans and shoving johnnycakes into their mouths. Barely chewing his supper, Titus pushed at least half a dozen corncakes inside his shirt for the road.

Neddy watched Titus and Jack galloping their supper like pigs at a trough and warned, "Eating thataway afore a trek'll put a tangle in your gut."

Isaac agreed with a shake of his head. "White folk always eat too fast."

"White!" Titus spewed out a stream of cornbread crumbs. "I'm five times darker than you on any day, Isaac Onenshontie—and, for that matter, so is Jack." They all laughed, for it was true—living wild in the open had deepened the tone of Jack's complexion to a honeyed brown.

Once the men finished their supper, they began collecting their bedding and gear for the hike back to the Continental Army Command in Albany. Joining the others sitting around the fire distributing the common gear among their pouches and haversacks, Titus said, "Ned—don't forget to burn those pages and pack the candle."

Ned picked up one of the pages lying beside him on the log seat, and held the paper to the stubby candle still burning in its holder. But rather than set the damning evidence alight, as he was told, Ned began moving the page from side to side, just as he'd seen Jack do earlier.

Titus looked up from securing his bedroll with a length of rope. "Quit fooling around and burn the thing."

Ned turned the paper upside down, and brought it close to his eye. "There's something more writ here . . . on the bottom. Look . . ."

Titus took the page, studied it for a moment, then hooted, "Ooooh, Neddy boy! You've uncovered some vital information here—a most urgent love note."

"You see, Jack," Ned declared, lifting his chin and folding his arms across his chest. "And I didn't scorch nothing."

"Let me have that . . ." Jack leaned in for the paper, but Titus swept the page up and out of reach. Ned and Isaac laughed as the two men tussled like boys over a ball—Jack chasing after Titus, who circled backward around the fire, switching the paper from hand to hand—his height and the length of his arms keeping the page just out of Jack's grasp—all the while teasing in a silly falsetto, "Oh my sweetie darling, I love you so!" In mock swoon, he dropped back in his seat, fanning himself with the page.

Jack snatched the paper from Titus and sank down onto his hunkers to read the message Ned had revealed. But there were no words. Centered along the bottom edge, and no more than half an inch high, Anne had drawn in simple lines an image of their two love tokens fitted together to form a full crown, flanked by the initials *J* and *A*.

"I'd never figure to find anything down along the bottom edge. I never search beyond 'message ends.'" Jack looked up at Titus. "How'd she ever expect me to see it? What does it mean?"

"It means she didn't expect for you to see it at all. That scribble is naught but a woman's silly fancy." Titus resumed stuffing gear into his haversack and gave Jack a nudge with the toe of his moccasin. "Get busy."

Jack stayed on his haunches, still eyeing the drawing. "You're right, Titus. She put this here knowing full well I would most probably never see it."

Ned retrieved the hat Jack lost in the tussle with Titus. With a grin, he playfully exchanged headgear, plopping his turkey-feathered *gustoweh* onto Jack's head. "Look, Uncle—Jack is one of us—*ukwehu-wé*—an Oneida man."

So fixated on the scrap of paper in his hand, Jack didn't even notice the exchange of hats.

"Time's a-wastin' . . ." Titus swapped the hats back onto the proper heads. "Let's go, Jack. Shred it, burn it, swallow it—I don't care—but we need to make tracks, and I'm not about to travel with those pages."

Jack looked up. "You all can go on without me . . . I'll meet up with you tomorrow night in Stillwater."

"I knew it!" Titus brought his fist down onto the haversack he was packing. "You are truly love-cracked, and seeing that Britisher captain talking with Mrs. Anne has put the devil in your head . . ."

"It's not that, Titus." Jack stood upright, tapping his finger to the drawing at the bottom of the page. "Something's amiss—something troubling her—I know it."

"Flapdoodle." Titus threaded Jack's arm through his rifle strap, settling the weapon on his friend's shoulder. "You're coming with us."

"No—I'm going to see Anne." Jack slipped the rifle off, letting it thud to the ground at his feet. "You are more than capable of delivering the message to Stillwater on your own."

"And you are more than common stupid, Jack Hampton, to be even thinking about sneakin' into that camp on your own." Titus tugged hard at the red kerchief Jack wore tied about his neck, exposing a ribbon of angry scar tissue rippling round his throat. "Odds are against your cheating the hangman twice, brother."

"Don't you fret, Titus; I've a few lives left in me yet." Jack jerked away, righting his kerchief and shirt collar to conceal his noose scar. "I don't see why you're putting up such a kick and stram, anyway. My staying behind is no more dangerous than anything else we've been at these past few weeks."

Titus settled his bedroll diagonally across his back. "There's no time for this nonsense. We've got to get this message to David's ear, toot sweet."

"Anne's message has my eye—and I know, for some reason, she wants us together." Jack held up the page with the crown, his dark brows knit in determination. "I pray you're right, and it is just a silly fancy on her part—but there's a chance she's in some trouble, and I can't leave before finding out which it is. I'm all for our cause, Titus, but I will not lose Anne to it."

Titus whipped the leather strap through the buckle on his haversack, wrenching it tight. "What's your plan, then?"

"I'll go into the camp after dark . . ."

"Just stroll right in, will you?" Titus interrupted. "Alright. Let's say somehow you manage to get past the pickets and the guardsmen—how do you expect to find Mrs. Anne in the dark, among thousands?"

"I'll . . . I'll find the baggage train, and then I'll find Anne. I know her barrow. Once I find her and make sure all's well, I'll be on the road."

"And if all isn't well with Mrs. Anne?"

"Then we bring this business to a halt, and she and Sally come with me to Stillwater."

Fully accoutered and ready to travel, Isaac said, "Your friend's a hardheaded man, Titus."

"Yep. Hard as hickory." Titus poked Neddy in the shoulder. "This is all your doing—messin' with that candle—so you can stay with him now, and see he keeps a scalp attached to his hard head."

"Alright." Neddy shrugged. "I'll stay."

Titus shouldered his haversack and took up his rifle. "I expect to see you both in Stillwater by twilight tomorrow—y' hear me, Jack?"

"Don't you worry, brother. We'll be there." Jack thumbed a cross over his heart. "I swear."

Without a backward glance, Titus and Isaac took off at a trot and disappeared in a churn of greenery. Neddy shed his gear and announced, "I'm still hungry . . . You?"

Jack shrugged and took a seat at the fire ring, contemplating the little drawing at the bottom of the page he still held.

With tomahawk in hand, Ned left the fire, returning after a moment with a fair-sized sheet of bark he'd peeled from a nearby white pine. He sat next to Jack and nudged his griddle stone over the hottest coals. With a broad-blade knife honed to a razor edge, Ned proceeded to peel free the edible inner layer of bark from the rough outer bark. He cut the thin sheath of inner bark into uniform rectangles, each the width of two fingers, and no longer than the length of his hand.

Creasing a sharp fold just above Anne's drawing, Jack tore the bottom inch from the page and tucked the scrap safe behind the leather band circling the crown of his hat. He floated the damning pages onto the coals, and sat motionless, watching the paper squirm and writhe and burst into flames.

"Titus has the right of it," Ned said, breaking the silence. "Lots of coats down there—red, green, blue—won't be no easy task, finding one little woman amid all that."

Jack grunted in assent.

Ned arranged a dozen of the pine bark chips onto the hot stone, flipping each to toast both sides to a crisp golden brown. He plucked a cooked chip from the stone, and handed it to Jack.

"Eat."

"Really? Tree bark?" Jack eyed the offer. The Indian scouts were prone to eating the oddest fare, but he found the wilderness edibles they harvested usually provided a welcome addition to their army rations of cornmeal and beans.

"G'won." Ned smiled. "Roasted, it's sweet."

After taking the first bite, Jack reached for a second chip, and Ned asked, "*Yawéku ka?* Tastes good?"

"*Yawéku ka.*" Jack nodded. "First you got me to wearing moccasins, then making birdcalls, and now I'm eating tree bark—and liking it. Afore you know it, I'll be forgoing breeches for a breechclout."

Laughing, the Oneidan arranged another batch of chips on his griddle. "I aim to make you *ukwehu-wé*, Jack. When I'm done, your own woman won't know you . . ." Ned glanced up at Jack. "*Oho!* That's the way in, isn't it? You're sure dark enough for it . . ."

"Goddamn, Neddy Sharontakawas! If you aren't one slippery Indian." Jack tossed his hat off, fit Ned's turkey-feather cap onto his head, and crossed his arms over his chest. "*Shekóli*, you bloodyback bastards!"

✺ FOUR ✺

What we obtain too cheap, we esteem too lightly:—
'Tis dearness only that gives everything its value.

THOMAS PAINE, *The American Crisis*

IN CAMP—DARNING AND SCHOOLING

Evenfall found Anne and Sally cloistered inside their tent. They'd pitched their canvas alongside an orderly camp of Hessian dragoons, amid a sparse grove of popple and pine trees bordering the deepwood. A lone whippoorwill perched nearby and added comfort to the quiet night, trilling its name over the rough chorus of katydids and crickets.

Released from the stricture of her stays, and stripped down to muslinet shift, Anne settled cross-legged on her cot with her mending basket and hairbrush. After sweeping the boar bristles through her hair one hundred times, she plaited it for sleep, flipping the thick braid over her shoulder where it hugged the ridge of her spine. She stretched a silk stocking over a wooden darning egg and angled the eye of her needle toward the lantern light, pinching the thread through.

Down to her shift as well, Sally sat on her bed facing Anne, bare feet flat to the ground. Chewing on the fuzzy end of her braid, she tapped a chalk pencil to the writing slate on her lap in time to the rolling chant of the whippoorwill's call. *Taap-tap-tap. Taap-tap-tap.*

"I never paid much mind to birds back at the Cup and Quill," Sally said, "but out here, I find I'm grown partial t' th' whippoorwill. It seems she follows us from camp to camp, na?"

"Mm-hmm . . ." Anne did not glance up from the series of satin stitches she sewed to bridge the small hole in the toe of her best pair of stockings. "She sings a pretty song, our whippoorwill."

Sally dropped her chalk and leaned back on her hands. "Bab Pennybrig tells me she dreads the whippoorwill's call. 'Tis a portent of death, she claims, and swears she heard it the night her Bill fell at Breed's Hill."

Anne began weaving the tip of her needle up and under the satin stitches. "Bab Pennybrig saying a thing doesn't make it so."

"Aye, tha's true. Better to hear the whippoorwill's sweet call than the snake's rattle, I tolt her." Sally set her slate aside. "Th' snake's rattle— now, there's a true portent of death. Ye ken tha as well as I, d'ye not, Annie?"

Anne looked up from her darning. "I ken you ought take up your chalk and turn your mind to finishing your sums."

Sally dragged her slate back onto her lap. "I *hate* sums! I'll never be an arithmetician. I've no th' knack for it."

Six years before, when Sally was only fourteen years old, shod in wooden clogs and wrapped in a threadbare woolen shawl, she boarded a ship in Glasgow. Upon landfall in New York, Old Merrick purchased her indenture at the auction block and set the girl to work as a scullery maid in his household. Anne soon recognized that Sally owned a keen mind, and even though she knew it would rile her husband—for Merrick was not given to cosseting his servants—she determined to teach the illiterate girl to read and write.

Sally was an eager student and she quickly developed into a voracious reader, but the war had put a pause in the progress they had been making. Once ensconced in the British encampment, Anne seized on the idle night hours between supper and sleep as time devoted to expanding Sally's schooling with the practice of penmanship and ciphering.

"For God's sake, Sal, no one is expecting for you to become an arithmetician," Anne said. "One day soon you'll be helping David to run the Peabody Press, and I should think you might want to learn enough to manage and keep your own accounts. This war won't last forever, you know."

"Aye, Annie." Resigned, Sally brought her legs up to sit tailor style and bent her head to the problems Anne had written out on her slate.

Ho-hoo . . . hoo . . . hooooh! An owl's sudden hoot put an end to the whippoorwill's soothing refrain.

Sally slapped her chalk down. "Fegs! Tha' owl's gone and scared our sweet whippoorwill away . . ."

Ho-hoo . . . hoo . . . hooooh!

"My!" Anne gazed upward. "Sounds as if he's perched right above our heads."

Ho-hoo . . . hoo . . . hooooh!

Sally groaned.

"Never mind the owl," Anne said. "Just concentrate on finishing your sums."

Tossing her slate to the side, Sally heaved a dramatic sigh. "I'm tellin' you true, Annie, I canna muster a single thought for all this racket."

Ho-hoo . . . hoo . . . HOOOOOH!

Sally hopped off her cot, gathering several pinecones from the floor. "I'll chase him off . . ." Before Anne could stop her, she scooted through the tent flaps emitting a high-pitched, *"Shoo! Shoo!"*—the shrill cries followed by the thwack and roll of pinecones landing on the taut canvas overhead. *"Shoo! Sho . . . mmmmph!!!"*

Anne looked up at the odd stifled squeal. The tent flaps swept open, and with blue eyes as round as Dutch dinner plates, Sally was pushed inside, locked in the arms of a befeathered and tattooed Indian. Crouched in the tight confines of the wedge tent, the fierce savage struggled to keep squirming Sally constrained within the vise of his arms. With one hand clapped tight across her mouth, he muffled her distress.

The lantern hanging from the shaking ridgepole swung mad shadows over the quaking canvas. Anne fumbled under her pillow and, in an instant, produced her pistol. Arm extended ramrod stiff and the gun clasped in a two-handed grasp, she clacked back the hammer.

The Indian jerked his head back, his wild black hair flying. Flinging off his feathered headgear, he whispered, "Don't shoot, Annie!"

Sally visibly calmed at the voice. Heart a-race, Anne leaned forward, her pistol trained as she focused on the savage's tattooed face blinking in and out of the swinging light. She reached up to still the lamp, shining light on features made friendly by a familiar smile.

"Jack?!"

Jack flashed an even wider grin and gave Sally a little shake. "I'm going to let you loose, Sal," he said in her ear. "Promise you won't put up a fuss?"

Sally answered with a vigorous nod. As soon as Jack relaxed his hold, she stomped her heel down on his moccasined foot and sent a sharp elbow straight to his brisket.

"Ow!" Jack's tattooed face renewed its fierceness in grimace.

"Tha's what ye get fer scarin' us witless." Sally plopped down beside Anne.

"Goddamn it, Jack!" Anne uncocked her weapon and let it drop to her lap. "I was about to shoot!"

Jack positioned himself under the ridgepole with feet planted wide in order to fit his tall frame fully upright. Swiping back his long hair away from his face, he posed with fists resting at hips. "Convincing, eh?"

Anne and Sally shagged their heads up and down in brisk unison in admiration for Jack's clever disguise.

The faded indigo shirt he wore was belted at the waist with a sash woven in a pattern of red and yellow braided wool. Voluminous shirtsleeves were cuffed with horn buttons, and cinched at biceps with armbands worked in pierced silver. His woolen breechclout was trimmed with a scallop of colorful bead- and ribbon work, and extended several inches beyond his long shirttails. Utilitarian buckskin leggings came to mid-thigh, and were secured below the knee with finger-woven garters. Anne was relieved to see he wisely kept the telltale noose scar concealed with a knotted red kerchief.

"At long last . . ." Sally stifled a giggle with her hand. "Yer bedecked and festooned like the heathen ye are."

Worn loose as it was, Jack's black hair was perhaps a bit too wavy for a full-blooded Indian, but the two thin braids he'd plaited at his right temple and tied off with beads and feathers helped aid the deception. To complete his disguise, three diagonal hatched lines rendered in indigo ink crossed his tanned face from hairline to jawline, and a stylized drawing of a bird in flight adorned his right cheek.

Brow furled, Anne stood and pointed to his face. "You didn't really . . . ?"

"Not to worry . . ." Jack pressed his index finger to the tattoo and transferred a blue smudge to Anne's face. "Paint. Neddy made it by boiling a scrap of sugar paper in bear fat."

Anne sank back on her cot. "Neddy?"

"The younger of our Oneidan scouts. David charged two of them to work with us."

Sally gave Jack's shirttail a tug. "Yiv been with David? How's he fare?"

"David's fit as a fiddle and busy being Schuyler's right hand, keeping what passes for the Continental Army of the North together—no easy task, that. I saw him last when we delivered the courier you two uncovered."

"And it was David who put you in the company of savages?" Anne asked.

"Ned and Isaac are no savages. I'd wager pounds to pennies they know their Bible better than any in this tent."

Sally was skeptical. "The British claim th' tribes all gather beneath the King's banner . . ."

"Except the Oneida and Tuscarora have fallen in with us rebels." Dropping down, Jack took a cross-legged seat at the women's feet. "Good thing, too—they're valuable allies—master woodsmen, crack shots, fierce fighters, and now, good friends. Titus and I learn daily from Isaac and Ned." Jack hooked a thumb under the beaded strap crossing his chest. "These are Ned's clothes."

Anne shifted forward in her seat. "What happened with the courier you delivered to David?"

"We found a message hidden in his canteen, just as you said we would. Due to your good work here, General Howe will never receive that message."

"And the courier . . . ?"

"Captured as a spy and hung for one."

"Och!" Sally drew her shawl over slumped shoulders.

"We were hoping that maybe he'd be spared. You see," Anne explained, "the courier's sweetheart was the one who revealed his true purpose to us."

"Th' poor lass." Sally sighed. "So worried for her man, she is, and doesna ken it was she who sealed her lover's ill fate . . ."

"Strung up like a common criminal . . ." Anne said with a shake of her head.

Sally added, "And they were soon to wed . . ."

"Stop it!" Grabbing them each by the knee, Jack said, "We are spies. We lie, we cheat, we steal, we take advantage—our task is dangerous and thankless, but every bit of information we glean and anything we can exploit is crucial to our country's survival." He took in a big breath. "Ensconced among these British, you two have no ken to how desperate our cause has become. Our army is outmatched and outgunned at every turn and sorely lacks supply and matériel. Our soldiers are daily deserting by the drove. The only way we can ever hope to defeat the British Empire is by our wits, and without intelligence, we are doomed to fail. You must both keep your minds, eyes, and ears ever tuned to that which aids our cause, no matter the unsavory consequences. Do you hear me?"

Duly chastised, Sally and Anne both nodded vigorously, and Anne slipped her hand over Jack's. "We left an important message today . . ."

"Under a big maple—with a ribbon marker. Did ye no' find it?" Sally asked.

"We found it—awful important it is, too. Titus and Isaac are on their way to David. I was set to travel with 'em but when I saw this . . ."

Jack dug into the pouch at his hip and produced the drawing of the reunited crown. "I thought maybe you needed to see me . . ."

"Oh no!" Anne tipped the slip of paper to the light, and winced. "An aimless, silly scratching . . ."

"Which is unlike you," Jack interrupted. "I worried maybe something was amiss."

"I didn't expect for you to even see this, much less have it induce you to risk your neck in coming here." Anne handed the drawing back to Jack, and it made her heart skip to see how carefully he returned the little scrap of paper to his pouch. "I was missing you—feeling lonely and more than a little sorry for myself, and drawing our little crown made me feel better."

"Caw!" Sally gave Anne a little shove. "Yer a softhearted lass, fer all yer stoic brash!"

Jack smiled. "I'm glad to hear that's all there is to it."

"You are a madman to have come here"—Anne touched the silver disk hanging from his pierced earlobe—"but I'm so glad you did."

"Ahoy, Mrs. Merrick!"

Anne and Sally locked eyes, and Sally whispered, "What's he want?"

"I've no idea!" Rising to her feet, Anne pressed a fingertip to Jack's lips in silent warning.

Jack grabbed her by the hand. "It's Captain Feather Hat, isn't it? What was it he gave you today?"

Anne dropped back to her seat. "What?"

"Ahoy, Anne Merrick—Geoff Pepperell come to call—"

"It *is* him." Jack growled under his breath, pushing off to rise up to his feet.

Sally lurched forward and shoved him by the shoulders, sending him back onto his hind end. Her index finger like a dart to his forehead, she hissed between gritted teeth, "Stay down an' shet yer hole, or it's the three of us dancin' a jig at rope's end by sunup."

"Ahoy, Mrs. Merrick!"

Anne stumbled forward and banged into the lantern, sending the light swinging. Rubbing her forehead, she gave Sally a pull. "Get rid of him—but nicely."

Sally nodded, drew a deep breath in, breathed it out slow, and poked her head between the tent flaps, clutching the canvas beneath her chin.

"Good evening, Captain," she said in a loud and cheery voice.

"Hullo, Sal. May I have a word with your mistress, please?"

Sally pulled inside, keeping the canvas crimped closed in white-knuckled fists. "He wants to talk to you."

"*No!*" Anne and Jack hissed in unison and waved her back.

Sally once again inserted her head between the flaps, her twin plaits swinging. "Apologies, Captain, but th' hour is dark, and my mistress bids ye t' pay yer call in the light of day."

"Tell your mistress this matter cannot wait. I must speak with her now."

Sally pulled inside. "Maybe ye ought . . ."

"*No!*" Anne and Jack whispered together.

Sally's head emerged once again. "I'm so sorry," she told the Captain, "but Mrs. Merrick is not prepared t' receive callers at this late hour . . ."

"This is absolutely ridiculous . . ." Pepperell raised his voice. "Please inform your mistress that I will wait right here while she collects herself to speak with me direct."

Sally popped back in. "Ye heard. He willna budge."

Anne slipped her feet into shoes. "I'd better see what he wants."

Jack grabbed Anne by the hand and pulled her down, their cheeks brushing. He growled in her ear, "I know what he wants, and so do you."

Anne jerked free, and hissed, "That man is the fount of our intelligence—every bit of it crucial—you said so yourself." She tugged a striped skirt over her shift, twirled a shawl over bare shoulders, and slipped outside.

Lantern in hand, dressed in casual shirtsleeves and buff breeches protected by black gaiters, Pepperell kept himself at a discreet distance from the tent, as any gentleman should. Anne noted the brace of pistols tucked into the sash at his waist, and she rushed forward to keep him as far from the tent as possible.

"I apologize for the lateness of the hour . . ." he began, setting the lantern on the ground.

"Indeed." Anne held tight her shawl and managed a smile. "Sally and I are about to douse the light."

"Were you at your letters? You've a bit of ink there . . ." Geoffrey stepped close, and brushed the back of his hand to her cheek.

Anne stumbled back a step, scrubbing the blue pigment with the tail of her shawl. At the exact moment, Sally squawked a distressing yelp. Pepperell made a move toward the tent, but Sally's ginger head popped forth in an instant, stopping him in his tracks. She sputtered, "A huge, *ugly* spider crawlin' about in here—he needs *squashin'* . . . I could use your help, Annie." And she disappeared.

"Captain Pepperell." Anne resorted to her vexed-widow voice. "Paying call at this hour—most unseemly, sir. I must bid you good night."

"Wait . . ." The Captain grabbed her by the hand, curtailing her retreat. "I have come with only wholesome intent. Lennox has set out his telescope—a beautiful instrument—and Mrs. Lennox sends an invitation for you to join us in our stargazing. I've come to escort you to our camp."

"S-s-stargazing!" Anne struggled to shift her tack from angry to reasonable. "How . . . how very kind of you, Captain . . . and, of course, kind of Mrs. Lennox as well—to think of me." Any other time she would have leapt at this sort of opportunity, for Lucy Lennox had already proven to be a valuable resource. Eyes darting to Jack's silhouette in a hunker near the canvas tent flaps, she was nonetheless compelled to cultivate Pepperell's good graces. Tugging the Captain along, she guided him to stand with his back toward the tent.

"A telescope, you say? I've always wanted to learn more about the night sky . . ."

"Good! I'll wait while you dress."

"No! I couldn't . . . wouldn't want to trouble you." Anne could not keep her hands from flailing about. "After all—well—it's very late. And of course . . . there's Sally and the spider . . ."

"The spider!" Geoffrey laughed. "It's a moonless night—perfect for stargazing—and the views are fantastic. Please say you'll come."

Anne glanced over Pepperell's shoulder at the tent, horribly aware of Jack and Sally watching her every move and listening to her every word. She moved in closer, kept her eyes cast demure, and lowered her voice to a more seductive tone. "Oh, Geoff, I would truly love to spend the night with you . . . stargazing." Letting go of her shawl ends for a moment, she allowed the Redcoat captain the briefest glimpse of her dishabille, before collecting the soft wool in a modest clutch at her breast. "But it has been one long day after another, and I am"—she let out a breathy sigh—"quite spent. Could you possibly come calling to-morrow night, when I can promise to be better company?"

"Of course I understand. Tomorrow it is, then." Smiling, Geoffrey Pepperell moved in to claim a kiss, which Anne managed to avoid with an adroit step out of his orbit, and an offer of her hand.

"Until tomorrow, Captain."

Pepperell placed a tender kiss at the very center of her palm. "I'll call for you at dusk . . . and I will hold you to your promise." Bowing with a courtly sweep of his arm, he snatched up his lantern and threw her a kiss. "Sleep well, my sweet."

"Convey my regrets to Mrs. Lennox . . ." Anne waved. Pepperell spun an about-face and marched away with a chipper bounce in his step.

Keeping her eye on the British captain, Anne backed away to take a stand at the tent door, until the glow from his lantern disappeared among the many pinpricks of yellow light in the distance. Ducking inside the tent, she found her writing box thrown open, and Sally scribbling like mad with a lead pencil on a sheet of foolscap.

Anne puffed out a breath. "He's gone."

Grim-faced, Jack stood upright and, without a word, snapped a mean-looking blade back into the beaded scabbard hanging from his belt.

"I got rid of him," Anne added. "He won't be back."

Jack looked up, his dark brows knit into a single line. "At least not until tomorrow—*my sweet*—"

"Don't . . ." Anne held up a hand. "I have no choice but to court the man's favor. He's our best source—"

"And no wonder . . ." Jack interrupted, aping her voice with exaggerated inflection. "'Oh, Geoff! I would truly love to spend the night with you!'"

"Mind yer wicked tongue." Sally slammed her pencil down, her eyes fierce. "Annie's but doin' the work she was sent to do. Ye ought t' be proud of her—be it the camp laundress, sutler, or Burgoyne himself, she kens exact how to gull these Britishers to eatin' out of her hand . . ."

"Literally." Jack swiped his hair from his face, his glare unforgiving.

Anne flinched as if she'd been dealt a slap to the face. Mired in a muck of guilt and regret for kissing the Redcoat captain the night before, she scrubbed the palm of her hand to her skirt, unable to muster any defense. Sally, however, held no such compunctions.

"D'ye hear yerself, Jack Hampton? Ye can oft times be sech an utter arsehead."

Jack's shoulders sagged a bit, and his mouth lost its hard edge. Closing his eyes for a moment, he sucked in a deep breath, and let it out in a slow whistle.

"You've only the half of it, Sal. I'm a thoughtless, stupid, and selfish arsehead." Clasping his hands behind his back like a contrite schoolboy, he turned to face Anne direct. "I'm so sorry, Annie. I *am* awful proud of you and the work you do, and the good that comes from it, and that's the God's honest truth." He shrugged. "It was probably not a good idea—my coming here. I should go."

"Already?" Anne's voice wavered on the single word, and she dropped down to sit on the edge of the bed, lacing her hands tight to keep from bursting into tears.

"No call to linger—" Jack retrieved the *gustoweh* from where it rolled under Sally's bed, and offered it up with a weak smile. "Ned'll have my hide if I leave this behind—said it took him a year to collect the proper feathers . . ."

Anne nodded, the lump in her throat too great to overcome with words.

Jack brushed dirt from the hat and fiddled with straightening the feathers. "I'm wondering—though my borrowed plumage is nowhere near as fancy as your Captain Feather Hat's . . ."

Anne groaned. "He's *not* my captain!"

Jack winced. ". . . And though I continue to be a first-rate arsehead to boot—maybe, Annie . . . Maybe you might consider going for a walk with me this night?"

The sincere earnestness of his apology combined with the self-deprecating invitation washed all the ill feeling from her heart. Anne looked up into his soft brown eyes. "I'd like nothing better."

Sally threw up her arms. "Now, tha's a brilliant scheme, in't it? Him an Indian, and you a white woman, strollin' about the camp the-gither la-di-da—are yiz both daft?"

"Not to worry, Sal." Jack grinned. "I have it all figured, and I'll have Anne back safe before the drummer boys beat reveille."

"You see, Sal? Jack has a plan . . ."

"Why am I not surprised?" Sally creased the letter she'd written into a square, and handed it to Jack. "Not a single damning word—ye'll no' hang for anything writ on this page. Carry it to David for me?"

"Gladly." Jack stuffed it into his pouch. "Handing off a letter is preferable to answering his thousand and one questions."

Sally jumped up and gave Jack a hug and a two-handed shove to the chest in quick succession. "Have Annie back as promised, ye blackguard, or I'll hunt ye down, scoop yer still-beating heart out with a spoon, an' leave it t' pickle in yon Hessian cabbage barrel."

"Aye, aye, sir!" After saluting Sally with a knuckle to his brow, he turned and grasped Anne by the shoulders. "Wait a little time after I'm gone, then take your leave and head straight north." He pointed to the back of the tent. "Do not carry a light; you don't want anyone following you. Once you breach the tree line, count one hundred paces, and I'll find you there. You understand?"

"I do."

Jack slipped out of the tent. A moment didn't pass before he popped his head back in and, with a wag of his brows, added, "Best bring your blanket!" before disappearing in a flap of canvas.

"Good earth and seas!" Anne flung herself to lie flat on her back. "Could that damned Redcoat have picked a worse time to come calling?"

Sally plopped onto her cot. "Ye had it easy. I was the one stuck inside this tent with a madman."

Anne bolted upright. "Do you have my brush?" She pulled the ribbon from her plait, finger-combing her hair to separate the braid-crimped tresses. "Why do you goad him so, Sal?" Exaggerating Sally's brogue, Anne singsonged, " 'She kens exact how to get these Redcoats to eatin' out of her hand.' "

"Och! It's no secret what we're about here." Sally found the brush, and tossed it over.

Anne put the brush to work. "Did you hear him call Pepperell 'Captain Feather Hat'? I can only assume he was watching us at the bridge this morning . . ."

Sally groaned. "And saw the kiss, no doubt."

Anne stopped brushing. "Then he comes into camp at great risk, and finds the same man calling on my tent after dark." She resumed the brisk strokes. "In this instance I have to allow Jack some understanding. I know it would be awful difficult for me, if our roles were reversed."

"I swear, Annie, when Pepperell touched your cheek, Jack near went out of his senses."

"I know." Anne pressed a palm to her chest. "My heart's still pounding double time."

"If Jack means for us all t' remain a success at this business with necks unstretched, he must learn t' curb his jealous heart. 'Twas all I could do t' keep yer man from leaping out with tha' huge sticker he carries. 'I'll separate the bastard from his bollocks,' says he, very near bringing the British Empire down upon us all. Poor Titus," Sally clucked. "No doubt he has his hands full."

Anne stood, her chestnut tresses falling in a crescendo of soft waves to the small of her back. "Do I look a fright?"

"Och! Yer only gorgeous!" Sally dug a blue ribbon from the mending basket. "Should we pull yer locks up?"

"I think not. I know it's altogether brazen, but he likes when I wear my hair loose." Anne pinched her cheeks, splashed lavender water on her neck, and poured a drop down her décolletage, shivering as it trailed a cool trickle down to her navel. She dug under her pillow for her little half crown. Realizing she had neglected to tie on her pocket, she simply dropped the token down the front of her shift. Tossing on her shawl, she announced, "I'm off!"

"Wait!" Sally jumped up and rolled the woolen blanket on Anne's cot into a sausage, handing over the bundle with a smile and a wink.

Tucking the blanket under one arm, Anne smiled. "You are the *finest* kind of friend." Giving Sally a shoulder squeeze and a peck on the cheek, she scooted out the doorway. Careful to keep the tent betwixt herself and the neighboring Hessians, Anne ran the few yards to the looming wall of trees at the forest's perimeter, her heart near bursting with joy that she would soon be in Jack's arms.

She began counting her paces. *One, two, three, four . . .*

The friendly, sun-dappled forest by day was transformed by a moonless night into an endless black cave. To assure she wasn't being followed, Anne glanced back every few steps until the cheerful glow of illuminated canvas was swallowed in the inky wake of her trail.

Twenty-two . . . twenty-three . . .

Without a lantern to light her way, Anne stumbled forward through fern beds and shrubbery with arms outstretched—bumping into trees and low-hanging limbs with almost every other step. Once ensconced under the thick canopy of leaves, she was so completely night-blind, she could not make out her hand before her face. Forced to a complete standstill, she took a deep breath and blinked, willing her eyes to adjust to the spare starlight filtering through the overstory of leaves.

Awful quiet.

This thought very loud in her head. Even the constant cricket and tree-frog din seemed faint and muffled under the dense canopy, the night sounds absorbed by damp greenery, massive tree trunks, and the soft forest floor. The stillness, in company with the all-enveloping darkness set Anne on edge, and she shifted from joyful to wary. To prove her mettle and to fill the silence, she began to whisper-sing a brash rebel song. Hugging the bedroll to her chest, and swaying from side to side, her voice grew in volume with every line—

> *With Loyalty, Liberty let us entwine,*
> *Our blood shall for both, flow free as our wine.*
> *Let us set an example, what all men should be,*
> *And a toast give the world—*
> *To those who dare to be free.*
> *Hearts of oak we are still;*
> *For we're sons of those men*
> *Who always are ready,*
> *Steady, boys, steady—*
> *To fight for their freedom again and . . .*

A deep wing thumping suddenly skimmed right over her head— *fffoom, fffoom, fffoom*—sending her down in a squeal and squat and raising instant gooseflesh to race over her forearms and up the nape of her neck.

Just an owl, common sense assured.

A big hairy, nasty bat, unreasonable fear insisted.

"No more singing," Anne decided with a shiver, drawing her shawl up to protect her hair from airborne nocturnals. Her eyesight had adjusted somewhat and infinite pitch black began to transform into an environment formed of shapes and shadows in shades of gray, purple, and deep blue. *Jack's waiting.* She set out once again.

Thirty-one . . . thirty-two . . . thirty-three . . .

She pulled to a sudden stop. The sound of tumbling pebbles reached her ear, and she could hear a creature scratching and rooting around in the crunch of dead leaves just to her left—its musky odor wafting up to crinkle her nose.

"Thirty-four . . . thirty-five . . ." Anne scurried forward, counting aloud, cringing at the sound of her panic-tinged voice. At the forty-pace mark, she let loose a squeal and was roughly jerked to a standstill—her shawl caught in the claws of a brambly thicket.

"Drat! Damn! *Bloody-damn-hell-shit!!*" Stringing together a stream of the foulest curse words she could utter, Anne yearned for a light as she untangled her shawl from the bramble's clutches. It was hard to see, but she was certain she'd torn at least three holes in the only summer-weight shawl she'd brought on campaign, assuring a long evening spent in the company of her darning needle.

Resisting the urge to hurry, Anne narrowed her focus to the immediate path, and moved in a more deliberate wend through the monochromatic world of shifting shadows.

Where is he? The uneasy twist carried in her chest was wrung tight and tighter with every step forward. Wrestling with the wisps of spider silk sliding over her face and arms, she kept her eyes on the path, maneuvering under jutting limbs, around grasping brush, and over tangles of deadfall—trying to avoid bumping her noggin, snagging her clothes, or tripping flat on her face.

"Goddamn it!" Anne stopped dead in her tracks, and, throwing her head back, she stomped her foot and railed at the dark. "I forgot to keep count."

Spinning around, she gazed back into the black hole from whence she'd come, unable to see anything to help gauge the progress made since the encounter with the thornbush. She turned back, and her breath caught in her throat.

"*Hohh . . .*"

Ten paces ahead, haloed by a ghostly blue-green light, a monstrous hand rose up from the forest floor, pointing straight up to the heavens.

"What in the . . . ?" Anne leaned in, blinking and squinting. A few cautious steps forward provided eyes and brain with the information required to override wild imagination, and she heaved the answer in relief.

"A tree."

The jagged, broken remains of a huge old tree—*a maple?* She moved closer.

Hard to tell. Definitely one of the grandfathers of the forest by the great girth it had attained before being snapped in two by rot and wind. The frightening apparition being in actuality a tree in no way explained where the curious blue-green light was coming from.

Just your eyes playing tricks . . .

Anne closed her eyes and counted to ten before blinking them open. The otherworldly light had not dissipated and she resisted the urge to run.

Jack is nearby. He'll come and find me, and we'll . . .

Anne unhunched her shoulders and smiled. She tucked her bedroll under the crook of her left arm, and took a few steps toward the glowing tree, calling in a loud voice, "I know that's you, Jack Hampton."

No reply.

Anne tried once again. "This isn't funny, Jack."

Like a tinker's monkey attracted to a shiny object, she inched toward the glowing old tree, drawn to the comforting light it cast upon the surrounding phalanx of slim saplings and leafy branches. Close enough to see that there was a large patch of lady's slippers in bloom near the base of the old tree, she reached out and dared to poke a fingertip to the trunk.

"Jack?" she whispered. "That you, Jack?"

Her palm flat to the rough bark, the old, broken tree became the center point to her circle, and her outstretched arm, the compass. Moving in a slow arc toward the light source, she rounded the apex, and gasped, careening back a step, dropping her bedroll, shielding her eyes to the uncommon brightness.

"Whoa!"

The back side of the tree trunk was covered in a tumble of flat-capped mushrooms emitting blue-green light.

Mushroom lights? Anne had never heard tell of such a thing. Just as a laundress would test a hot iron, she licked her fingertip and quickly touched it to one of the broad caps. Curiously cool, the glowing fungus put Anne in mind of the lamp end on the fireflies she and her brother, David, would capture as children. Snapping one of the shining mushrooms free, she moved away from the tree, fascinated to see every line on her palm illuminated in eerie clarity by the light cast from a single mushroom.

"I could write by this light—I could read by it!"

Anne looked around, entranced by the enchanted scene created by the phosphorescent tree fungus. The leaves on the surrounding trees reflected a thousand shades of blue and green, shimmering as if fashioned of taffeta and bombazine. The downed upper portion of the rotten tree had—in falling over—created a rift in the dense canopy overhead, exposing a narrow patch of star-strewn sky. The luminescence cast by the fungus and the added starlight turned the huge fallen snarl of twiggy branches into a dense swath of silver-blue lace draped over the black velvet of the forest floor.

"Ho-hoo . . . hoo . . . hooooh!"

Anne spun round to the owl's call. In the distance, bobbing golden lights playing on the branches and canopy overhead preceded a figure carrying a torch. Weaving through the trees, he was wearing a broad-brimmed felt hat.

The figure stopped and circled the torch over his head in a *whoosh*. He cupped hand to mouth and once again mimicked an owl's call. A second figure appeared alongside the torchbearer.

Jack and Titus!

Waving her mushroom lamp, Anne called, "Hoo-hoo!" and the torchless figure came bounding toward her.

Like something out of a dream, Jack met her in the glow of the odd mushroom light, dressed in Indian garb and carrying a long rifle strapped over his shoulder. Exclaiming, "There you are!" he swooped her up into his arms and kissed her twice, soft on the lips. "You were so long in coming—I worried maybe you'd changed your mind."

Slipping his hand into his shirtfront, he pulled forth his half of the crown token worn strung on a leather thong round his neck. Anne quickly dipped down her shift to retrieve the token she carried, and fit her piece to his.

"There!"

"I don't know why," Jack admitted, "but it makes me feel good to see it whole."

Laughing, Anne wrapped her arms around his waist and pressed her ear to the real-world steadiness of his heartbeat. The familiarity of his strong arms, his breath on her hair, the smell of woodsmoke on his skin—it all rooted Anne in time and place. Jack was hers and she was his, and her heart, tipped askew in his absence, was set aright by his presence.

"A hundred paces is an awful long way in the dark—" She held up the mushroom, and with the light she could see he'd washed his face clean of the painted tattoos. "See how it shines even when plucked? Have you ever seen such a thing?"

"I have—but never so much in one place." Hand in hand they went to examine the mushrooms up close. "I know some folk call them fairy sparks," he said, "but we always called it foxfire—grows on rotten wood, especially after the kind of rain we've been having."

"Foxfire," she repeated, thinking the name very fitting.

Jack poked one of the mushrooms. "I remember being scared to death as a boy the first time I ever spied foxfire. I ran inside and told my brothers there was a ghost living in our woodpile."

"Koué!" a strange voice proclaimed.

Anne startled to see Jack's torch-bearing companion had joined them, and was not Titus at all. The strange man was wearing Jack's hat. "That's a very big patch," he said. "Watch . . ." The man put the torch close to the tree, and in the light, the fungus instantly lost its luminous quality, reverting to a drab, mushroomy hue.

"Oh no!" Anne cried.

"Don't fret. The green fire never shows in the light," Jack's companion explained as he tossed the torch down and stomped out the flame. The mushroom light at once began to glow in verdant intensity. "There's why it's best to see it when the moon is hiding."

"Anne Merrick, I'm pleased for you to meet my friend Ned Sharontakawas." Jack clapped the man on the back.

Anne took Ned's proffered hand and regarded with some amazement his very gallant bow. He was a tall and handsome young fellow, Jack's Indian guide, and seemed nothing at all akin to the often gruff and surly Indians who wandered in and out of the British camp. There was an exotic quality to his facial features, but dressed as he was in

Jack's hunting shirt and breeches, Anne would have been hard-pressed to figure he was an Indian at all. *A Frenchman, perhaps . . .*

"*Shé-ku,* Jack's woman." Ned's smile was shy but friendly. "I found the crown you drew beneath the recipe for snake stew."

"And Jack is wearing your clothes . . ." Anne said.

"And I wear his," Ned replied with a tip of Jack's hat.

The men got busy using their tomahawks to prize free two chunks of mushroom-covered bark.

"Let's get a move on." Scooping up Anne's blanket, Jack set forth. "Our camp's up the hill a ways."

Anne fell in behind Jack, and was surprised to see Ned follow after, both men lighting the narrow footpath with their mushroom lights. They traveled with speed and assurance up a narrow, switching trail—pausing for brief moments to check bearings invisible to Anne's ignorant eye—easily covering five times the ground in the same time it had taken her to stumble-bumble less than one hundred paces.

"I don't understand how you can navigate," she said, impressed to see Jack not only take the lead, but know where he was heading, and how to get there.

"Without a moon, this forest is as black as the Earl of Hell's weskit, but we're pretty good at getting around in the dark," Jack said over his shoulder. "Aren't we, Neddy?"

"Yup." The trail widened and the Indian scooted forward to walk two abreast with Anne. "Like big cats, Jack and me work our mischief in the dark," he said.

An instant tension stiffened her neck and shoulders. Anne pulled her shawl up to cover her hair and moved as far to the right as possible. Putting a little skip in her step, she tried without success to catch up to Jack. But no matter how slow or quick she moved, the Indian matched her pace, lighting her path, ready with the support of a gentle hand at her elbow when required to negotiate a tangle of tree roots or a tumble of stone.

Nothing but kind . . .

"Mind your head, now, miss," Ned warned, shining his mushrooms on a low-slung limb crossing the path.

Anne ducked under. *Small-minded I am . . . and fearful.*

Jack was never either. Anne suffered a moment of silent shame hooded in the depths of her shawl. Perhaps she'd been too long amongst the British . . . *Always looking down on those of inferior rank.*

With a twist of guilt Anne was put in mind of her dearest friends— a slave-born black man and a lowborn Scots servant girl—two of the best people relegated to the very bottom of the social order. She determined if Jack found Ned Sharontakawas worthy of being called "friend," then she could do the same.

Anne drew her shawl down. "Your torch was such a welcome sight, Ned."

"Made it to help Jack find you," he said.

"I was sorry to see you put it out."

"It's risky traveling with a light," Jack explained over his shoulder.

Ned added, "Don't want to draw the enemy."

"You both must be very skilled at avoiding British patrols."

"Dodging Burgoyne's soldiers is easy enough . . ." Jack said matter-of-factly.

Ned added, "Them stomping around in boots with torches and swords like they do."

"But Burgoyne's Indians—" Jack began, and Ned finished, "Oho! That's another matter altogether."

Jack turned around, walking backward for a moment to announce with a smile, "Our camp's just up ahead."

They burst through the brush onto a wide ridge shelf under an open sky at the base of a steep cliff. Facing east, the view of the valley below was filtered through a curtain of close-growing white pines. An outcropping of jagged stones and scrubby brush buttressed the cliff at an angle offering a natural windbreak for the fire ring and the low log seat beside it. Opposite the seat, on the other side of the fire ring, a curious mound of green balsam boughs were arranged in careful order, one atop another, and neatly corralled within a six-foot-square log frame.

She followed the men straight to the ring of stones, where Jack dropped Anne's blanket down onto a small pile of gear stowed behind the log. In the glow of blue-green mushrooms, both men shed their weapons and pouches. Dropping down to one knee, Jack used his tomahawk to split a piece of firewood into lath, while Ned raked up the ashes. Jack arranged the kindling in a fretwork and Ned fanned the smoldering coals with a scrap of birchbark. The thin strips of oozing pine caught fire at once.

Amazed by their wordless cooperation, and the speed with which a fire had been kindled, Anne sidled up to the friendly light. "I'm happy to see you keep a fire."

Jack admitted, "We rarely do."

"This camp is well sheltered from view," Ned said, as he selected a few pieces of wood from their supply of gathered deadfall and dropped them beside Jack.

"And it's too dark to see smoke rising." Jack broke a thin branch in two, crisscrossing the wood over the burning kindling. Yellow-orange flames curled over the fuel, encouraging the flecks of glassy quartz embedded in the sheer granite cliff to sparkle and shine like citrine and topaz.

Swiping his hands on his shirtfront, Jack rose to his feet. "It's time to say good-bye to our Iroquois friend, Annie."

"Iroquois?" Twin lines creased the bridge of Anne's nose. "You said he was Oneida . . ."

"He's both."

Ned gathered up some gear and a haversack. "English, French, and Dutch call us Iroquois, but we say *Haudenosaunee*—people of the Long House."

Anne grabbed ahold of Jack's forearm. "The Iroquois fight with Burgoyne, Jack . . ."

"The Iroquois are a league of six nations"—Jack counted off on his fingers—"Oneida, Mohawk, Seneca, Cayuga, Onandagas, and Tuscarora. Some Iroquois fight with us rebels, and some Iroquois fight for the King . . ."

"*Most* Iroquois fight for the King," Ned corrected, slinging his pack on one shoulder. "Just like you English, choosing sides in this war has divided our people."

"Enough of that . . ." Jack draped a four-point blanket over Ned's shoulders like a cape. "We don't want to keep you here discussing politics. I know you have important business to attend to."

"I hear you, *at-uhló*, I hear you . . ." Ned laughed and squatted down beside the fire. "I'll take a piece of this fire and be on my way." Using a twig, he herded two egg-sized coals into a tin cup. Weapon on shoulder, he toasted them both with the cup of fire starter. "I'll be back when the redbreast sings in the day. *Ona kí wahe*—till next time."

Anne stood beside Jack and waved Ned off as he disappeared in the darkness beyond the glow of the campfire, oddly uncertain as to whether the Indian's presence or departure was more discomfiting.

"All right!" Jack clapped his hands together and began digging through a haversack. Producing a leathern flask, he sat down and swung his legs around to face the fire. "Peachy?" he offered.

Anne came to sit beside him. "I could use a drink of water."

Jack took a quick gulp from the flask, then leaned back and rifled through the gear to come up swinging a barrel-shaped canteen into her lap.

"Water . . . such as it is."

Anne took one swallow, grimaced, and recorked the vessel. The inside of the wooden canteen was made tight with a coating of pitch, imparting an unpleasant, turpentinish flavor to the water.

"Maybe I'll have a drink of your brandy, after all."

Jack handed over the flask. Though she was careful to take but a small sip, the strong liquor still stung her throat. She handed the bottle back, sputtering, "Never quite as peachy as the name would imply."

Jack laughed. "You made that same funny face after drinking your share of the Quaker's Armagnac, and there's no finer brandy in the world than French Armagnac."

Anne shrugged. "I'm not one for hard spirits."

"Oh, I don't know about that." Jack scooted close and wrapped an arm around her waist, his grin devilish. "As I recall, the evening drinking Armagnac ended with you and me carried away—doing the deed right there atop the press!" He took another scoof from his flask. "Ha! I won't soon forget that night."

"Seems like forever ago . . ." Anne could feel the blush sprung to her cheeks. "The night we printed the counterfeit banknotes . . ."

Jack grew suddenly somber and took another good gulp from his flask. "What started out a good and clever idea didn't end all that well, did it?"

Anne shook her head. The recollection of the unsuccessful counterfeiting scheme sent a torrent of troublesome memories through her brain—from the awful sight of Jack, bound at wrists and ankles, swinging from the prison-yard gallows, to Titus carrying Patsy Quinn's lifeless body through Canvastown, to the haunting look of betrayal in Edward Blankenship's eyes when she pulled the trigger to fire a musket ball point-blank to his head.

Giving her head a shake to banish her disturbing thoughts, she rested her hand in the spot between Jack's shoulder blades and asked, "How have you been faring? How's your arm?"

"Lucky thing I'm left-handed, eh?" Jack perked up a bit, flexing his right hand, stiffly opening and closing his fist. "Blankenship did me the favor of keeping a well-honed blade. Sliced to the bone, but a clean cut. The wound's healed well and gives me but little trouble. Working the ax as much as we do has helped me regain strength—that's for certain."

"And Titus is well?"

"Titus has taken to this life like a pig to the muck. He says running these hills puts him in mind of his boyhood in Virginia." Jack stood, unbuckled his belt, and dropped it into his open haversack.

Anne stared into the black hole of Jack's haversack, murmuring, "I never knew Titus was from Virginia . . ." She turned in her seat, and cast her eyes around the campsite. "So where've you pitched your tent?"

"You're under it, darling girl." Jack smiled and swept his arms up to the star-strewn sky.

"No! *Really?*" She squeaked out the last syllable.

"Canvas is too burdensome to tote around. Most days we just curl up in our blankets and catch sleep where we can." Jack gathered up a pair of woolen blankets, including the one Anne had brought along.

She beat back a flutter of panic, and brought reason to her tone. "With the storms we've been having . . ."

"Oh, when it rains we try to find shelter, or make one with deadfall and tree boughs." With a snap of the wrists, Jack unfurled the blankets one by one, floating them over the collected mass of balsam boughs. He turned to find Anne staring up at the sky, her brow woven in concern.

"Ah, now . . . you've no cause to fret, little noodle. We're blessed with a crystal clear night—not a cloud in the sky— and Ned helped me make us this nice balsam bed."

Anne eyed the blanket-draped boughs. "Pine branches?"

"Almost as soft as your lovely goose-down tick back at the Cup and Quill." Jack bounced his hand on the balsam mattress to demonstrate the springy quality.

"Jack! You don't really expect we're going to"—she sputtered—"on a pile of tree branches?"

"What were you expecting? Marquee tents and camp beds? Crystal goblets and Canary wine? Well, balsam boughs, peachy, and a starry night are the best I can offer." Jack flopped onto the bed, folding hands under head. "This is a sight better than most mattresses I've laid my bones upon—and for our purpose, certainly better than the hard ground."

"Our purpose . . ." Anne repeated under her breath.

Jack flipped onto his side, his head propped on his elbow. "C'mon, Annie! We oughtn't quibble. As always, our time together is small."

"As always . . ." she repeated. He was right. This rendezvous in the starlit woodland bore the same brand of uncertainty and limited time frame as the handful of nights they'd spent together back in New York town. Furtive, danger-fraught trysts requiring Jack to climb from the kitchenhouse rooftop with grappling hook and rope to the window of her tiny garret room, where they would whisper the short hours away, making love in the dark—literally over the heads of the British officers she'd been forced to quarter on the floor below.

Disappointment jammed her throat, and she was suddenly exhausted by the complicated machinations required to snatch a few simple moments together. Scrinching her eyes to abate her tears, she pulled her shawl tight to her shoulders, almost wishing she'd stayed back with Sally and saved herself the inevitable pain of yet another parting.

"What's troubling you, Annie?"

She shrugged. "I just wish . . ." She completed her thought with another shrug.

"I know . . ." Jack came to plop down beside her. "I so wish I could do better than tree boughs and brack canteen water . . ."

Anne sat up, pushing her hair back. "It's not that . . . It's not about the bed. I just wish things were different for us. Less complicated. More normal."

"Things will be different soon. This war can't last forever, and the way it's been going . . . Well, no matter who wins, once the war's over we'll be wed and living back at the Cup and Quill, frolicking on a proper feather tick under a proper roof. I promise." Jack crisscrossed his thumb over his heart. "But this is how it is for us here and now—and for now, lying with you in my arms on a bed of sweet balsam under a beautiful sky is truly my idea of heaven on earth." He brought her hand up and placed a kiss on the inside of her wrist.

"Mine, too," she said, drying her tears with the hem end of her shift.

Jack waggled his brow in the way that always made her laugh. "Then let's get to it!" Hopping to his feet, he pried open the jaws of the silver armbands at his biceps, tossing them one by one into his sack.

Anne let her shawl fall away as she stood to kick off her shoes and fiddle with the tie on the waistband of her skirt. She struggled with the knot, keeping an eye on Jack through downcast lashes, watching as he undid the buttons at his cuffs and tugged the frock shirt over his head.

Ranging the Adirondack foothills with an aim to wreak havoc on the British army had added a quality of tough durability to Jack's tall frame. The firelight illuminated his body, tanned Indian brown, his muscles tempered and hardened by a life lived on the run in the wilderness. As outlandish and heathen as he appeared in his Indian cos-

tume, Anne found herself quite taken with the allure of watching her
man strip down to beaded breechclout.

He looks as if he could move a mountain . . .

With heart beating a war dance in her breast, Anne swiped the
back of her hand to the perspiration collected on her brow, and tried
to regain a semblance of normal breathing. Successful in untying the
knot at her waistband, she dropped her skirt and stepped free from
the heavy yardage, quelling a brazen urge to peel off the thin shift she
wore as well. Lifting her heavy hair up off her neck, Anne backed
away from the fire, and caught Jack in an unabashed stare. Letting her
hair drop in a cascade, she fanned her flushed face with both hands.

"The fire's so warm . . ."

"The night chill is settling in, and when the dew falls, you'll be
happy for the heat cast from the coals." Jack braced one foot to a large
branch. Cracking it into manageable sizes, he tossed the pieces onto
the embers, sending flakes of fire borne on heated air blinking around
him in a glittery halo. Jack dropped down on hunkers, his half-crown
necklet swaying to and fro as he tended to the fire. It pleased Anne to
see him carry his love token near his heart, but other things not so
pleasing—and some things quite strange—were also brought to light
by the rising flames.

There were the recently acquired marks earned by his devotion to
the cause of liberty—the thin pink scar curving from his left eye to the
corner of his mouth, the rough scapegallows scar circling his neck,
and the vicious saber slash across his forearm—all his injuries yet raw
and raised. Trade silver dangling from his pierced ear flickered within
the tousle of long dark hair, and Anne reached out and brushed her
fingers over the curious drawing revealed on his bare shoulder—a
wing-spread eagle with a bunch of arrows clutched in one talon.

"Paint?" she asked.

"No . . ." He turned and flashed a shamefaced smile. "Rum—too
much of it, I'm afraid. That one is mine to keep forever." Standing upright, he clapped the dirt from his hands. "Well, our hearth is banked
for the night . . ."

Heart quickening, Anne took a step forward. Pulling her close,

Jack slid his hands around to encompass her waist and caress the small of her back. Twining her arms about his neck, she swayed into his embrace.

Jack nosed the top of her head. "Mmm . . . lavender . . ." he murmured. He bent to nuzzle her cheek, and whisper hoarse in her ear, "Come and lie with me?"

Rising on tiptoes, Anne answered his question with a kiss and, kissing and spinning, they twirled a slow and erratic path to the bed. Jack pulled Anne onto the blanketed boughs in a puff of balsam fragrance, deepening their kiss with a hungry groan. Rolling to lie side by side, he ran his hand up under the hem of her shift, his rough, work-calloused palm and fingers following a slow curve from thigh to hip. Caressing the dip at her waist for a moment, Jack moved upward to cup one breast before his hand fell back to course the same slow path in retreat, ending with an impelling nudge to urge her thighs apart.

A moan caught in her throat, and Anne began a struggle with the unfamiliar workings of his breechclout, finally tugging the swath of fabric loose enough to let slip her hand between his legs.

"*I-gods!*" Jack groaned, and rolled to cover her body with his.

Anne fluttered her eyes open to see the heavens bending over Jack's broad-muscled shoulders, and she watched a sparkling star shoot across the sky as their bodies joined in close embrace.

"It is a wonder, isn't it?" she whispered. "Loving, and being loved . . ."

Jack rose up to blot out the sparkling sky, and the only glimmer she could see was the amber firelight dancing in the dark of his eye.

"Like our little crown," he said, "fit together, we are complete."

"*Hurry!* It's so cold without you."

Jack shook off the last few drops before tucking himself back into his breechclout. Tugging on the front flap to settle the fabric snug in the straddle, he went to stir the embers to life and added a few chunks of wood, then grabbed his shirt and scuttled back between the warm blankets. "Here, you can put this on."

Anne sat up and wriggled into the shirt. Once she'd negotiated the ridiculously long sleeves, she dove back into their nest, snuggling up against Jack to loop her leg over his and make a pillow of his shoulder.

"Ooh! You are so nice and *toasty* . . ."

Their every shift of limb, shoulder, and hip sent up wafts of sweet balsam, and Jack relished the scent with a deep, indrawn breath. "Ahhh! I think from now on, I'll never pass a fir tree without pining for you . . ."

Anne couldn't help but laugh at his silly pun. She tipped her head to Jack's, and they both gazed up into the heavens. "That's a sight to see. It looks as if the angels spilled the salt cellar over the sky."

"You see this dusty swath arcing right over us?" Jack asked. "The astronomers call it the Milky Way—so many stars clustered so far away, it appears as mist to our eyes."

"A mist of stars," Anne said. "Imagine that . . ."

"Captain Feather Hat had the right of it—this is one fine night for stargazing." Still staring up at the sky, he asked, "What was it Feather Head gave you this morning, wrapped up with a red ribbon?"

Jolted by his sudden shift, Anne kept her tone level and her answer honest. "A dagger and sheath his Indian friend fashioned from the skin of the snake Sally and I killed."

"Hmmmphf . . ." Jack grunted. "He has an Indian friend?"

Anne nodded. "But not near as nice as Ned. In truth I'd rather not talk about Pepperell or anything else to do with the damned British. Tomorrow will be here soon enough."

Jack lay quiet for such a long time, Anne startled a bit when he pointed to the northeast and asked, "Do you see the brilliant star— right above the tip-top of the tallest pine tree?"

"I do . . ."

"The brightest stars in the sky are Sirius, Canopus, Alpha Centauri, Arturus, Vega, and Capella. That brilliant star right there is Capella."

"Capella," she repeated. "How is it you know so much about the stars?"

"At Parker's Press we printed a celestial map—a star chart of all the constellations—a beautiful copper engraving with hand-colored illustrations of all the mythological creatures and real gilt borders. Mr. Parker allowed me to take a plain copy to color on my own, and I have to say, I did a fair job of it. I have it still—packed away with my things at my brother's farm."

"One day we can hang it in our print shop."

"On a clear night like this one, I would bring my chart up to Parker's rooftop and sort out the business of the sky." Jack rubbed his bristly cheek to Anne's hair. "The time I first kissed you, the day the Stamp Act was repealed—I remember how I wished I could show the stars to a girl like you."

Anne pressed a kiss to his cheek. "And here you are—your wish come true."

Jack sat up. "I'd wager that's why Feather Head's offer to take you stargazing sent me more than a bit mad . . ."

"None of that! Not tonight." Anne pulled him to lie flat, and settled her head back on his shoulder. Once she could feel him relaxing to enjoy the sky, she asked, "The bright star up and to the right of Capella—what's it called?"

"That is . . . Alpheratz." He leaned his cheek to her head, and pointed. "Now follow on a diagonal down from Alpheratz—those next two stars are Mirach and Almach. The string of three belongs to the constellation Andromeda." Jack tipped his head away, and back again. "Makes no sense to me, but by the illustration on my chart, the Greeks determined those stars formed the image of a naked woman chained to a rock . . ."

"Why is she chained to a rock?"

Jack turned to face her, resting his head on the crook of his arm. "Because, like you, Andromeda was very beautiful, but unlike you, Andromeda had a very vain mother—Cassiopeia, Queen of Ethiopia." Jack turned onto his back, drawing a zigzag on the sky with his finger. "There's the constellation Cassiopeia—just above Andromeda."

Anne tugged his arm down. "But the *story* . . ."

"The story. Let's see . . ." Jack pushed a swath of hair from his face. "Though Cassiopeia was a queen, she was still a mere mortal woman—and a stupid woman at that. Stupid enough to boast to all and sundry about her daughter's beauty, and even claim Andromeda was more beautiful than the Nereids . . ."

"The Nereids?"

"The daughters of Poseidon—the nymphs of the sea."

Very solemn, Anne said, "Never a good idea to taunt the gods."

"As you have so wisely discerned, Cassiopeia's bragging is a terrible affront to Poseidon. In anger, he unleashed a horrible, hideous sea monster named Cetus, directing him to wreak havoc on the land and people of Ethiopia. Cetus is . . ." Jack sat up abruptly and craned his neck. "I don't see where Cetus is—hidden by the pines, I think . . ."

Anne pulled him to lie down. "Finish the story."

Jack settled back into his warm place. "The Oracle warns the King and Queen of the coming catastrophe, and tells them the only way to save their land and people is to give their daughter to the monster in sacrifice."

"They don't . . ."

"They do. They strip poor Andromeda naked and chain her to a rock out on a barren island, far from shore."

"What terrible parents . . ."

Jack shrugged. "Should they have sacrificed the multitude of their people for the life of one daughter? If they did, you would say, 'What terrible monarchs.'"

Anne gave him a thump to the chest. "So she's chained naked to a rock, and Cetus is on the way . . ."

Jack picked up the thread. ". . . And Perseus the Hero just happens to fly by and see Andromeda . . ."

"Fly by?"

"Perseus is just returning from a quest to kill Medusa and he has a pair of magic winged sandals—but that's another story. Anyway, Perseus falls instantly in love with Andromeda."

"And he rescues her!"

"Not exactly. A canny fellow, he first flies to Ethiopia and wrangles a deal with the King and Queen: He agrees to destroy Cetus in exchange for Andromeda's hand in marriage. Of course, they agree. Perseus flies back to Andromeda just as Cetus is about to gobble her up. Perseus goads Cetus into rising out of the water, and makes him gaze upon the Medusa's decapitated head, which he happens to carry in a magic sack . . ."

"How handy!" Anne giggled.

"Cetus is instantly turned to stone, Andromeda and Perseus are married, and they live happily ever after. When they died of ripe old age, Athena placed them in the sky as constellations."

Anne asked, "Which one is Perseus?"

"Right there, just below and to the left of Andromeda." Jack snaked his arm beneath Anne's shoulders, and pulled her close. "Keep your eye on Perseus and you might see a shooting star this time of year."

They lay quiet, watching the sky for some time, when Jack whispered in her ear. "I'll rescue you from any monster—land or sea."

"I know."

Anne blinked awake to a deep violet dawn. The celestial mob had dispersed with the onset of daylight, leaving behind only a few twinkling stragglers—the brightest of these high in the sky overhead. She barely whispered its name.

"Capella."

Dreading the advent of daylight, like a magical incantation to keep the sun at bay, she whispered the names of all the stars that had climbed higher into the sky, calling them back to the horizon. "Capella. Almach. Mirach. Alpheratz."

Jack's arm lay warm and heavy across her middle. She turned to see his features masked by a blanket of her hair, tiny wisps flying up and down on the whistling in and out of his breath. Anne gathered her tresses into a tail over one shoulder, and turned to lie in a curl on her side. Sleeping Jack matched her movement, and without any words they settled in to nest together like two cups in the cupboard.

"Mmmghh . . ." Jack said to the back of her head. "We ought wake."

Fully awake, Anne said, "Not yet."

She lay warm on their balsam bed, relishing the rise and fall of his chest against her back when, to her horror, a robin fluttered down to land just beyond the fire ring, his rich red breast startling in the pre-dawn light.

The early bird, she thought, reminded of the red-coated regulars up at dawn readying for the day's march. She watched the robin hunting for its breakfast, hopping here and there to peck at the dew-soaked ground with its beak.

"A redbreast," Jack whispered into her neck.

"Mm-hmm . . ." she said. "Pay him no heed."

But the robin would not be ignored. Hopping to perch on the log seat, he began his morning song. *Cheerup, cheerup, cheerup, cheerio!*

Jack gave her shoulder a little shake. "Ned will be here soon."

Anne covered her ears, trying to shut out every sound and every reason signaling the time had come for them to leave their private universe.

"One night's not enough." Her voice wavered, near tears.

Jack leaned up on his elbow and stroked her hair. "You're right. It's not enough."

Cheerup, cheerup, cheerup, cheerio!

Reaching down, Anne scooped up a small rock and hurled it at the robin, sending it fluttering up into the trees.

"Oh, Annie . . ." Jack wrapped her tight in his arms, and she turned and buried her face in his chest, but she could still hear the damned robin singing in the distance. She peeked up at the sky, searching the cerulean blue. "I don't see it anymore . . ."

"See what, Annie?"

"Capella." A single hot tear trickled out the corner of her eye, and her chest ached with sudden panic. The earth was still spinning. Time had not stood still. She bolted up, unable to stay her tears. "I know I have to go back there—and I will—but I want—no—I *need* for you to understand this one thing . . ."

Jack shifted to sit facing her, and he brushed back the mad tangle of hair from her face, his eyes deep pools of worry. "What is it?"

Anne met his eye, and took hold of his hand. "In order to serve the cause we so believe in—to fight how I can to win our country's liberty—I find myself doing things that in any other world would seem untrue to you. To us. You must know I'm not." She pulled Jack's hand to lie over her heart. "I belong to *you*."

Jack nodded, and pressed Anne's hand to his heart. "And I to you."

A rattle of drums echoed up through the morning mist, and the two of them jumped out of bed like cats out of the woodbox.

Jack scrambled to pull on his leggings and moccasins. "I was supposed to have you back before reveille beating! Sally's going to have my hide . . ."

Anne struggled out of Jack's shirt, wriggled into her skirt, and found her shoes. They worked together to fold and roll both blankets into tight sausages. Jack rigged his bedroll with a rope strap and slung it over his back. Pulling on his pouch and haversack he said, "I have your crown piece here."

Anne took it from him, dropped it down her shift, and tied her shawl ends into a knot at her breast. "As fond as you are of this breech-clout," she said, tugging on the flap, "you ought change back into breeches before you travel south, lest the Continentals mistake you for one of Burgoyne's Indians."

"I almost forgot . . ." Jack dove into his pouch. "I made a present for you," he said, handing her a small packet wrapped in a maple leaf and tied with a scrap of blue grosgrain ribbon.

Anne undid the wrapping to find a plump heart, carved of wood as smooth as a peach and stained golden brown. Beautiful in its simplicity, the heart fit in the palm of her hand. She was struck dumb.

"Wood from an oak that was split in two by lightning," Jack said. "Sanded it for hours on end to get the polish. Go on, turn it over."

Anne flipped the heart over, and she lost her breath. Within a hatched border, three words were etched in neat block letters, and carefully stained a deep umber:

LOVE
NEVER
FAILS

"Oh, Jack!" Anne smiled and blinked back her tears. "This is the most beautiful thing anyone has ever given me. I will cherish it always." She flung her arms around his neck, and kissed him farewell. "You'll be back after Stillwater?"

"I think we'll be joining the fight at Bennington. I imagine they'll need every man they can get. I'll make sure David sends someone to watch for your messages." Jack shouldered his rifle and pack and, with a jerk of his chin, said, "There's Neddy now."

Discreet in a stance at the edge of the ridge with his back to them, Ned leaned on his rifle, eyeing the horizon. Anne and Jack walked hand in hand the few steps to the parting in the brush and the deer path they had climbed to reach their haven.

"This path zigs and zags straight down to your camp. It's not far." Anne nodded. "I'll be fine."

It was clear neither of them wanted to curse their parting with the word "good-bye." Their lips met in one last, simple kiss, and Jack walked off to join up with Ned. Giving his friend a slap on the shoulder, they took to the trees.

Anne called out, "Take care . . ."

Jack turned to flash a grin and wave. Anne forced a smile and blew him a kiss, and she watched until he and Ned were lost in the rising mist.

Taking up her blanket, and clutching the wooden heart to her own heart, Anne started down the path. Covered in a veil of morning fog, and cheered by birdsong, the dark and ominous woodland came into enchanted green focus with the onset of dawn. Anne stopped at the rotting tree to see the patch of foxfire fungus transformed by the daylight into a clump of plain, ordinary mushrooms. She smiled and brushed her fingers across the velvety caps.

Whoever would guess how you glowed in the night?

❧ FIVE ❧

I love the man that can smile in trouble, that can gather strength from distress, and grow brave by reflection. 'Tis the business of little minds to shrink; but he whose heart is firm, and whose conscience approves his conduct, will pursue his principles unto death.

THOMAS PAINE, *The American Crisis*

SCOUTING THE ENEMY ENCAMPMENT NEAR BENNINGTON

Jack leaned in to toss another chunk of wood on the fire just when a wayward gust ruffled the smoke to sting his eyes. He took a step back, narrowing his eyes at an opening in the forest canopy overhead and the gray clouds roiling by like turbid river water. A drop of rain landed splat on his forehead.

"Get ready," Jack said, swiping the wet from his face with the back of his hand. "It's about to weather hard."

Stretched out along the full length of their lean-to shelter, Titus turned onto his side. Hugging his bedroll like a boon companion, he muttered, "No battle today . . ."

Fat summer raindrops began to find their way through the leaves and boughs, driving into the soft duff of the forest floor like miniature cannon shells. Jack ducked under the lean-to and took a tailor-style seat before the fire.

"I think this as good a time as any to cast some ball."

"Mm-hmm . . ." Titus grunted. "Lord knows we'll soon need all we can get."

Hinging open his folding knife, Jack shaved the end of a green-wood stick to a taper, and twisted the makeshift extension into the socket end on the handle of his smelting ladle. Nestling the ladle's shallow bowl in the bed of white-hot coals raked from the fire, he propped the makeshift handle on a rock to extend beyond the fire ring, keeping it cool to the touch and safe from the flames.

Jack arranged the rest of his bullet-making supplies on the swath of soft buckskin to his left—a cake of beeswax, half a dozen finger-length bars of lead, a pliers-like bullet mold with handles wrapped in leather strapping, a scotch polishing stone, and a battered copper spoon, its shank sharpened to a point. He placed one of the lead bars into the hot ladle and settled deeper under the shelter to wait and watch the metal melt into a blue-gray puddle.

They began the day's scout at dawn, but the clear blue skies did not fool Isaac, who soon noted the leaves on the ash tree had turned to show their white undersides. "Bad storm's on the way," he predicted. "No battle today."

Soon enough, huge thunderheads massed on the eastern horizon as the scouting party hurried through the woods to circle around the high ground occupied by Colonel Baum and his regiment. When they saw the enemy's contingent included a cohort of Mohawk warriors, Ned and Isaac altered their *gustoweh* in keeping with the Mohawk style, showing three feathers pointing upright, and broke away to infiltrate the German encampment.

With an eye on staying dry while they waited for the Oneidans to return, Jack and Titus set about constructing a simple shelter. Harvesting several lengths of spruce root, they lashed a sturdy ridgepole five feet off the ground between a huge pair of red spruce trees. Together, they assembled a square frame braced with a rough gridwork of sapling wood. The completed frame was propped and lashed to the ridgepole at a forty-five-degree angle with the open face away from the wind, providing space enough for four to sit, and plenty of cover to protect a fire.

Jack and Titus thatched the lean-to with a weaving of spruce boughs and pads of absorbent moss, and used the same to carpet the shelter floor. A small ring of stones was arranged at the open face, and a quantity of firewood was stockpiled. Combined with the natural windbreak afforded by the flanking tree trunks, and the living spruce umbrellas overhead, the hasty bower would provide plenty of shelter from the oncoming tempest.

A blast of wind whipped through the trees in a skirling rush, broadcasting a spray of mist and setting the shelter to rustle and quake. The pleasant patter of rain instantly shifted in intensity, and the new din was akin to thousands of anxious fingers drumming on hundreds of tabletops. Jack eyed the veracity of the structure.

Thunder rumbled overhead, sounding all the world like someone dragging a heavy chest across the floorboards of the heavens. Jack screwed a greenwood handle onto the spoon's pointy shank, setting it and the bullet mold on the coals to heat.

"D' you think it's storming by Annie and Sal?"

Titus didn't answer. Jack glanced back to see his friend snoring softly. No matter day or night, wind or rain, thunder or lightning, Titus was a great one for grabbing snatches of sleep whenever and wherever he could—a valuable wartime skill—a skill Jack often wished he could develop. A fretful sleeper, Jack never slept so sound as he did when holding Anne Merrick wrapped in his arms . . . *Was it the way her hair smelled of lavender? Or maybe something to do with the rhythm of her breath . . .*

He'd bedded more than a fair share of women in his time, and no other but Annie had ever managed to soothe his restless soul. Jack pinched off a bit of beeswax and worried it into a pea-sized ball between thumb and forefinger, the corners of his mouth turning up in a smile. One day, when the war was over, he would sleep to that sound every night.

One day . . .

He dropped the wax pea into the molten lead, and a gray cloudlet puffed up from the ladle like magic smoke from a sorcerer's cauldron. The bit of beeswax flux brought the metal's impurities to the surface.

One day soon . . . Jack flashed a smile, and just as quickly lost it. It was both naïve and stupid to believe anything but British victory would come soon. Using the spoon, he skimmed the dross from the molten metal, leaving behind a silvery puddle of pure lead.

We are at war with the world's most formidable foe . . .

He'd witnessed the vast British armada crowding New York's harbor—hundreds of ships armed with enough cannon to flatten any city in their sites. He and Titus had scouted on Long Island to see the first wave of the invasion—thousands of soldiers and massive amounts of artillery and matériel landing ashore. And when they infiltrated the British forces, they saw the Redcoats exact a *tour de force* in military strategy, outflanking the Continental Army's fortified position on Brooklyn Heights.

By all rights the war should have ended right then and there . . .

And it would have but not for a fortuitous fog allowing Washington to stage a stealthy nighttime retreat, saving what was left of his army to fight another day.

Pulling off a miracle to survive the year after the disastrous defeat on Long Island, the American rebel forces were now wedged between Burgoyne's well-trained army coming from the north, Howe and his army on the move, and Clinton with a sizable force occupying New York town. The unstoppable might of the Empire was on a collision course with a Continental Army desperate to increase ranks decimated by sickness and desertion.

When Jack and his fellow scouts caught up to the ragtag brigade of New Hampshire militiamen that had been deployed to prevent Burgoyne's Germans from raiding the stores at Bennington, he could not help but feel his heart sink. Though strong in numbers and spirit, and led by an ardent and experienced commander, the Patriot soldiers rallied to wage war on professional Hessian and Brunswicker troops without a piece of artillery, nor a single bayonet among the lot of them.

Outgunned, outtrained, without steady support to feed, clothe, and arm those willing to fight . . . Jack heaved a sigh. "We don't stand a chance."

He poured a thin stream of molten lead into the opening of the bullet mold. The lead hardened in a matter of moments. He swung open the mold, and rapped it with the flat of his knife, knocking the hot bullet out onto the buckskin.

Staring at the solitary ball, he thought, *Like flies on a bull, we are to the British . . . annoying, but easily banished with the flick of a tail.*

Why the British Army did not flick their tail was the question befuddling the minds of many. Giving his head a shake, Jack turned to his task, developing a rhythm to pouring and knocking the molded pieces out onto the buckskin to cool. The balls rolled to settle in a depression on the leather, and began to look like a bowl of just-picked silver cherries, the flared stems a by-product of the molding process. Jack clipped off these sprues, rubbing each finished sphere against his scotch stone to erase the resulting nub, assuring his ammunition would fly straight and true to the target.

Waste not, want not . . . Jack gathered up the severed sprues along with the now-hardened drips and drops of lead that had drizzled onto the ground during the pouring. The tick of the lead bits dropping into his cupped hand recalled his days at Parker's Press, where he apprenticed and worked as a journeyman printer before the war. He sprinkled the lead bits into the ladle, as if adding pepper to a stew, thinking how he ought to be setting lead type, not making lead bullets. Watching the hardened lead consumed by the molten puddle, he muttered, "I wish the British would just have done with us already. Then Annie and me could . . ."

He regretted the awful wish almost as soon as it had coalesced in his brain, and he couldn't believe he'd let the words escape his lips. Jack glanced back at Titus, worried his sleeping friend might have heard him utter such treason. Surprised and dismayed to find himself gone so out of heart for his cause, Jack ground a knuckled fist at the bridge of his nose, telling himself, "Stop it!"

Too much in blood and treasure had been sacrificed to give up now. *Too much.* Throwing back his head, he shouted out to the wind, "Bugger King George's royal arse, and *fuck* the British Army as well!"

Jack snatched up his mold, and returned to the business of making ammunition with methodical frenzy. Pour. Knock. Pour. Knock.

Pour. Knock. Pour. Knock. Add more lead. Add the flux. Clip sprues. Pour. Knock. Pour. Knock . . .

A blinding flash of lightning split the sky, and almost simultaneous earsplitting thunder cracked so loud as to startle the bullet mold from his hand and roust Titus to snap upright. Jack pulled a deep breath to check his racing heart.

"How long have I been asleep?" Titus asked, eyeing the large pile of newly minted musket balls.

"Not long."

Titus stretched, sniffing at the sulfurous smell in the air. "Your face is white as gypsum paste."

"A close strike, that . . ." Jack pulled the ladle away from the coals to cool.

"You know, they say carrying a laurel leaf will keep the lightning away . . ."

"Who says? Old wives?" Jack laughed, gathering his bullet-making tools into his haversack. "And how exactly is a leaf in your pocket supposed to stave off a strike like the one we just heard?"

"I don't know exactly—but there is a science to dealing with lightning." Titus would not be swayed. "Mr. Fraunces would have us lay iron bars on the beer barrels stored in the cellar, to keep the beer from turning sour during a thunderstorm."

"Pish. Another old wives' tale."

Titus scooted forward, dragging his pack along to sit beside Jack. He untied the camp kettle strung there and handed it to Jack. "Put this out to catch some water. Isaac and Ned will be back soon, and as long as we have fire, I'll make us some soup for our supper."

"Soup? Really?" Jack stretched to set the kettle out beyond the shelter, raindrops beating a bright tune on the hollow brass.

Titus nodded with a wicked twinkle in his eye as he undid the buckles on his pack. "Back in Stillwater, the quartermaster was distributing officers' rations. I fell in the queue with the other mess servants and came away with a share for us." He laid out the bounty gained by clever deception—four turnips, a dozen onions braided together, one thick yellow carrot the size of a baby's leg, a small sack of oatmeal, and a package wrapped in brown paper and tied with jute string.

Jack tugged at the string on the package. "Pocket soup?"

"It is."

The package contained eight pieces of "soup." Able to fit in a soldier's pocket, each cake of concentrated meat stock was roughly four inches square and one inch thick, and as dense and brown as chewy molasses candy.

Jack laughed and slapped his friend on the back. "I surely do benefit by your knack for seeing to your belly."

Titus grinned. "On rare occasion, this black face comes in handy."

Jack set the full kettle to heat on hot embers. Titus dropped in a soup cake and two handfuls of oatmeal into the simmering rainwater. Four onions, two turnips, and a third of the carrot were chopped and added to the pot.

Waiting on their supper, the pair used the time to see to their weapons. The worst of the thunderstorm blew over, and gradually the rain diminished to a drizzle, and all the while their soup bubbled into a wholesome potage. On hearing a familiar turkey call, Jack and Titus grabbed their guns and scooted out from under the shelter to see Isaac and Ned trotting through the trees, dressed in naught but breechclouts and bare chests.

"*Shekóli.*" The smiling Indians slipped under the shelter, and took seats close to the fire, dark eyes sparkling with pleasure to see supper had been seen to in their absence.

Jack once again admired the tattoo on Ned's shoulder. In one talon the spread eagle clutched six arrows—one arrow for every nation in the Iroquois Confederacy. As Isaac had explained, "Many arrows bundled together are stronger than one arrow alone." On an idle day, bolstered with plenty of pain-numbing rum, Jack had Isaac tattoo a similar design on his shoulder, except the eagle that was pricked into his skin with a needle and rubbed with lampblack was clutching a bundle of thirteen arrows, one for each of the thirteen states in his new nation.

The men all found their spoons and dipped their cups into the kettle.

"Mmmm . . . *yawéku ka*," Isaac said, with an appreciative nod.

Jack waited until both Isaac and Ned finished eating before asking, "Did you get into the German camp?"

The Indians cast him a look that would curdle sweet milk, and both of them dipped in for another helping without answering his question. After slurping down seconds, Ned was the first to speak. "The German colonel—he chose good ground."

Isaac began smoothing the space between himself and Jack. "This is the enemy camp." Pushing a small pile of spruce needles into a hill at the center, he began illustrating the details of the German encampment on a canvas of dirt and duff. Using a small stick, he drew a sinewy line curving past the hill to indicate the river. Crossing the line with a short stroke he said, "The bridge." He placed his tin cup within a bend of the river. "The American militia camp is here." Putting a small stone a ways behind the hill he added, "We are here, on the wooded ridge."

With their bearings thus defined, Jack and Titus nodded and scooted closer.

Ned balanced a small twig atop the spruce-needle hill. "One three-pound cannon on the high ground aimed west, well protected with a breastwork of logs." He placed another twig, saying, "A second three-pounder aimed at the bridge. I counted only a dozen artillerymen in all."

"A strength and a weakness," Jack noted.

Ned shrugged. "They say Burgoyne is sending more soldiers and cannon. Once reinforced, they move forward to Bennington."

Titus asked, "How many men do they have now?"

Placing one of the lead balls from Jack's pile of ammunition near the hill, Isaac said, "One hundred Indians are camped near the bottom of the hill." Keeping to the scale of one ball per hundred soldiers, Isaac continued to place bullets to illustrate troop strength and position. "Three hundred Hessian grenadiers and dragoons—green and blue coats—protecting the high ground. Two hundred Redcoats with the baggage. Two hundred Loyalist militia—Canadians and Americans—defending the bridge."

"You can tell them by the paper badges pinned to their hats," Ned added.

"Paper badges?"

Ned dug into his pouch for a damp and wrinkled scrap of foolscap. "The German Colonel ordered it, so they can tell Loyalist from rebel in the heat of battle."

Jack examined the simple badge—nothing more than an inch-wide strip of white paper folded at the center to flap like a pair of wings—then he turned back to study the map for a moment before looking up with a big smile. "It's almost too easy, isn't it?"

Anne walked in step with Geoffrey Pepperell, elbows linked, her skirts draped over her free arm. Even so, the wind coupled with the disparity in their heights rendered useless the waxcloth umbrella he had borrowed from Lucy Lennox. What seemed a trifling drizzle when they departed the manor house General Burgoyne had commandeered as his headquarters, developed into quite a downpour.

The path along the river's edge was a thick stew of mud, and Anne's every step was taken with effort, as if she were shod in lead boots. She tugged a foot free from the sucking morass, almost losing one of the sturdy walking shoes she'd had sense enough to wear to the General's table this night.

Geoffrey set their lantern on the ground, handed the umbrella off to Anne, and unsheathed his sword. Prodding with the tip of the blade, he succeeded in dislodging a great glop caught between the sole and heel of his boot. "This substance is more akin to mortar than to mud," he said, scraping the soles off with the edge of his blade. "Let me have at yours now . . ." He motioned for Anne to lift her foot.

Anne braced a hand to the Captain's shoulder as he bent to take practical hold of her silk-stockinged ankle to clear the muck caked on her shoes.

"That's better, no?" Geoffrey stood to sheathe his sword. Armed once again with lantern and umbrella, he offered the crook of his elbow. "Let's make for higher ground."

Awaiting the supply train on its way from Lake George, the army encamped along the curving east bank of the Hudson at a place called Fort Miller. Once restocked with provisions, the entire army would traverse the pontoon bridge Burgoyne's clever engineers had built, and then advance toward Albany.

Anne flinched at a huge bolt of lightning splitting the sky over the river. She buried her face in a red wool–clad shoulder to weather the companion clap of thunder.

"A close strike . . ." Pepperell wrapped an arm about her. Another bright bolt shot across the black sky, and the accompanying thunder rumbled like the roll of battle drums, signaling a blast of wicked wind to race up the river, jostling the trees and dousing their light.

Geoffrey shouted over the tumult of the storm, "We'll take cover in the fort!" With umbrella turned as a shield to the wind, he pulled Anne toward the dilapidated ruins silhouetted against a sky alive with flash and crackle.

Fort Miller once guarded the fording place just below a series of rapids on the Hudson, and a huge stone fireplace and forlorn chimney were all that remained of the old wilderness blockhouse. They ducked in to hunker inside the vast fireplace.

"I think we are wise to wait out this tempest." Pepperell stuffed the half-open umbrella up the chimney's throat to block the rain making its way through the opening.

"There's not much time between the lightning and thunder." Anne dropped to haunches, wringing water from her hems, casting a fretful glance to the north where the baggage train was encamped. "I hope Sally's faring well . . ."

"You needn't worry. Your tent's staked high enough, and the trees will break the wind." Setting sword to the side, Pepperell sat down beside her, back pressed to the firebox wall. "We'll go forth as soon as it ceases lightning."

The rain turned almost horizontal, and moved in waves on staccato blasts of wind, punctuated by flashes and crashes of lightning and thunder. Water sprayed through the open face of their shelter, but the huge old fireplace was deep enough to offer protection from the worst of the storm.

Anne settled to sit beside Geoffrey, hugging her knees to her chest. "That was a rather somber table this evening. The General in particular seemed to be treading a razor's edge."

With eyes never wavering from the curtain of water falling across the opening of the firebox, Geoffrey said, "We're all on edge since Colonel Baum sent troubling news regarding the strength of the rebel forces at Bennington. Two more battalions of Hessians have been dispatched; we can do naught but wait on tenterhooks, hoping the relief forces arrive in time to mitigate a disaster."

Of this Anne was well aware. She and Sally had stood with the hankie-waving crowd of weeping German wives flanking the sides of the road, counting the reinforcements as they marched out of camp to go to the aid of Colonel Baum.

"You really oughtn't fret so. The Germans are assured victory."

"What care these mercenaries, I wonder?" Pepperell leaned his head back, brow knit, eyes shut, then shrugged. "Win or lose, they earn their pay regardless."

Taken aback by his embittered tone, Anne asked, "You doubt the fidelity of the German troops?"

"I've no doubt their officers are honorable fighting men," he said. "But the German common soldiers lack a backbone stiffened by love of country and cause. Every day, more and more of them desert— more willing to brave the unknown wilderness than the inevitable battle at the end of our march."

"Have you voiced your concerns to your commander?"

Pepperell shook his head. "Fraser detests officers who cavil and question the judgment of their superiors, and I don't blame him."

Anne persisted. "If you believe there's a problem, it would ease your mind to point it out to General Fraser."

Geoffrey heaved a weary sigh. "I'm afraid my malaise regarding the Germans is but a single symptom of a much more complex corruption."

Though most anxious to learn what could cause an officer in Burgoyne's command to be so troubled, Anne found she was yet hard-pressed to not feel sorry for the man regardless the color of his coat.

"Giving voice to your concerns can help to unburden a heavy heart. If you'd like"—Anne scooted closer—"I can lend an ear."

Pepperell shot a weak smile. "I wouldn't want to bother you . . ."

Anne gave him a jab with her elbow. "Come, now—it's a poor friend indeed that can't be bothered."

Geoffrey turned, and with all the earnestness of a young boy he said, "Then you must swear to never repeat what I'm about to say—not to Sally, not to anyone."

With no little guilt, Anne crossed a thumb over her heart. "As if you whispered your cares down a well."

Geoffrey drew a great in-and-out breath. "So, you know I'm no stranger to these colonies. I was all of fifteen years old when my father bought my first commission in the Forty-fourth Regiment of Foot back in . . ." He pondered for a moment. " 'Fifty-nine, it was."

Surprised to find such a seasoned officer of high rank was only three years her senior, Anne said, "You were but a boy."

"Discipline, hard marching, and self-reliance quick made a man of me. I was there when we took Fort Niagara, and I was at the siege to see de Cavagnal surrender Montreal to Amherst, and the whole of Canada added to the Empire." Geoffrey tugged the soggy ribbon from his queue, and raked fingers through his wet hair. "So enamored with this country was I, once back home in England, I resigned the Forty-fourth for the Forty-first so I could come back and garrison at Niagara."

"Is that where you met Ohaweio?"

Pepperell nodded. "And where I learned to speak Mohawk. When I caught wind of Gentleman Johnny's Army of Canada, I left Niagara to join the Twenty-fourth. I simply had to be part of this campaign."

Anne said, "I'm sure your familiarity with the country, and ability to communicate direct with the natives, made you a perfect addition to his corps . . ."

"Because of my experience, I always knew the army's progress would be much more difficult than Burgoyne anticipated. And I knew the Indians would be difficult to control. But with the ultimate aim of uniting our forces with Howe's army, I never questioned that we would succeed in crushing the rebellion to put an end to this bloody civil war." His voice fell very quiet, his eyes downcast. "Things have changed since. Now I question the methods we use to wage war on our brethren Englishmen. The answers to my questions leave me with naught but a dreadful feeling of doom—and it hangs like a flaming sword over my head."

There was a terrible crashing accompanied by wood snapping and splintering, like the sound of axmen felling trees in the forest.

"Stay put," Geoffrey said, jumping to his feet. "I'll be right back."

Pepperell made a dash toward the river, disappearing beyond Anne's sight. In a short time, he reappeared in a full-on gallop, skittering to a halt as he stamped the mud from his boots and dropped into a dripping crouch beside her.

"You should see the Hudson! A raging torrent . . ." Geoffrey panted, swiping water from his face.

"The awful noise . . . ?"

"Our pontoon bridge being washed away." Plopping to sit with legs sprawled before him, he puffed out a great breath, and leaned back against the wall. "What are we doing here?"

"We're waiting out the storm . . ."

He heaved an exhausted sigh and turned to Anne with grief-filled eyes. "I mean what are we doing *here*—hiring mercenaries to fight our battles—giving our native allies stretch to scalp and pillage at will—" His mouth went grim and he waved his hands to the sky. "It is clear to me God Himself does not favor our position."

In all the time she'd spent with Geoffrey he'd never been anything but a cheerful, stalwart, and devoted officer. *If Geoffrey Pepperell harbors doubts, there must be others of good conscience who feel the same,* she thought, with an initial glee that shifted straight to guilt. The man's obvious misery should not cause such delight.

Anne laid a hand on Pepperell's shoulder. "Remember, this war is man's doing, and so men must suffer the consequences of it. The same storm causing grief to British intentions is no doubt harrying the rebels as well."

His shoulders slumped. "True enough. I've no call blaming God for our misfortunes"—Pepperell snorted a halfhearted chuckle—"when we are proving so adept at mucking up the whole affair quite handily on our own."

"Take heart," Anne said, forcing conviction to her tone. "Surely when General Howe's army converges with ours in Albany everything will be set aright."

Geoffrey shagged his head from side to side. "Howe's not coming."

Anne could feel her heart flutter in her chest. "What? Why not?"

Geoffrey shrugged. "He's rallied his forces to Pennsylvania. He intends to engage Washington there."

"Oh." Anne stammered, "Why . . . th-that is quite a turn . . ."

"And it seems my General has been aware of this turn for some time." Geoffrey pinched the bridge of his nose. "My head aches to think of it. Our entire stratagem is based upon the two armies forming a junction to crush the rebels once and for all, and Burgoyne only informed us of Howe's Judas kiss in meeting *today*." In a practiced and precise imitation of Gentleman Johnny's very posh accent, he mimicked, " 'And oh, by the way, my good fellows, we are betrayed by the bastard Howe, and are to be left spinning in the wind, as it were . . .' "

"He said *that*?"

"No . . ." Geoffrey flashed a sheepish grin. "But it's exactly where we stand."

Anne drew a deep breath. "What's to be done?"

"We ought commence a strategic withdrawal. We are in a damned bad way, and our ridiculous supply line will be our undoing. We are at half rations now, and still we have difficulties provisioning the troops. All the while, our scouts tell us the Continentals are daily growing their forces. Without Howe, we are badly outnumbered."

"Do you think Burgoyne will fall back?"

"He will not, and, swords in hand, my brothers-in-arms and I will follow wherever he leads." Geoffrey took Anne by the hand. "But I admit this to your ears only, in the dark, in a raging storm." Squeezing it tight, he kept his eyes forward. "We cannot conquer this land."

Anne shook her head. "This pending confrontation with the Continentals is perhaps questionable, but the King has deep coffers. He will send all the supplies and soldiers needed to secure his colonies . . ."

"No matter," Pepperell said. "We will not win and here's why: If I were as American as I am an Englishman, and foreign troops landed in my country, I would never lay down my arms. *Never!* And our army fights a country filled with a relentless multitude of such Americans."

To hear this brand of thinking existed among the British officer corps! Anne sat quiet, loath to say anything that might lead Pepperell astray from this line of reasoning. Together they sat for some time, listening as the thunder faded and watching the rain slow to a reasonable patter. She tugged at Geoffrey's hand. "I'm worried for Sally . . ."

"You're right. We should be on our way."

They walked in silence to the baggage camp. Protected by a buffer of tall pines, her tent seemed unruffled by the storm. Standing before the doorway, Anne offered her hand. "Good night, Captain."

"You must be aware, Mrs. Merrick, there are not many in this world I make privy to my thoughts." Geoffrey brought her hand to his lips. "Thank you for putting up with this soldier's ramblings."

Anne reached up on tiptoe and planted a kiss on his cheek, whispering in his ear. "Try not to carry all the burdens of the world upon your shoulders, Mr. Pepperell. Some things are simply beyond control." She slipped inside her tent.

Sally bolted upright, wide-awake. Unshuttering their lantern, she exclaimed, "Och! Yer soaked t' th' bone!" Snatching up the seam ripper, she hopped up to help Anne undress.

Anne took the ripper from Sally's hand. "While I undress, you mix up a batch of hartshorn ink and ready my writing box."

Sally swung the writing box out, flipping open the lid. "It must be dire news indeed for yer Redcoat rascal to forgo all attempts at wheedlin' ye intae his bed."

Anne peeked through the tent flaps and watched Pepperell wend his way back to the river path. "It would be a crime, but I think with a little effort, I would be able to turn that man to our cause."

"G'won! What's happened?"

Anne stepped out of her soaking wet gown. "Howe and his army are in Pennsylvania, and he intends to stay there!"

"*Gweeshtie!*" Sally dropped onto her cot. "Ye think we might actually stand a chance of beating Burgoyne?"

Anne tugged on a dry shift. "At the least, we stand a better chance."

After preparing her message in the bottle, Anne extinguished the light and lay down to sleep. She worried the smooth curves of the little wooden heart she now kept beneath her pillow, thinking about the secret doubts Geoffrey Pepperell admitted to owning, and wondered how many of the Redcoats might feel the same. *Perhaps even Howe himself. Poor Geoffrey.* No whip bit so sharp as the lash of one's own conscience.

Anne glanced over to Sally, sleeping so soundly, her soft snore buzzing in time with the steady rain on the tent top. She always envied Sally's knack for not allowing the day's events to trouble a good night's sleep. Tossing onto her side, Anne had a hard time finding a comfortable position, and was amused to find she craved the springy balsam bed she'd so derided.

The steady rain drumming on the taut canvas slowed and dwindled to a random scattering of heavy drops loosened by the wind traveling through the treetops. Anne gathered her shawl about her shoulders and stepped outside.

But for the constant shush of the river rushing by, the camp was dead quiet. Here and there she could see the yellow glow of fires kindled by pickets on guard duty. A refreshing breeze blew in off the river, and the storm clouds slipped quickly across the face of an almost-full moon, like a herd of misty horses racing across the sky.

Ho-hoo . . . hoo . . . hooooh!

Anne spun to the direction of the owl's call, heart a-race, half expecting Jack to come sauntering from the trees decked out in befeathered Oneidan finery. She sighed, and pinched back tears.

Just an owl being an owl.

Pockets of starry sky became exposed by the wind chasing the storm clouds to the west. Anne faced east, searching for and finding Capella. Pulling her shawl tight to her shoulders, she imagined Jack somewhere looking up at the same bright star.

One day soon, she thought, smiling.

Jack handed the paper to General Stark. "And this is the badge the Loyalist militia wear pinned to their hats."

A refreshing breeze blew in through the wagon doors at either end of the old Dutch barn serving as headquarters for the American forces, sending the lights into a flicker. The Loyalist badge fluttered from Stark's grasp like a butterfly.

The general from New Hampshire turned his attention back to the makeshift table contrived of planking and a pair of sawhorses. He pushed the tin lamp to shine upon the detailed schematic of the German camp Isaac had drawn there with a chunk of charcoal.

John Stark was taller than most men crowding around the table, including Jack and Titus, who both stood over six feet tall. All bones and sinner, Stark was leaner than a piece of venison jerky. His hawk nose was the fulcrum to craggy features and a pair of belligerent blue eyes—all topped off with a shock of contrary white hair. Well regarded as a ruthless fighter in the French and Indian War, and most recently a valiant commander in the battle at Breed's Hill, John Stark was a better man than most to follow into battle.

"A-yuh . . . so these Hessians have planted *two* pieces of artillery. A very cautious position." Stark spoke with a strong Yankee twang. He circled the table in silence. "The bastards have fortified and wait on reinforcements from Burgoyne. With their big guns and bayonets—of which we have none—they are confident that they can easily withstand any conventional charge we might launch." Again, the General slowly shuffled around the drawing, his concentrated gaze assessing the lay of the land from all angles. Stamping to a halt, he looked up to address his officers. "Caution is best answered with feats of derring-do. With our strength in numbers, we shall divide ourselves into four columns, surround the enemy, and attack as one overwhelming body before the damned Germans have chance to be reinforced."

The General zinged sword from scabbard and used it to delineate his battle plan in swooping strokes of steel. "Colonel Herrick, you will lead your men around through the woodland, to attack from the west. Nichol—the north. Hobart—south. Stickney and I will take the bridge from the east. As Herrick has the farthest to march his troops into position, he will begin the attack. We will snap our trap closed on your signal, Sam."

All heads were bobbing at the brilliance of the bold plan of attack—and that quickly, there was a potent smell of victory in the air.

Stark touched the tip of his sword to the black bars Isaac had drawn to indicate the German artillery positions. "Grapeshot sprayed from these three-pounders can do us all a world of hurt no matter what our formation. Our plan hinges on silencing their cannons. Are you an able man with that rifle, Mr. Hampton?"

"Titus and I can do some damage. Isaac and Ned here can shoot the eye from an owl on a moonless night."

"Your scouting party will leave in advance of our flanking columns and gain position to pick off every one of their artillerymen."

"Yes, sir!" Titus gave Jack a slap on the back, and they both grinned. This was exactly the kind of irregular warfare they excelled at.

A sudden hullabaloo interrupted the staff meeting—pistol fire and shouting as a mob poured through the doorway, crowding into the barn. Stark leapt up onto the trestle table, calling the tumultuous crowd to order with sword upraised.

"Arrah! Explain yourselves!"

The crowd hushed and one man was pushed to the fore.

"We've come in answer to your call to arms, General! One hundred and fifty Massachusetts fighting men ready to feed the bloody-backs and their goddamn Hessian lackeys a supper of lead."

"We welcome Massachusetts to our fold," Stark shouted over their cheering. "And we admire your spirit, sir, but would you fight now on this dark and rainy night?"

"We'll fight the Redcoats wherever and whenever we can find 'em, sir!"

This bravado drew a second rousing cheer, and Stark shouted out, "Oh, there'll be fighting aplenty tomorrow. If the Lord gives us sunshine, the battle will be hotter than love at haying time."

The men burst into laughter, and with a wave of his arm Stark brought them to order. "I promise you all this—if I do not give you fighting enough, I will never call on you to come again. Go back to your people, Massachusetts, and tell them to get some rest while they can."

Abuzz with excitement, the Massachusetts men shuffled out, and the General ordered lights out, bidding good night to all as he left to his bed in the farmhouse. Ned and Isaac called to Jack and Titus, pointing to the loft, and they clambered up the ladder to make soft beds of the hayrick.

Jack could swear Titus began snoring before his head hit the bedroll he used for a pillow. Though his bed was comfortable and dry, Jack could not find sleep as easy as his fellows. Tossing and turning, too keyed up by the prospect of battle in the morning, he went over the details of the daring plan in his mind.

We are going to prevail.

The drumming of the rain on the roof shakes slowed to a stop. Jack rose to open the shutters and gaze out on the sea of men who would, on the morrow, become his brothers-in-arms.

By God, these men have come to fight!

Compared to Burgoyne's encampments where tents and equipage were formed and arranged in an organized manner, the Patriot soldiers sprawled out across the fallow field in a haphazard jumble, making their beds under wagons, oiled tarps, and greenwood shelters.

Jack's gaze wandered up to the heavens where patches of star-filled sky emerged between great, misty swathes of disbursing clouds, reminding him of Anne's loose hair caught up on a breeze. It was easy to imagine her standing somewhere, in her gauzy shift, head thrown back, looking up at the same night sky. The wind worked to comb the clouds into thin strands, exposing the brightest star in Andromeda. He smiled and whispered, "Capella."

✣ SIX ✣

Tyranny, like hell, is not easily conquered; yet we have this consolation with us, that the harder the conflict, the more glorious the triumph.

THOMAS PAINE, *The American Crisis*

ON THE HUDSON, AFTER THE STORM

"There!" Anne floated a clean napkin over Sally's basket. "We're off!"

With hems tucked into waistbands to protect them from the mud, Anne and Sally made their way from the kitchen fires with three dozen scones hot off the iron, ready for use as bribe or reward.

Happy fat white cumuli floated lazily across the crisp blue sky, and it was already a hot and sultry day. The strong sun steamed what Anne had earlier classified as soupy mud into an easier-to-negotiate cakey paste.

The camp was a hive of activity recuperating from the stormy night. Sodden clothing, bedding, and gear were laid over brush, hung from every available tree limb, and strung from webs of impromptu clothesline. Door flaps were thrown open, airing out waterlogged tents. Canvas, line, and poles damaged by the strong winds were being repaired and restaked.

Anne ran up to knock at the door of the small farmhouse occupied by the officers' wives. When the Baroness answered, Anne pressed a dozen scones tied up in a napkin into her hands.

"Fresh-baked this morning by my girl, Sally—with raisins to please small bellies." Anne winked at the two girls peeking out from behind their mother's skirts.

"How wonderfully kind of you, Mrs. Merrick," the Baroness exclaimed. "Friedrich relished the last batch immensely."

"Is the Baron at home?"

"*Nein.*" Irritation furrowed the woman's brow. "Called from his breakfast to headquarters early this morning."

"A soldier's duty knows no clock." Anne put on a sympathetic face. "I'm sure everyone is on pins and needles waiting to hear of Colonel Baum's success at Bennington—is there news?"

"None yet. My husband is most anxious."

"As are we all." Anne stepped off the stoop. "Good day, Baroness."

Anne and Sally marched toward the manor house Burgoyne commandeered for his headquarters, and joined the loose crowd gathering in the yard. Slowing to a stroll, the women assessed the available soldiers, and, spotting a likely target, Sally elbowed Anne.

"The sergeant leanin' against th' newel post—that's Pennybrig."

With a nod Anne said, "Let's go."

Sally waved, and called out, "Hoy! Sergeant Pennybrig!"

The particularly grizzled veteran turned and his face near broke in two for a smile missing an incisor and the molar beside it. Excepting for the salt-and-pepper stubble edging toward being branded a full-on beard, Pennybrig was strapped and buttoned into his full dress regimentals.

"We're on our way to pay a visit to yer woman," Sally said in a thicker-than-usual brogue. "How d'ye fend this bright an' cheery morn?"

Thin streams of powder-tinged sweat ran from under his side-curl wig to stain the black leather stock buckled about his jowly neck. Handkerchief wadded in his fist, the sergeant mopped his brow and lamented, "I'm as hot as a bride in a featherbed and as wet as her—" Catching himself, his eyes went wide, and he stammered, "Beg pardon, ladies. I've an ugly soldier's tongue on me."

Anne smiled. "It *is* very hot today, Sergeant. Would you care for some water?"

Sally offered the man a tin bottle from their basket. As he guzzled half the contents, she asked, "What are ye after, all busked out in full fig on a day like today, anyway?"

Puffing out an exasperated sigh, he jerked a thumb to the house. "Court-martialing. I bore witness in one case. Wasting a good chunk o' my day on cowards and deserters."

Sally tsked. "Och, a soldier's duty knows no clock."

"Ohhh . . ." Anne said, "When we saw the crowd we thought there might be word on the success of the expedition to Bennington."

Pennybrig took another drink, swiping his sleeve over the mouth of the bottle before handing it back. "The scouts tolt me our reinforcements are still on the road, bogged down in the muck an' mire."

Picking two scones out of the basket, Anne handed them to the Sergeant. "Here's something to add a bit of pleasure to your day, Sergeant. Fresh-baked this morning."

In shagging his head negative, Pennybrig's wig slipped precariously to the left, and was quickly righted with a deft tug. "I've no coin on me, mistress."

"Not to worry . . ." Anne pressed the scones into his hands. "You've earned them."

The door to the house was flung open and two desolate soldiers shackled in wrist and leg irons were shuffled down the stairs under guard.

"What did they do?" Sally asked.

"Deserters." Pennybrig produced a clean handkerchief, in which he carefully wrapped the scones before slipping them into his pocket. "Sentenced to a striping—five hundred lashes each with the cat-o'-nine."

"They're but boys!" Anne hated to contemplate the damage to be wrought on their young backs and spirits.

"There's no cosseting of deserters in the King's army." The sergeant pointed to a third man being prodded down the stairs, leg irons clanking. "Here's the poor bugger I was called to testify against—quit his sentinel post to desert! Scouting party picked him up some twenty miles away, just wandering along the road, la-di-da." Pennybrig tapped a grubby-nailed forefinger to his temple. "Not right in the head, that one. Thick as manure and only half as useful, if ye ask me. Says he deserted because the washwomen refused t' tend to his laundry. Pah! I know for a fact Bab Pennybrig is not prone to refusing any man's coin."

"What's to become of him?"

"That one's earned the full measure of Johnny's wrath—firing squad."

"My!" Anne said. "Discipline has grown harsh indeed."

"Especially harsh," Sally added, "if the lad is as thick as ye say."

"Aye, 'tis harsh, but the man quit his post and Gentleman Johnny's making a fair example of him." The drummers began beating the call to assemble, and like a dog to the whistle, Pennybrig snapped to attention. "The Forty-seventh is being paraded t' witness the execution, ladies—many thanks fer th' drink and th' scones."

While the regiment was drummed into formation, the shackled prisoner was marched out to the far end of the pasture. They stripped the man's regimental jacket from his back, and his white shirt was daubed with an X over his heart, in bootblack. The rhythm of the drum call shifted into a steady roll, and a tow sack was drawn over his head.

Anne grabbed Sally by the hand and they hurried away. The tension in Anne's neck was as tight as the cords on the drums, and it seemed they could not move fast enough to escape the shouts of, "Ready— aim—"

Cracckkkkk.

The women flinched in unison—shoulders to ears. Anne stopped and turned. Eight puffs of smoke floated like a string of pearls above the head of the onlookers, the shots yet echoing up the river valley.

Sally pulled Anne by the apron strings. "C'mon . . ."

They picked their way down a sloppy path to the river and the laundrywomen working the steaming cauldrons. The children crowded around Sally, and she distributed the remaining scones among them, breaking them in two. "Share, ye wee imps," she admonished, "or I'll take a switch to yer hurdies." Swinging the empty basket overhead,

Sally called, "Hoy, Bab! We spied yer man over t' headquarters. He cuts a fine figure in his fancy coat."

Bright as a beet, Bab stirred the wash on the boil. "Was that th' crack of the firing squad just then?"

"Aye." Sally nodded.

"God rest the poor lad's soul." Bab stepped away from the wash to make a sign of the cross. Leaning on her battledore, she closed her eyes and fanned the back of her neck with her hand. "I swan, it's hotter than two cats fighting in a wool sock today."

Anne and Sally sat on a tree stump to slip off their shoes and roll off their stockings. "Come wading with us," Anne said. "It'll do you some good."

Bab kicked off her wooden clogs and the three of them kilted their skirts high and ran down to cool their feet. Anne pointed upriver to a gang of shirtless soldiers splashing around, who were shouting in German and tossing wood and shards of sodden canvas onto the shore.

"What are they up to?"

"Salvaging pontoons and bridge decking scattered by the storm," Bab said, her eyes wandering warily to gaze at the opposite shore. "There'll be no retreat. Gentleman Johnny means to build us another bridge."

Jack squinted in the bright sunlight and watched the column of stoic Indians armed with gun and tomahawk marching into the barnyard, many of them dressed in British red coats. "What have we here?"

Ned shaded his eyes with one hand. "Those are Stockbridge Indians."

"Mahicans so loyal to the British they were near wiped out fighting in the French War," Isaac explained. "So few in numbers now, they live with the support of the Oneida."

"I heard the Stockbridge fought with the Americans at Breed's Hill, but I didn't believe it." Ned folded his arms across his chest, head shaking in wonder. "*Koué!* Never thought to see the day when Mahicans would take up arms against the Redcoat . . ."

The new influx of manpower was quickly welcomed and integrated into the four columns forming on the fallow field, more than two thousand men ready and eager to do battle. Scraps of foolscap were passed along the lines, and the militiamen pinned the counterfeit Loyalist badges to their hats with plenty of high-spirited laughter and bravado. Jack, Titus, Ned, and Isaac stood off to the side, divested of all heavy gear—traveling light with but weapons, pouch, and powder horn. Ned bounced on the balls of his feet, and Jack saw Isaac quiet his nephew with a hand to his shoulder.

The troops pulled to full attention when General Stark emerged from the barn. Mounted on a big gray gelding, back ramrod straight, he traversed up and down the ranks, his face a craggy and serious study. Rising up on his stirrups, Stark pointed west and shouted for all to hear. "There are your enemies—and they are ours, or this night Molly Stark sleeps a widow!"

"Huzzah!" Fists and rifles punched the air, and Jack bellowed his cheer, feeling as if his lungs would burst from his chest. On Stark's signal the drummer boys beat a marching cadence, and in a thump and a clankety-clank, the first two columns were set in motion, splitting like fish from the bone into opposite directions.

On the same signal, Jack and his fellow scouts peeled off in a trot. Running along the river flats, they splashed across a small creek feeding into the Walloomsac River, and parted ways—Titus and Isaac heading toward the bridge, Jack and Ned toward the wooded ridge.

Rifles strapped across their backs, Jack and Neddy ran up and along the ridgeline to a place northeast of the German artillery redoubt. Stopping to search for a suitable tree at the edge of the woodland, Ned leapt to grab hold of a branch on an age-old sugar maple, swinging up to straddle its lowest limb. "This is the one."

Leaning down with arm outstretched, Ned pulled Jack along, and then clambered up the ladder of limbs with the speed and agility of a squirrel. When breathless Jack caught up, he found Ned sitting comfortable on a sturdy limb, about three-quarters of the way up, his rifle laid across his lap, and without a word he pointed to the clear view of the German cannon seated behind a breastwork of logs about two hundred yards away. Jack settled onto a limb just below Ned.

"I've never seen any human climb a tree with your kind of speed."

Ned began swinging his legs. "My Oneida name—Sharontaka-was—it means 'tree shaker.' On a hunt, I was always the one chosen to climb up to scout from on high."

"Tree Shaker." Jack laughed. "After today, they will call you 'Widow Maker.'"

Ned grinned. "That's a good name, too."

Neither Jack nor Ned suffered any qualms applying their hands and eyes to a battle tactic decried by the British as uncivilized and barbaric. Charged with nervous energy, they both reviewed the condition of their weapons, and arranged their shooting accoutrements.

When compared to a British smoothbore Brown Bess, Jack's rifle seemed ill suited for the battlefield. Lacking a bayonet, its rifle barrel took twice as long to load, making it a senseless weapon for use in European-style warfare. But the range and accuracy of an American rifle made it the perfect sharpshooter's weapon. In the hands of a marksman shooting from under cover at a distance, the rifle wrought pinpoint damage, and this woodsman's skill was an advantage the rebels were learning to exploit.

To make for quicker loading and improve their rate of fire, both Jack and Ned had prepared a bullet block. Nothing more than a paddle of wood augered through with a dozen holes matching the caliber of the weapon, each hole fitted with a lead ball wrapped in a greased patch of fabric. In the heat of battle, the board could be handily positioned over the bore, the bullet more quickly rammed down the tight-fitting grooved barrel to the breech. Their bullet blocks were attached to sturdy shoulder straps crossing over chest, nestled alongside powder horns filled to the brim with perfectly dry gunpowder.

Jack followed Ned's example, and wore his priming horn fashioned from the pointed tip of a deer antler on a stout thong around his neck. The hollowed-out antler contained the fine-grained gunpowder granules to be tapped into the frizzen on the flintlock to catch the spark when flint struck steel to charge the shot. A shooter had to carefully control the prime—not enough would result in a misfire; too much could severely damage one's weapon and person.

Jack studied the redoubt through his spyglass, counting heads. "We have seven gunners to dispatch." He passed the glass to Ned.

Ned peered through, one eye asquint. "Hmmm . . . those blue coats aren't as easy to mark as the red on a day like today."

From their vantage point, they had a good view of the overall encampment, renewing Jack's admiration for Stark's daring strategy to divide his force and completely surround the enemy. He fingered the paper pinned to his hat and only hoped the subterfuge would fool the Brunswicker pickets into allowing the militiamen to gain their positions according to the battle plan.

He and Ned set their flintlocks at half cock and settled in to wait for the rebel forces to encircle the enemy, sharing what was left of their pemmican and a few stale wheat cakes—not a bad breakfast when washed down with a gulp of peachy from Jack's flask.

Their backbones were instantly stiffened by cracklings of sporadic gunfire coming from the west. Standing to peer out beyond their cover of branches, Jack could see flashes and puffs of smoke coming from gunfire in the clearing around the bridge to the east.

"They've begun."

Within the cannon redoubt, the German gunners lurched to their feet to peer over the breastwork. Another volley of shot sent them scrambling to ready their cannon.

Ned and Jack regained solid seats on their tree limbs and brought rifles to full cock and stocks to shoulders, settling on their targets. Jack looked up, the mottled pattern of shadow and sunlight coming through the maple leaves dancing across Ned's brown face. "The sergeant using the quadrant is in my sights," he said.

Ned nodded. "I have a clear shot at the gunner with the ram."

In a unison crack and boom of rifle fire, the man with the quadrant and the man with the ram dropped from sight. The Germans were rattled for a moment, confused by the direction of the attack.

Discipline willed out, and the artillery commander quickly reorganized his crew into a more defensive posture, working low behind the cover of the breastwork. At the same time, Jack and Ned reloaded.

"Keep your eye on those red puffballs they have on the tops of their hats," Jack advised.

Ned pulled the trigger, and dispatched the crew commander. "Four left," he said, pouring a measure of powder down the smoking barrel of his rifle.

Jack pulled his trigger. "Three."

As Jack and Ned concentrated on the time-consuming process of reloading their weapons—swiping the barrels clean, pouring powder, ramming patch and ball, charging the frizzen pan—the Germans whisked off their hats and shaded their eyes from the sun, using what they knew to be but a minute or two at the most to try to locate their far-off assailants. One man shouted and pointed to the telltale smoke trail floating away from the sugar maple. The artillerymen ducked low and swiveled the cannon around, taking aim at the revealed position.

Heart a-race, Jack pulled weapon to shoulder and peered along his sights, methodically moving the barrel from spot to spot, searching for a good target. A plume of smoke wiggled up from the redoubt, and Ned gave Jack's shirttail a yank as he scrambled down the tree. "Move!" he shouted.

They leapt from limb to limb, catching clothing on branches, scraping skin on rough bark. The boom of the three-pounder was followed by the unmistakable whirr of a heavy iron ball hurtling with unimaginable speed through the air. The ball hit the mark dead-on in a crash and crack of wood, shaking the two men out to tumble and roll onto the ground like ripe fruit in a shower of wood shards, branches, and leaves.

Ned did not waste a second. Leaping to his feet, he scrambled back up the damaged tree. Jack gave his head a shake to resettle his brains and followed after.

Shouts and heavy musket fire resounded from the opposite direction. Stark's two columns charged across the bridge. The dragoon squadrons holding the redoubt on the high ground beneath the cannon were forming to withstand a mighty rebel assault.

With admirable German tenacity, the three remaining gunners heaved their gun around toward this new threat, swabbing the steaming muzzle and ramming powder charge and muslin bags filled with deadly grapeshot with machinelike precision. Not bothering with instruments, they simply pointed the muzzle at the charging mass of patriot soldiers.

His face a study in calm and steady deliberation, Ned took aim and dropped the gunner holding the linstock—the long rod wrapped with the slow match fuse used to light the charge.

"Neddy!"

Like jugglers at the fair, Jack tossed up his loaded rifle at the same time the spent weapon was dropped down. With a calm grace, Ned cocked the gun, pulled quick aim, and picked off a courageous gunner just as he lunged forward to pluck the smoking linstock from the hands of his fallen comrade. The sole surviving artilleryman cast a panicked glance toward the maple tree, and hurled himself over the breastwork, abandoning the cannon.

"Done!" Jack shouted. They scrambled down the tree, finished reloading, and ran to join the chaos at the foot of the hill.

Gunfire rang out fast and furious. The encampment was shrouded in smoke, and the field was littered with blue-coated humps of fallen soldiers.

"Jack Hampton!" Titus shouted from behind a choice cluster of tree stumps and rubble, waving his hat. "Over here!"

Jack and Ned ran in a crouch, dodging around the fallen. With musket fire whizzing overhead, they slid in to join their fellows.

"What took you so long?" Titus said with a grin, ramming a load down the barrel of his rifle.

"Damn Germans managed to shake us out of our perch." Rolling over to lie on his stomach, Jack waited for a blue jacket to move into his sights and he fired.

A rifle was best used from a position of cover, where the shooter could maintain protection while reloading. Jack and his fellow scouts quickly spent the ammunition on their bullet boards, and were forced to resort to fumbling with individual patches and lead balls.

Assaulted from every direction, the Brunswickers' steady fire began to slow, and then, after a few sporadic pops and flares, the German line went quiet.

Jack rolled to lean back against their cover. He drew a deep breath, and coughed, lungs burning from breathing in acrid sulfur smoke. His shirt stuck to his skin with a glue of sweat, dust, and dirt, and his rifle was blazing hot in his hands. Mouth equally gummy, he longed for a drink from his flask to wash away the coppery taste of blood in his mouth where he'd bitten his tongue in the fall from the tree. "Sounds like they've run out of either powder or ammunition."

"Or both," said Titus. "If our fellows have taken their ammunition wagons as planned."

"Good." Isaac wiped the sweat from his face on his sleeve and laid his rifle aside. "My gun is useless—fouled."

"Mine, too." Ned strapped his rifle across his back and unhooked the tomahawk from his belt.

In the sudden quiet Jack became aware of the ringing in his ears. "You think they'll surrender?"

Isaac tugged his battle club free. "I wouldn't."

Jack and Titus followed suit. Armed with tomahawks and razor-sharp knives slipped inside knee garters, they coiled into a crouch, ready for anything.

A breeze swept across the field, lifting the heavy gun smoke. As if on this signal, three sharp blasts of a whistle accompanied by orders shouted in a guttural tongue snapped all rebel eyes to the redoubt. With a barbaric battle cry that Jack imagined must have once sent a chill up the spine of Roman centurions ages ago, the besieged Brunswickers charged down from their defensive position in a whirl and fury, bright sabers upraised, bayonets honed and shining glorious in the sunshine. These hardened faces looked determined to cut a way through the rebel lines. The Patriot militiamen sprang forward and met the enemy with a flash of musket fire and a clank of edged steel.

The clash was fierce, but short-lived. The outnumbered Germans were soon vanquished by the overwhelming rebel force. As Burgoyne's mercenaries tossed aside their weapons and fell to their knees with arms upraised in surrender, the scruffy Patriot army—in all their homespun, nut-dyed glory—raised their old and mismatched weapons, and shouted in victorious salute.

"LIBERTY!!"

In wonder, toothy smiles began to brighten the grimy and breathless Patriot faces with the realization that they had not only outwitted and outfought professional, trained troops; they had protected what was theirs at the Bennington depot, and also prospered greatly to the tune of hundreds of muskets, wagonloads of ammunition, swords, and two much-coveted artillery pieces.

"We won!!!!" Jack linked arms with Titus. Laughing and spinning round and round, they danced a noisy jig.

Sally whisked the tent flap open. "There's a havoc in th' camp!"

Anne tossed stockings and garters to the side, slipped shoes on bare feet, hoisted her skirts, and ran to catch up with Sally, following the river path toward the General's headquarters and the sound of drums beating the call to assemble.

The commotion centered on the makeshift parade ground at the manor house, where Burgoyne sat mounted straight and handsome in full and sparkling regalia on a prancing steed, leading the 47th Foot in formation from the camp.

Anne and Sally pushed their way through the throng to find Bab Pennybrig and the Crisps waving bits of pure white linen edged with lace as the regiment marched past.

"What's happened?" Anne asked.

"A complete disaster!" Emma Crisp wailed.

Bab Pennybrig did not contradict her friend's hysterics. "Baum's Brunswickers and the Hessian reinforcements Burgoyne sent have all been crushed in a rebel onslaught. Pennybrig says nine hundred are killed or captured!"

Anne's breath caught in her throat. "My gracious!"

"Never trusted these Germans, not me," Emma Crisp declared. "A fushionless, mim-mouthed lot, always singing their dreary hymns."

"So where's yer man an' th' Forty-seventh off to?" Sally asked Bab Pennybrig.

"Rescue force." Even stoic Bab seemed stricken to the core, the corners of her mouth dragged downward with worry. "Gentleman Johnny's leading it himself to recover and escort stragglers who may have escaped capture. As things stand now, our general's lost a full seventh of his corps on this escapade, and gained nary and naught for the effort."

"What a dismal turn of events . . . I'm . . . Oh . . ." Anne tugged the hankie from her pocket, pressing it over her mouth to conceal her inexcusable happiness, and she slumped against Sally for support.

Sally clutched her by the hand. "Are ye unwell?"

"The heat, I think . . . combined with the ill news." Anne heaved a ragged sigh. "I'm feeling . . . overcome."

The laundrywomen turned and cooed, whisking out their hankies to fan Anne's flushed face. "Best take yer mistress for a lie-down, Sally," Bab advised.

"Aye—look at her," Emma Crisp concurred. "Th' poor thing's gone as red as a cardinal's cloak."

Sally wound a supporting arm around Anne's waist. "Dinna fash, ladies. She's prone to going all egg-shelly. A cool cloth to the brow and a tot of rum will put her to rights."

Anne leaned her head on her friend's sturdy shoulder and they headed slowly back to their tent with somber, downcast faces, matching the mood of the soldiers and officers gathered throughout the camp muttering in worried groups. Dipping into their tent, Sally pulled the door flaps shut and tied the ties tight. She turned to face Anne.

They both burst into wide grins, and in the narrow aisle between their camp beds, the women kicked off their sensible shoes, lifted their skirts, and danced a silent jig.

❧ SEVEN ❧

We have put, Sir, our hands to the plough, and cursed be he
that looketh back.

THOMAS PAINE, *The American Crisis*

SEPTEMBER 18, 1777
HAVING CROSSED OVER THE HUDSON

The young grenadier dug down into his pocket, pulling forth a two-penny piece. Holding it pinched between thumb and forefinger, he offered the precious coin to Anne in exchange for the letter she'd written on his behalf.

"No charge." Anne rejected his payment with a shake of her head, handing over the sheet of foolscap. No matter the color of their coats, she could not bring herself to accept any payment for writing the letters some of the soldiers readied before marching into battle.

The Redcoat didn't argue the point, relieved to slip his hard-earned silver and the folded page into his breast pocket. "My thanks t' ye, Widow Merrick. It's true what they say—yer possessed of a kind soul."

Since the army crossed the Hudson into what was solid rebel territory, Anne's pen was kept busy writing these letters bidding farewell to dear mothers, beloved wives, and sweethearts—often begging forgiveness for some slight or real transgression, or giving instruction on how to disburse personal possessions. Every letter assumed the worst, and every letter asked for prayers.

The onset of twilight brought with it a horde of mosquitoes to further plague the Redcoat army, and Anne killed the leviathan feasting on her forearm with a smack. She licked her thumb, and swiped away the sticky smear left behind. Even the mosquitoes seemed bolder and fiercer on this side of the river.

She packed her wares. Peddler's box on her back, and her hands left free to swat at will, she marched a quickstep back to the crowded site at the very outskirts of the camp where sutlers, peddlers, and campwives were cloistered by order of Burgoyne. Anne was careful to note the placement of every sentry on picket duty along the way. Posted at close and regular intervals, the new picket line was quite a gauntlet, and she could not figure a way to get beyond it without being seen.

After the sound trouncing received at Bennington, Burgoyne tarried for several weeks at the Fort Miller camp, rebuilding the pontoon bridge and—most important—gathering provisions via his tenuous supply line stretching all the way back to Canada. Once ten tons of provisions had been horded, and careful rationing instituted, Burgoyne led his army across the Hudson. The General was intent on getting to Albany, as ordered, whether Howe was there to meet him or not.

Three days before, mounted on his charger, Burgoyne greeted each regiment as it stepped off the bridge, with his hat raised high and a shouted, "Britons never retreat!" His soldiers cheered in response.

Once the army, artillery, and resupplied baggage train completed the crossing, General Burgoyne ordered the floating bridge dismantled. From her position at the tail end of the snaking column crossing over the Hudson, Anne watched the engineers release the pontoons from their moorings. As the last link to supply and communication tumbled past on the current, she could not help but admire the dogged purpose these British exhibited. Burgoyne had made certain there would be no turning back.

The bravado displayed at the river crossing was soon squashed flatter than the mosquito on her arm. The Patriot army owned the west bank of the river, and Burgoyne's progress forward was at once relegated to worse than a snail's pace.

The only road was so severely damaged, the British columns were forced to march in a tortuous single file most of the way. To further bedevil the Redcoat advance, the bridges crossing over the many creeks and streams feeding the Hudson had all been destroyed, causing long periods of complete standstill, waiting for the engineers to jury-rig new crossings.

The vulnerable and drawn-out column was hemmed in on the right by the Hudson, and on the left by very steep, menacing, tree-covered hills. Redcoat scouts and foragers had little room in which to reconnoiter, and they were so immediately harried, ambushed, or captured by the rebels, Burgoyne was soon forced to put an end to sending out any scouting parties. He and his seven-thousand-man army stumbled forward veritably blindfolded, not knowing the whereabouts or numbers of the rebel army, or how it was preparing to engage.

Every step forward contributed to a palpable unease. There was not a single beast of any type to be seen—cattle, sheep, pigs, even deer were all missing from the landscape. The few wilderness farm fields the army passed stood burned or thoroughly gleaned by their unseen enemy.

A terrifying rumor warning of rebel sharpshooters lurking behind every tree and stone soon spread up and down the column like wildfire, putting everyone on edge. The rumor was soon affirmed as fact when a group of soldiers—lured by the prospect of a likely potato patch—breached the picket line and were mown down in an instant crack and flash of rifle fire.

With no way or hope of replenishing his precious supply of fighting men, Burgoyne railed at this loss for "the pitiful consideration of potatoes." Orders were issued for all corps to proceed completely armed and fit out for instant action. To guard against rebel infiltration and maintain control over his troops, a dense picket line was mandated in camp and a complex system of passwords instituted. It was made clear to one and all, man or woman—cross the picket line, and, if the rebels didn't plant a lead ball between your eyes, Gentleman Johnny would see you hanged for disobeying orders.

Anne stopped to reposition leather straps on her peddler's pack. She'd hiked three miles to the front lines and learned nothing of value.

What a waste of time.

Burgoyne's high-command officers were so deeply embroiled in preparing for conflict with the rebel army, she hadn't even seen Geoffrey Pepperell, much less spoken to him, since they'd crossed the Hudson. The Baroness and Lucy Lennox were equally sequestered from their husbands, and Anne found her main streams of intelligence had run bone-dry.

No matter. Impossible to pass any messages, anyway. Up ahead, she spied Sally walking along the very edge of the path in a listless stroll, her basket dangling by two fingers. Anne called out, "Sally!" and ran to catch up with her friend.

"Any news?"

Sally shrugged. "More of the same. Everyone's on pins and needles. The soldiers ready for battle. Their womenfolk dread it."

Anne nodded. "I walked all the way up to the front line where the Twenty-fourth is camped. You can actually hear the Continental drums echoing from their works somewhere on the heights."

"We're tha' close?" Sally's voice wavered, and her big blue eyes went watery.

Anne nodded. "There's bound to be a clash any day."

Choking back a sob, Sally hiked her skirt and darted off in a sprint. Anne chased after, and slowed to a walk upon seeing her friend duck inside their tent. She took a deep breath before following her inside.

Sally lay on her cot facing the tent wall, a single creased page in her hand. From the sad sighs and sniffling, Anne knew Sally was reading, for perhaps the thousandth time, the last letter she'd received from David back in Peekskill.

Poor thing! The closer they moved toward the Continental Army and the inevitable battle, the harder it was on her.

"Landsakes!" Anne clapped her hands together, killing a mosquito hovering over Sally's head. "These beasts are big enough to be harnessed." Wielding a damp towel she'd twirled into a whip, Anne went on a hunt, killing half a dozen biters lurking along the canvas roof. She then uncorked a bottle of lavender oil, and massaged the scent onto her arms, face, and neck to keep the bugs at bay. She offered the oil to Sally. "You should put some on."

Sally didn't budge, so Anne poured a dab onto her friend's exposed forearm, rubbing it in. "You don't want to catch a fever, do you, Sal?"

"Och, Annie, can ye leave me be?" Sally drew her blanket over her head. "If ye want to be a help, go and see to the wee ones next door. The poor things are being et alive."

"Come with me."

"I've no' th' temper for any more idle chatter this day." Sally's voice was very tired, and she waved Anne off. "G'won—off wi' ye. There are scones for them . . . there . . . in my basket."

Relieved to have an excuse to escape the thickening brew of doom and gloom percolating inside their tent, Anne dropped the lavender oil into the basket and snatched up a lantern before heading out the door. "I'll see to our light as well."

General Burgoyne had the camp followers confined to a small flat area along the river shore, organizing the usual helter-skelter camp into a tight military order, creating a very crowded and noisome tent city.

Sally and Anne had acquainted themselves with their close neighbors, and had taken a special liking of the campwives on their left. Cheerful, tiny things with dark hair, pixie faces, and lilting Welsh accents, the two sisters were married to a pair of brothers serving in the 47th. The Sandiland women lived on the strength of the regiment, and were allowed to draw rations from army stores by working alongside Bab Pennybrig in the laundry.

With a baby balanced on one knee, Viney Sandiland sat near the smoke of a small fire, forming handfuls of unleavened wheat dough into flat cakes to bake on the broken blade of a spade-turned-griddle. She greeted Anne with a smile.

"'Ullo, there, Mrs. Merrick! How're ye keeping?"

Anne held up the basket. "I've lavender and scones for the children."

"*Ust!*" With a snap of her apron, Viney shooed off the two little boys squabbling over the only other campstool. "Have a sit-down, missus—please. This is a surprise. Where's your Sally today?"

Anne sat down, catching one of the boys by the shirttail, she trapped him between her knees. She quickly broke off a piece of scone and handed it to him, putting an instant halt to her captive's wriggling. "Sally's not feeling up to the mark today."

"Poor dab! Coming onto her monthly, is she?"

Anne nodded. "I suspect so."

"Good evening t' ye, Mrs. Merrick." Viney's younger sister, Prue, waddled out from inside the tent. About to give birth at any moment, she looked as if she'd hidden a ripe melon under her skirt. Prue's advanced pregnancy did not deter her from chasing after three assorted wee Sandilands, lining them up to wait their turn for scones and lavender.

"It's good you have your own fire today," Anne noted. "The mosquitoes are especially voracious, and the smoke will help to keep them away."

"Voracious," Viney repeated in a way Anne could tell the word was being set aside for future use.

Prue swiped a loose tendril of dark hair back under her mobcap, and bent over the fire to give stir to a kettle of pease porridge simmering over the hot coals. "Our men brought us a supply of firewood so's we wouldn't have to fight for a place amongst the mob at the kitchen fire."

Anne poured lavender oil onto her palms, and got to work on the boy she'd trapped, briskly rubbing it onto his face and neck. "You know," she said to him, moving down to his scabby arms, "I once was Mama to a sturdy little boy like you."

Prue glanced over. "What happened to him—your lad?"

"The smallpox. Jemmy was but six when he was stricken," Anne said, surprising herself with how matter-of-fact her loss sounded. It didn't seem so long ago she wouldn't have been able to speak Jemmy's name without choking back tears. "He's gone from me five years this spring."

"Did ye have any others?"

"No. Only the one boy."

"How sad for you." Viney pushed the shovel blade onto the embers. "I lost my eldest girl to the pox last summer."

Prue stepped around and gave her sister's shoulder a squeeze. "All of us caught it—every one."

"How awful." Anne winced. Not counting the baby on the way, the sisters had five boys between them.

"Don't know how we pulled through," Prue said. "And I suppose we were lucky to lose only one, but we do miss our little Mary . . ."

"That we do, sister." Viney blew out a sad sigh. "It's hard, sometimes—this army life."

Anne gave the boy a hug and a pat on the bum, and lured the next little Sandiland into position with half a scone. "These past few days since crossing the river have been more than trying."

"Poor Prue." Viney nodded. "About to hatch, and here we're on the move again. The heat is so wearin' on her."

"It seems t' be gettin' cooler by night, though." The violet circles beneath Prue's eyes told the tale of sleepless nights in their hot and crowded tent. She arched her back and ground her knuckles into her spine. "The trees are beginning to turn—I spied more than a few red leaves on the maples along the river, and last night I slept like the dead, din't I?"

Anne stood and used a stout stick to move the porridge kettle from the embers. "I suspect your sleeping sound has less to do with the weather, and more to do with your being exhausted."

"Exhausted," Viney repeated with a nod to her sister.

Anne gestured to the stool. "You ought sit and rest a bit—raise your feet up . . ."

"I'm afeart th' stool won't bear my weight." Prue laughed as she sank down to sit on the ground with legs outstretched, the space between them immediately filled with a tumble of wrestling boys.

Anne divided a scone between the boys, quickly rubbed them down, and sent them off to play. "Lavender is said to make one sleepy." She handed the bottle to Prue, who, with eyes closed, rubbed oil into the back of her neck.

Viney shifted to cradle her fussing baby. Untying the string on her blouse, she put him to breast. "I haven't had a tidy night's sleep myself since before we crossed the river—toss and turn with worry, I do."

"Our Viney cannot abide the not knowing." Prue massaged the last of the oil onto swollen ankles and feet.

"Maddening, it is. I but close my eyes and my brains take off in a spinning reel." Viney ticked off her worries on her fingers. "When will our men be ordered into battle? When will Prue's baby decide to be born? How on earth are we to stretch half rations to fill so many bellies? Where will we winter? How are we to find shoes for all the boys?" Viney gave her head a shake to dispel her worries. "Fain would I be back home in Swansea with Mum and Dad . . ."

Prue's pretty blue eyes snapped open. "Tripe! Not only would you be about committing murder after two days with Mum nipping at your neck; being apart from Sam for more than a fortnight would find you drowned in a sea of your own tears."

"You tell true, sister." Viney giggled. "I could never stand to be parted overlong from my Sam. And I truly couldn't bear not being able t' wish my man Godspeed afore he marches into battle."

"And if, heaven forbid, either of our lads are wounded," Prue added, "with us here, they are certain t' be tended by the most loving hands . . ."

"Aye, that," Viney agreed. "But yet, army life is hard on woman-kind, in't it?"

"'Tis," Prue agreed with a single and emphatic nod. "Awful hard."

Anne lit the wick on her lamp, bid the Sandiland women good evening, and went back to her tent, finding Sally curled on her side under a blanket, the letter from David still gripped between her fingers. She hung the lantern from the ridgepole, and adjusted the wick to bathe the tent in light. "That's better for reading, isn't it?"

"I don't need any light." Sally's voice was gruff with tears. "David's words are etched on my heart."

Anne began rifling through their dwindling stores, coming up with an almost empty sack of dried peas, and a shriveled rind of bacon. "The Sandilands have a fire. What say I cook us up a little porridge?"

"Not on my account. I've no stomach for food of any sort."

Anne sank down on her cot. "Neither do I."

She fell back, staring up at the canvas. Every scrap of information they unearthed since crossing the river pointed to the inevitability of the upcoming battle. She and Sally both knew the temper of these Redcoats. No matter the hardships that must be endured, nor the odds for success, they were determined to prevail.

And somewhere in those hills, only a few miles distant, David, Jack, and Titus, as well, were committed to joining in the fight that was bound to ensue. Anne so wished she could, like the Sandiland sisters, be there to bid her men Godspeed before the battle.

No matter how swift and desperate their last tryst had been, she was happy and grateful for the precious night spent under the stars wrapped in her lover's arms, but it was troubling to think the sight of Jack following Ned into the mist might be the last she'd ever see of him.

No good comes from thinking the worst.

Anne turned to see Sally's cot trembling with her stifled sobbing. The war left Sally and David separated for more days than they'd ever been together. It was no wonder she grew so upset at the news of the Continental drums. The last time David engaged in a battle, he'd barely come out alive.

It was a good thing she and Sally had decided not to flee New York as most had, and were there to tend to his wounds properly. Anne shuddered. Her brother would have certainly perished otherwise.

"I've been thinking, Sally," she whispered. "Since crossing the river, we haven't been able to cull any sort of information, and with the picket line so tight, we've no way to pass along what we might learn, anyway. Burgoyne's situation and actions are just as clear to the Patriot scouts as they are to us—probably more so."

Sally whimpered and waved her hand, as if shooing off a mosquito.

"What I'm saying is I see no point in our staying on any longer." Anne jumped up to her feet and untied her apron. "As a matter of fact, I'm going right now to ask Burgoyne for a pass to leave the camp."

Sally bolted upright and, swinging her legs to the side, she sniffed and swiped the wet from her pillow-creased cheek with the back of her hand. "D'ye think he'll let us go?"

"I don't see why not. After all, the sale of scones and foolscap are not essential to his efforts here." Anne slipped off her mobcap, smoothed her hair, and tied the ribbons of her best straw hat under her chin.

"Bide a wee." Sally rummaged through her pocket and brought out the rouge pot and thumbed a little color onto Anne's lips and cheeks.

Anne pulled her friend in for a hard hug. "Wipe your tears and start packing—we'll leave at first light. By sunset tomorrow, we'll be with David and Jack in the Continental camp."

Jack, Titus, Isaac, and Ned finished strapping on their gear and ran to catch up with David Peabody. Regardless of his bad leg, Anne's brother led them through the camp at a quick pace.

"Did I hear right?" Jack asked. "Did you say Stark has *quit* the fight?"

"That's right," David said over his shoulder. "Packed up and left, taking his men with him . . . said their time was up."

"I don't understand," Jack said. "Why'd Stark even bother marching his militia here?"

David pushed a loose shock of hair behind his ear. "Stark's a goddamn prickly bastard, always finding cause for slight. He's made a big show of it this time, marching in as the heroes of Bennington, only to turn and take his men home."

"Why does General Gates let them leave when you say we need every man we can get?" Titus asked.

"Gates and Stark are always at each other." David punched the flats of his fists together to illustrate the relationship. "Stark thinks he ought to be in charge of this army, and carries a grudge about being passed over for promotion."

Jack shrugged. "The man is a great field commander—proved it at Breed's Hill and Bennington, didn't he?"

"Yes, but this is neither the time nor place for such theatrics," David said. "Not with the likes of John Burgoyne knocking on our door."

Titus said, "General Stark knows how to fight and win . . ."

"Will you two stop?" David snapped. "Stark is gone and you've been reassigned to scout for Colonel Morgan. Take my word for it— you won't miss that bastard Stark for a moment. Morgan is of the same ornery ilk."

David Peabody was so like his sister, Anne, and Jack could not help but sometimes smile at their similarities in both look and temperament. From the way his brow furrowed in irritation, to his impatience with perceived foolishness, to the rich shade and texture of his chestnut hair, it was clear they were siblings. David's face was more drawn since last they'd met, with deep, dark circles beneath his eyes. Anne would think him too thin, and Sally would be compelled to fatten him up.

That David was alive, let alone back serving as an officer in Washington's army, was a wonder of sorts. Jack and Titus had found him unconscious and badly shot in the shoulder and leg after the battle on Long Island. They'd tended to his wounds and fever as best they could and were able to smuggle him back to New York and into Anne's and Sally's more capable hands. Captain David Peabody survived his wounds with a definite limp, but he'd managed to somehow incorporate this handicap into a swinging gait at a speed suited to a young soldier of twenty-six years.

Regardless of his limp, once recovered and returned to duty, General Washington made use of David's keen mind and organizational skills, assigning him to the task of maintaining the league of scouts and spies that were the eyes and ears of the Continental Army in this contest with Burgoyne.

"Here they are," David announced with a sweep of his arm. "Morgan's Provisional Rifle Corps. Five hundred of the best crack shots in these United States."

The trek through the Continental Army camp gave evidence that none of the American regiments could come close to the tight order that exemplified a Redcoat camp, but Morgan's Rifle Corps encampment had even more of a rough frontier quality about it.

There was little tentage in evidence. Dressed in a hodgepodge array of fringed hunting shirts, Indian-style leggings, and breechclouts, the rangers lounged around their fires under brush bowers and lean-tos. As David coursed a path betwixt and between the variety of makeshift shelters, Jack could see the everyday habits of these men were similar to those he and Titus had developed in their time spent with Isaac and Ned.

Thin strips of venison dried on racks over smoky fires. One barefoot soldier stood upon a stretched-out hide, while his mate traced the outline of his foot for a new pair of moccasins. Camp women mingled freely with these soldiers, cooking, washing, and mending, and the men whiled away the time playing games of buttons and beans, fine-tuning their flintlocks, casting supplies of lead ball, and sharpening their tomahawks and knives.

Jack and Titus grinned at each other, and Ned and Isaac nodded in approval.

"See the tent and the fellow standing afore it? Under the big oak?" David pointed ahead.

"The one shaving?" Neddy asked.

David nodded. "That's him—Daniel Morgan."

The Colonel's standard-issue wedge tent was located on a high patch at the edge of a stubbly cornfield. In the shade of the oak, a plank-and-trestle table was covered with a scatter of maps and papers kept from flying off with strategically placed stones. A young man—the Colonel's aide—sat on a rock with a rag, spit-polishing a pair of half boots.

"Captain Morgan." David swept off his tricorn in salute, and tucked it under his arm. "Here are the scouts I promised. They've been working the area for several months now, making life difficult for Gentleman Johnny."

Standing shirtless and shoeless in a pair of brown leather breeches, it was plain to see Colonel Morgan was a big man—a very fit man—a solid man accustomed to the rigors of hard work. The graying hair on his thick chest matched the thatch on his head, which he wore pulled back in a stubby braid. He eyed them all with suspicion, at the same time swirling his shaving brush into a thick lather on his face. "Scouts . . ." he said, swiping the soap from his lips with a flick of his thumb. "Have any of you fellows ever ventured in to where the bullets fly?"

Jack let his rifle slip from his shoulder, dropping it to rest breech end in the dirt. "We've just come from Bennington."

"Hmmmph." Morgan grunted. "Been scouting long for Stark?"

"Not long at all," Jack said. "We've been working on our own— mostly harrying Burgoyne's advance and passing along intelligence. David—I mean, Captain Peabody—he sent us to scout for Stark. After Ned and Isaac here were able to infiltrate the German camp, we gave him the lay of the land. Stark figured his battle plan, then used us to take out the Hessian artillery."

"After dispatching the artillery, we joined the general mayhem," Titus added.

"You his slave?" Morgan asked Titus, pointing to Jack.

"No, sir. I'm a free man."

"And my friend," Jack was quick to add.

"Friends, you say?" Morgan tossed his soap brush into the steaming bowl. "Spare me a moment, boys, but this crooked face of mine requires some attention when put to razor's edge."

The Colonel turned to concentrate on the small looking glass hanging by a thong from a nail pounded into the tree trunk. Watching him swipe the edge of the razor across his skin with quick deliberation, it seemed to Jack the man was very familiar with all the nooks and crannies of his face, and could no doubt give himself a close shave in the dark.

Just as Morgan turned, wiping his face clean with a linen towel,

Ned gave Jack a poke with his rifle, and gestured to the web of silvery scars crisscrossing the Colonel's broad back.

"Wondering how I earned these stripes?" Morgan asked.

Ned nodded. Titus shrugged. Isaac and Jack said nothing.

"Army discipline—a British lash—they don't call them 'bloody-backs' for naught, you know." The Colonel pulled on a spotless white linsey hunting shirt and tied it about the waist with a red satin sash. "I was a teamster with Braddock's army back in 'fifty-eight. Young, hotheaded, and more than a bit of a natural cuss, I never took too well to being ordered about, and ended up knocking a captain bung-end to the dirt with a sound fist to the gut. Assault on an officer earned me five hundred lashes."

"Foh . . ." Titus groaned. "Five hundred'll kill a man."

"I never did get the full five hundred. My flogger tired and quit at four ninety-nine. How I despised that horse's arse of a captain . . ." The recollection brought on a big smile, and Jack could see Dan Morgan's face was indeed "crooked," his features thrown off-kilter by a thick scar that formed a deep cleft along his left cheek. "Still worth every stripe, I think."

"That's a good story," Ned said. "But the Redcoats might say you owe them a stripe."

"Ha! I'd like to see 'em try to collect." Without putting aside his razor, Colonel Morgan pointed to Isaac. "You and your war club are familiar to me, friend . . ."

"From our days with Braddock, when our hair was not so white," Isaac said, obviously proud to have found a place in this man's memory. "I remember you were a good fighter of Redcoats even then."

Morgan laughed, a big booming laugh, and though Jack could well imagine the man's spirit had perhaps mellowed some with age, there was yet a truly wild look in his eye.

The Colonel suddenly reached out to him with his open razor, and Jack was hard-pressed not to flinch, allowing Morgan to trace the wet steel along the saber scar on his cheek.

"And what might your name be, brother?"

"Hampton. Jack Hampton."

Morgan moved his blade, using the tip to push aside Jack's necker-chief. He took a long look at the hanged man's scar snaking up the side of his neck.

"Dear, dear, bread and beer—I'd wager you might have a few good stories to tell, Jack Hampton."

Of the same height, Jack smiled and met the Colonel's gaze, eye to eye. "I suppose do."

"Scars . . ." Morgan snapped his razor shut. "A man with none has about as much worth as a hole in the snow—ain't that so, Isaac?"

Morgan sat down on a campstool, pulled on a pair of woolen socks, and laced his feet into his polished boots. "We're light infantry here—skirmishers mainly—trained troops. Not a ragtag militia like those who serve with Stark. My corps is made up of the bettermost marks-men from every regiment, and every man serving in it passed a test—and so must all of you. Except for Isaac there. I already have the measure of his mettle."

"What kind of test?" Ned asked.

"A shooting test." Morgan got up and rummaged through the table for a plain sheet of foolscap. "First, we establish the target." To their amusement, rather than a standard bull's-eye, he took a pencil and drew a comical head of King George in profile, complete with crown. He handed the page to his aide, who took off running across the corn-field and affixed the target to a big elm tree.

"You'll each take three shots," Morgan said.

Jack squinted at the target, gauging the distance at more than two hundred yards. He, Titus, and Ned readied their rifles, taking note of the direction and velocity of the wind as they figured and poured the exact number of gunpowder grains to prime the pans on their weapons.

Ned was the first to shoot, followed by Titus and Jack. After three rounds, the aide ran back, and handed the target page to the Colonel.

Morgan studied the paper made ragged by nine lead balls punch-ing through where he had penciled in King George's eye, and grinned his crooked grin. "Well, Captain Peabody—these scouts will suit."

★ ★ ★

Twilight was quickly ebbing into nightfall, and Anne walked as fast as she could toward Burgoyne's headquarters in the family farmhouse he had commandeered. Skirting the edges of the Rear Guard encampment, Anne was surprised to see the 47th abuzz with activity at a time when most soldiers might gather with their messmates to share a bite and a tot of rum before finding their beds for the night.

Every fire had a kettle on the boil. Red wool coats were being vigorously brushed. Soldiers were busy polishing boots and gaiters with blackball, while others brightened white britches and crossbelts with a sponging of pipe clay. Sheet-draped men sat softening their beards with steamy towels, and their makeshift barbers whipped up bowls of frothy lather with badger-bristle brushes.

As she passed by Riedesel's first battalion, Anne's ears rang with the *shing-shing* of bayonets and curved sabers being drawn over whetstones and honed to a hairsplitting edge. With looking glasses propped, the Brunswicker mercenaries trimmed their mustaches and dressed their hair in their odd fashion.

Rat tails, Anne thought, as she passed a grenadier tightly wrapping his queue in black linen tape, leaving the long whip of a tail to trail down to the middle of his back.

Off in the distance, centered in a clearing and surrounded by a scattering of crude log outbuildings, the ochre-painted farmhouse was shining like a pumpkin lantern on All Hallow's Eve, its square window eyes yellowed with candlelight. The dirt path leading to headquarters and the farmhouse yard was thick with soldiers milling about. A queasiness squirmed into her belly, and Anne felt as if she'd eaten a bad oyster.

"Mrs. Merrick!"

Anne glanced over her shoulder to see Sergeant Pennybrig waving. She waited for him to catch up. "Good evening, Sergeant . . ."

"You shouldn't be about on your own this night, Mrs. Merrick. It can get ugly. Johnny's ordered an extra ration of rum for one and all." Pennybrig offered his arm. "I'd best see you back to your quarters . . ."

The queasiness in her belly hardened into a leaden lump. "An *extra* ration?"

"Aye. The sure sign," Pennybrig said with a nod. "No doubt we'll be ordered into battle on the morrow."

Ignoring Pennybrig's offer, Anne took off in a run, weaving a path around the cadres of soldiers lining up to collect their bonus rum. She pushed through the officers gathered around the porch of the farmhouse, ran up the steps, and peered through the window.

The front parlor was mobbed with white linen and braided red jackets—the polished brass and silver gorgets the officers wore on their chests glinting in the candlelight. Anne spied a laughing Geoffrey Pepperell in his dress regimentals, standing off to the side with Lennox and a few others, a goblet of claret in his hand.

She rapped on the glass with her knuckles, her voice frantic to her ear. "Geoffrey! *Geoffrey Pepperell!*" One of the officers nudged Pepperell and drew his attention to the window where Anne stood. She waved, and he came rushing out to the porch, his blue eyes twinkling with excitement.

"Anne!" Pepperell glanced over his shoulder at his smirking fellows. "How sweet! This is quite a surprise."

"Geoffrey, please." She grasped him by the forearm. "I must speak with General Burgoyne. I need but a moment of his time."

Disappointment coupled with annoyance to flash cross Pepperell's handsome features. "It's Burgoyne you want? Whatever for?"

"I need a pass. Sally and I are leaving for Albany tomorrow, and we need permission to get across the picket line."

"Leaving?" Geoffrey shook his head. "That's impossible."

Anne rose up on tiptoes, catching a glimpse of the General and Simon Fraser sitting side by side at a table in the corner of the parlor, sipping on flutes of champagne.

"There he is! I see him . . ."

"Officers only." Pepperell grabbed Anne by the shoulder before she could squeeze through the doorway, and pulled her back. "I understand you are anxious to get to Albany—as are we all—but Burgoyne will not see you—not tonight."

"Ask him for me, then. Tell him that Sally and I are quite capable; after all, Albany is but a long day's walk from here . . ."

"A long . . . Are you daft? I'll do no such thing!"

Anne tugged at the facings on his jacket. "Please, Geoff. All I need is a pass through the picket line. Tell Burgoyne Sally and I know how to take care of ourselves. Tell him we'll be fine."

"Don't be ridiculous. We've been given our marching orders. There will be a battle tomorrow and no one will be safe on that road, Anne. No one." Geoffrey took her by the hand. "I'll take you back to your camp."

The reality of the situation tumbled down upon her like a cartload of cannonballs, pinning her in place. The day had come—battle eve— and she would not be gathered together with Jack, David, Sally, and Titus. She and Sally would not be able to bid their men farewell with a kiss, or care for them if they should need care.

Pepperell tugged at her hand. "Come along, now."

Unable to speak, Anne jerked free from his grasp and covered her face with both hands, pressing her fingertips into her eyes to staunch a flood of tears. How on earth would she break this news to Sally after raising her hopes so high? Her voice cracked. "No one will be safe."

"There, now . . ." Pepperell pulled her into his arms.

Anne leaned into his embrace, buried her face in the musty red wool of his jacket, and sobbed, "I hate—*hate* this war!"

Pepperell rubbed circles into her back and crooned into her ear, "Dear, dear Anne—don't fret so. I'll be fine. You'll see . . . We shall route these cowardly rebel rascals, and then you and I will be together in Albany with the whole of the winter season before us."

Though spoken as a comfort, his words served to thump Anne over the head like blows from a stout cudgel. With a firm hand to his chest, Anne pushed the Redcoat captain back.

"Of course. You're right." She swiped at her tears, and with complete sincerity said, "Take care tomorrow, Geoffrey." Rising up on tiptoes, she kissed him light on the lips, twirled away, and skittered down the steps.

Pepperell began to follow. "I'll come with you . . ."

"I can make my way back on my own." Anne held him at bay with a shake of her head. "Your place is in there—together with your fellows—your band of brothers."

Geoffrey shot a glance back to his friends, laughing in the golden light with glasses upraised. "Are you certain?"

Anne nodded. "I am."

Daniel Morgan's riflemen rushed in to take their positions within the cover of the trees, forming an irregular line at the edge of Freeman's field. Some of the soldiers took their stand behind tree trunks and some lay on the flats of their bellies, hidden within thickets of brush. The lithe scrambled up into the branches. Jack followed Ned up into the arms of a sprawling chestnut oak.

"This is a good place," Ned said, making himself comfortable on his perch.

Jack settled on a wide limb beneath Ned, laying his rifle across his lap. It was a good place, not so high that he couldn't jump down if he needed to, but high enough to offer a good view of the open field before them. He reached up and slapped at Ned's dangling foot.

"The Redcoats are almost here."

Ned shaded his eyes as he stared into the field. "Do you see 'em?"

"No . . . but I can smell 'em." Jack lifted his chin, drawing in a deep breath. "Bootblack, and"—he drew another breath—"bagpipes, and"—he wrinkled his nose, sniffing—"yep . . . beshitted britches."

Ned guffawed, drawing a "shush" from Titus and an evil glare from Isaac, both sitting at the base of the oak.

The day began cold with a heavy fog clinging to the landscape like sheep's wool to a thornbush. Once the fog began to break, scouting parties returned with reports of British troops no more than three miles away, moving toward the Continental works. Morgan's riflemen, along with Dearborn's light infantry, were out to blunt any possible advance.

Maybe two hours past noon . . . Jack squinted up at the sun shining hot and bright in a clear blue sky. "I sure wish the damn lobsters would show," he whispered, tugging at Ned's foot. "My inner spring is wound tighter than an eight-day clock."

Ned leaned over to whisper, "That's how it always is, brother . . . Hurry up and wait."

Jack tipped his head to rest against the tree trunk and closed his eyes, filling his lungs in through his nose, and out in a slow puff. A cool breeze skirled across the open field, brushing over his face like a ghostly hand and whirling through the branches to shake a flurry of acorns rattling down through the leaves. He smiled, hearing the tiny dull thuds of the nuts landing on the ground and on the felt of Titus's hat. The woods were very quiet, considering it was teeming with close to five hundred men just like him, itching for a fight.

Settling deeper into his seat, Jack heaved another breath, relaxing sweaty fists clutched tight to the barrel and stock of his weapon. There was a rustling in the leaves to his right—a bird flitting among the branches.

A cardinal or a jay gathering acorns. Jack opened one eye and just caught a flash of blue against the rich mottle of green. *Jay it is.*

"*Hao*—get ready." Ned gave Jack a kick to the shoulder. "Here they come."

Jack snapped erect. "That didn't take so long, now, did it?" Squinting through a filter of insects, chaff, and motes dancing on the sunlight, he could see a line of red-clad figures emerge from the forest at the opposite end of the field, moving forward at a wary pace.

Bringing his rifle to full cock, Jack propped the stock against his shoulder. As ordered, he slowly swept the barrel of his rifle from left to right, searching for just the right target. His worldview became very small and, with the enemy's every step forward, the details in it, crisp and clear. Like a divining rod to water, the blink of an officer's brass gorget drew the attention of Jack's weapon—and he held the Redcoat captain in his sights, finger on the trigger.

A turkey call rang out, and on this signal, hundreds of rebel rifles exploded in frightening unison. Every Redcoat in the front ranks fell—dead or wounded. The British line broke, retreating in panic.

The riflemen's wild cheer reverberated in the trees. Jack, Ned, and every other soldier sitting in a tree leapt down, and Morgan's corps moved forward. The crunch of moccasined feet kept time with the scrape of ramrods seating lead ball to a charge of black powder. They left the cover of the trees and entered the open field.

At the far end, the Redcoats shouted and scrambled to re-form their lines to the rattling call of the drums. Jack finished reloading, slipping his ramrod back into place beneath the gun barrel. He and Titus ran after Ned and Isaac, and the foursome all dropped to one knee in a patch of tall grass. This time Jack was not so discerning with his aim. He drew a bead on a blur of red and pulled the trigger.

"Fire!"

The British volley whizzed across the field, and all around, rebel fighters were knocked to the ground like ninepins.

"Fire!"

The second barrage sheared Jack's hat from his head, sending it flying. Another lead ball buzzed past his ear, and another whistled straight through the loose fabric at his hip. All around, riflemen toppled, groaning and writhing. A heavy veil of sulfurous smoke drifted across the field, clouding Jack's vision, burning his throat.

"Fire!"

Someone punched him hard in the arm, and Jack fell flat on his back.

The turkey call yelped once again and voices shouted, "Take cover! Fall back!"

Jack jumped up and stumbled into Titus, who was struggling to lift a wounded man to his feet. Together, they half dragged, half carried the soldier back beyond the tree line, to the deeper cover of the forest, laying him flat beneath the umbrella of a balsam fir. The man's shirt was soaked dark with blood, his eyes fluttering, barely conscious.

Jack fell to one knee and examined the wound, then looked up at Titus. "Gut shot."

British artillery boomed, and chained iron ball sliced through the branches overhead, casting up great clouds of dirt and debris as it pounded into the forest floor. Jack and Titus ducked, covering their heads.

"Their big guns are in range," Titus said, giving Jack a shove. "We need to make tracks before they reload."

Jack began to hoist the wounded soldier, but Titus stopped him. "There's nothing we can do for him but add to his misery."

Jack put his ear to the wounded man's chest. "You're right. He's dead."

"At least the poor fella didn't have to suffer overlong."

They took off, running an erratic course in a crouch, back to the cover of the chestnut oak. Jack tore the kerchief from his neck, wiping the sweat and grime from his face. "Do you have any water?"

Titus slipped the strap over his head, and handed over his canteen. "Save a swallow for me. My throat's dry as dust." Touching the side of his head, Titus's fingertips came up sticky with blood. "I guess I lost my hat," he said.

"Looks like you're lucky you didn't lose your head." Jack took a gulp of water, and poured a drizzle onto a four-inch-long furrow carved through the spongy hair just above Titus's right ear.

"Looks like you took a ball to the shoulder," Titus said.

"Huh!" Jack grunted, plucking at the blood-sodden linsey clinging to his right biceps. "Doesn't hurt much . . ."

"It will. Give me that kerchief." Titus wrapped the scrap of fabric tight over Jack's wound and tied it tight. "There. Another scar in the making."

Ned and Isaac came running in from the field, sliding in to tumble and duck behind the big chestnut oak. "Take cover!" Ned shouted, and they all turtled up, arms over heads.

A sharp crack of musketry, and a spray of lead ball whizzed in an instant later, drilling into the tree trunks and sawing off branchlets—sending shards of bark and rough splinters hurtling through the air.

Isaac sat up and bit the cork from his powder horn, poured a charge down the barrel of his rifle, and uttered one frightening word. "Bayonets."

Jack concentrated on reloading his weapon—*powder, ram, cock the hammer.* A soft breeze came across the field to lift the cloud of smoke, exposing the disciplined line of British infantry on a forward march, their fearsome bayonets affixed. An artillery crew was dragging a cannon over the rough ground. Jack found a mark, and pulled the trigger.

The riflemen all worked with a steady rhythm—pour powder, ram the ball down, cock the hammer, take aim, and fire—powder, ram, aim, fire—powder, ram, aim, fire—the dead accuracy of their every shot taking a horrific toll on the Redcoat advance.

Powder, ram, aim—Jack pulled his trigger and picked off an artilleryman struggling to load the six-pounder under heavy fire. Titus fired and sent the gunner wielding the linstock flying.

Jack and Titus spun back to sit with their backs to the oak. In unison they began to reload. Titus chuckled, his grin so white Jack jabbed him with the butt of his rifle, and laughed. "What's so funny?"

"By God, I think we're holding the bastards!!"

❧ EIGHT ❧

*Danger and deliverance make their advances together, and it
is only at the last push, that one or the other takes the lead.*

THOMAS PAINE, *The American Crisis*

OCTOBER 6, 1777
BRITISH FIELD HOSPITAL

Raindrops began pattering a steady tune on the painted canvas
stretched overhead. Anne peeked out beyond the tarp at a murky dusk
sky, thinking it was almost as dull and dreary as the barley gruel simmering on the hospital kitchen fire. She drew her woolen shawl up
over her head, tying the ends in a bulky knot on her chest.

Following suit, Sally sighed. "Och—just what we need—more
rain."

At their turn, Anne laid claim to one of the mess kettles, cushion-
ing the wire bale handle with a flannel pad to hoist the steaming pot
from the hearth. Sally collected three paper-wrapped packages of
ship's biscuit into the basket looped over her left arm, and hooked her
thumb through the handle on a jug of spruce beer.

The wet weather combined with all the comings and goings
around the barn-turned-hospital to churn the grounds into a gummy
slurry. At the end of a long day's work, with skirt hems heavy and
caked in mud, the slippery slope down to the convalescent tents be-

hind the barn was made even more treacherous. Using mincing steps, the women carried the rations over to the third tent from the right. Like swimmers making ready to dive underwater, Anne and Sally each sucked in lungfuls of fresh air before shouldering a way through the door flaps.

A misling cloud of sweat, sick, and bloody bandages hung in the air. Anne squelched a gag as she tugged her shawl loose, turning her head to take relief from the lavender-infused hankie she kept tucked at her left shoulder.

"Belay that wambly belly," Sally ordered, setting the brimming latrine bucket outside the doorway. "The quicker we see to this lot, the quicker we can find our beds."

Two rows of straw-stuffed pallets and soldier's gear flanked either side of the big marquee tent, leaving a narrow aisle down the middle. Sally tied the tent flaps open to encourage a bit of fresh air as Anne evaluated the state of their charges.

Most of the patients were too debilitated to do anything but lie prone on their pallets. The tent's ranking officer, Captain Thomas Thorn of the Royal Artillery, sat listless against his field chest, a thick book open on his lap, his right leg ending in a bandaged stump at the knee. The Captain's face was ruddy and his eyes bloodshot, leaving Anne to worry if his fever had returned. In the far corner, three of their healthier convalescents huddled around a broken shard of planking, playing a game of Hazard with dice they fashioned from a pair of musket balls.

Banging a ladle to the mess kettle, Sally announced, "Dinnertime, lads!"

Like schoolboys called in from play, the gaming soldiers put their dice away, scooting on rear ends to their own places to fumble in packs for mess kits and spoons. Anne took in another bracing breath of lavender. Exhuming a stubby lead pencil and small tablet from her pocket, she proceeded to count heads.

"Ye'll be missing Lieutenants B-B-Bowman and K-K-Kinnear. They're . . . they're . . . they're . . ." Foley, a left gunner who ironically lost his left arm to the surgeon's saw, was always eager to offer up pertinent information. Anne waited patiently for the end of his sentence, her pencil poised.

"D-d-dead," Foley finished.

"Moanin' and groanin' all through the night, them two." A blunt, squatty man, Sergeant Burgus was brought to hospital four days earlier, his left foot having been crushed under an ox's hoof. "Not a one of us caught a wink o' sleep."

Foley jerked his only thumb toward his neighbor. "C-c-captain Thorn's sad in his heart, p-p-poor soul."

Anne went to the officer's side, drawing down onto her haunches. "My condolences, Captain Thorn. I know Lieutenants Kinnear and Bowman were good friends of yours."

"Good friends . . . yes." Captain Thorn closed his book. "Did you know they came by their grievous wounds carrying me from the field?"

Anne nodded. "I know."

"John Bowman and James Kinnear were fine soldiers—courageous men—imbued with every quality that can create esteem." The artillery Captain eyed the tablet Anne held in her hand, his voice so very tired and pained. "And now, Mrs. Merrick, you may draw a line through their names, as if they never existed."

Blinking back sudden tears, Anne rose to her feet and left the Captain to his grief. When she agreed to infiltrate Burgoyne's army, the one thing she never figured on was becoming so enmeshed in the suffering of her enemies. Knowing men like Jack and David were responsible for the carnage she'd seen carted in from the battlefield was very difficult to bear. With a heavy heart, Anne forced herself to remember that the men she nursed, whose wounds she tended, and whose names she daily crossed from her list—these soldiers were fighting with all their might to crush a just cause, and kill the good, brave people who supported it.

People like Jack and David . . . and Sally . . . and me.

Sally banged once again on her kettle. "Bowls up!"

"Ye can divvy up the extra rations amongst us . . ." Will Crisp held out his bowl. "No one will be the wiser." Emma Crisp's eldest was wounded on picket duty during a rebel ambush the night before. Knocked flat by a rifle shot to the leg, he was lucky the lead ball zinged through his thigh muscle without doing any damage to the bone.

With a fierce look in her eye, Sally poured a double ration of gruel into the boy's bowl, daring Sergeant Burgus to voice a complaint. "Thin as a needle, this lad is—not enough meat on him to even stop a bullet."

Anne pointed to the end of the row, where a man bundled in a blue jacket lay curled on his side, facing away from the others. "Who's that there?"

Foley gave it a good try. "M-m-mooo . . . moo . . . moo . . ." Taking a deep breath, he tried again. "M-mm-moo-mooo . . ."

Captain Thorn leaned over and clasped his gunner by the shoulder. "Moved him in today—right, Foley?"

The gunner nodded. "A German."

Anne went down the aisle to give the toe of the new arrival's mud-crusted boot a shake. "I need your name and regiment."

The Hessian rolled onto his back. Strips of clean linen were tied to his head, holding a fresh padding of cotton lint over his right eye. He wore gold braid looped over one blood-splashed shoulder, and an ornate scabbard and sword lay atop his field chest.

"Yer wastin' yer breath." Sergeant Burgus sneered. "Th' cabbage-licker don't speak a word o' the King's English."

Putting pencil to paper, Anne softened the timbre of her voice, and spoke slowly. "Please, sir, your name and regiment?"

The Hessian officer rose up on one elbow, pushing long, matted tangles of straw-colored hair over his shoulder. Though equipped with but one working eye, the officer still managed to cast Burgus a withering glare as he said in a firm voice, *"Kapitän Andréas Hoffman—erste brigade, regiment von Rhetz."*

While she scribbled the Hessian's name onto her roster, Sally mimicked spooning food into her mouth. "Are ye able t' feed yerself, Capeetan?"

"Ja . . . ja . . ." The German sat up and fished a shining brass mess kit from his pack.

"Good," Sally muttered, ladling a helping into his bowl. "One less for us to cosset."

Anne and Sally finished dishing up the soldiers' dinner—a bowl of gruel, three round ship's biscuits, and a cup of spruce beer.

Knocking one of his biscuits to the side of his wooden bowl, Burgus said, "Hard as a woman's heart, these biscuits." The Sergeant scooped up a spoonful of gruel, letting it drizzle and plop back into his bowl without eating it. "And would ye look at this pap? How's a man expected to get back into fighting fit on this pig swill, I ask ye?"

"Thank ye, sir." Sally snatched the bowl from his hands and, with great flourish, spilled the contents back into the kettle. "Plenty will be grateful for yer share of pig swill." She tossed his empty bowl back into his lap.

"You've no call to deny me my victuals." Burgus held his bowl out. "I'm a wounded soldier . . ."

"Wounded? *Fiech!*" Sally sneered. "Over-friendly with the oxen is what ye are."

Captain Thorn snorted into his beer.

"I'm a King's man, Mrs. Merrick, and I fight for rations and six-pence a day." Burgus shifted in his seat, turning to Anne, his voice raising in pitch. "Your girl has no call to withhold my victuals. I was but sayin'—a man needs a piece of proper meat and a cup of proper grog in these desperate times . . ."

"In desperate times, Sergeant," Anne replied, "a real man keeps such thoughts to himself."

"Hear, hear!" Captain Thorn perked up, and raised his cup to Anne.

"I'm owed rations, Mrs. Merrick," Burgus insisted, making a big show of wincing and lifting his bandaged foot onto a bolster. "I'm a King's man, wounded in the line of duty."

Anne could not bear to hear another word drop from the man's selfish mouth. She closed her eyes and huffed a sigh. "Just give him his share," she said.

"So pleased wi' yerself, aren't ye?" Sally jerked the bowl from Burgus. "Th' face on ye—like a bulldog lickin' piss off a nettle." She ladled out a portion of gruel and shoved the bowl back into his hands. "There—ye wee whinging snivelard. Choke on it."

Will Crisp hooted. Foley slapped his knee and stuttered, "Yer a rare one, S-S-Sally." Even the Hessian was laughing.

"Never tangle with a redhead, Sergeant," Captain Thorn advised. "They're known to carry a sting in their tails."

The women settled in to spoon-feed the invalids, and Captain Thorn broke a biscuit into his bowl. "So, ladies . . . what news?"

Sally shrugged, using the corner of her apron to wipe the spittle dribbling from her patient's mouth. "There's little good to tell."

Anne rolled a blanket into a bolster, propping her charge up at an angle. "Burgoyne has cut rations once again."

One-handed, Foley used the socket end of his bayonet to pound a biscuit into bits before stirring it into his gruel. "That b-b-bodes ill."

"I tell you what bodes ill . . ." Burgus did not hesitate to join in the conversation. "It's been over a fortnight since the battle and we do naught but sit and wait while the damn rebels gain in numbers and strength. By all rights we ought be in full retreat—back to Canada to winter."

"Britons never retreat," Sally said.

Anne shot her friend a warning look, to which Sally flashed a grin and a wink. No one else seemed to catch the sneer in Sally's tone.

"There's talk of reinforcements on the way," Will Crisp offered. "General Clinton's forces from New York, maybe General Howe, some say."

"Don't believe it. No one is coming." Captain Thorn traced the brim of his bowl with his spoon. "We're on our own out here."

A low-pitched, mournful drone pierced the stillness punctuating the Captain's dour pronouncement. Echoing over the tree-covered hills, the lone call was joined in by a higher-pitched howl, and another, and another. Sounding much like a winter's wind screaming through chinks in a wall, the eerie harmonic wail sent a shiver up Anne's spine.

"D'ye hear that, young Will?" Burgus cocked his head to the side, one bushy brow raised. "Reinforcements!"

Foley's bony shoulders hunched up around his ears. "Hellhounds."

"Is that what they are?" Will Crisp went goggle-eyed. "The woods are filled with the reek of 'em by day—and by night you can actually see the glint of their fiery eyes as they dart among the trees." His voice cracked on the word "trees."

Sally leapt up to raise the wick in the oil lantern hanging from the center pole, brightening the light. "Dinna speak of th' hellhounds, Will Crisp, lest ye bring ill fortune upon yerself."

Foley nodded vigorous in agreement. "G-g-gaze into the eyes of a hellhound three t-t-times, and yer certain t' meet with d-d-death."

"Nonsense." Captain Thorn crushed another biscuit into his bowl. "It's nothing but the howling of wolves drawn in by the smell of war."

"With the wounded left behind on the field, and the pitiful graves that were dug under fire"—Burgus shoved a spoonful into his mouth, spattering gruelly gobs of biscuit as he spoke—"it's certain those wolves are eating better than we are."

The rain began falling in earnest, thrumming on the canvas roof in rapid fire. Anne was compelled to close the tent flaps to save those closest to the door a drenching. A staccato flash of lightning produced a bone-shaking crack of thunder, startling Foley so, he upset his bowl, spilling his dinner out onto his pallet.

"S-s-s-s-sorry. Th-th-th—"

"Don't fret, Mr. Foley." Anne took the empty bowl from the gunner's trembling hand. Thorn shimmied over to draw a blanket over Foley's shaking shoulders. Sally came over to pour the last of the gruel into the gunner's empty bowl when the sharp report of a hunter's rifle resounded, causing them all to jerk. The single shot was followed by a hue and cry, and the ragged crackle of musket fire.

"Sounds like another sharpshooter hit his target," Thorn said.

Will nodded. "Puffing a pipe on picket duty, I bet. No better way to draw a rebel bullet to your brain."

"They brought a dozen dead in from Breyman's redoubt today," Sally said. "Every one of 'em picked off by rebel sharpshooters."

"You mean rebel cowards. Targeting officers and artillerymen from a distance—" Burgus grumbled, gathering his blanket about his shoulders. "Where's the gallantry in that?"

Foley shrugged. "G-g-gallantry don't win wars."

"I've heard tell these American boys are given rifles when still in leading strings. By the time they're full grown, they can shoot the winking eye from a man at two hundred yards." Will jerked his head over toward the Hessian.

Burgus laughed. "For once it don't pay to be an officer, does it?"

"Whether you agree with their methods or no, the rebels have dogged our progress since Ticonderoga, and on the field of battle, they managed to repulse every one of our charges." Captain Thorn toyed with the last of his biscuits, spinning it like a coin on the cover of his book. "There's something to admire in how they've figured a way to fight us. I never thought they stood a chance, but a fortnight ago I saw untrained, ill-armed, backwoods farmers hold back the might of the Empire."

"What a load of old bollocks! 'Something to admire,'" Burgus mimicked. "Sounds like a rebel in the making."

"Poltroon!" Thorn whipped his biscuit across the aisle, hitting Burgus square on his big greasy pate. "You forget yourself, Sergeant!"

Anne laughed, and Sally clapped her hands, exclaiming, "Bull's-eye!"

"How dare you question my loyalty, sir?" Captain Thorn leaned forward, his bloodshot eyes hooded in fury. "If you were any kind of a soldier, you'd know to study your enemy's strengths. If you were a smart soldier, you'd know to respect them. But you, Sergeant Burgus, are akin to a fingerpost on the road, pointing the way to a place you've never been." The Captain pounded a fist to his chest. "I was on that battlefield and know what I saw—an enemy fighting with fierce determination—men fighting for something more than sixpence a day."

"Sorry, Cap'n." Burgus mumbled his apology, fished out the flung biscuit caught in the folds of his blanket, and crumbled it into his bowl. "But I stand by what I said—Americans are cowards, through and through."

"If the Americans are cowards, why do they flock to the rebel standard, while our fellows desert in droves?" Will Crisp asked. "Just the other day, a whole company of Brunswickers snuck off in the night."

Burgus snorted. "What d' ye expect from Germans?"

Kapitän Hoffman bolted upright. *"Arschloch!"* he shouted, and a bright patch of red burst like a blossom on the pad covering his eye. "It *vas* German *soldaten* who saved *die Englische flanke* . . . German *soldaten!"*

Burgus scooted backward, putting as much space as he could between himself and the Hessian's fury, wagging a stubby finger. "You just better shut your kraut-hole. No one here gives a shite about your gibberish."

"Lie back, lad." Sally rushed over to soothe the Hessian back to the pillow. "There's no use gettin' in a twist over the likes of him."

"What do you know, anyway, B-B-Burgus?" Foley stuttered. "Like Cap'n says—you-you-you weren't there."

The Sergeant folded his arms across his chest, his jaw set tight and jutting forward. "I know what I hear."

"Then hear this—" Thorn raised his cup in toast. "To our German comrades-in-arms! Without whose courage and fortitude we here may well have ended up as wolf's meat."

"Aye that!" Foley leaned over to tap his cup to the Captain's. "T' th' Ger-Ger-Germans!"

Anne pushed through the canvas, sank down onto her cot with a groan, and swiped the mobcap from her head. "This place is sucking the very life from me." Shoulders in a slump, she stared down at skirts, shoes, stockings—all saturated and crusted with mud. "What's the point of changing out of muddy clothes?"

Sally hung the lantern from the ridgepole, dropped her basket, and plunked down onto her bed. "No point."

Anne tottered over like a felled tree, landing on her side in a thump. "I don't think I can bear another day in that hospital."

"I canna bear another day in this bloody camp." Sally flopped onto her back. "But we're trapped in this hellhole until Burgoyne makes a move. Who'd a' thought th' bastard would sit on his fat English arse doing nothing?"

"And what in bloody hell is General Gates waiting for?" Anne whispered. "Why doesn't he attack? The British have never been as weak."

"Bastards, th' lot of them!!" Sally flung her pillow at the ridgepole, sending the lantern in a wild swing.

"Shhh . . ." Anne warned. "Keep your voice down. Remember where we are."

"How can I forget?" Sally hissed. "I'm just about ready t' go bloody mad, Annie. A wee skirmish here, and a few shots in the night—as if Gates thinks Burgoyne and his army will just dribble away on their own. It's a foolish strategy, and we've no way to get word to our lads."

"And Burgoyne is nobody's fool. I fear there is method to his madness, and reinforcements are on the way. Goddamn it!" Anne pounded the stretched canvas of her cot. "Gates ought to seize advantage and attack with full force now!"

"Wheesht, Annie!" Sally began to giggle. "Would ye listen to us two? Swearin' and cursin' like a pair o' drunken troopers!"

Anne smiled. "Jack would call it honest language."

The whispered conversations within the protection of their own canvas served as a relief to the exhausting pretense they were forced to carry on without respite. Living out each day in constant dread, guilt, and worry had taken a toll.

Back when they were able to pass along intelligence, there was a great purpose served by their deception—but since the battle at Freeman's Farm, they floated aimlessly in a maddening limbo, like lost souls, with no aim or direction.

Anne fussed with her pillow, kneading it into a doughy ball. There wasn't even any pleasure to be found in the comfort of her bed, as sleeping served only to hasten yet another awful day among the enemy. "That's it." She shot up to her feet. "I'm sick and tired of living at the whim of generals. I will not do it a single day more." She pulled out the basket stored beneath her cot. "What food do we have put by?"

"Quit raiblin' nonsense." Sally waved an abject hand. "We're caught aqueesh two armies with no way out. No way."

Anne dug into her pocket, separating a few pieces of silver and copper from the bits and bobs she carried. "How much coin do we have in the till?"

Sally rolled her eyes. "Two pounds, and some odd shillings and pence . . . muckle good may it do ye."

"More than enough." Anne snatched up the blanket crumpled at the end of her cot, and snapped it out, folding it longwise into a neat rectangle.

"We've been over this time and time again, Annie." Sally recited her reasoning by rote. "Anyone caught crossing the picket line is shot on sight. Ye'll get a bullet in your brain afore ye have a chance t' offer a bribe to any sentry men. And where a Redcoat bullet doesn't kill us, a Patriot bullet will."

Anne rolled her blanket into a sausage and tied it into a compact bundle with a length of cordage, leaving enough slack to serve as a strap. She slipped the bedroll over head and shoulder, wearing it on a diagonal across her back like she'd seen Jack and Ned do. "Neat and tidy, no?" She tugged at Sally's sleeve. "Come on. Get packing."

Sally turned on her side, propping her head on her elbow. "Until someone makes a move—Burgoyne or Gates—we're stuck here amongst th' bloody lobsterbacks, and that's that. Be sensible, Annie. There's no way for us to get to the Continental lines unscathed."

Sitting down on her cot, Anne picked through the things in her storage basket, and found the dagger sheathed in snakeskin Geoffrey had given her. "What if we don't go to the Continental lines? In fact, what if we go the opposite direction—north to Saratoga?"

"Aye . . ." Sally sat up. "Ye might have something there . . . Only th' Loyalist camp and a single picket line to cross to th' north . . ."

"And I expect it is stretched thin at that."

"Still," Sally said with a shake of her head. "We'd be heading north—farther away from our lads."

"No one is minding the river. Once we get to Saratoga, we can pay a boatman to take us downriver to Stillwater." Anne strapped the dagger to her thigh with a length of grosgrain ribbon. "By this time tomorrow, you could be with David."

Digging down between her breasts, Sally came up with a small leather sack. She tossed it onto Anne's cot. "There's all our coin." She slipped down onto her knees to scramble through her stores. "I've one packet of ship's biscuit, a sack of raisins, and an odd sausage Pepperell's Indian once traded me for a scone . . ." She held the withered length of pemmican up for inspection. "I've never been desperate enough t' take a bite."

"That's enough food to get us by for a couple of days." Anne flipped over her pillow and pocketed her firearm.

Sally stripped the case from her pillow, and deposited the foodstuffs and her pistol into the empty pillowslip. Anne added their mess kits, a tin water bottle, and two pairs of clean stockings. Sally wrapped the letters from David in a silk scarf and slipped the packet into her pocket. Anne pinned the mourning brooch containing a lock of her son's hair to the inside of her stays, close to her heart, and tucked the two keepsakes from Jack between her breasts. They tied their hair up with dark-colored kerchiefs, and swirled into somber plaid shawls, draping the wool over their heads.

Anne grabbed Sally by the shoulders. "Ready?"

Sally answered with a grin and a vigorous nod. "This time on the morrow we'll be within th' lovin' arms of our lads!"

"We're off." Anne stepped out and gazed up and down the avenue of tents. There were a few campfires spotted here and there in the baggage camp, but the majority of the camp was dark and quiet, with only a handful of tents glowing soft with yellow lantern light. Taking Sally by the hand, Anne scurried through the rows to hug the edge of the forest that lay between the camp and the river road.

"We stay in the shadows as much as we can. Once we get a good ways beyond the Loyalist camp, we'll cross over to the river road, and the going will be easier." Anne eyed a spot along the horizon where the faint glow of the setting moon filtered through dense cloud cover. "I hope it doesn't rain."

Sally sidled up to Anne, linking arms. "A darksome night," she whispered. "Nary a star in the sky."

"A good thing." Anne gave Sally a squeeze. "A dark night favors our purpose."

They held on to each other, at first startling and stopping at every sound and movement, every step taken so as not to stumble or fall. As eyes adjusted, they gained speed, darting along the shadows to the Loyalist encampment at the army's northern reaches.

Moonlight peeked through breaks in the clouds, and a mist crawled up the arc of an open field as the saw-toothed silhouette of the Loyalist camp came into view. Row upon row of wedge tents rose up in the clearing, shining soft with the glow of many campfires and faint voices in song, far enough away that neither Anne nor Sally could make out the words.

"Ulch! What a reek!" Sally squeaked and pinched her nose. "Hellhounds, ye think?"

"Don't be silly . . ." Anne crinkled her nose at the sudden stench. Slipping her right hand into her pocket, she wrapped her fingers around the pistol grip, and grabbed Sally with her left. "Let's get past this camp and—"

A grunting and rustling in the brush to their right caused Anne to clip her sentence short. Both women froze in their tracks as a pointy-headed creature with long arms and legs stomped out from the shadows, no more than ten yards ahead.

Sally hissed, "A wraith! Tha's the smell . . ."

"Hush!" Anne jerked her down into a crouch, neither of them daring to breathe.

The wraith began to bend, turn, and stretch its limbs, and he suddenly jerked around and called out, "Pinch it off, Liam, and let's get back. This damp's creepin' intae m' bones. I can feel m' joints rusting over."

"Waesacks, Dougal!" Another pointy-headed wraith rose up from the fog, tugging up his britches. "Can ye no' leave a mon take his shite in peace?"

The almost-full moon broke free of the clouds, reflecting an eerie light on the low-lying fog crawling over the ground. Mitered fur caps and white crossbelts became apparent in the moonlight. Anne nudged Sally and whispered, "Grenadiers."

Swinging his musket from his shoulder, Liam shouted, "Who goes there?"

Musket hammers clacked back and the sentries raised their weapons. Edging forward, Dougal shouted, "Friend or foe?"

Sally squeezed Anne by the hand and whispered, "We've no choice, aye?"

Liam warned, "Show yerself, or we shoot."

Sally leapt up, waving her arms. "Hold yer fire!" She ran toward the sentries, arms flailing, flinging herself into an abject supplication at the soldiers' feet, wailing and sobbing. "Praise th' Lord on High! Happy to be found, we are! Thanks be t' Saint Anthony and all the saints in heaven! Thanks be!"

Stuffing her pistol back into her pocket, Anne ran after Sally with arms raised over her head. The sentries swung the barrels of their muskets to target the new threat.

"A friend! A friend! Don't shoot, sir!" Anne joined in the hysterical babble. "Hopelessly lost . . . Came late off our duty shift—"

"At hospital, mind," Sally squeaked.

"We got turned around—"

"Our light was doused . . . ye ken?"

"Couldn't see our hands before our eyes—"

"Flummoxed. Nary a star in the sky—"

"Thought for certain we'd be picked off by rebels—"

"—or torn to bits by hellhounds—"

"HOLD YER WHEESHT, WOMEN!" Liam ordered.

A big man, as grenadiers were wont to be, Dougal towered over Sally. He gave her a nudge with his foot. "Get up." Strapping musket to shoulder, he snatched the pillow sack from her grip, and pulled forth the packet of ship's biscuit. "Filching rations from the hospital?"

"Earned—never filched," Sally countered.

Anne nodded vigorously. "We're each given a share in exchange for nursing the wounded."

"Carrying rations and blankets . . ." Liam used the muzzle of his weapon to push Anne's shawl aside, eyeing the bedroll. "If ye were men, I'd peg yiz both as deserters."

"Dinna tell me yiv lived amongst the English for so long ye can no longer discern man from woman?" Sally giggled, and gave Liam a playful bump with her hip.

"Maybe they're spies," Dougal offered, pulling Sally's pistol from the sack.

"Spies!" Sally laughed. "An' what should we report t' the rebels? Tha' we found a pair of Scotsmen havin' a shite in the field?"

"We both carry pistols." Anne revealed the gun in her pocket. "My departed husband's dueling pair. You can't expect a decent woman to work in camp without some sort of protection, can you?"

Dougal shook his head. "Why're ye headin' north, when th' camp lies in the other direction?"

"North! I told ye, Annie, din't I?" Sally scolded, snatching her sack from Liam's grip. "But ye never listen, do ye?"

"Thank you, trooper." Anne took the pistol from Dougal's hand. "Now that we know the way home, we will fly like pigeons and trouble you no more. Good evening to you both!" Anne and Sally linked arms and began the march south.

"Hold." Dougal grabbed Sally by the back of her skirt.

Anne put on her best bluster. "Really! You've no call to detain us any longer. We are citizens of the Crown—we have rights."

Dougal spoke over Anne's head. "These might be decoys. Sent tae us by tha' bleatin' miser bitch of a sergeant."

"Aye . . ." Liam worried the stubble on his chin. "Testing our mettle—like he did Darby . . ."

"We're no decoys!" Sally cried.

"An' what became of poor Darby, aye?" Dougal said. "Dealt fifty bloody stripes, na?"

Liam grabbed Anne by the arm. "Best we take 'em t' th' Sergeant."

"If you must take us somewhere," Anne said, jerking free, "take us to Captain Geoffrey Pepperell of His Majesty's Twenty-fourth Foot. You'll find him in the High Command at Burgoyne's headquarters."

"Friend of yours, he is?" Dougal asked.

Anne took a step back, the leer in the grenadier's eye making her most uneasy.

Sally wagged a finger in Dougal's face. "Aye, she's his mistress, ye great gobshite—and the Captain'll be none too pleased to find his woman manhandled."

Heart thumping in her chest, Anne pulled her shawl tight. "We have their names. What is their regiment, Sally?"

Sally leaned close and read the numbers embossed on the buttons of their jackets. "Thirty-fourth."

With an imperious jut of the chin, Anne said, "I insist you bring us to headquarters where Captain Pepperell can vouch for us, or I will report you both."

Flanked by the grenadiers, they set off on the long march all the way to Burgoyne's camp near the Great Redoubt—the earthworks the British had built as a last line of defense. The grenadiers turned the women over to the duty officer, who ordered Anne and Sally to wait under the watchful eye of their captors, on a bench outside the large, lantern-lit marquee tent the High Command was using for headquarters.

Sally muttered, "I saw two butter knives crossed on the kitchen table at hospital this morning—a sure sign no good would come to me today." She leaned forward, propping chin on fists. "We are doomed to live out our days trapped in this circle of hell."

Anne wrapped an arm around Sally's shoulders. "Ah, now, it could be worse."

"Aye . . ." Sally leaned her head on Anne's shoulder. "We could be shot or hanged, I s'pose."

Pepperell followed the duty officer out of the tent, Sally's pillow sack in one hand, his hat tucked under his arm. "Anne! What on earth . . . ?"

"Geoffrey!" Anne jumped up to her feet, allowing the Redcoat captain to claim a quick peck on the cheek. Off to the side, Liam and Dougal came to attention, shouldering their muskets.

Other than a brief sighting at the hospital just after the battle, she'd not spent any time with Pepperell, but she'd never seen him looking so disheveled. He hadn't shaved for days. The hair he always kept meticulously queued and beribboned hung lank about his shoulders. His red coat was tattered and scuffed with soot. Anne noticed three bullet holes scorched through the heavy cuff on the right sleeve, and two more torn through the skirting.

"It's been ages, hasn't it?" she said.

He flashed a tired smile. "I've been very busy. They tell me you were lost—?"

Anne shook her head, deciding in that instant not to bother with a lie. "Not lost—we've had enough, Sally and me. We were on our way home."

"On your way . . ." Geoffrey swept back his hair. "Are you daft, madam? The area is teeming with rebels, wolves, deserters—Indians!"

Shrugging and nodding at the same time, Anne said, "We acted on a mad impulse."

Pepperell dismissed the sentries, and turned back to Anne. "I really do not have time for this kind of nonsense. If you haven't noticed, we are at war."

Anne heaved a sigh. "I no longer wish to be part of your war. I only want to get to my brother. A pass and escort to Saratoga is all I need. We can make our own way from there."

"Maybe an escort can be spared once reinforcements arrive, but for now, what you are asking is absolutely impossible."

"Reinforcements, Geoffrey? Is that likely?"

"No, but it's our best hope." Pepperell glanced over his shoulder at a hearty cheer and the sound of glasses clinking coming from inside the marquee. "I must get back. There's a teamster delivering a load in the artillery park. Have him give you a ride back to the baggage camp." Geoffrey pressed the pillow sack into Anne's hand and pulled her in for a quick hug and kiss. "Everything will be better after tomorrow, I promise."

"What do you suppose is going on?" Anne watched Pepperell hurry back into the tent where more than a dozen officers, Lennox, Fraser, and Riedesel among them, crowded around a map-covered table with glasses of champagne in hand.

"Mischief, to be sure," Sally said, flinging her sack over her shoulder.

They trudged across a rutted, mucky field to the artillery park illuminated by numerous cressets ablaze. The thickening fog swirled between the artillery carriages like a ghostly specter as gunnery crews tugged the cannon into new formations. Soldiers bearing pine-pitch torches aglow in misty halos were streaming in from all directions while sergeants shouted company names, herding the men into groups.

Sally bounced up and down on tiptoes, craning her neck. "I hope we can find a ride. My legs are cooked noodles—I'd wager we've marched at least eight miles this night."

"And have gotten nowhere for it." Anne grabbed Sally by the arm. "It's odd, don't you think? Quite a lively scene for so late an hour. Something is afoot . . ."

"There's our teamster." Sally waved and called, "Mr. Noonan!" steering Anne toward a group of soldiers off-loading rum casks from a cart. Noonan leaned against his wagon, his tricorn pushed to the back of his head, puffing on a long-stemmed clay pipe.

"D'ye mind, Mr. Noonan, if we ride in your wagon back to baggage camp?"

"No skin off'n my nose. Hop aboard."

With a jerk of her thumb, Anne asked, "What do we have going on here, Mr. Noonan, an extra rum ration?"

"A-yup!" The teamster took a deep draw on his pipe.

Sally asked, "Then it's battle tomorrow, ye think?"

"I shouldn't wonder, miss. Gentleman Johnny's known for treating his men to a tot afore a fight. These twelve barrels are the last of the rum stores—rousted from me bed to bring it here, too. These English don't fare well without their grog, no, sir! Like mother's milk to 'em, eh? Mother's milk!"

"Did ye hear that, Annie?" Sally beamed, and tugged the tin cup from her sack. "I'll be back in a tic."

Ignoring all complaints and resistance, she muscled her way to the front of the queue where the first cask was being tapped, and held her cup out for a share.

"My friend and I've been breakin' our backs day in and day out for over a fortnight now, tendin' th' wounded and sick in hospital," she announced, staring down the protesters with redheaded ire. "I dare th' meanest among ye to step up and say our service doesna warrant a good, stiff drink."

The soldiers all cheered and laughed, and Sally's rum ration was dispensed with great ceremony. Noonan helped the women to climb up into the empty wagon bed, and they made themselves comfortable, sitting with backs resting up against the headboard, facing the tail end.

The withy mite of a wagoneer was dwarfed by the massive horned beasts he mastered with nothing more than the aid of a hickory rod. Goading the left-lead ox into motion with a light tap to the forehead, he shouted, "Haw!" and walked alongside the oxen, driving the pair with constant pokes and prods.

Sally clutched her cup with both hands. To keep from losing any of her drink, she swayed with the pitch as the wagon lurched forward and rumbled from the artillery park.

Anne unfurled the blankets to cover their legs, and she snuggled in beside Sally.

Sally said, "Give over your cup."

Anne fished it from the pillow slip, and Sally carefully doled out a share of rum. Before they could take a sip, a shout rang out—

"FIRE!"

Anne and Sally grabbed hold of the sideboards at the order. The accompanying cannon blast shattered the night—reverberating through the very ground, sending the wagon into a creaky shudder, bringing the oxen to a lowing and uneasy standstill.

"Burgoyne's signal to reinforcements," Noonan shouted over his shoulder as he hawed and goaded the oxen back into motion.

"I'm struck deaf." Sally thumped her ear with the heel of her palm. "I'm certain th' rebels heard it as well."

"That's the point," Anne said. "The signal serves as both a desperate plea to any British forces that might be coming, and a desperate ploy . . ."

"I see . . . to make the Continentals think reinforcements are arriving, and trick them into retreating," Sally finished. "Och, Burgoyne's a cunning one; I'll give him that."

Anne nodded. "But I think he's run out of time."

Three signal rockets screamed up into the sky—one right after another—bursting in a bang and a glittering shower of silvery sparks, casting flashes of bright light over the landscape. Anne leaned her head on her friend's shoulder, watching the sparks float, twinkling, to their demise.

"Tomorrow's the day, Sally."

Sally raised her cup. "To our good lads, Annie . . . and to us!"

Anne tapped her cup to Sally's, whispering, "To Liberty!"

❧ NINE ❧

Here, in this *spot is our business to be accomplished, our felicity secured. What we have now to do is as clear as light, and the way to do it is as strait as a line.*

THOMAS PAINE, *The American Crisis*

OCTOBER 7, 1777
IN THE WOODS, NEAR A WHEAT FIELD

Think of something else . . . something good . . . Jack wiped the sweat from the back of his neck. *A thunderstorm on a summer night . . .* Eyes closed, he worried the cast-iron token he wore on a leather thong about his neck and smiled.

A thunderstorm on a summer night with Annie curled warm at my side. The gale wind sweeps in and cools our skin . . . banging the shutters open and closed . . . open and closed . . .

The constant crackle of musket fire in the distance almost sounded like raindrops on the roof tiles over Anne's garret room above the Cup and Quill—the sharp report of rifles, the shutters; the boom of cannon, thunder. Jack imagined Anne's chestnut curls in a tangle on sun-bleached linen—he could almost smell the lavender water used to press the pillow slips. He took a slow breath in through his nose, and whistled it out, calming his racing heart, and easing the tension bunched between shoulders.

Owk! Owk! Owk!

Jack's eyes snapped open. Squinting west at the sun flashing in and out between the flutter of gold and orange maple leaves, he could see a dark chevron of migrating geese flying by, dispelling his pleasant daydream with their grating call.

Along with the whole of Morgan's rifle corps and Dearborn's light infantry, Jack waited on tenterhooks in the forest at the edge of a wheat field—listening to the battle being waged in the distance, waiting for the order to unleash American fury on Burgoyne's right flank.

Jack massaged his right upper arm where he took a musket ball during the last clash with the Redcoats. Loath to pay a visit to the surgeon's tent with what was a minor wound in the grand scheme of things, he had Titus pry out the lead ball with the tip of his folding knife. Isaac applied an odd plaster he made with water and the powdered bark of the slippery elm tree, and though the wound was healing nicely, his arm was still feeling a bit stiff and bruised.

He sucked in another deep breath. It was a perfect autumn afternoon. The crisp blue sky served as a backdrop to the fiery fall foliage, and every now and then a cool breeze played through the treetops, sending torrents of leaves dancing down upon them.

"What a beautiful day," Jack said.

Standing at his left, Titus grunted, his loaded rifle in a two-fisted grip, the brim of his felt hat drawn down to shade his eyes. "It's about to get very ugly, very soon."

Ned waited in front of them, head bobbing, shifting from foot to foot, as if he were standing with bare feet on a sheet of ice. Jack laid a hand on the young Oneidan's shoulder.

"Close your eyes and take in a breath, Tree Shaker. Imagine you're up in the branches."

Standing beside Titus, bare-chested Isaac pulled the hammer on his rifle to full cock. "Get ready, my brothers," he said.

Sure enough, Isaac's instincts proved spot-on. Morgan's turkey call sounded twice in succession—the signal to move forward at the quickstep.

The rhythmic *scrunch scrunch scrunch* of moccasined footfalls on the thick carpet of leaves blotted out the sound of the distant battle.

The moving force gained in speed and noise—the woodland resounding with the steely riot of six hundred flintlock weapons clacking back.

As they drew closer, the British artillery began to thunder, shaking the ground, rocking the foot soldiers with a bone-rattling vibration. In no more than a blink of the eye, a hail of grapeshot flew through the treetops, tearing through the leaves and branches, ricocheting off thick limbs, but doing little to slow the momentum of the Patriot onslaught.

Titus shouted over his shoulder, pointing up at the sky with a grin. "The lobsters have their guns cranked up a notch too high!"

Jack was among the first to break through the trees, running full speed into the open field. The world closed in and then zoomed past in a blur. He flew over a rail fence as if he wore winged sandals like Perseus. Running straight at the Redcoat formation, he raced along with Titus, Ned, and Isaac, on a collision course with the solid wall of stiff-spined musket-bearing infantrymen. Jack's feet pounded the ground and he shouted the Iroquois war cry at the top of his lungs: *"Kohe! Kohe! Kohe!"*

A volley of lead buzzed past his ears. Cannon boomed and heavy ball came smashing into the ground, sending giant plumes of dirt and debris flying up into the air. Some soldiers fell—some dove for cover—but most, like Jack, just kept on running.

With the advantage of numbers, the massive wave of yowling rebels charging across the field was impossible to stop. The British line faltered, then broke completely. The Redcoats turned and ran in disordered retreat, scrambling to drag artillery carriages and keep their big guns from being captured.

Having yet to fire a shot, Jack was intent on getting into range and finding a target. Speedy Ned took the point, and Jack followed in phalanx with Titus and Isaac. Dodging and leaping over the dead and wounded, they moved across the field like a pack of howling wolves on the hunt, focused on their prey.

Enemy gun crews working from behind redoubt defenses began to cover their comrades' retreat, bombarding the field with iron shot.

Drawn into the ebb of the retreating tide, the rebel riflemen swarmed past the big gun trajectory, pursuing their enemies virtually unscathed.

"Shoot!"

On Isaac's order, they all dropped to one knee and took aim. Jack brushed back his hair, drew a bead on the intersection of white crossbelts on a red coat, and pulled the trigger. He hit the mark. His target dropped from sight.

"Into the trees! Into the trees!" Jack croaked, his throat rough from breathing in sulfurous gun smoke. He and his fellows ran an evasive pattern, veering back into the forest to join the majority of their company reloading and catching a clean breath in the thick timber. Jack fell in with Ned behind the trunk of a middling oak tree, happy to see Titus and Isaac skitter in as well.

Colonel Morgan ran into the woods, waving his sword over his head, shouting, "Hold your positions!" His order swept through the trees.

British drums began pounding the call to assemble and willow green regimental colors were raised along with the Union Jack behind a rail fence at the far end of the field, where saber-swinging Redcoat officers shouted and directed their scattered infantry into ordered ranks, two deep.

Jack watched the Redcoat progress while reloading—measuring his powder, ramming in a patched ball, priming the pan—doing all on reflex. He had to admire the British bulldog tenacity. There was no way for a rifleman to match the speed with which a trained regular could load and fire his musket using paper cartridges. If Morgan meant to avoid a tangle with a British bayonet, his riflemen had to break the back of the Redcoat attack before it could become fully formed and on the forward move.

Titus whistled and pointed. "Take a look at that!"

A soldier wearing the Continental blue and buff jacket was racing pell-mell at full gallop across the battlefield, riding up in the stirrups, bent over the neck of his brown horse. Covering the considerable distance between the enemy's right and left flanks, the reckless fellow exposed himself to fire from both sides—and he was heading straight for their position.

Jack held his breath, not believing his own eyes when the valiant rider came tearing into the woods without a scratch. Morgan's riflemen greeted the man with cheers and hats waving.

The breathless officer leapt from his mount. "Colonel Morgan!" he shouted. "Dan Morgan, where are you?!"

"Ben Arnold!" Morgan pushed to the fore, a huge grin on his crooked face. "You're either drunk or crazy to pull a mad prank like that!"

"I'm both." General Benedict Arnold threw an arm around the frontiersman. "General Poor's men have exposed Burgoyne's left, and the enemy is falling back at all points. We have an advantage in numbers. We must press forward. If we keep them on the run, we may yet force a surrender."

"They're readying another assault." Morgan handed Arnold a telescoping spyglass and pointed to the second rail fence where frantic, retreating Redcoats were being rallied into order by an officer on an imposing gray stallion.

Arnold peered through the eyepiece. "The man on the gray horse is General Simon Fraser. He's a host in himself—worth your whole regiment . . ." He snapped the glass shut. "He must be disposed of."

Morgan nodded and called out, "Send me Sergeant Tim Murphy!"

Jack'd heard of Murphy. The man was legend in the rifle corps—a veteran who proved his skill at the siege in Boston, and battles at Long Island, Trenton, and Princeton—Tim Murphy was the best marksman in a regiment of crack shots.

When the sharpshooter reported to duty a few minutes later, Jack almost burst out laughing. Tim Murphy was about six inches shorter than the double-barrel rifle he carried. Small and skinny as a beanpole, the ginger-headed Irishman wore a farmer's smock shirt, his cheerful, elfish grin belying a reputation as the deadliest shot in the corps. Jack edged in close to get a better look at the man's gun. It was a beautiful piece—the polished metal fittings were engraved with meticulous scrollwork, and the stock was embedded with three silver shamrocks.

Morgan grabbed the sharpshooter by the shoulder and pointed.

"See the man on the gray horse? That gallant officer is General Simon Fraser—a devilish brave fellow—but he should die. Pick a tree and do your duty, Murphy."

After a moment gauging the distance to his mark, judging the position of the trees and the strength of the wind, Murphy scrambled up onto the jutting limb of a grandfather maple.

"Good choice," Ned muttered.

The sharpshooter did not waste any time. He settled in, aimed, and fired off a shot.

General Arnold peered through the glass. "Miss."

Murphy raised rifle to shoulder and took a second shot.

"That double barrel sure is a handy thing, ain't it?" Titus noted.

"Goddamn it!" Morgan said. "Grazed his mount's mane! The bastard won't keep still, will he? Give it another go."

Tim Murphy had already bit the stopper from his powder horn, and was recharging both barrels.

"You haven't spooked him yet, Murphy," Arnold announced, still peering through the glass. "Your mark is staying in range . . ."

"FIX!" General Fraser shouted to his Redcoats, and the order was repeated down the line.

"Fix!"

"Fix!"

"Fix!"

Morgan ordered, "Pour some fire on them, boys!"

The riflemen peppered the Redcoats with lead. Titus dropped a regular. Ned picked off the soldier who stepped forward to fill the gap in the line. Isaac targeted a horseman. Jack rushed his shot, and only managed to knock the furry hat from a grenadier.

General Fraser rose up in his stirrups, and ordered, "BAYONETS!"

"Bayonets!"

"Bayonets!"

"Bayonets!"

The Redcoats locked deadly blades to the muzzle ends of their muskets, and the British line was suddenly bristling with the formidable glint of honed steel.

Jack rammed a bullet down his rifle muzzle, and watched Tim Murphy wait for his shot. One eye asquint, the tip of the sharpshooter's tongue poked out the corner of his mouth, weapon held steady, as he waited for the veil of smoke to lift. Murphy squeezed the trigger and, after a moment, cast a grin over his shoulder.

"Got him!"

Simon Fraser slumped in his saddle. Several mounted officers maneuvered in, ensconcing their wounded commander in a protective cocoon to lead him off the field.

"Well done!" Benedict Arnold swung back onto his horse, sword in hand. "If the day is long enough, my brothers, we'll have them in hell before nightfall. Victory or death!"

"Victory or death!" They all cheered as the General tore back across the field to rally the Continental forces on the left.

"Make ready to advance!" Morgan stood with his arm upstretched, his blade raised high.

Jack looked down at his feet and muttered, "Good legs, do your duty now!"

The sword fell and the order rang out. "Charge!"

A furious mass of riflemen streamed out onto the field, shouting, shooting, and loading on the run. The enemy soldiers at the center of the formation were the first to collapse, toppling over like the wooden skittles in a game of ninepins. Redcoat discipline held out long enough for the British company to fire off a single volley, before grabbing their colors and turning tail to run harum-scarum back to the safety of the main lines.

Jack and Titus ran through the abandoned field strewn with the bodies of horses and men, wounded and dying, and took cover behind one of two twelve-pounders the British had left behind.

Jack blew at a tendril of smoke still trickling from his rifle, and pushed a sweaty hank of hair from his eyes. "I lost my hat."

"Take your pick," Titus said, jerking his thumb toward the field they'd just crossed, littered with tricorns, bearskin caps, and jacked leather helmets.

Jack got busy reloading. "Do you see where Ned and Isaac have landed?"

Titus peered over the carriage wheel. "Yep. I see 'em . . ." A musket ball whistled past his ear, spinning him around and down onto his knees. "Shit!" he cursed, hunkering down between the big wooden wheels with Jack. "Where'd that come from?"

Another spate of lead ball came squealing by, pinging off the cannon and thunking into the artillery carriage, sending off a spray of splinters. Titus inched up and peered out above the wheel rim with his spyglass. "A bloodyback platoon making a stand," he said, pointing to the right. "At least a dozen muskets in close array, no more than fifty yards away. Something tells me they don't favor our position here, with their big gun."

Jack wheedled under the carriage to lie flat on his belly beneath the axletree. "Let 'em come and root us out. I'm not budging, Titus. This gun is ours."

"Too bad our gun ain't pointed in the other direction," Titus muttered, scooching in to lie beside Jack. "Start picking 'em off. I'll reload. We don't want any of them lobsters getting close enough to soil their bayonets in our carcasses, right?"

"That's a fact." Jack scooted to sit up crouched against the wheel hub, poking the barrel of his rifle out between the spokes.

Another volley of lead buzzed by like a swarm of angry bees, whittling away at the carriage. One missile ricocheted off the cannon, grazing Titus on the cheek. He swiped at the trickle of blood. "Get to it, Jack! Take a shot."

"Keep your breeches on. I can't see anything to shoot at just yet . . ." Jack peered down the sights at an enemy shrouded in a thick veil of gun smoke. A breeze swirled by, breaking through the smoke screen, and a small cadre of red jackets came into view. Jack trolled along the line and found his mark—a saber-wielding officer with a large ostrich plume adorning his hat, shouting the firing orders.

"Well, I'll be!" Jack pulled his eye away. "It's Captain Feather Hat."

"You sure?"

"Yep. It's him." Jack kept a bead on the man, following Pepperell's movement up and down the red line. "I have to admit, he's one brave bastard. He's got sure command of those men—has 'em firing in two directions."

"Get rid of him," Titus advised, "and maybe the others will scatter."

Jack smiled and pulled the trigger, sending a ball whizzing to shear the fancy feather from the Captain's hat. The man barely flinched. Removing his hat, he first considered the frowzy stub of a feather, then looked up in Jack's direction. The distance was too great, the smoke too dense, and the action too hot, but Jack could swear he and Pepperell met eye to eye in that moment.

The pause was brief. With a shout and a wave of his sword, Pepperell turned the attention of his company's muskets and ordered, "Fire!"

Jack and Titus flattened, faces into the earth, as a curtain of lead came flying across the field to scour their position.

"What happened?" Titus asked, brushing flakes of wood from his hair.

Jack shrugged. "I guess I missed."

Titus snatched the smoking rifle from Jack, and handed over his fully loaded weapon. "Quit playing. Knock the man down."

British drums began to beat the retreat as Jack took aim. The dense smoke lifted, he could see Pepperell's company had abandoned their stand, and were running off at full speed toward the redoubts, with Pepperell trailing the pack, driving his men forward. Jack kept his sights on the Captain, the muzzle end of his rifle slowly tracking his moving target. He fired.

"Did you get him?" Titus asked.

"Hard to tell," Jack answered. Squinting through the smoke, all he could make out were red jackets disappearing one by one, into the trees. "They ran off."

Jack and Titus crawled out from beneath the carriage and sprinted to join up with Isaac and Ned and the rest of Morgan's riflemen coming out from behind their cover to give chase to the retreating British forces. Dashing through trees, hurdling a small creek, they broke through to a clearing, and charged across the field heading straight toward the enemy redoubt on a slight hill.

Through a barrage of blazing iron, the Americans stormed the fortification, scrambling up and over eight-foot earth and log walls with a fearsome battle cry. Overwhelmed by American numbers and ferocity, the defenders turned and ran, only to be met by more Patriot forces attacking through the sally point at the rear of the redoubt. Outnumbered and surrounded, most of the German regulars sensibly dropped their weapons, threw off heavy brass helmets, and flung their arms up in surrender. Hessian officers railed and prodded their soldiers to stand and fight. One frustrated officer—much braided and bedecked in a golden satin sash—berated and slapped his surrendering Hessians with the flat of his saber, until he was felled by a bullet to his back—shot dead by one of his own men.

The redoubt enclosure was strewn with forsaken snarls of regimental colors, drums, brass helmets, muskets, cartridge boxes, and haversacks, and writhing with the throes and groans of the wounded and dying. Scores of German prisoners were being herded at bayonet point while American soldiers began plundering the spoils, tugging the boots off of Hessian corpses, gathering swords and pistols from the dead officers.

Rifles shouldered and tomahawks in play, Jack, Titus, Ned, and Isaac skirted the chaos and ran to the sally port, encountering no resistance. Once through the breach, they slowed to a halt at fifty yards. But for a few sporadic shots, the gunfire had all but ceased, and there was no more fight to be had.

The foursome gathered on a small rise, side by side, breathing hard, watching British Redcoats, German blue coats, and Loyalist green coats streaming from fortifications like ants from anthills, disappearing into the darkening forests, retreating back to their base camp on the Hudson.

"What the hell?" Jack raised his rifle over his head and shouted, his throat raw, his voice hoarse, "Come back, you bloodyback bastards! Come back here and fight!"

No one answered his challenge.

Jack dropped his rifle breech-end in the dirt, and leaned in on the hot iron. Panting, he caught his breath, and wondered at the handful of stars shining on the deepening twilight in the eastern sky. Spinning about, he was surprised at how dark it had become—not even a sliver of sun shone above the glowing western horizon. From the first turkey call in the woods to this moment, time had hurtled along at breakneck speed, and the battle that seemed to rush by in a few minutes had actually lasted hours.

"I guess that's that." Titus slipped his tomahawk back into a loop on his belt, and brought out a leathern flask from inside his shirt. After taking a hearty sip, he wiped the rim on his shirtsleeve and, with a poke of the elbow, offered the bottle to Jack. "Peachy?"

Jack took a deep swig and passed the bottle on to Isaac, who took a gulp and handed the brandy to Ned with a nudge.

"*Kwe*. Have a drink, nephew—this battle is won."

Anne stopped mid-pour. She glanced up at the sound of sporadic gunfire, and checked the position of the sun lowering on the western horizon. The day began and progressed with such order and quiet, she feared all the conclusions drawn the evening before were in error, making the plans she and Sally devised pointless. *A wasted effort.*

Sally dumped an armload of wood and looked to the western hills, one hand on her hip, the other shading her eyes. "Did ye hear tha'? Sounds like a battle in the making, na?"

"Just see to your chores," Anne snapped, "and leave the soldiering to the soldiers." Shaking off the twinge of remorse brought on by Sally's crestfallen expression, she moved on to fill the next kettle. *Best to squash such thoughts before they have a chance to take root . . .* She was tired of rising up on waves of optimism only to be dashed on the rocks of false hope. *Tired of the whole mess . . .*

"Most likely skirmishers," Bab offered, coming over to help Sally feed the kitchen fire. "A reconnaissance force went out this noon. Pennybrig said Burgoyne was taking a few regiments forward to get the lay of the rebel works on the Bemis Heights."

Anne finished filling the kettles with water, and moved on to measuring in the salt and cornmeal for the dinner porridge. Growing in intensity, the gunfire not only continued, it became amplified by artillery barrage. *More than skirmishing, I think.*

She moved from kettle to kettle, stirring the thickening mush with a paddle, listening to the pounding artillery and watching swathes of smoke rise up to hover over the hills. Once the porridge was cooked, Anne moved the kettles off the fire, and noticed the cannonade had become so incessant, the women working the hospital kitchen no longer flinched at the blasts. She and Sally carried the porridge, biscuits, and beer down the slope to their assigned tent, neither of them daring to utter an encouraging word.

Best not to raise hopes . . .

"Only a reconnaissance force," Anne repeated as Sally ladled out corn porridge to the tent full of soldiers on edge.

"Reconnaissance, my arse!" Sergeant Foley declared without a stutter.

"Sergeant Foley," Captain Thorn reprimanded, "mind your language."

"Beg p-p-pardon, missus," Foley said. "But I've served a g-g-gun for three and twenty years—I k-ken the sound of battle when I hear it."

Captain Thorn took the bowl Anne passed over. "The guns do tell a story. That is a fierce bombardment. Sounds like the rebels are taking quite a beating."

Burgus laughed. "Burgoyne is blowin' the damn rebels to bloody bits."

"It's the rebels in peril for certain, ye think?" Sally asked, scraping the last of the porridge into Will Crisp's bowl with sudden tears welling up in her blue eyes.

"Never you fear, Sally," Will said. "Our lads are trouncing 'em."

Anne and Sally hurried through feeding their charges and finishing up their hospital chores. Neither of them said a word as they trudged back to their tent in the deepening twilight, but when the noise from the far-off guns dwindled away, they both stopped in their tracks and stood squinting at the horizon, flinching at the now-and-then crack of a rifle shot echoing over the hills.

Sally pulled her shawl up over her head. "I dinna care what ye say, something is going on, and I mean to find out what."

"You're right. I'll go see the Baroness." Anne nodded. "She might know. I'll meet you back at the tent."

Frederika von Riedesel and her young daughters were quartered in a gambrel-roofed farmhouse not too far from the hospital. Anne stepped up onto the wide, covered stoop to peer through the window, and her heart sank. *A dinner party . . .*

Inside, Lucy Lennox, the Baroness, and a very pregnant Lady Harriet Acland were orbiting a candlelit dining table, setting the service with china and crystal. Anne tapped on the glass.

The Baroness waved her in. "Mrs. Merrick, what a surprise. As you can see, I am hosting a *diné* for Generals Burgoyne and Fraser," she explained while making minute adjustments to every plate, fork, spoon, and knife in the place settings. "I'm afraid I've no time for visiting."

"It all looks lovely," Anne said.

Harriet Acland snapped, "What is it you want here?"

Anne took a step back. "I—I apologize for the interruption. It's just that with all the shooting earlier, I worried that perhaps something had gone amiss . . ."

"Amiss? Nothing's amiss. Why in heaven's name would you say such a thing?" Harriet Acland snatched up a crystal goblet and set to polishing the glass with such fervor, Anne feared it would shatter in her hand.

"If you wouldn't mind, Mrs. Merrick . . ." The Baroness pointed to the door. "The Generals will be arriving at any minute . . ."

Lucy turned Anne with an arm around her shoulders and led her back out onto the stoop. "Pay them no mind. They are wound tighter than a German clock . . ."

"Because of the guns?"

Lucy nodded. "The reconnaissance force was due back over two hours ago." She tried to put on a brave smile. "But this is the lot of a soldier's wife, isn't it? On pins and needles until we see our men come back safe and sound . . ."

A loud shout drew their attention. Escorted by a few clusters of men on foot and several riders on horseback, a wagon had turned up the road leading to the house.

"Look!" Lucy waved. "Here they come now."

None of the riders waved back. Heads were hanging low, and some of the men on foot were helping others stumble along. As the train drew closer Anne recognized only Burgoyne and Gordon Lennox among the riders. A man lay prone in the wagon bed with a blanket thrown over him.

Frederika and Harriet came out onto the stoop, shawls clutched around shoulders. The Baroness called out, her voice pitched high. "Is it my husband?"

"No, madam. It is General Fraser." Burgoyne leapt from his horse, looking oddly frantic. "A grievous wound—the doctor is on his way. Please be so kind as to make a place for him to rest."

"Here?" The Baroness blanched. "Should you not take him to the hospital?"

"I think not." Burgoyne shook his head. "The hospital will be over-run in no time."

Anne ran back into the dining room and whisked the candelabra from the table. Lucy dragged the chairs over to the side, and in a clatter of metal and glass, they bundled up the place settings into the tablecloth, clearing everything just as the litter bearers barreled through the doorway to deposit Simon Fraser onto the tabletop.

Burgoyne followed them in and said, "Best prepare. More are on the way."

The women all turned to look out the window. A steady parade of soldiers interspersed with wagons, carts, and artillery carriages was straggling in from the west. With a face as white as her bone china, the Baroness grasped Burgoyne by the arm. "My husband?"

"I couldn't say, madam."

Burgoyne had lost all luster. Bareheaded, his hair was in disarray, with long strands escaping from his usually fastidious queue. The golden braid adorning his slumped shoulders was dusty with dirt and soot, and his handsome, confident features were turned harsh and ashen. He took Harriet Acland by the elbow. "Lady Acland, might we have a word?"

Burgoyne led the stricken woman to a chair. Gordon Lennox came in, directing Anne, Lucy, and the Baroness to stand back against the wall, making way for litter bearers carrying more wounded inside.

"Take them to the back rooms," Lennox ordered. "Push the furnishings aside and clear the floors . . . Make room for more . . ."

The Baroness sank into the corner, her girls running in from their beds in nightdresses to cling to her silk skirts. With trembling hands and features pinched with worry, she reminded Anne of a frightened bird that had toppled from its nest with a broken wing.

"Lieutenant Lennox," the Baroness asked, "any word on my husband?"

"General von Riedesel is with the left flank, and I can only pray his troops have fared better than the Twenty-fourth."

Anne could wait no longer. "Did you win the field, Mr. Lennox?"

"No, we did not." Gordon closed his eyes for a moment. "Our lads fought valiantly, but we were outnumbered at least three to one. We abandoned the Balcarres and Breymann redoubts to the rebels and lost many of our big guns—all forsaken in retreat."

Anne masked the joy that sprung to her heart, and pushed the Patriot victory to the back of her brain. Eyeing the puddle of blood accumulating beneath the dining room table General Fraser lay upon, all she could think was, *Do not become entangled here . . . Get out . . .*

Lucy whimpered, and touched her husband's sleeve, torn and bloody at the shoulder. "Gordon, you're *bleeding!*"

"It's nothing—" Lennox stayed his wife's panic with a hand on her shoulder. "I'm lucky to be only grazed; the sharpshooters were on a mission to spare no officer. Look at Fraser—and poor Acland—both legs shot out from under him and taken prisoner." He nodded to the opposite corner, where Harriet Acland sat sobbing in a chair, General Burgoyne down on one knee, her hands in his.

Lucy linked elbows with Anne, and pulled her close. "What of Geoffrey? Mrs. Merrick came seeking word . . ."

Anne felt her head nodding, but her mind resounded with the

words *heartless* and *selfish*. She was engulfed by a wave of guilt—so centered on getting away and leaving the enemy encampment far behind, she hadn't given Geoffrey Pepperell or his well-being a single thought.

Lennox shrugged. "When Fraser was shot, all semblance and order was lost. Geoffrey's company became separated . . ."

The surgeon just then arrived in a great hubbub, his aide trailing along bearing an instrument chest on his back. Shouting, "Make way!" the surgeon pushed in and took command of the situation at the dining room table. Ordering his aide off to fetch water and rags, he first measured the General's pulse, then drew the blood-saturated blanket aside. After rattling through his case for a pair of shears, he began to snip away at the General's bloody clothing and expose the wound. Simon Fraser managed to grasp the surgeon by the hand.

"Do not conceal a thing from me," he said. "Must I die?"

The surgeon nodded, and in a very even tone said, "The bullet has pierced your bowel, General. I'm afraid it is a mortal wound, sir."

Fraser let loose of the doctor's hand and sighed. "My poor wife."

Tears were streaming down Lucy's cheeks as she turned to peer out the window. "There are many, many wagons coming down the road . . ."

Lennox kissed his wife. "I must go and see to my men . . ." He twisted away, disappearing out the door.

Anne's mind raced. Concern for Jack, her brother, and her friends on the Patriot side was overwhelmed by the noise of soldiers shouting directives at one another and the pathetic cries of the wounded calling out for mothers and to God. She forced herself to close her ears to all but the single voice clamoring in her head.

Get out—now!

The Baroness grabbed Anne by the arm. "Rebel scoundrels! Murderers! To target our officers in such a way—it is uncivilized."

Hemmed in between Lucy and the Baroness, Anne sputtered, "I'm going back to the hospital . . . They must need all hands . . ." She tugged free and wriggled a way through the crowd, breaking free through the doorway to find Ohaweio stepping up onto the stoop, carrying Geoffrey Pepperell in his arms.

Anne's heart stopped for a moment; then she glanced over her shoulder and grabbed the Indian by the sleeve. "Don't take him in there—it's a madhouse." She steered Ohaweio to the far end of the stoop, and gestured. "Here. Lay him here . . ."

Ohaweio very carefully laid Geoffrey down onto the boards, centered in the skewed rectangle of candlelight streaming out the window. The Indian bent down and placed Pepperell's cavalier hat on his chest, the once-proud ostrich plume reduced to a sad little remnant.

Anne's world went suddenly quiet, and she dropped down to her knees, eyes scanning Pepperell's blood-covered form from head to toe. *He's a sieve* . . . Blood was seeping from every part of him. She brushed the hat aside. Candlelight flickered on his handsome face and his quite peaceful features were drained of all color. She pressed a finger to his neck, and felt the feeble pulse of his heart. "He's alive!"

"Yes." Ohaweio sat opposite, legs crossed. "You fix."

"*Fix?!* He needs a surgeon . . ." Anne began to stand.

Ohaweio leaned across Geoffrey's unconscious form and grabbed Anne hard by the upper arm. Dark eyes serious, with a voice deliberate and stern, he repeated, "*You* fix."

Anne spoke very slowly, pointing to the most obvious wounds. "He's shot in the shoulder here—the arm—this knee is shattered—this leg, shot through . . . *I can't fix.* He needs a *doctor*. I'm going to fetch a doctor . . ."

"He means for you to stay with me, Anne."

She looked down to see Geoffrey, smiling up at her, the charming sparkle in his blue eyes dulled by pain. Anne sank down onto her heels.

"How happy I am to see you." His voice was a whisper. He flailed and managed to grasp her hand for a moment before losing strength.

"You need tending, Geoff." Anne rose up on her knees. "I'm getting a doctor . . ."

"No point . . ." With erratic fingers, he grasped the bloody buttonhole edge of his jacket and flipped it aside. The waistcoat and shirt beneath were ripped open. A hasty field dressing had slipped and she could see blood burbling up and his insides spilling from a ragged hole—the length of two handspans—torn in his side.

"Oh no . . . Oh, God!" Anne pulled off her apron. Folding it into a pad, she placed it over the awful wound. The linen was imbrued with blood in an instant, and she shouted, "We need a doctor here! *A doctor!*"

"Shhhhhh . . ." Geoffrey cautioned with one trembling finger upraised. "I've little time. Please—no doctor."

Anne slumped down to sit with her legs curled to the side. She took a breath and wiped the tears from her eyes with the back of her forearm. She looked through the door to see the Baroness sitting with one of her girls on her lap, reading to Simon Fraser from the Bible.

"Do you want me to read some prayers for you?" Anne asked.

"God, no!" Geoffrey laughed, then coughed.

Anne used her skirt hem to swipe away the blood trickling from his mouth. "What would you have me do?"

"Just promise you'll stay."

Anne took Geoffrey by the hand. "I promise. I won't leave you."

She sat by his side as he drifted in and out of consciousness, and witnessed three times the wondrous smile come to his face as he opened his eyes to see she was still there—as she said she'd be—holding his hand. The look in his eye was so sweet and childlike, she was reminded of the vigil she kept at her son's bedside. *The night Jemmy slipped away . . .*

Anne sat and watched the twilight deepen and the endless stream of lights and shadows bouncing along the road as carts and wagons and foot soldiers came rolling and trudging in from the battlefield. A horse and rider peeled away from the parade, galloping through the field up to the farmhouse. General von Riedesel swung down from the saddle and stomped right past without seeming to notice the man dying on his front stoop.

The Baron's entrance was greeted with a wild scream from the Baroness, and squeals of glee from his little daughters. Anne leaned back and watched the happy family reunion through the doorway. She turned back to find Geoffrey awake, and said, "The Baroness is much relieved. An odd couple, those two."

"He's such a toad, and she's . . ." Geoffrey closed his eyes for a moment. "She's mad in love with him, though, isn't she?"

There was such a heartfelt ache in his voice and such sad yearning in his blue eyes, Anne was compelled to ease his way onward. In another place, at another time, Geoffrey Pepperell might well have been her one true love. She smoothed a tendril of bloody hair away from his forehead, and brushed his cheek with the back of her fingers.

"Now, you and I, Geoff . . ." she said, choking back her tears. "We are the most perfect couple, don't you think? A true love match."

"Love match," Geoffrey repeated with a smile, and squeezed her hand. "I knew you were the one, the moment I saw you lop the head off that snake."

Anne leaned in and pressed a soft kiss to his lips. "And I knew you were the one when you swooped me up into your arms and carried me across that mud puddle."

Geoffrey's once-easy laugh turned into a choking cough. Anne slipped her arms under his shoulders and said to the Indian, "Help me raise him up . . ."

Ohaweio stripped the blanket from his shoulders and rolled it into a bolster to support Pepperell's shoulders and head. The coughing eased, and Geoffrey was able to catch his breath. He managed to pat Ohaweio on the knee. "Much better . . . Leave it to you, my old friend."

Ohaweio reached in and rested a hand on Pepperell's shoulder. "Good Pepperell. Brave man."

"Oh, Anne." Geoffrey blinked, held tight to her hand. "You are so very beautiful in the light . . ." His grip relaxed. His smile faded, and the bright of his eye waned, like a candle being carried off into the distance, diminishing until it disappeared.

Anne looked up at Ohaweio, her throat aching so, she could barely utter the words, "He's gone."

Ohaweio said nothing as he closed his friend's eyes, salty tears tracking a trail through the smoky grime and paint on his cheeks.

Anne stood and smoothed her skirts, unable to stay the tears streaming down her face. "He needs to be seen to. I'll find Gordon." Pushing her way through the crowd standing vigil around Fraser's deathbed, Anne went from room to room, looking for Lennox.

The house was in turmoil, the floors of every room crowded with the wounded. Some wives had come to find their husbands, and one woman grabbed Anne by the hand as she passed by. "Bring water," she said.

Anne pulled away and stumbled out into the hallway to lean against the wall. The farmhouse was stuffy with the unwholesome smell of blood and fear, and cauterized flesh.

The smell of war. Anne covered her eyes. *How . . . How could I have ever wished for this?*

She lurched out the back door and, leaning over the back stoop railing, sucked clean fresh air into her lungs. The gray hills in the distance seemed so round and soft and peaceful against the clear black, star-filled night, but Anne knew the book-match to the British aftermath was being played out beyond them, on the Patriot side. Victorious or vanquished, men on both sides were wounded, maimed, dead, and dying in pain. The living were suffering the loss of their loved ones, and if lucky, brave men like Geoffrey Pepperell clung tight to the hand of a stranger for comfort in their last moments.

For possession of a patch of ground. No . . . it isn't that simple. Anne puffed out a breath, and remembered what Jack had once said, when she questioned his commitment to the cause of liberty. *Blood has been shed, and our countrymen are dying. I do all I can for our cause—wholly in it, heart, mind, and soul, for I will not have our men perish for naught.*

She fixed her gaze upon a bright star and pressed her fists to her breast, beginning her prayer by whispering the names of her love, her brother, and her good friend. "Jack. David. Titus . . . be whole and safe . . ." She gulped another breath, and finished by saying, "Peace be with you, Geoffrey. Ohaweio has the right of it—no matter the color of your coat, you were a good and brave man."

"Mrs. Merrick . . ." A hand fell heavy on her shoulder. Anne turned and blinked through tears. It was Gordon Lennox.

"Geoffrey's dead," she said.

Gordon leaned with both hands on the railing, and heaved a shuddering sigh. "He went right into the thick of it without a thought. So reckless . . . so courageous . . ."

"Ohaweio is with him on the front stoop. You need to see to him,

Gordon." Anne stepped down and took a few backward steps. "You were a true friend to him."

Anne ran. She ran as fast as her legs could carry her, all the way to the baggage camp. There was a light in their tent, and she fumbled at the ties on the flaps, her lungs aching, unable to catch her breath. Sally pulled the tent open.

"Annie! Yer drenched in blood!"

"There was a battle. A bad one." Anne sank down onto her cot, her palms open on her lap. "Pepperell's dead. He died holding my hand . . ."

Sally sat down, not saying a word, her eyes bloodshot and swollen.

"What's the matter with you? It's what we've been hoping for, isn't it?" Anne plucked at her bloodstained skirt, unable to temper the note of hysteria in her voice. "Now's our chance—what are we waiting for? Let's go. Let's get out of here."

"Th' chances of our getting back t' David and Jack are less to none. Burgoyne's pulled what's left of his regiments to this position. We are now at the front, and the Continentals will no doubt press their attack at daybreak. The defenses are set and solid—there's no getting through in any direction." Sally bit her lip, trying very hard not to cry. "What are we t' do? It's all such an awful mommick . . ."

Anne shrugged. "Trapped on a sinking ship . . ."

"Aye." Sally nodded. "A sinking, pocky British ship."

Anne stared for a moment at the flame flickering in the lantern, and she smiled. "Would you listen to the two of us? By all our sniffling and whining, you'd never know our side came out victors in the mess."

"Aye—'tis true . . ." Sally's smile was weak. "Our lads did well, did they na?"

"They did! And reinforcements or no, Burgoyne will be hardpressed to recover from this defeat. It is the beginning of the end for them . . ."

"I s'pose . . ." Sally wiped her face with a tear-drenched hankie. "I s'pose I thought victory would feel better than it does . . ."

Anne fingered a sticky smear of blood on her forearm, and said, "So did I."

*   *   *

The day broke with cannon booming.

All British forces had retreated back behind the safety of the Great Redoubt, the hilltop fortifications built to protect the artillery park and baggage camp. The rebels turned their newly acquired cannon on these defenses. The Continental Army was closing in.

Carted, carried, or staggering in all through the night, there was not enough shelter under which to house the multitude of wounded soldiers, and all able hands were pressed into service to deal with the massive influx of battlefield casualties. The drummer boys organized the camp children into a bucket brigade, passing endless buckets of water up from the river to the hospital. The laundrywomen fashioned shrouds for the corpses, and the teamsters piled the dead onto wagons like cordwood, to be taken and buried in a mass grave. Armed with water and packets of ship's biscuit, Anne and Sally were among the brigade of camp women giving succor to row upon row of wounded men lying in the open field near the hospital. Given no time to mourn their dead husbands lying among the bodies awaiting burial, many a tearful wife coursed these rows, stoic in performing her duty to the regiment.

Throughout the day, Anne and Sally gleaned information from the soldiers and officers they tended. The tales often shifted with the storyteller, but certain constants remained—the rebels fought ferociously and in great number. Burgoyne's forces were routed, and the army's position with its back to the river was untenable, with little hope for reinforcement.

Anne knelt down beside a wounded ensign lying on a scrap of oiled canvas, head cradled on his furry goatskin pack. The surgeon managed to dig the lead out of his hip, but the young officer was fevering. She offered him a dipper of water.

Sally ran up and crouched down beside Anne, keeping her voice low. "Burgoyne has ordered the entire army to retreat north."

Anne drew a rag from her pocket and dipped it into the water. "When?"

"Now."

"Now? But the wounded . . ."

Sally leaned in and whispered in her ear, "They're leaving the wounded behind."

Anne wrung out the cloth and sponged the soot from the ensign's face. Setting the bucket beside him, she placed a packet of ship's biscuit in the crook of his arm. "Remember to drink," she told him, tugging his woolen blanket up to his chin.

"Away—" Sally gave Anne a pull. "This mess is beyond your fixing. Look—" She pointed to the row of artillery carriages being assembled on the flat. "They've brought the great guns down from the Heights."

Burgeoning with all regiments in residence, the camp was in motion as never before. From hospital, to artillery park, to baggage camp, the urgency to get the army packed and under way was palpable. Teamsters were frantic, yoking and hitching their draft animals to wagons being loaded with provisions and matériel. Officers shouted orders to soldiers rolling casks of meal and flour down to the riverside, where the provisions were loaded onto bateaus and floated upriver. Women ran about, searching for and gathering their children. By the time Anne and Sally reached the baggage camp, more than half of the tents had been struck and packed for the march.

"It's goin' t' be a sharp night," Sally noted. "I can already see my breath."

They hurried to change into more suitable clothes, augmenting petticoats and skirts with a second layer. Loose linen jackets were belted at the waist with cotton sashes. They tied their hair up in checkered kerchiefs, and swirled hooded cloaks of cardinal red wool over the entire ensemble. Handled baskets prepacked with their few rations, and other odds and ends, were brought up from under beds. Sally tucked the leather coin purse between her breasts. After doing the same with her keepsakes, Anne held the tent flap open for Sally and said, "This is it—we're leaving."

The neighboring Sandiland sisters were also preparing for the retreat. The two young women and their boys were dressed in several layers of clothing, and Sally smiled at the sight. "Like a family of roly-poly bugs, they are."

Viney carried the heavy canvas tent folded and strapped to a wooden frame she wore on her back. Prue hefted their bundle of bedding onto her shoulders, tied her toddler's leading strings to her wrist, and adjusted the sling she used to carry her new baby girl on her chest. Tent poles became walking staffs, and like good shepherds, the women used them to prod the children into order.

"Viney!" Anne called. "Make use of our barrow, and take whatever you want—the tent and anything within."

Viney's eyes popped wide. "For truth? Won't you be needin' yer things, missus?"

Anne held up her basket. "We're traveling light. Sally and I are heading south, to my brother."

Viney and Prue ran to the barrow, unloading their packs and parcels into it. They turned to quickly strike the wedge tent, stuffing it into the barrow as well. The cots were all they left behind.

"Husbands wouldn't care for those," Prue explained with a shy smile.

"But we'll each have our own tent now, sister!" Viney sighed. "What a luxury!"

Anne hoisted the two smaller boys to sit atop the cargo pile, and Sally took the Indian sausage she'd saved and snapped it into five even pieces, giving one to each of the boys.

"A little something to chew might keep them quiet for a mile or two," Anne said, stuffing a sack of raisins and a packet of ship's biscuit into Prue's pocket.

Prue said, "Yiv worn a soft spot into my heart with all your kindnesses."

Anne and Sally bid the Sandilands farewell in an onslaught of hugs and kisses from the teary-eyed sisters—Prue and Viney turned back every now and then to wave or blow a kiss as they bumped the barrow along, disappearing in the human mass funneling down to the river road.

Sally waved and said, "Ye ken we just gave away all our food."

"I know," Anne said, waving as well. "They'll be needing it more than we."

"True enough."

As the sun melted into the horizon, they stood and watched the exodus on its northern path until nightfall, when the long snaking column disappeared beyond their sight. But for the lights at hospital, where a few physicians and some women stayed behind to care for the wounded and infirm, the camp seemed deserted.

Anne slapped Sally on the back, and, baskets in hand, they set off down the muddy track that, only a few hours before, had been flanked by crowds of tents and wagons. Drainage ditches carved into the ground and piles of unused firewood beside river stones gathered into circle hearths were the only signs marking where the Redcoat army had, for a short time, laid claim to the land.

"Mrs. Merrick! Sally!"

Anne turned to see Sergeant Pennybrig running toward them, a company of soldiers with muskets in hand trotting right behind.

"Should we make a run for the trees?" Sally asked.

"They're armed." Anne sighed. "Best wait and see what it is he wants."

Pennybrig pulled up huffing and puffing. He shouldered his musket and ordered the rest of his company off with a terse, "Get to it." The soldiers scattered to the abandoned campsites, tossing firewood onto the deserted hearths, sprinkling it with lamp oil and setting it alight.

"What are they up to?" Anne asked.

"A ruse for the rebels, to make the camp seem inhabited." Pennybrig crossed his arms over his chest, his countenance stern. "Why is it you two have strayed so far behind the others?"

Anne gripped tight to her basket. "We're heading south, Sergeant, to my brother, as was always my destination."

"Ah no, that's a very dangerous course, missus," Pennybrig said, with a gruff shake of his head. "Not wise. Very dangerous."

"Pardon my bluntness, Sergeant, but it makes no sense for Sally and I to follow a defeated army north on a desperate retreat with the enemy in pursuit. I'm willing to wage the southern course is the safer path for us."

"Still . . . it's not right . . ." Pennybrig's brows merged into one. "Women traveling alone in enemy country . . ."

Anne laughed. "In this instance, Sergeant, enemy country also happens to be our own country."

"Aye, you've a point there . . ."

"Dinna fash for us, Pennybrig." Sally gave the sergeant a slap on the shoulder. "We're willing t' take our chances with the rebels."

"Pray it's rebels you find, Miss Sally, for these woods are filled with deserters both British and German—cowardly, desperate men—if it's them you meet with, they will not treat you so kind." Pennybrig pulled the dirk from the sheath at his waist belt and offered it to Anne. "I want for you t' take this blade. It'd ease my conscious some if at least one of you were armed."

"Och, d'ye take us for simpletons, Pennybrig? O' course we're armed." Sally nudged Anne and the women swept open their cloaks, displaying the loaded dueling pistols tucked in at the sashes they'd wound at waistlines. "And . . ." Pushing back jacket sleeves, they unveiled sheathed daggers strapped to forearms with blue grosgrain ribbon.

Pennybrig broke into a grin, resheathing his weapon. "I pity th' ill-willie who might think to tangle with the two of you." In a tone more serious he added, "Avoid the river road. I'd expect trouble to be lurking there in droves. D'ye know the trailhead just behind where Johnny'd pitched his big marquee?"

Anne said, "I do."

"Follow it," Pennybrig said. "That path will take you south through a cover of trees as far as Stillwater."

"You've been a good friend to us, Sergeant." Anne popped up and gave the man a kiss on the scruffy cheek. "Take care, and keep Bab safe—bid her farewell from us."

"I've no scones for ye—so here's my kiss instead." Sally tiptoed up and planted her kiss on the opposite cheek.

"I prefer kisses to scones any day." Pennybrig grinned and waved as they set off. "Fare thee well, ladies—watch and ward—and keep to the trees!"

Anne and Sally marched toward the Great Redoubt, ducking into the shadow of the tree line as they approached Burgoyne's headquarters camp. The General's lavish marquee tents were no longer standing, and were no doubt among the items packed into five covered wagons parked in a long line, waiting on oxen teams, and blocking the entrance to the trail. The pair of soldiers guarding Burgoyne's baggage train sat crouched in the circle of light from a lantern dangling from the lead wagon, very intent on the game of dice played between them.

Anne set her basket down and glanced up at the crescent moon casting scant light on the open field they needed to cross. Pulling up her hood, she said, "Toward the tail end, fast and quiet—on the count of three . . ."

Sally tugged her hood up. "Ready . . . one, two, three!"

They darted across the field at a quickstep, ducking behind the last wagon to catch their breath. Anne panted, "They didn't see us."

Sally nodded. "Never once looked up from their dice."

A high-pitched giggle sounded, and a voice exclaimed, "Hal*looo!*"

Anne grabbed Sally by the arm and they hunkered in the shadow of the wagon, but it was too late—they'd been spotted. Dressed in a beautiful blue gown and velvet cape, sucking on a bottle of Champagne, Fanny Loescher came staggering out of the trees. She threw her arms up and squealed, "Company!"

"*Shush!*" Anne dropped her basket, rushed over, and slapped a hand over Fanny's mouth, whispering, "We don't want to call the guards down upon us—understand?"

Wide-eyed, Fanny's nod was emphatic, and Anne removed her hand, regretting it instantly as Fanny exclaimed, "Hiding from the guards! What fun! What an adventure!"

"Shhhh!" Anne and Sally shushed in unison.

"Oh, I forgot!" Fanny giggled, and put a finger to her lips, whispering, "Quiet as a mouse, is me. But those guards? Not to worry—they really don't give a shite." She tipped the bottle back and, finding it empty, tossed it aside to clatter over a patch of gravel.

Anne winced, shoulders to ears, and Sally cursed, *"Fiech!"* leaning out to see the guards still at their game and paying no notice to the goings-on at the back end of the wagon train.

"Maybe she's right." Sally shrugged. "Maybe they dinna give a shite."

"Of course I'm right." Fanny bent over the tailboard of the wagon and came up with another bottle of Champagne. With a dexterous expertise reserved for the most craven, she removed the wire bale and popped the cork. Slurping at the geyser of froth that bubbled up, she offered the bottle to Anne. "It's French . . ." she said.

"Come on . . . away with us . . ." Sally handed Anne her basket, and as they turned to leave, Fanny caught hold a fistful of Anne's cloak.

"Hey . . . why aren't you gone with the rest of 'em?"

"Let go—" Anne tugged and pulled, trying to wrench free, dragging Fanny along. Sally dropped her basket to help Anne disengage, but Fanny maintained a clawlike grip on the fabric—clinging like a stubborn burr, she would not be plucked off.

"Tell me where you're going," Fanny said, "and I'll let go."

"We're going south," Anne whispered, trying to prize Fanny's fingers open.

Fanny dropped the Champagne bottle in a resounding thunk. Grasping Anne's cloak with both hands, she cried, "I want to go with!" In a voice rising in volume and pitch, she began to chant, "Take me with! Take me with! TAKE ME WITH! TAKE ME WITH!"

Anne managed to twist around and behind, gagging the woman's bleating with the palm of her hand. Spitting, squealing, and kicking up a fuss, Fanny struggled. Sally engaged in the tangle of cloaks, trying to keep Fanny's arms pinned to her side, suffering a number of kicks to the shins in the process.

"She's going t' bring the guards down on us, Annie!"

Anne heaved a deep breath, and gave the woman a violent shake. "Enough! Listen—you can come with us, but only if you promise to be very quiet and behave. Promise?"

Fanny's nod was vigorous. Anne let loose, and Fanny twirled free.

"Ha!" She sneered at Sally, and in an exaggerated whisper she sing-songed, "Fanny and Annie going on a great adventure. Fanny and Annie—it *rhymes*!"

"Are you daft?" Sally bristled with teeth clenched. "I'm no' goin' anywhere with that drunken whore . . ."

Fanny reached in and poked Sally in the chest. "Who're you calling a drunk?"

Sally gave her a rough, two-handed shove. "I'm callin' you a drunk, ye stupid cow!"

"*The guards!*" Anne glanced around the corner.

The hissed reminder caused Sally to take a step back. All in a pucker, she stuffed loose strands of hair back under her headscarf. "Bringing that one along is madness—utter madness."

"Come, now, Sal—the more, the merrier . . ." Anne bent to pick up the discarded Champagne bottle and pressed it into Sally's hand with a nudge and a wink. "Come on—join in the fun."

Anne threw her arm around Fanny's shoulder and whispered, "Fanny and Annie are off on a great adventure!" Giving her a spin, she steered the drunken woman toward the trailhead, and with a know-ing glance over her shoulder, she called, "Come on, Sal."

Sally came up from behind and knocked Fanny over the head with the heavy bottle. Fanny crumpled in a heap of velvet and taffeta. They dragged the unconscious woman back to the wagon and propped her up against the wheel.

Anne said, "I feel bad leaving her this way. It is a cold night, and who knows when they might find her . . ."

"Och, she'll be fine." Sally halfheartedly tugged at Fanny's skirts to cover her exposed legs.

Anne positioned Fanny's lolling head to rest between the spokes, and pointed up to the tailgate of the wagon. "Climb in there and see if you can find a blanket or something we might cover her with."

Sally climbed up into the wagon, muttering, "I'd wager th' whore's drunk enough to keep herself and a whole regiment warm . . ." After a moment's shuffling around, a pair of blankets came sailing out, one after the other.

Anne spread and tucked the wool over Fanny's still form. "Alright, Sally . . . this'll do . . . Let's be off."

Sally leaned out of the wagon. "Fetch the baskets, Annie—it's a treasure trove!"

The wagon was packed with Burgoyne's personal stock of comestibles. Fanny had pilfered bottles from one of three cases of Champagne. One wooden crate contained wheels of Dutch cheese coated in beeswax and packed in straw. Another was filled with strings of smoked sausages coiled like rope. There were bushels of apples and quince. Sally opened the lid on a chest filled with tins of fine biscuits. "Whole tins!" she said, tucking a few into her basket.

Acting as lookout, Anne leaned out to check the status of the guards. "Hurry up! We oughtn't press our luck . . ."

Sally held out a lantern. "Look!"

Anne took the lantern, moving the shutter up slightly to expose a sliver of light. Pushing the shutter back down, she hid the flame within. "A dark lantern—it might come in handy."

"Fanny's, no doubt . . ." Sally whispered. "Th' wee sneak thief . . ."

"A pot calling a kettle black, wouldn't you say?"

"Och, no! *I'm* capturing enemy supplies." Sally handed out the two baskets, heavy with plunder. "That one thieved goods from her lover." She jumped down from the wagon and took up a load.

"Either way," Anne said, grabbing the lantern with one hand and her basket with the other, "Burgoyne is poorer for provisions."

"*Hold!*" Sally stopped short. She snatched up the half-empty Champagne bottle and ran back to tuck it in the crook of Fanny's arm. "For when she wakes—a bit of the hair of the dog that bit her."

Arm in arm, Anne and Sally entered the dark maw of the forest, excited to be at last setting out on the road that would lead them to the American camp. The good feeling was instantly squashed by the woodland's oppressive embrace. It didn't take long for Sally to beg

Anne to open the dark lantern "but a chink," or for Anne to acquiesce. Paned with amber-hued isinglass, the narrow band of golden light cast by the lantern offered them little comfort.

Sally clung to Anne's cloak, and every few steps forward brought muffled rustlings and indistinct flappings, sending new tendrils of tension creeping up Anne's neck.

To steady Sally's nerve and keep them both moving forward, Anne blathered commonsense explanations. "Naught but tree frogs," she said. "That's only dry leaves falling from the trees," or, "But an owl on the wing," she whispered, struggling to believe in the veracity of her own words.

Coming to a sudden stop, Sally let out a whimper, pointing ahead to a limb arching over the trail. A long dark object was hanging maybe five feet out from the trunk of the tree. The thing turned to and fro ever so slightly—like a body suspended from a gallows—and a shiver slithered up Anne's spine.

"A wraith, ye think?" Sally rasped in her ear. "No—*a Ban Shidh!*"

"Don't be ridiculous." Anne squinted in the dark, her bravado ringing false in her ear. She mustered up the pluck to take a few cautious steps, opening the lantern a smidge wider and angling the light at the object. Anne took one step closer, and heaved a sigh.

"It's only a coat!"

Sally did not budge. "Are ye certain? Why would a man leave his coat behind on a cold night?"

"It's a red coat—left behind by a deserter, I suspect." Anne walked up to the coat with lantern raised to read the regimental number embossed on the pewter buttons. "Forty-seventh Foot—the Rear Guard . . ."

Something sharp poked into her belly, and Anne hopped back to swing her light toward the awful clack of a flintlock. She could see a squat figure standing beside the tree trunk, a blanket drawn over his shoulders like an Indian. The musket in his hands was fitted with a bayonet, and his familiar voice grated.

"Drop the basket, Sally Tucker, and up wi' yer hands or I tear a hole in this one's belly."

"Annie." Sally set her basket down and raised her hands. "It's tha' wee pigwidgeon, Burgus."

"I'm putting down my goods, Mr. Burgus," Anne said, slowly lowering down to set the lantern and basket on the ground. She rose with hands held out, and used her reasonable, motherly tone. "We have no quarrel with you, Sergeant. You are welcome to any and all we have . . ."

Gesturing with his musket, Burgus ordered Sally, "Come forward, you—come stand beside yer mistress here." He warned, "Keep those hands up . . . both of ye."

Sally stepped forward, and scrunched her nose. "*Ulch*, what a reek! Has the order to retreat caused ye t' both piss and shit yerself like a proper Englishman?"

"Shut it!" Burgus growled and hobbled into a position nearer to Sally, dragging his broken foot bound up in a bulky bandage. In a clumsy balance he kept the musket aimed on Anne, freed a flask from his pocket, and took a sip.

"You've our goods, and our promise not to tell a soul we ever set eyes on you," Anne said. "Put by your musket, and we can all be on our merry way."

Burgus hurled the flask aside. "I said shut it!"

Sally's eyes narrowed, and she muttered, "Spineless wee smatchett."

"I'll show you spineless . . ." He began to fumble with undoing the buttons on his breeches. A dark malevolence played across a face scathed by pockmarks, and he said, "Get down on your knees."

"*Pfft!*" Sally squared her shoulders. "I'll see ye as maggot meat afore I ever go down on my knees to the likes of you."

Burgus squinted, and his stance wavered. "I said, *down on your knees!*"

"Don't do this, Sergeant," Anne warned. "It will not end well for you."

"Shut yer fuckin' gob!" Burgus snapped, jabbing at her with the point of his bayonet.

Anne glanced up to see Sally's hands cross at the wrists for the briefest moment, the right hand slipping down into the sleeve on her left arm.

Burgus turned his attention back to Sally. "Yid better do as I say, for I can gut her like a Christmas pig and plant a ball in yer brain in a blink of the eye, and not think twice of it."

Anne kept her eye on Burgus. "Maybe you should do as the man says, Sally."

Sally laughed. "I see no man. I see naught but a snivelin', ox-buggerin' deserter."

"Bitch!" Burgus growled and swung the bayonet toward Sally.

Sally leapt backward and Anne leapt forward, at once stomping down on the Sergeant's broken foot, and bringing her arm down like a hatchet on his musket. Burgus yowled a high-pitched scream, losing hold of his weapon; the gun discharged in a bounce and flash of powder, the shot flying wild. Anne and Burgus dove to gain control of the musket, both laying hands on it, each trying to twist it from the other. Dagger in hand, Sally entered the tussle, burying six inches of cold steel between the Sergeant's shoulder blades.

"*Garrrrgh!*" Burgus yowled. Jerking the musket away from Anne, he spun around, pounding the breech end into Sally's middle, sending her to the dirt, curled on her side, helpless, gulping for air. Anne flung her cloak over her shoulder and pulled her pistol.

Panting for breath, Burgus spun his weapon around, and drew the musket back over his shoulder to drive the bayonet end home. Cocking the hammer and pulling the trigger in one fluid motion, Anne sent the man flying with arms flung wide to land on his back with a bloody, smoking hole in his chest. Flinging the spent pistol away, she ran to Sally's side.

"Just need t' catch my wind," Sally gasped, arms crossed over her middle. "Go . . . make certain he's dead."

Anne found the lantern and brought it over to shine a light on Sergeant Burgus. His eyes were open and lifeless, and his gaping mouth brimmed with a puddle of blood. "That is the second man I've had to kill . . ."

"Yer certain he's dead?"

"I am." With a trembling hand, she retrieved her spent pistol, and tucked it back into her sash. "There's nothing so empty as a dead man's eyes."

"We both had a hand in it." Sally struggled up to her feet. "I stove my blade intae him, an' I'll not fash a moment over it. Th' world's well rid of th' spawn."

An indistinct shout rang out in the distance, followed by the crackle of musket fire.

"This is not a good place for us . . ." Anne scurried to gather the baskets, offering one to Sally. "Are you able, or ought we leave it behind?"

"Are ye daft? These baskets are filled with good cheer." Sally took the one. "No doubt I'll be sore on the morrow, but I'm fine for now."

They started up the path only to pull to an immediate halt when two figures stepped out from the trees no more than ten yards ahead—shadowy men, each wearing a tall hat and carrying long guns.

"Grenadiers!" Anne moaned.

Sally dropped her basket and freed her pistol and, extending her arm, she clacked back the hammer and shouted, "Who comes there?"

Anne slapped open the shutter on the lantern, the soft beam swinging wildly on a pair of befeathered Indians shading their eyes. The taller Indian waved.

"*Shé-ku*, Jack's woman!"

Anne reached up to steady the swinging light, and squinted. "Neddy?" Sally lowered her weapon, and they both jerked at the crackle of musket fire flashing in the trees to the east.

"Deserters," Isaac said.

Sally turned to Anne. "These are our friends, na?"

"Friends . . ." Anne said, shuttering her lantern. "And a sight for sore eyes."

"*Hoa.*" Ned set off, waving them along. "We'll show you the way home."

❧ TEN ❧

Here are laurels, come and share them.

THOMAS PAINE, *The American Crisis*

DECEMBER 17, 1777
SARATOGA

"Up-a-daisy!"

Skirts in a bundle over one arm, Anne grabbed hold of Jack's hand, and he helped her scramble up the last few steps to a hilltop overlooking the place where Fishkill Creek drained into the Hudson, near the town of Saratoga.

The wind was brisk, but for the first time since the battle at Bemis Heights, the sun shone bright and unfettered by clouds. Anne tossed back the hood of her red cloak, and took in the view. The clear sky was reflected in the water, turning the river into a blue satin ribbon wending north and south through a beautiful tapestry of trees at the apex of change—iridescent yellow and orange broadleaves mingled with mellow reds and browns, tempered by stands of deep green conifers. "What a grand day!" she exclaimed.

Jack said, "Looks like we're the last to arrive to this party . . ."

Anne held back for a moment, watching her man as he strode away to greet the others with a shout and a wave. Jack, and the men he

fought alongside with, had become woven into the cloth of the colorful landscape spread before her.

They are the weft to the warp of this weaver's loom . . .

Jack's dark hair had grown so long and unruly, he took to plaiting
it into a single thick braid bound with a leather lace, and even at that,
the breeze still managed to coax several strands loose. He wore a
length of soft red wool wrapped around his neck against the chill, the
loose ends tucked into his homespun hunting shirt. A long rifle was
slung over his shoulder, an Indian tomahawk dangled from his belt,
and his feet were shod in moccasins he'd made for himself. But the
changes most notable were not wrought in his dress. The battles he'd
survived had chiseled him stronger—a more thoughtful, cautious
strength—a strength Anne knew she could rely on.

Since their joyful reunion under the stars at the Continental camp
on Bemis Heights, they'd managed to snatch only scant moments of
time together. Anne and Sally joined the cadre of Patriot camp followers as the Continental Army continued to press Burgoyne's army to
the point of surrender. At last, completely surrounded, severely outnumbered, and without any other recourse, Gentleman Johnny agreed
to the terms of an honorable surrender, and on this day, the capitula-
tion would be completed in formal ceremony.

Grown to number more than twenty thousand, General Gates's
entire force marched across the Fishkill that morning to witness the
surrender. Always-prudent and ever-cautious David was unwilling to
risk exposing Anne and Sally's true allegiance to any on the British
side, and he deemed it unwise for them to attend the ceremony. Instead, he proposed a picnic, and promised them all a "wondrous sight."

Ned and Isaac were sitting before a fire they'd kindled, roasting sausage links on sharp green sticks. The Indians were garbed in full array
for the celebration—moccasins, leggings, and breechclouts heavy with
beaded embellishments—with trade silver strewn over chests, and dangling from ears. Isaac's *gustoweh* was adorned with the bright feathers
of a male cardinal, and was edged with a band of wampum beads. As
Anne drew close, she was surprised by the friendly design ringing the
brim—white figures on a purple ground, linked hand in hand in hand.

Sally sat beside the Oneidans on a striped wool blanket, cutting a wheel of cheese into slim wedges. Handing each Indian a piece, she said, "It's good. It's Dutch!"

Jack asked, "Where's David?"

"Wagin' war on th' bramble." Sally jerked a thumb. "Making ready for the surprise, he says."

Saber in hand, dressed in polished black boots and his blue and buff. dress uniform, David was hacking away at a bramble, creating a break in the thicket to the north of the picnic site.

Jack shouted, "Hoy, Captain!"

David looked up and waved as well, and Anne couldn't help but smile. It had been some time since she'd seen her brother so happy and carefree. "Lately, I forget he's but six and twenty," she said to Jack. "It's a pleasure to see the boy in him once again."

Titus came out of the break, tossing an armful of cut brush into a pile, and he waved to Anne and Jack. Though his clothes were a home-spun match to what Jack wore, he sported an elaborate tricorn, pinned with a green silk cockade, edged in silver braid, and topped off with a tall white plume.

"He certainly has a fondness for hats, our Titus," Anne said.

"He's amassed a collection," Jack said. "That one's plundered from the German redoubt."

"Come here, everyone! It's time!" David waved them over to the promontory. Once assembled, he announced, "From this vantage point, we will be able to see what no other Patriot eyes are allowed to see by order of the final Treaty of Convention—the vanquished Brit-ish army grounding its arms." David handed Sally and Anne each a spyglass. "Aim toward the flats by the river."

Anne could already hear the roll and thump of the regimental drums and the trill of fifes carried on the breeze. With the aid of the spyglass, she could see a throng of red coats assembling into ranks, blue coats in formation marching in, and she was able to pick out Gen-eral Burgoyne on horseback, looking very handsome in his splendid dress uniform, reviewing his vanquished army.

It was a massive assemblage, more than five thousand soldiers. As she panned across the ranks, Anne thought she might spy a familiar face or two, but other than Burgoyne, she couldn't find any of the significant faces she hoped she might see.

"Do you see any you know?" Ned asked.

"I dinna see any I cared for. Do you, Annie?" Sally said

"No." Anne shook her head. "I don't."

"They all look the same, don't they?" Titus said, his glass to his eye. "Sad and grim."

Jack took the glass from Titus and had a look. "We sure know that feeling, don't we?"

Row by row, the soldiers came forward to surrender their arms. Infantrymen tossed muskets and cartridge boxes into growing piles. Artillerymen brought the cannon forward. Officers relinquished sidearms and swords, and even the drummers stacked their drums. Then General Burgoyne led the entire parade north, beyond their sight, to where he would meet with General Gates, and hand over his sword in defeat.

Titus was the first to snap his spyglass shut. "There it is. We beat him. Beat Burgoyne with all his Germans and Indians. Beat him bad."

David's grin was wide. "The French are bound to sit up and take notice of us now . . ."

"*French!*" Sally yelped and ran off to the campfire. She came running back brandishing a green bottle and a stack of tin cups. "Champagne filched and carried over hill and dale for just such an occasion," she said, passing around the cups. "Compliments of Gentleman Johnny Burgoyne!"

"Perfect! Give it here!" David opened the bottle—whacking off wire bale, cork, and all with one swing of his sword. They all swooped in, giggling and laughing, trying to catch the spilling froth. Even reserved Isaac shouted, "*Oho!*" and captured a share.

Anne said, "Raise your cups!"

Jack held his high. "To us here—and to all who peril their lives for Liberty—'tis to Glory we steer!"

Part Two

VALLEY FORGE

Then cheer up, my lads, to your country be firm
Like kings of the ocean, we'll weather each storm!
Integrity calls—fair Liberty see,
Waves her flag o'er our heads,
And her words are "Be Free!"
Hearts of oak we are still;
For we're sons of those men
Who always are ready—
Steady, boys, steady—
To fight for their freedom again and again.

HEARTS OF OAK, Author Unknown

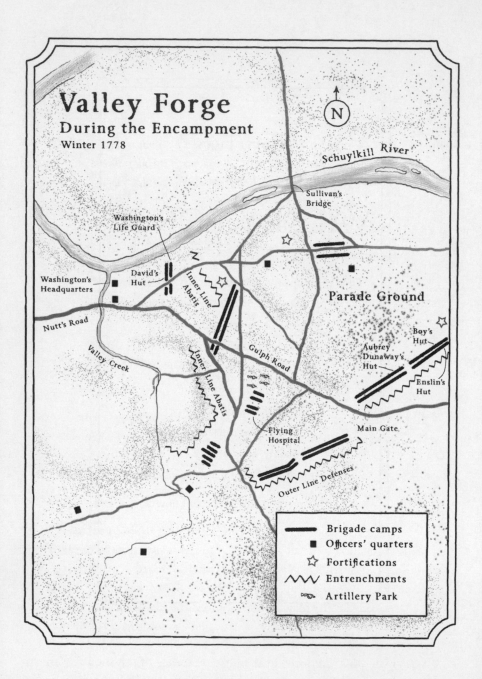

Valley Forge
During the Encampment
Winter 1778

N

Schuylkill River

Sullivan's
Bridge

Washington's
Life Guard

David's
Hut

Inner Line Abatis

Washington's
Headquarters

Parade Ground

Nutt's Road

Boy's
Hut

Valley Creek

Inner Line Abatis

Gulph Road

Aubrey
Dunaway's
Hut

Enslin's
Hut

Flying
Hospital

Main Gate

Outer Line Defenses

Brigade camps
■ **Officers' quarters**
☆ **Fortifications**
∧∧∧ **Entrenchments**
⌐⌐ **Artillery Park**

✎ ELEVEN ✎

These are the times that try men's souls: The summer soldier
and the sunshine patriot will, in this crisis, shrink from the
service of his country; but he that stands it NOW, deserves the
love and thanks of man and woman.

THOMAS PAINE, *The American Crisis*

JANUARY 1778
ON THE GULPH ROAD IN PENNSYLVANIA

"What a pretty snow!"

Big, buoyant flakes floated on the frigid air, much like loose down from a burst featherbed. Slouched inside a cocoon of woolen garments, Anne swayed with the motion of the mule-drawn wagon in time to the creak and turn of the wheels. She pulled down the muffler tied over nose and mouth and, with a giggle, caught a single snowflake with the tip of her tongue.

Jack laughed and pulled at his muffler, trying to catch some snow in similar fashion without any success. Anne brushed away the fluffy flakes that clung to his black mustache and beard like burrs on a hound dog. "Best cover up, or your beard will be ice again."

"Don't fret for my beard." Jack pointed ahead. "See those hills rising up at the crest of the road? Valley Forge and the promise of a warm fire lay just beyond . . ."

A crash of musket fire cut through the peace of the snowfall, the discordant echo ringing as lead shot pinged off the iron-banded wheels on their wagon. "What the . . . ?" Jack twisted around, trying hard to maintain control over the agitated mule team and see beyond the hooped canvas cover protecting their cargo.

Holding tight to the edge of her seat, Anne leaned out as far as she could to see a company of red-jacketed horsemen with sabers drawn, closing in at full gallop—long madder-dyed horsehair tails snapping from the top of their leather helmets like pennants in the wind.

"Dragoons!"

"Goddamn it!" Jack tossed the reins into Anne's lap and tugged one of the pistols from his belt.

Anne shouted, *"HYAH!"* sending their two-mule team into a full-on gallop with a hard smack of leather.

Spinning around in his seat, Jack made his way to the very back of the wagon bed in a lurching half crawl, half bumble over the load of crates, barrels, and meal sacks, tearing down the canvas cover as he went.

With the cover down, Anne could see Sally right behind in the second wagon, the hood of her cloak flung back, red braids flying, as she urged her team to speed while Titus with his stubby blunderbuss slung over his back struggled to get to the rear. Anne shouted over the rumble of wheels and jangling harness chains. "Mind you don't shoot Sally or Titus!"

"Mind your driving!" Jack shouted back. Situated in a semi-crouch with legs acting as springs to absorb the bumps and jerks as the wagon clattered across the frozen, rutted road, he tugged a few meal sacks into a pile. Dropping down behind this rough cover, he used it to prop and steady his aim as best he could in the bouncing wagon. Anne steered the mules around a bend in the road, giving Jack a clear shot at the pursuers. He fired, shouted, "Blast!" and ducked down immediately to reload, pouring powder and ramming shot down the barrel of his weapon. "Ride's too rough—target's too swift."

Titus's blunderbuss boomed. Jack whooped and yelled, "The blunderbuss knocked Titus back on his arse, but knocked a Redcoat onto his as well!"

Soon a riderless horse came bounding off the road to their left, racing—wild-eyed, mane, reins, and tail flying—surpassing them all.

Titus bellowed, *"Down!"* and another shot rang out. One of the dragoons managed to fire his pistol on the run, sending a flurry of shot thunking into wagon boards and whistling overhead—one buzzed past Anne's ear like an annoying fly.

Jack popped up, shouting, "You all right, Annie?" as he fired off another shot.

Anne rose up to her feet and encouraged her mules with another *"Hyah!"* and a snap of the reins. "I think I can see the Continental earthworks."

"I hope our fellows can see us . . ." Jack tossed his spent gun and tugged the other pistol from his belt. "Those dragoons are relentless—and they're closing in."

As if in answer to Jack's wish, rifle fire flashed along the line of Patriot entrenchments like a lit string of crackers, the welcome noise crisp in the cold air. Jack clambered back over the cargo and regained his seat beside Anne. "Let's test their mettle in range of Patriot sharpshooters."

Anne handed over the reins, and checked over her shoulder. "The dragoons are drawing to a halt—"

Titus whistled and shook his fist in the air, and Sally screamed, "Huzzah!"

With much relief, Anne watched the Redcoats growing smaller and smaller, until, with a swing of his saber, the dragoon captain wheeled his company around, and they headed back to the British winter camp in Philadelphia.

The two wagons careened through the opening in the hills, following the road into a wooded valley. "Whoa!" Jack tugged on the reins, easing his team into a canter. He and Anne waved and shouted, "Halloo!" to the sentries manning the fortifications, and the soldiers whistled and cheered with guns raised overhead as the wagons passed by. The mules slowed, their lathered sides heaving and great puffs of steam spewing from their noses. Anne turned in her seat and shouted to Sally, "Are you all right?"

"I'm nothin' but grand since those dragoons turned arse about," she replied. "But poor Titus lost his hat to the wind . . ."

"Not the Canadian one with the fur?"

Sitting beside Sally with his muffler tied over his ears, Titus nodded and called, "I'll go back later and see if I can find it."

Anne secured the woolly muffler she used to keep her felt hat from blowing away, tucking the free ends down the front of the Brunswicker coat she wore. She stuffed each gloved hand up the opposite sleeve, forming a makeshift muff of the big cuffs. Not given the time to alter the too-long sleeves and too-wide girth, Anne had not relished wearing one of the heavy officer's coats Titus had scavenged for her and Sally back in Stillwater. But in traveling the miles from Albany to Valley Forge by river and road in the dead of winter, she'd grown to appreciate the volume and quality of the dense German wool. With a combination of wool and flannel layers beneath the coat, hot bricks at feet, and hooded cloak thrown over all, the women weathered the worst of the journey bundled in good comfort.

As the wagons passed deeper into the Patriot army encampment, the rolling landscape flanking the Gulph Road became crowded with hundreds and hundreds of little log cabins. Like the buttons on a general's coat, the cabins were situated in neat rows.

The woodsmoke tumbling from the multitude of mud and timber chimneys hovered between the earth and the cloud-heavy sky, stinging her eyes. Anne swiped at tears, shifting around in her seat, looking in all directions. "It feels like it will storm soon. Everyone must be hunkered in." Washington's winter quarters housed more than eleven thousand soldiers and officers, but there were not many within sight. The American camp seemed almost deserted.

Jack slowed the mules to a trot, and the new pace matched the slow motion of the odd world they'd entered. Up ahead, situated amid a legion of tree stumps, they could see a few bundled figures huddled around a large fire and a steaming cauldron.

Anne sniffed the air, crinkling her nose. "Soap making."

A few men in shirtsleeves filtered out of doorways, waving and shouting greetings. Anne and Jack waved back. They passed by cluster after cluster of the little log cabins, the mule hoofbeats plodding to a steady metronome of ax steel biting into wood—the noise of construction—the *thwack, thwack, thwack* resounding from either side of the road. One ax was halted by shouts, and followed by the distinct popping, crackling, and crash of the tree falling somewhere in the distant woods to their left. Anne could only imagine how many trees were felled to build this miniature city in a wilderness where practically nothing had existed the month before.

Jack pulled his team to a halt, giving way to a man tugging a heavy sled loaded with deadfall across the rutted road. Once across, the man stopped in the knee-deep snow to catch his breath, and Jack urged the mules forward with a double click of his tongue.

Anne could not help but stare. Bandaged against the cold, the man's face was wound in strips of wool torn from a dingy blanket, leaving nothing but his eyes exposed to the icy wind. The rest of his costume was a raggedy puzzle of parts and pieces that even the poorest beggar on the meanest street in New York would be shamed to wear. This tatterdemalion wore a flannel nightshirt beneath a frazzled-edged jacket cut from blanket wool, the pieces of which were sewn together with thick, coarse thread in stitches big enough for Anne to see at a distance of ten paces. Rather than britches, he wore loose trousers patched together from tent canvas of varying hues, and the entire ensemble was topped off with a tasseled nightcap pulled down low to cover his ears.

The man pulled aside the scraps of wool tied over his mouth and nose, and called out, "Got any shoes in them wagons?"

"No shoes," Jack answered. "Meal, beans, salt pork, and blankets."

"All good, and we are grateful for it, but what you brung there is but a fart in a gale wind, mister. We've no meat. No shoes. No clothes. No pay. Naught here but fire cake to eat and misery aplenty." The soldier grasped the leather harness strapped over his shoulders with hands chapped pink and raw and renewed his trek.

Jack called, "Wait!" He reached back into the wagon bed and tugged a blanket free from one of the bales, and tossed it over. "Take this, friend. Come find me and I'll make certain you get a fair share of what we brought."

"I *will* find you, mister. Thank you—thank you, kindly." He twirled the gift over head and shoulders. As he trudged away, they could see his feet stepping in and out of the snow were shoeless and bound in a few filthy strips of wool.

Jack snapped the reins, the muscles in his jaw set tight. "It's a crooked and fretful country that treats its fighting men with such disregard."

They passed the army's artillery park—piles of shot and shells alongside rows of cannon foundered in the deep snow. Anne eyed one of many odd hummocks dotting the open flats along the roadside near the artillery park. The wind had swept the snow away from one to reveal a fuzzy dark patch—an equine head. Her brow furrowed. "Horses?"

"Dead horses . . ." Jack said.

The small convoy approached a long man-made tangle of tree limbs and branches pinioned to the ground in front of a long trench. The abatis stretched out from either side of the road, and there were more cabins laid out in neat avenues beyond the obstacles, a few yet incomplete. At the farthest end of the Gulph Road, a two-story stone house stood with its back to the junction of a small creek and the Schuylkill River.

"The General's headquarters, Annie!" Sally shouted and clapped her mittened hands. "We'll find David there."

They pulled to a halt near the house, drawing onlookers from the nearby cabins. Jack hopped down and helped Anne from her seat. The crowd of curious men gathered around the wagons, most of them in the same sad and ragged condition as the man they'd seen crossing the road. The door of the stone house swung open and a smiling David came running out. Pulling on a heavy overcoat, he waved and shouted, "Sally!"

Before Titus could bring his team to a full stop, Sally squeaked, scrambled down from the wagon seat, and ran into his arms. David swooped her up as if she were no more than a child and swung her around before setting her on her feet to kiss her soundly.

"I missed ye so!" Sally cried.

"Not anywhere near as much as I've missed you!" David pulled her close, but after only a moment's embrace, he twisted around to sneeze three times into his sleeve.

"Ochone! Look at ye—yiv grown thin as a noodle! Snifflin' and sneezing . . ." She stripped off the woolly muffler she wore.

"A bit of catarrh, is all," he said.

"Once we're settled in I'll make you a nice soup." Winding the muffler around David's ears and throat, Sally brushed away the snow collecting on his chestnut hair. "See to yer buttons—an' where's yer hat gone to?"

"I suppose I left it inside." David smiled, dutifully buttoning up his coat.

Whisking a hankie from the depths of her sleeve, Sally ordered, "Blow!"

David made use of the handkerchief as directed, then turned to give Anne a hug and shake hands with Jack and Titus. "I can't tell you how happy I am to see you made it through with the goods in tow. Manna from heaven, you are." With clear delight he walked around the wagon beds inspecting the cargo, running his hand over the sacks of cornmeal and beans—knocking knuckles to the barrels of salt pork.

"We brought what we could lay hands on, but I see now we should have brought more. No one told us you were suffering such privation," Jack said, waving his hand to the gathering crowd.

"No one knows—and that is how the General would like to keep it. The British might be tempted from the comfort of their winter quarters if they knew our weak and downtrodden state."

"They know, David," Titus said. "We were almost waylaid on the road by a company of dragoons."

"Waylaid!"

"Dinna fash." Sally looped her arm through David's to dispel the worry in his eye. "Fire from yer pickets gave them pause, thanks be, and we managed t' ride in unmolested."

"Sergeant Caufield . . ." David called a soldier over. "See to these animals and place a guard on these stores. Spread the word—a severe flogging will be dealt to anyone suspected of thievery."

How her brother was able to recognize rank or identity was a mys-

tery to Anne. The sergeant who stepped forward at David's command
was one of the many desperate onlookers wearing a patchwork of rags
nowhere near resembling any kind of uniform.

"What's going on with this army?" Jack asked. "A soldier we spoke
to on the road said he lives on naught but fire cake."

"He told true. The British passed this way before us, and stripped
the landscape clean. Forced to supply two armies, the locals are suffering. Our foragers wander far and wide for victuals, straw for our beds,
clothing and shoes, fodder for horses—and they have little success
dealing with suppliers who prefer British silver to Continental dollars." David glanced at the crowd, and lowered his voice. "Though the
hills and hollows provide good defense, this is probably not the best
choice of sites, but the General wanted to stay close to Philadelphia."

Anne said, "But surely Congress can . . ."

"*Pffft!*" David snorted. "Congress! Run off to Yorktown with tails
tucked when Howe took Philadelphia, and our Department of Commissary is now a shambles and of little use." He closed his eyes and
took a breath, struggling to control his temper. "When the bunglers
do manage to obtain needed supplies, they can't deliver. They claim
lack of wagons and draft animals. When they do manage to cobble
together a wagon train, it is either hampered by weather or captured
by British raiders. As of this morning we were down to the last
twenty-five barrels of flour." David put his arm around Sally. "I'm so
sorry . . . It's not the best of circumstances you've come to."

"Don't fret, brother." Jack gave David a slap on the back. "We're all
happy to be here."

Titus added, "I know Miss Sally'd rather be in the middle pits of
hell at your side than in the comfort of heaven on her lonesome."

"Titus tells true . . ." Sally clung to David's arm. "God's eye on it."

"Jack! Jaaack! *Jaaaaackkk!*" Two screaming boys came tearing
through the crowd. The smaller of the two leapt onto Jack's back,
clinging like a monkey. The taller boy threw his arms around Jack in
a dancing, exuberant embrace, causing the collection of three to wobble and totter off-balance, all of them falling into a deep snowdrift.

Jack sat up and grabbed the taller boy by the shoulders. "Is that you, Brian?" The boy grinned wide and shagged his head up and down. Jack turned to the smaller boy. "And Jim!"

"See? I told you he wasn't hung!" Jim swept a handful of snow into Brian's face. "Jack's alive and there's his woman," he said, pointing to Anne. "She's the one what sent him the soft gingerbread with the magic writing message, and she saved him from the bastard Cunningham's gallows."

Jack threw his arms around both boys and drew them into a bear hug. "I can't believe you're both alive!"

"We did like you tolt us," Brian said. "Joined the damned Redcoat army—the Twenty-third Foot."

"Signed up as drummer boys in the Royal Fusiliers," Jim said. "As soon as the recruiting sergeant stood us to our pint, we collected our shilling, a new set of duds, and snuck right off."

The boys jumped up and, in fine imitation of a British regular, offered a salute to show off their blue coats with red facings and cuffs.

Laughing, they pulled Jack up to his feet, and he made the introductions, slapping each boy on the back. "Brian Eliot and Jim Griffin—brothers-in-arms and old veterans of the Long Island campaign. This here is Mrs. Anne Merrick, her brother, Captain David Peabody, and our good friends Sally Tucker and Titus Gilmore."

Old veterans . . . Anne thought with a wince. Painfully thin, the crack in the taller boy's voice left her gauging he was no more than fifteen years old, and the smaller boy couldn't be older than twelve.

Jack went on. "These boys were my mates when I was imprisoned in Cortlandt's sugar house."

"They called it a sugar house, all right," Brian said. "'Tweren't sweet at all, for a fact."

" 'Twas a shit hole," Jim added.

Brian gave him a shove. "Mind your goddamn tongue in front of the ladies."

Though their British uniforms were in tolerably good condition, there was not a button on either coat. Beneath the open coats, the gangly boys wore oversized undershirts made of thin muslinet. Hatless and shoeless, they'd drawn their long hair back in a queue to cover their ears, and their bare feet and calves were shod and stockinged with long, narrow strips cut from a blanket.

Anne suppressed a shiver, and resisted a strong urge to bundle the boys into the folds of her cloak. "Did the British not issue you any shoes or stockings?"

Both boys grew glum, and Jim said, "We had sturdy shoes and warm woolen socks . . ."

"Good linen shirts, as well . . ." Brian said. "But they was wrested away."

Jack bristled. "Wrested away? By who?"

The boys shrugged, their mouths set in grim lines. Brian drawled, "More of them than of us, that's for dang sure."

"They're lucky to be left with coats and breeches," David said. "This man's army is in dire, desperate straits."

Titus said, "I've got a hide of sole leather in my bundle. We can make them moccasins and gaiters right off."

"And what's become of your buttons, lads?" Sally asked.

Brian scrunched his gaunt face. "Didn't care for those—all bedizened with crowns and such."

"Cut 'em off," Jim said. "To rid our nice coats of the royal taint."

"We made us a new set—see?" Brian dug a handful of new buttons out from his pocket—each perfect circle smoothed and drilled through with two tiny holes. An ornate "USA" was incised onto the face of each. "Carved from a cow bone," he said. "I made a paste with rust scraped from a cannonball to get the letters darkish-like."

"They're lovely buttons!" Sally exclaimed.

"Trouble is, we ain't found us no needle to sew 'em on with as yet," Jim explained.

"We've both needle and thread. Once we settle into our lodgings, come pay a call, and Sally and I will see to it those buttons get sewed on."

"And there's the problem . . . la . . . la . . ." David paused to sneeze, and blow his nose. "Lodgings. We're awful short on beds around here, and the women's huts are packed full. Let's bring your gear into head-quarters where you can warm up while I sort it all out."

"If it helps any, Cap'n, Jack and his nigra friend can bunk with us." Jim took Jack by the hand. "Our hut's warm and tight as bark on hickory."

Brian nodded. "We chinked in every crack and laid in a good supply of firewood. You'll be as snug as a bug in a rug in our hut."

"There're empty beds in your hut?" David seemed surprised.

Jim wagged his head up and down. "Only me and Brian in there now. Some died, and the others were taken away to hospital."

"Died?" Titus folded his arms across his chest, his eyes narrowed. "Camp fever?"

"Naw . . . The doctor fella said they was sick with the pleurisy," Brian said. "Don't fret none. We swept out the old straw and burned the herbs Pink give us to clean the air."

"Who's Pink?" Anne asked.

"She tends to her master in the brigade next to ours," Brian said.

"A slave woman?"

Jim nodded. "Pink knows all about ailments and remedies and such."

"Our company weren't all fever-ridden, anyhow," Brian was quick to assure. "Our sergeant, for one, caught a ball at Brandywine, and the wound never did stop festerin' . . ."

"And Jed Scovill's feet got frostbit so bad they blistered up and turned black," Jim said. "They took him away to hospital this morning."

"No matter. A hut is better than a tent on any day." David seemed relieved. "My officer's hut houses two, and my cabinmate is out on an extended forage. I'll move in with Jack and the boys, and the girls can share my cabin."

All agreed to the sense of the arrangements. Jack and Titus separated the personal gear from the cargo. Anne and Sally found their trunks, and David ordered a pair of soldiers to carry the baggage to his cabin.

Anne bid farewell to Jack with a kiss on the cheek, and watched as he and Titus trotted off with the boys. "And here I was fretting about how I would while away an entire winter in camp."

"Aye, there's work aplenty." Sally eyed David blowing his nose. "Remedies t' brew, soups to cook, bread to bake . . ."

"Shirts to be sewed, caps and stockings to be knit." Anne folded her arms. "I think this *man's* army could use a few more women."

❧ TWELVE ❧

Vigor and determination will do any thing and every thing.

Thomas Paine, *The American Crisis*

.

Gathering Water at First Light

Dawn's glow edged above the eastern horizon, hugging the snow-covered hilltops in soft halos of copper and purple. Bundled into her Hessian coat, and wrapped in warm mufflers, Anne tramped off to collect the morning's water, a pair of tin pails in hand.

She was not the first to blaze a path through the new-fallen snow. Lost in an overlarge coat with caped shoulders, a sentry paced in front of Washington's headquarters. Musket on shoulder, head ensconced in a big badger-fur cap, he shuffled to and fro in a pair of tall jackboots. Anne waved to him with her clatter of tin pails and called, "Halloo!" before skittering down the incline to the creek.

The bitter-cold morning was filled with the soft clacking beaks and throaty rattle of wintering crows roosting in the chestnuts at creekside. Nestled together with their glossy black feathers reflecting soft daylight, it looked as if someone had decorated the snow-covered branches with lumps of shiny coal.

Crows. Anne set her pails down, and eyed the trees with dismay, unreasonable fear balling up in the pit of her stomach.

Carrion feeders—such ugly things. From their guttural *caw* to their greasy black feathers—always hovering, searching, waiting on death— Anne bore a strong dislike for the creatures.

A picture of her mother, young and smiling, popped into Anne's mind, crisp and clear. If she were here, she would laugh and say, "Let's count the crows, children, and tell our fortunes!" Anne suddenly began to recite aloud the old nursery rhyme her mother would chant whenever a crow was spied.

> *One for sadness, two for mirth;*
> *Three for marriage, four for birth;*
> *Five for laughing, six for crying:*
> *Seven for sickness, eight for dying;*
> *Nine for silver, ten for gold;*
> *Eleven a secret that will never be told.*

David hated the game, and though Anne never would admit it, the rhyme frightened her as well. No matter the mention of mirth or silver or gold, she always dreaded counting crows—dreaded having a secret so awful, that it could never be told.

But there were way more than eleven crows roosting in these trees. Anne tossed off her mittens and scooped up some snow. Packing a ball with bare hands, the warmth of her skin made for a good, hard missile. She hurled the snowball into the branches, and watched with satisfaction and relief as the noisy mob lifted up into the sky, flying away like a black veil caught on a breeze.

The spring-fed creek was frozen over, but for a thin ribbon of water running deep and fast down its center. Anne ventured carefully out to the ice-crusted edge to pull up two pails of ice-cold water.

The trek back to the cabin was a slow, serious affair, requiring concentration to maintain footing up the slippery incline, and keep from sloshing too much water from the pails. Anne reached the crest of the creek bank at the changing of the guard, and witnessed the slender young sentry handing off the communal overcoat, boots, and hat to the new man coming on duty. Wrapping up in an old blanket, the relieved soldier took off in stocking feet, kicking up a cyclone of snow as he galloped across the valley to his hut.

Shrugging into the overcoat, the new sentry set the fur cap aright, and snatched up his musket. "Halt!" he ordered. "Who goes there?"

Anne pulled to a stop, and called, "It's Mrs. Merrick—a woman belonging to this army."

The sentry leveled his weapon. "Advance to be recognized."

Anne marched up to the sentry and set her heavy pails down. The new guard was a grizzled veteran—his cheeks bristled with steel gray stubble, and his keen blue eyes were hooded with brows so wild and bushy, they melded seamlessly into the badger fur of his cap. He took a step forward and leaned in. With a low, gruff whisper he said, "Sparta."

The parole word! Anne racked her brain for the day's countersign, a place-name, usually beginning with the same letter as the parole. She quizzled her forehead and guessed, "Springfield?"

"Na," the sentry said with a shake of his head.

Anne could not recall the password her brother had told them only the night before. Her toes were going numb, and she shifted from foot to foot, fiddling with her wet mittens, the thumbs already beginning to stiffen with the cold. "Why don't you just let me pass, soldier? It's too cold for this nonsense."

The sentry clacked back the hammer on his musket. "Protectin' our camp from enemy spies is no nonsense."

"I assure you, I'm no spy," Anne said, pointing to her pails. "You can see I went down to fetch water."

"A clever ruse, mebbe, used by a clever spy."

"Heavens!" Anne threw up her arms. "If I were truly a clever spy, I'd know the bloody countersign, wouldn't I?"

The sentry stood firm, and offered the challenge once again. *"Spaar-*ta."

"I'm the least likely spy," Anne said.

"It's the least likely who make the best of spies," he said, and repeated the parole word. "Sparta."

Anne could not argue with his logic. "Give me a moment. These

daily countersigns are all so alike, they are a jumble in my brain."
Eyes squinched tight, she repeated, *"Spaarta aaaannnd . . ."* Her eyes
popped open, and she blurted, *"Spain!"*

"Aye. 'Tis Spain." The sentry shouldered his weapon. "Ye can
advance."

Anne gathered up her water and headed toward the first row of
eight officers' huts strung out in a straight row not too far from the
stone house headquarters. She set the pails down to yank on the latchstring to lift the bar on the inside. Putting her shoulder into it, she
pushed the heavy plank door open. Hung not quite square to the
floor, the swing of the door rode in a perfect semicircle carved into
the dirt floor. Anne grabbed her pails and hurried into the dark cabin,
kicking the door shut.

"Tha' wind is sharp as the devil's teeth!" Sally shivered on a small
stool near the hearth, fanning the coals to flame and feeding the fire
slim pieces of kindling.

Anne deposited her pails and went to lay wet mittens on the hearth-
stones. She hung her muffler and coat on one of the many pegs driven
into the wall. "It is so cold, the stream is almost completely frozen
over," she said, stomping her boots and shaking loose the snow caked
to the hems of her skirts.

Sally pulled a stumpy candle from her pocket and set it alight.
Reaching up on tiptoes, she touched candle flame to the wick of the
oil lamp hanging from the rafters, bathing the room with light.

All of the soldier cabins were supposed to have been built to the
same simple specifications—twelve by fourteen feet, sidewalls no less
than six and a half feet high, with plank roofs pitching up to the center. According to the General's plan, each cabin was to have two windows to provide cross ventilation and promote a healthy atmosphere.
From what Anne could tell, no one paid much heed to Washington's
directives. There were as many different cabins as there were build-
ers, and Anne had yet to see one with windows.

Her brother's hut was built to quarter two officers, and was much
more spacious than the common soldier huts meant to house twelve.
The roof planking was tight and kept out the snow, the door was

heavy to keep out the wind, and the thick timber walls were well chinked with straw and mud to allay drafts. David's cabinmate had scavenged an iron plate from the old ruined forge that gave the valley its name, and installed it at the back of the fireplace to radiate warmth back into the room. Well supplied with firewood, the little cabin was a toasty sanctuary even in the worst weather.

The single room was sparsely furnished. The fireplace, fitted with an iron grate and flagstone hearth, was centered opposite the doorway, and took up most of the wall. Tucked into the corner to the right of it were two simple plank platforms—built one atop the other—with straw-stuffed ticks for mattresses. David and his cabinmate stowed their chests and other gear in the space remaining at the foot of the bunk bed. A rough table with bench seats occupied the other wall, where Anne and Sally kept their trunks. They situated one of the benches close to the hearth, where they would sit and sew at night by the light and warmth of the fire.

Anne set a pail of water on the grate to boil. "I expect the boys will be here soon. I'll make some chocolate."

"Set th' griddle to heat on th' grate," Sally said and, arranging two good-sized logs onto the fire, she went to forage through her trunk for the breakfast makings. "I promised th' young lads a batch of scones."

Brian Eliot and Jim Griffin fit neatly under Anne's and Sally's wings. The women spent the week alternately fattening the boys up and working on augmenting their pitiful wardrobes. Right off, Jack and Titus made good on their promise, producing two pairs each of leather moccasins and gaiters. Though there was no wool for knitting, the women managed to fashion socks, caps, and mufflers by unraveling shawls Anne and Sally donated to the cause. One old blanket became two new weskits. A green-striped quilted petticoat was turned into soft, warm shirts.

There was a rap on the door and Anne answered with a cheery, "Come in!"

The door scraped open, and in tumbled hungry men and boys, stomping snow from feet and hanging coats on pegs in a chaotic exchange of howdy-dos and good mornings.

At the table, Sally patted her floury dough into two thick, raisin-speckled disks, cutting each into eight even wedges with a razor-sharp knife. In transferring the wedges onto the hot griddle, young Jim reached in and pinched off a piece of dough, popping it into his mouth.

"Och, ye wee glutton!" Sally slapped his hand.

Jim grinned. "Why d'you bother with the baking—it tastes good as is . . ."

"Ye'll earn a sour stomach—eatin' raw dough . . ." Sally handed the boy a broad-bladed knife and plunked him down onto the bench. "Keep yer eye on those scones, and when the edges go golden, give 'em a turn."

David sidled next to Sally, wrapping his arm about her waist. "Scones!" he said, planting a loud kiss on her cheek. "Yum!"

Anne set meticulous Brian to shaving a cake of chocolate with a paring knife, and when she went to dig up some maple sugar from the chest, Jack came up from behind and pulled her into a bear hug, nuzzling his scruffy face in her neck. "Chocolate!" he said. "You are spoiling us all!"

Anne shrugged. "The chocolate does no one any good stored away."

Titus sat down at the fire, scratching inside his shirt. "Nothing better than a hot, sweet drink on a bitter-cold morning."

Once the water was brought to a boil, Anne dumped in the chocolate shavings and a fistful of maple sugar, beating the mixture to a froth with a wooden spoon.

Jack and Titus arranged the two benches in a V before the hearth, and David threw a couple big logs in. They all sat with feet stretched to the crackling fire, sipping on tin cups of steaming chocolate and munching their scones, when there was a rap on the door.

David pulled the door open to a blast of snow, and revealed a small man wearing a fur-trimmed roquelaure cloak and matching tricorn, hunched in the wind.

"Come. Come," David urged, simultaneously rushing the visitor into the room and pushing the door shut.

The man whisked off his hat, slung back his cloak, and bowed.

With a soft Norfolkian accent he said, "I beg pardon, but I was told I might find writing paper for purchase within?"

He owned a long, sharp nose, and there was a quality to his smile that reminded Anne of an illustration in one of her son Jemmy's storybooks. *An elf,* she thought. Rising to her feet, she offered, "I've a supply of writing bond for sale—penny a sheet."

"Much obliged. I'll take all you can spare."

Anne went to dig in her trunk, and Jack called, "Join us, friend. Our fire will warm you without, and a cup of chocolate will warm you within."

The man smiled his impish smile, and raised one eyebrow. "I confess to being quite fond of chocolate."

He took a seat, cup, and scone without saying much other than murmuring, "Delicious!" and "What a treat!"

Anne held up a paper-wrapped ream. "I could let you have as much as half a ream . . ."

"I'll take it." The man nodded happily, brushing crumbs from his front. He delved into his breast pocket, pulling forth a squat, oval-shaped brass case. "Might you also be supplied with ink?"

"Enough to fill your writing set," Anne said.

With a big smile and ink-stained fingers, he snapped open the brass cover and revealed a compact kit that included a corked glass bottle and a stubby little quill pen. Anne filled the inkwell to the brim and handed him a packet of paper. He, in turn, handed over three continentals, and tucked the writing set back into his breast pocket.

"That's quite a bit of paper," David noted. "You must have a lot of correspondence."

The man wagged his head. "Though I'm yet farming my thoughts, I'm at present composing a letter to General Sir William Howe."

"To General Howe!" Titus burst out laughing.

"When you write that letter," Jack said, as he snatched up a piece of kindling, and used it to scratch his back, "tell ol' Howe Jack Hampton says 'Go to hell!'"

They all laughed, and, bidding them adieu with a wave of his hat, the man scurried out the door.

"What an odd little fellow," Anne said.

"But he's surely able with that bitty little pen," Jim said, plucking what would be his third scone from the griddle. "Did you see the size of it?"

Brian piped up. "I like how he writes—Common Sense."

Titus gave Jack a nudge. "Didn't seem to have much sense to me, writing a letter to Howe."

"Oh, he's a fine writer," Brian said.

"When we first got here, the General had Common Sense read to us all. You remember, Cap'n . . ." Jim stood up and with a deepened voice intoned, " 'These are the times that try men's souls . . .' "

"That was *him*?" David asked. "Thomas Paine?"

"No!" Jack ran to the door, swinging it wide-open, but the man was nowhere to be seen. He came back and sat in a slump. "I can't believe we had Thomas Paine himself, sitting right here in our cabin, without our knowing it."

"I knew it," Jim said.

"Shame!" Sally chided, finger waving. "All o' yiz all laughing at th' man . . ."

"I saw you laughing as well," David reminded. "And who wouldn't think it a jest? Writing a letter to General Howe . . ."

"Och!" Sally gave David a shove. "Come summer, I'll be paying a bonny penny for a copy of that letter."

Jack went back to scratching his chest. "He was mad for your scones, Sal. Maybe he'll be back."

Anne leaned over and rapped both Jack and Titus with a wooden spoon, the two of them scratching with hands deep down their shirt-fronts. "Stop it! You're driving me mad, clawing at yourselves all morning like a pair of flea-bit pups."

"It's driving *me* mad." Jack snarled, and continued scratching.

"Can't help it, Mrs. Anne . . ." Titus twisted around, trying to reach a spot under his arm.

"They have the Itch," Jim said, and Brian agreed with a knowing nod.

"The Itch!" Anne groaned.

"Most everyone here comes down with the Itch," Brian said. "Pay a call on Pink. She has a balm for it."

Old friends, Captain Aubrey Dunaway and First Lieutenant Erasmus Gill shared a cabin. Unlike the officer's cabin Anne shared with Sally, theirs boasted a separate bed in each corner. Jack and Titus sat shirtless on what was apparently Mr. Gill's bed, as the other bed was occupied by a coughing, wheezing, and feverish Captain Dunaway.

Anne sat beside Jack, sipping on the fragrant cup of Oswego tea Captain Dunaway's slave woman had pressed into her hand on arrival, and she watched Pink light the nub of a candle in a dish, and bring the bright light close to examine Jack's chest.

"Mm-hmm . . ." Pink murmured. "Y'all have the Itch, all right . . ." She moved to sit beside Titus, and said, "Could you tilt your head t' the left a bit, please . . ."

Pink touched him beside the ear, tracing her fingertips down the side of his neck. Titus's eyes popped wide. Muscles tensing, his chest began to heave, and the bed boards creaked with his squirming. Anne feared Titus was about ready to bolt out the door when Pink looked up with an apologetic smile and said, "On dark skin like ours, I get a better sense of the rash by touch."

Titus blurted, "But you aren't dark at all, Miss Pink. I expect that's why they call you that . . . Pink . . ."

"I'm not as dark as some." Pink laughed. "But I'm sure not pink."

"No . . ." Titus flashed a shy grin. "I'd say you're sugar brown."

Jack snorted.

Anne gave Jack a bump with her shoulder and leaned forward with a smile. "I must say, Miss Pink, I am enjoying your bayberry candles. Such a pleasant, homey scent—isn't it, Titus?"

"Mm-hmm," was all Titus could manage.

"I used to help my mother make bayberry candles when I was a girl," Anne said.

"I make 'em . . ." Pink said as she slowly traced around to the front of Titus's chest, fingertips slipping down toward the waistband of his breeches. "It's not hard."

"Oh." Jack raised an eyebrow. "I bet it is hard, isn't it, Titus?"

Titus shot Jack an elbow, and Anne dealt him a kick.

Jack leaned down, glaring at Anne, rubbing his leg. "Did you hear that, Titus? Miss Pink makes her own bayberry candles!"

"That's . . . fine," Titus managed through clenched teeth.

Pink looked up from her examination. "Am I causing you pain, sir?"

Jack snorted again, and Titus muttered, "No," with a very vigorous shake of his head.

Pink rose to her feet. "I'll go an' mix up some balm for you both."

Anne watched Titus, his eyes following the woman as she crossed over to the table near her master's, and she whispered in Jack's ear, "They'd make for a perfect couple."

Tall and willow slim, the slave woman was much younger than Anne expected she'd be. Excited by the prospect of engineering a match, Anne asked, "How old are you, Pink?"

Pink glanced up from measuring a dark powder into a bowl. "Me? I'm nine and twenty—I know fo' sure 'cause I was birthed the same day as Master Aubrey here." She reached down and squeezed Captain Dunaway's arm.

Jack leaned and whispered, "See that? She's missing the little finger on her left hand."

"Her only flaw," Anne said. "I think Titus is smitten."

"Titus can't tear his eyes from her," Jack whispered with a jerk of his head. "He's watching her like a hawk following a chicken."

There was an exotic cast to the woman's features—dark, knowing eyes, expressive black brows, a generous mouth—all arranged in perfect harmony. Pink had cleverly altered the dour gray hand-me-downs from an older mistress to suit her shapely form, extending the too-short sleeves and hems with bright bands of scarlet calico. Though her hair was twisted up in a tight turban of matching red fabric, the tiny dark corkscrews escaping at the nape of her neck gave hint to its color and texture.

"The bestest cure for the Itch is sulfur flour mixed with simple un-
guent." Smiling, Pink brought over two small clay pots, handing one
to Anne. "But in this misbegotten place, I'm afraid gunpowder and
hog fat make do. I'll show y'all how to apply it." Scooping up a finger-
ful of the gray sludge, she sat beside Titus.

Anne stood up to watch Pink apply the balm. Titus visibly flinched
at her touch. Brow furrowed, Pink asked, "Does it sting?"

"It stinks some," Titus said, "but it don't sting at all. In fact, it feels
real good—soothing."

"I know it do stink, but this balm will kill all the scabies what have
burrowed under your skin. You don't have to lay it on thick, but make
certain you cover every inch . . ." She looked up into Titus's eyes, and
you could almost see the spark struck between them, like the powder
flash from a pistol shot.

Aubrey Dunaway called to his slave in a wheezing sigh, "Pink . . ."

Pink startled. "I'm a-comin'," she said, rushing over to his side.

Jack shot Titus an elbow. "She fancies you."

Titus went grim. His gaze was locked on Pink, watching as she
propped her master up and fed him water with a teaspoon. His whisper was monotone. "No point in her fancying anyone. She belongs to
that man there."

"She cares for him gently . . ." Anne said. "Captain Dunaway must
be a kind master . . . I'm sure he wouldn't mind if . . ."

"Kind master?" Jaw clenched, Titus pulled on his shirt, and pointed
to the straw pallet and pillow at the foot of the bed. "So kind that he
has her sleep at the foot of his bed like a dog?"

"Titus has the right of it. There's no such thing as a kind slave
owner." Jack stood up and tugged his shirt over his head. "I'll never
understand these men who fight for the cause of liberty, yet they keep
human beings in bondage for their own selfish purpose."

"General Washington is numbered among these slave owners,"
Anne reminded.

"I know," Jack said, "and that has always been troublesome to me."

Pink returned, her brow puckered with distress to see them slipping on their coats. "You're leaving?"

"What do we owe for the balm?" Titus asked, holding up the clay pot.

Pink shook her head. "No charge, sir. Naught but gunpowder and hog fat, anyway." She followed after Titus as he turned to lift the door latch, saying, "Your rash might seem to get worse afore it gets better, but in five days or so, you should see the cure. Remember to rub the balm on every day . . ."

"I will." Titus kept his eyes downcast and muttered, "Thank you."

Pink grasped him by the hand. "If you run out, I can mix up more . . . no bother."

Bed boards knocked and creaked as the Captain turned onto his side, calling, "Pink . . ."

Pink tightened her grip on Titus's hand. "Best change your bed-straw as well . . . and boil your bedding . . ."

"*Pink—*" Dunaway groaned.

"Your master calls, Miss Pink." Titus tugged open the door, and the winter wind swept into the room, parting the pair of them like a sharp knife. Titus fled into the cold, and Jack ran after him.

Anne put a hand on Pink's shoulder. "Maybe you can come and pay me a call? The boys can show you my cabin . . ."

"*Piiink!*"

"I'm comin'!" Pink looked at Anne, dark eyes blinking back tears. "There's a whole mess of bayberry down by the covered bridge. If you want, I can show you . . . and Titus."

"Bayberries." Anne smiled. "That will work." She pulled her shawl up over her head, and ran to catch up with Jack.

❧ THIRTEEN ❧

*What we contend for is worthy the affliction we may
go through.*

THOMAS PAINE, *The American Crisis*

PAROLE WORD: PERSEVERANCE
COUNTERSIGN: PEACE

Anne tramped back to the cabin with two pails full of bayberries. The
day dawned clear and sunny, and not only did it look warmer; it *felt*
warmer. Snow dropped from the trees in clumps, and well-trod pathways had gone to mud and slush. The thaw trickled from the very
peak down the roof shakes to *drip drip drip* from a comb of icicles
formed along the eaves. Both hands occupied, Anne shouted, "Open
up!" and kicked the door, inciting a torrent of ice-cold droplets to rain
down on her head.

With a "Make way! Make way!" she scurried past Sally as she
pulled the door open, and set the heavy buckets down on the hearth.
"That ought be enough for a candle or two."

"Ahhh!" Sally drew a deep breath. "Yer candleberries have the
cabin smelling fresh already!"

The chandler in Albany had assured Anne the candles she purchased from him were the best quality, made with 100 percent sheep's

tallow. But from the moment she set the first candle alight, Anne knew she'd been duped. The cheap hemp wicks constantly guttered, and the smoke emitted was dense with an odor like rancid burnt pork drippings that clung to clothes and hair.

Evil-smelling things . . . Anne stripped off her coat and eyed the half-gone tallow candle in its dish. *I wager there's more of pig than sheep in those candles* . . .

Though costlier, Anne preferred to burn oil or beeswax. The light from either was brighter and better smelling than even the best quality tallow candle. Every time she was forced to light one of her foul candles, she was put in mind of the fresh-smelling tapers Pink manufactured from berries she gathered right here in camp.

When a week went by without the promised call from Pink, Anne learned from the boys that Captain Dunaway had taken a bad turn for the worse, so she decided to go on a hunt for bayberries on her own. She followed the path to the covered bridge crossing over the Valley Creek, found the thicket of bayberry shrubs Pink spoke of, and had no problem filling her pails to the brim.

"Hey-ho, Annie," Sally said, peering into the big kettle they borrowed from one of the washwomen. "Th' water's on the boil."

Sally stoked the fire, and after sifting both buckets of berries into the pot, the women sat down to a midday meal of quince jam and johnnycakes left over from breakfast.

"A wagon train come intae camp whilst ye were berry pickin'." Sally relayed this news, pouring them each a cup of liberty tea. "Oneida Indians all the way from Fort Stanwix bearing sacks and sacks of cornmeal. Such a welcome sight!"

"Lord knows this army can use every bit of it," Anne said. "The Oneidans are proving a good ally in many ways."

"I ran over to see if I might catch sight of Ned and Isaac," Sally said, "but no, I didna see 'em amongst this lot."

"I expect Isaac and Ned have gone off to their winter hunting camp. Isaac has a wife and children to provide for, and it's time Ned found a wife for himself as well." Anne dipped a piece of kindling into the pot, and showed Sally the resulting dirty green substance coating the stick. "The berries are waxing!" she said. "Help me pull the pot from the grate."

Using slats of wood slipped through the looped handles, they managed to slide the heavy kettle from the hearth and onto the dirt floor. Once the pot cooled, the wax hardened into a thick slab floating on top of the water. Sally cracked the brittle stuff into manageable pieces and dropped them into a smaller kettle and set it on the grate to melt again.

Anne fashioned a sieve with hammer and awl by punching a series of small holes into the bottom of a tin cup. She poured the molten wax through the sieve to filter out the bits of bark, stem, and berry. Sally fetched the wicks they'd plaited the night before from lengths of cotton thread. Just as they were about to commence dipping candles, the latchstring was jerked hard, the crossbar crashed upward, the door opened, and winter swirled in.

A strange man stood in the doorway, his big silhouette framed in the rectangle of blue sky. He wore a long caped watchcoat and a flat-brimmed hat cocked up at one side. Under his left arm, he carried a saddle. A bulging pair of saddlebags were draped over his shoulder, and his right hand held a pair of squawking and flapping chickens by their yellow feet.

"Well, I'll be jiggered!" He stood for a moment, blinking, head roving from side to side scanning the room. "I must beg pardon, ladies—I could have sworn this was my hut."

"Wait!" Sally jumped up as he turned to leave. "'Tis yer hut, if yer name's McLane." Grabbing hold of his sleeve, she tugged him back into the cabin, and pushed the door shut.

"I *am* McLane." He seemed relieved. "Alan McLane. Captain Alan McLane."

"It's a pleasure to meet you, Captain. We've heard so much about you." Anne came forward offering her hand. "I'm Anne Merrick—David's sister—and this is Sally Tucker."

Captain McLane set the chickens on their feet, and gave Anne an exuberant handshake. "Of course you're Anne! And shouldn't I have known this was Sally by her freckles and forthright manner?"

"They're lovely chickens," Sally said, strewing a handful of parched corn for the birds. She plucked up her cloak and swung it around her shoulders. "Have a sit by the fire, and I'll go fetch David."

"Alright." Alan McLane dropped his saddle and gear in the corner, shrugged out of his coat, and hung it up on a peg.

"Cup of tea, Captain?" Anne offered.

"Black tea?" he asked, hopeful.

Anne's smile was apologetic. "No . . . Sally's liberty tea."

"Sounds grand." McLane grinned. "I haven't had a hot drink in days."

"There's no cream," Anne said, pouring him a cupful. "But we do have maple sugar . . ."

"No sugar or cream necessary, thank you. I take my tea barefoot."

The big man pulled a bench close to the hearth. Broad shoulders in a slump, he sat with elbows leaning on knees, holding his chapped hands out toward the flames, and sighed with pleasure. Captain Alan McLane led a company of foragers who scoured far and wide in search of provisions and supplies for the troops in Valley Forge. Always on the move either gathering foodstuffs and livestock, or harrying British supply convoys, Captain McLane was a man rarely out of the saddle or the weather.

Anne cobbled together a meal for the Captain—slices of pemmican with johnnycakes and jam—which he wolfed down with much relish. Sally soon returned with David, Jack, and Titus in tow. Introductions were made and they all settled on benches before the fire with steaming cups of fresh-brewed tea.

"I didn't expect you back so soon," David said, gesturing with his thumb to the chickens. "But as usual, you didn't come home empty-handed, you old rover!"

Anne said, "Sally and I regret putting you out of your bed, Captain."

"No need to make a great touse about it. It doesn't matter much to me where I lay my bones, and David says there's room for me to bunk in with these fine fellows," Alan said, giving Titus and Jack a nod. "I won't be in camp for more than a night or two at most, anyway. I've only come in to gather up a few wagons and drivers."

David thumped his friend on the back. "You've secured some supplies, hey?"

"A mother lode," McLane said. "Stumbled upon a pair of British supply ships run aground not too far from Wilmington—a brig and a sloop. We captured 'em both with just a few shots from a field piece." He scooted forward a bit in his seat, excitement clear on his friendly face. "The ships are filled to the brim with the finest kind of uniforms, arms, ammunition, pork, flour, butter"—he jerked his thumb to the two birds clucking and pecking about—"not to mention chickens!"

"Oooh!" Sally clapped her hands. "D'ye by chance bring any butter?"

"More than a pound in my saddlebag," Alan said with a grin. "You've had your eye on those birds since I came through the door, Miss Sally. I hope you're thinking along the lines of fried chicken . . ."

"Fried chicken with gravy and an Indian pudding wi' raisins." Sally set her cup down, and rolled up her sleeves. "If yiz will excuse me, it appears I've necks to wring and feathers t' pluck!"

David blew his nose, and looked worried. "I don't know, Alan. We've wagons aplenty, but damn few draft animals . . . How far of a trek would you say it is?"

"A hundred forty miles, more or less." Alan shrugged. "I expected we'd have to make several trips . . ."

Titus gave Jack a nudge. Jack took Anne by the hand, and they exchanged a barely discernable nod. He said, "Me and Titus are willing to bogue in and go to and fro. We have a pair of sturdy wagons, and our mule teams are fit."

Titus added, "Provide us fodder to keep the mules moving, and an escort to keep the Redcoat dragoons off our backs, and we can help you bring those supplies here, where folk are in desperate need."

"Agreed, my fellows!" McLane jumped up and gave Jack and Titus a slap on the back. "We'll leave at first light."

Arms overloaded with firewood, Anne kicked at the door, and shouted, "Open up!"

Sally jerked the door open with a peevish whisper. *"Wheesht! He's still sleepin'!"*

Anne winced, whispering, *"I forgot he was here."* Tripping over a divot in the dirt floor, she lost control of her load, and the cordwood fell from her arms in a noisy thumpety-thump.

David bolted upright, shouting, "WHAT?"

Poor David had fallen asleep with his head on Sally's lap the night before. Rather than send him packing into the frigid night—seeing as how he was so sick with a head cold—everyone thought it best to leave him be. So exhausted he was, he didn't stir when Jack and Titus helped Sally lift him onto the comfy straw pallet she fixed for him near the hearth. David snored the morning away, even sleeping through breakfast and the farewells when Jack, Titus, and Captain McLane left for Wilmington.

Sally crouched down at David's side and gentled him back to his pillow, crooning, "It's naught, sweetums . . . Annie dropped th' firewood, is all. Back to sleep, now . . ."

David lay back, blinking and yawning. Throwing his arms up over his head, he stretched and asked, "What is it you have cooking there?"

"A nice chicken broth." Sally got up to stir the pot on the grate, taking a sip of the soup. "Made from the bones and leavings from last night's dinner . . ."

David scratched his head. "Last night's dinner?"

"Mm-hmm." Sally stirred her soup. "Ye had a nice lie-in this morn."

David bolted up and, struggling to disengage from the tangle of blankets Sally had heaped upon him, exclaimed, "I've got to get to headquarters."

"Och!" Sally dropped the spoon in the pot, swung a leg over David, and with both hands pushed him flat to the pallet. Vowing, "Yer stayin' put!" she dropped to her knees and straddled his chest.

"Let—me—up!" Twisting and turning, David tried to wriggle free. "I've got to go. The Baron begins training the Model Company today . . ."

Sally cried, "Help me, Annie!"

Anne ran over from stacking the firewood and managed to gain control over her brother's bucking legs. Pinned like a bug in a specimen case, David ceased struggling, and in a very reasonable tone he said, "This is serious. The two of you *have* to let me up. I'll be court-martialed for failing to report to duty . . ."

"Don't worry . . ." Anne said.

Sally grinned. "We promise t' testify on yer behalf."

David switched to his most imperious tone. "Let me up right *now*—that's an order."

"An *order!*" Anne and Sally burst into laughter.

"I mean it," David insisted. "I'm a captain in this army."

"Sorry, Captain." Anne jumped up and ruffled her brother's hair. "We take our orders from General Washington, who has removed your name from the duty roster."

"Removed?"

David's shift from terse to worried was so distinct, Sally slipped off to sit beside him and stroke the wrinkles from his forehead. "Dinna fash so," she said. "I stopped by headquarters first light and let 'em know ye were under th' weather. Th' General values yer service, and aims t' see ye fit."

Anne added, "You've been battling a bad cold for days and days, and it's only gotten worse. You're a fine officer, but you'll be no good to Washington feverish or consumptive. A few days' rest and a dose of Sally's chicken broth will surely cure what ails you."

"Yer t' be coddled, *Captain* . . ." Sally planted a kiss on his cheek. "Tha's an order!"

"But . . ." David's attempt to stifle a cough erupted into a drawn-out coughing fit.

"*Waesacks!*" Sally hurried to dipper up a cup of water for him. "D'ye hear tha, Annie? We need to do something about that cough."

Anne pulled her coat down from the peg. "I'll go see if Pink has any onions we might trade for."

David put on a sore face and groaned, "Noooo . . ."

"Aye . . ." Sally said. "A warm onion poultice will drive th' cough from yer lungs."

"That's it!" David threw his arms up over his head in total surren-der. "I give up . . ."

Fully bundled, Anne set off chasing her shadow on a march across the valley toward Captain Dunaway's hut. It seemed the entire camp was out taking advantage of the clear sky and calm wind. She passed several crews of soldiers hard at work with ax and adze, hewing round logs into level and even squares. Thick plumes of smoke snaking up into the blue sky marked the multiple fires where washwomen worked their battledores, stirring steaming cauldrons of laundry.

Anne stopped at the parade ground to join a huddle of women and soldiers watching a large company of soldiers being drilled in battle formations. The drillmaster was a big officer wearing a splendid bi-corn hat adorned with a gold and red cockade. He marched up and down the lines barking in French. A young officer followed after him, and in a much less daunting voice translated the directives into En-glish, which were then executed by the American soldiers in the most pitiful manner.

The Baron and the Model Company.

This was the man David was so concerned about—the latest in a stream of soldiers of fortune shipping in from far-flung places like France, Poland, and Germany to volunteer their services for the Amer-ican cause. David told them one hundred and twenty soldiers had been handpicked from across all regiments to form a Model Company to be trained by this Prussian in the European manner of waging war.

The Baron presented a very authoritative figure in a caped over-coat, double-breasted with shiny brass buttons and gold-fringed epau-lettes. A large, long-snouted hound followed obediently at his heels as he marched with the company, shouting directives. In the officer's few quiet moments reviewing his new company's performance, the Prus-sian tapped the side of his polished leather knee boots with the riding crop he carried, and stroked his pet's nose.

The Model Company, on the other hand, couldn't be any less im-pressive. The Continental ranks with their mishmash weaponry and horribly ragtag clothing and footwear were in no way performing anything resembling the close-ordered military drill Anne'd witnessed while encamped among the British. The training process was made even more convoluted by the Baron's lack of English—every order first conceived in German, shouted in French, and relayed to the troops by his aide in English.

Marching back and forth waving his riding crop, the Prussian grew red in the face, trying to get the ten ranks of twelve to maneuver with some measure of unison and alignment. When he gave the order to wheel left, some did go left, others kept straight, some moved too slow, and others too fast. With one simple order, the entire company converged in a confounded mess. In complete frustration the Prussian tossed his crop into the air and emitted a sharp stream of German and French invectives that could lift a scalp, no translation offered or required.

"The Baron will need to learn a few English curse words, if he thinks to whip this lot into any semblance of an army," Anne said.

Arms folded across his chest, an officer standing to her left commented with a laugh, "I expect, madam, Steuben's few English words are most likely curse words."

The strapping young man's speech bore a soft Germanic accent. Anne noted the officer's dark blue coat and asked, "Are you Prussian as well, sir?"

"No. I come from Holland, but I consider myself American now." With a curt bow, he said, "Lieutenant Frederick Enslin—Malcolm's Regiment, Third Pennsylvania."

A pretty woman wearing a wicker peddler's pack on her back stopped to hawk her wares. "Needles. Thread. Buttons. Combs—I have a good selection of all at reasonable prices."

Anne and the Lieutenant both declined with shakes of their heads.

The peddler woman did not press her sale. Laying her hand on Enslin's arm, she asked, "It is odd, isn't it, Lieutenant Enslin? To see an officer—a baron, no less—taking such an active part in training regulars?"

"It is the Prussian way . . ." Enslin said, taking a step back to free himself of the woman's touch. "Steuben is the son of an officer. He spent most of his life in service to Frederick the Great, and he is an expert in the military sciences."

The peddler arched her brows. "Is that his name? Baron Steuben?"

"Steuben is his name, but whether he's a baron for fact—" Enslin smiled and shrugged. "It is not unknown for foreign soldiers to exaggerate their rank and status."

"I see . . . most interesting . . ." The pretty woman strolled away, flashing a smile to the next group of soldiers. "Needles, buttons . . ."

"The peddler," Anne asked. "Is she an acquaintance of yours, Lieutenant?"

"No," Enslin replied. "I thought perhaps she was a friend of yours."

"She's no friend of mine—but she is somehow familiar to me . . ." Anne kept her eye on the peddler. The woman threw back her shawl to show off rich dark hair pulled back in a knot, and said something to make her new audience laugh. She was wearing a British red coat, cut down to size, but like many who'd scavenged an enemy coat, she'd masked its true crimson with a dip in a walnut dye, changing the color to a more acceptable maroon.

"Annie!"

Anne turned to see Brian and Jim among Steuben's drummer corps, calling to her and waving their sticks. She waved back. At the same time, the Model Company maneuvered into another discombobulated tangle.

Steuben marched forward, whipping his crop through the air and shouting, *"Halt—HALT—HALT!"*

Without taking a breath he stormed up and down the lines, laying into the company—first with a rapid stream of German, then French—capping the tirade off with a string of good old English swearwords.

"BLOODY HELL! GODDAMN IT! SHIT! SHIT! SHIT!" Waving his aide over, Steuben said, "You—come here *und* swear for me!"

Smiles cracked the faces of the berated soldiers. The drummers began to giggle, and Steuben himself burst out with a contagious chuckle infecting everyone on the parade ground.

After a good laugh, the Prussian grew instantly stern and barked, *"Attention!"* Visibly pleased with how his company snapped to, he renewed the training with an order to, *"Schulter firelock!"*

Bidding farewell to Lieutenant Enslin, Anne followed a snow-packed path to the opposite end of the parade grounds, and Captain Dunaway's cabin.

The latchstring was out, and Anne knocked at the door, but no one answered. Knocking harder, she yelled through a chink between door boards, "It's Anne Merrick come to call!" but still there was no answer. Taking a step back, Anne noted the smokeless chimney. She gave the latchstring a tug and opened the door.

Met by an overwhelming smell of wet ashes, Anne stood in the doorway squinting and blinking. A candlewick sputtered in a puddle of wax pooled in a dish on the bedside table. In the flashing light Anne could just make out Pink, sitting ramrod straight on the edge of the bed, a dark shawl thrown over her shoulders. It was the first time Anne had seen the woman without a headdress, and untamed, Pink's hair formed a soft explosion of curls haloing her head.

"Pink . . . ?" As Anne drew closer she could better make out the prone figure on the bed. Captain Dunaway was laid out in his best uniform. Pink had carefully dressed her master's hair with side curls, and powdered it white. She'd arranged his hands on his chest clasping his ornate saber.

Pink sat very still beside the body, eyes swollen and sad with crying, hands with fingers laced and resting on a piece of foolscap on her lap. "Lieutenant Gill went to fetch a cart. He made a promise to Master Aubrey. Promised he'd see him home to be buried in the family place." She whispered, as if she were afraid he might wake. "He was always sickly as a boy."

Anne stepped closer. "You laid your master out very fine."

Pink turned her head and brushed her fingers along the dead man's cheek. "He's my brother. *Was* my brother . . ." She paused, and self-corrected again. "He was my *half* brother."

Anne stuttered for a moment trying to fathom the proper condolence. "I'm—I'm so very sorry for your loss." She looked around. "Is there anything I can do—anything you need? Maybe I could fetch in some firewood?"

Pink offered up the page in her lap. "Mr. Gill give me this paper. If it's no bother, missus, could you read it out to me?"

"Of course." Anne took a seat on the bedside stool, held the page close to the candlelight, and read aloud— " 'Be it known to all unto whom these present letters may come, that I, Captain Aubrey Dunaway of York County, Virginia, in consideration of the loyal service rendered to me, hereby Liberate and Manumit and set Free from bondage as slave, the woman called Pink, twenty-nine years of age. I do hereby declare her to be a free woman and I do renounce Right title Interest claim and Demand whatsoever to the said slave this Tenth day of the First month in the year of our Lord, One thousand Seven hundred and Seventy-eight. In testimony whereof I have hereunto set my hand and seal the day and year aforementioned.'" Anne pointed to the signatures. "There it is, properly witnessed. Signed in the presence of First Lieutenant Erasmus Gill."

"What does it mean?"

"It means your brother did not want to appear before his maker bearing the awful sin of leaving his sister in bondage . . ." Anne hopped up and gave Pink a hug. "It means you're a free woman!"

"Mr. Gill said the same." Pink heaved a sigh, and closed her eyes. "As if bein' free were a good thing."

Anne gave Pink's hand a squeeze. "It *is* a good thing!"

"There was a day when I would pray and pine for freedom . . ." Pink shivered, and drew her shawl tight. "Now that I have it, I'm flummoxed as to why I ever would wish for such a thing."

"You're free. You can go where you want, and do what you will."

"Go where I want and do what I will," Pink repeated. "I ain't never been nowhere but with Master Aubrey since the day I was birthed— and since the day I was birthed, I ain't ever done nothin' but be in service to Master Aubrey. What am I to do now? Where am I t' go?"

"Have you no people back in Virginia?"

"Master Aubrey's all that's left of my people." Pink rubbed the stump on her left hand where her little finger ought be. "Ol' Master sold my mama off soon after I was weaned, and young Master Aubrey got rid of most everyone and everything to pay off Ol' Master's debts— though the man was my father, I curse the mean ol' bastard for the terrible gamblin' man he was. Left Master Aubrey in a right pickle, he did."

"I can see why this might be a shock for you." Anne carefully folded the page in two and handed it to Pink. "But you are an intelligent and hardworking woman, and you *can* make a life for yourself. If you'd like, you're welcome to come to live with me and Sally, at least until you figure out exactly what to do."

Pink looked up. "For real and true?"

"Of course." Anne pulled Pink up to a stand.

Lieutenant Gill arrived just then with a cart and two men to help lift the corpse. Aubrey Dunaway was hoisted out of bed in a sling fashioned from his blanket, and the women followed the parade outside to see him placed in the cart.

Pink began sobbing as she floated a fine linen sheet over the body, and Anne rushed up to wrap a comforting arm around the woman. Like a lawyer making a case to the judge, Pink looked up to the sky and proclaimed, "He was always kind to me—never once was I whipped—and I have more than a few tender remembrances of when we played as children." She swiped at her tears with the back of her hand, and asked Anne, "Master Aubrey's up in heaven now, ain't he? He's up in heaven right now listening to the music of the angels . . ."

Anne nodded only to give some comfort to Pink, for in her heart she doubted whether any of the men who enslaved their fellow human beings—much less this man, who kept a sister in bondage for twenty-nine years—could ever earn a place amongst the angels.

Pink packed her few articles of clothing into an old leather portmanteau, and Anne took the iron kettle from the hearth and collected Pink's medicaments and herbs into it. Together, they bundled up her bedding and tied the bulky package with a rope.

Pink threw on a plain but good wool cloak, pulling the hood over her wild hair. Considering the three loads, and the distance back to her hut, Anne said, "I'm wearing sleeves; I can carry the bedding on my back, like a pack."

Taking hold of the pot bale, Pink bit her bottom lip. "I don't feel right taking these things. This kettle and bedding are Master Aubrey's property . . ."

"Fiddlesticks!" Anne slipped her arms through the ropes and adjusted the bundle to sit comfortably across her shoulders. "Wherever Aubrey Dunaway is, I can assure you he has no need of either kettles or bedding."

Pink flashed a little smile, the first Anne had seen since she'd come through the door.

"It's a habit, I s'pose," Pink said, "worrying for Master and his things."

Grabbing the portmanteau, Anne suggested, "Get in the habit of worrying about Pink."

She swung open the door, and Pink stepped out into the light.

"There!" Anne balanced the last length of firewood onto the stack she'd arranged next to the hearth. "That should get us through to morning, don't you think?"

Straddling a bench, David looked up from shuffling a deck of cards. "More than enough—now sit down and play."

Anne sat to face her brother, and snapped up the cards David tossed her way. She sniffed the air, saying, "The girls are spoiling you on your last day, brother . . . I smell chocolate *and* shortbread for our afternoon tea."

"*Shortbread!*" Sally dropped the stocking she was knitting and knelt at the hearth. Very carefully she lifted the lid from the Dutch oven so as not to spill any of the hot embers layered atop it.

"Is it burned?" David asked.

Using a long-handled spoon, Sally levered up a round tin of shortbread, proclaiming, "It's perfect—have a look-see!" She brought the tin over to show them the slightly golden sweet cake she'd marked into eight pie-shaped pieces using the tines of a fork.

Pink came out from behind a quilt hung from the rafters in the corner, a tin pail in hand. "I'm heading out, y'all," she warned.

David and Anne clapped hands down on their game of Whist, and Sally flipped her apron over the shortbread. As Pink scooted out the door to toss the content of the piss pot, an ice-cold wind came skirling through the cabin, whistling up the chimney, sending out a scatter of ashes.

In a blink of the eye, Pink came scurrying back. "Woo-*hooo!*" she exclaimed, pushing the door shut. "It's colder than a witch's tittie outside. So cold, there ain't nary a soul to be seen." She went over to the hearth and stirred the little pot simmering on the grate. "On a day like today, this here chocolate will surely hit the spot . . ."

David's hand shot up. "I'll have a cup!"

"Glutton!" Anne gave her brother a shove to the shoulder. "I'm sure we'd all enjoy a *share.*"

Pink poured a round of chocolate, and David was the first to take a sip. "Sorry, Annie. I always thought your chocolate the best, but I have to say, Pink's is better."

Anne agreed after taking a sip. "What's your secret?"

"Ain't no secret, Annie." Pink laughed. "I just stir in a bitty pinch of red pepper powder. Adds a little bite to the sweet."

Sally turned the shortbread out onto a cloth and broke it along the perforations into triangular pieces she called petticoat tails. "I'm surprised we didn't see our young lads today. It's been more'n three days since they've been round for a meal . . ."

"I hope they didn't catch sick." Pink took a seat beside Sally. "I heard tell there's pox in the camp."

"Smallpox?" Anne looked away from the game. "Who told you that?"

"One of the washwomen." Pink nodded. "Said a quarantine's been set up and they're lookin' for nurses. I had me the pox as a little one, so I was thinkin' to apply . . . Pays eight dollars a month, plus rations."

Anne popped up. She pulled her shawl up over her head and plucked her coat from the peg. "I'd better go and check on them . . ."

"Och, Annie!" Sally said. "Not a one of us meant for ye t' go traipsin' about in th' ice cold."

David lunged out and grabbed Anne by the skirts. "Sit down and finish the game. I'm sure they're fine . . . You saw them on parade just the other day."

"That was three days ago, David . . ." Anne jerked her skirts free, tugged on a woolly cap, and stuffed her hands into a pair of mittens. "If you recall, it took my Jemmy just short of three days to die from the pox."

"You're right." David nodded and gathered up the cards. "Though I wager they're both hunkered in with their messmates, I suppose there's no harm in your checking in."

Sally tied Anne's muffler snug, and handed over a small package wrapped in a bit of old sacking. "Petticoat tails for our young lads, na?"

Hands and shortbread tucked in pockets, head down, Anne took off marching a quickstep across the valley. *David's right . . . Anyone with a brain is hunkered in . . .*

It was a crackling cold—a stinging cold—one of those days when it hurt to take too deep a breath. Strong gusts of wind propelled Anne across the parade ground, and she could see the groups of huts hugging the entrenchments—the gray ribbons of smoke rising from the stubby stone chimneys streaming sideways with the wind. Anxious for the boys and a warm fire, she veered off the packed-down path to cut a shorter way through knee-deep snow, aiming for the second cluster from the left. *Weedon's brigade . . .*

She'd been there only once before, but she recalled the directions Brian had given her. *Third hut from the left in the first row you see . . .* Anne stopped and wiped the water from her eyes, counting again, *One—two—three huts from the left . . .*

Not a wisp of smoke puffed from that chimney. Anne jerked up her skirts and ran the rest of the way to pound at the door. When no one answered her knock, she yanked on the latchstring and found what she knew she'd find—the hut was cold, dark, and completely empty.

Spinning around in the doorway, Anne pulled at the moist wool covering her mouth and heaved big, cloudy breaths. *Where could they be?* She eyed the hilly horizon, and the winter sun—so pale and weak— hovered just above an angry slurry of storm clouds riding in from the west.

No time to waste . . . Anne hurried to the last row—the officer huts— and pounded on the first door she came to, surprised to be greeted by a familiar face.

"Lieutenant Enslin," she said. "I'm Mrs. Merrick. I hope you re- member—we spoke on the parade ground the other day . . ."

"Of course." Equally surprised, the Lieutenant waved her inside. "Come in . . . come in . . ."

"Thank you." Anne scurried straight to the hearth.

The Lieutenant's hut was similar to the hut Pink occupied with Captain Dunaway, except that it boasted a rectangular cast-iron stove of the type the Dutch were fond of, resting on a pad of flagstones within the fireplace. A young soldier with a slate in his hand and a blanket thrown over his shoulders was sitting on one of the pair of stools pulled close to the stove. There was something odd in the look on his face, and Anne thought for a moment he seemed frightened.

"I'm helping Private Monhort learn his sums." Enslin directed the soldier like a schoolmaster would. "Carry on, Private, while I speak with Mrs. Merrick."

Private Monhort smiled, and bent over his slate, the soft tick of chalk on the stone signaling he was back on task.

"I'm sorry to interrupt," Anne said, allowing Enslin to draw her into the orb of warm air radiating from the stove. "I won't be but a moment."

"Warm yourself"—Enslin gestured to the stove—"and tell me why you are here."

"Do you recall the two drummer boys who were waving to me on the parade ground?" Anne lifted her skirts above her boot tops, allow- ing a warm draft to move up her legs.

The Lieutenant nodded. "I know them. They are with the Thir- teenth Pennsylvanians."

Anne tugged off her cap. "I've just come from paying a call and found their hut completely deserted. I'm very concerned . . . They say smallpox is in the camp."

"Not to worry, Mrs. Merrick. Your drummer boys have been inoculated." Enslin opened the little door on the stove and tossed a chunk of wood on top of glowing embers. "They are in quarantine."

"Inoculated!"

"Yes. General Washington has ordered all soldiers who've never suffered smallpox to be inoculated before we begin campaigning in the spring." Enslin laid a hand on Anne's shoulder. "Do not be so alarmed. The process is proven and very scientific."

Anne grabbed Enslin by the arm. "Where's this quarantine?"

Patting Anne on the shoulder, the Lieutenant said, "I assure you, Mrs. Merrick, inoculation is quite safe . . . Very few die from the procedure. Inoculation is for the good of the soldier and the army as a whole . . ."

"I know well the danger posed by smallpox, and the merits of inoculation. Both my husband and young son died of smallpox." Anne tugged her hat back on. "Tell me where I can find the quarantine."

Marching over to the peg where his coat and tricorn were hanging, Enslin shrugged into his coat. "I will take you to there." Tying his tricorn secure to his head with a muffler, he said to his student, "I will return shortly, John."

They walked side by side on a well-tamped-down path following along the lines of entrenchments. As they crossed the Gulph Road, Anne asked, "Are you inoculated, Mr. Enslin?"

"After a fashion," he said. "The disease is very common in Holland. I suffered it as a boy, and survived. And you?"

"There was an outbreak in our town, and I was inoculated as a child," Anne said.

"Hmmm . . ." Enslin said. "Your parents were progressive thinkers . . ."

Anne shrugged. "In truth, my father thought my mother had gone mad when she but suggested inoculation. She'd lost all her family to the smallpox, and said she could not bear see it happen again. Father absolutely forbid it, but Mother was a stubborn and willful woman, and she called Dr. Walker to our house when my father was away."

"To defy husband and convention . . ." There was admiration in his tone. "Your mother was a very brave woman."

Anne nodded. "She was."

She walked along remembering the day Dr. Walker came to the house with his black satchel of frightening tools, remembering how he laid them out, one by one, on a swath of bloodred felt. *Mother was the first . . .*

David had cried watching as she submitted to the physician's knife, but Mother assured them it hurt only "a wee, little bit," and that they must be brave. Anne smiled. *I was brave for David.* It had been difficult to stand stoic but she barely flinched when the physician applied his lancet to her arm. But for one tiny whimper when he was cut, David, too, was brave.

Together they watched from the window when Dr. Walker went out to the poor wretch he had lying in his cart on the lane. The poor boy's face was so completely covered over with weeping pustules, David said he thought the boy looked like a warty old gourd. Anne gave him a hard shove for saying such a cruel thing, and she began to weep when the doctor scraped up some of the oozing matter from the sick boy's face with a silver teaspoon.

It didn't hurt much at all when Dr. Walker squeezed the pus he'd gathered into the open wounds on their arms, and Mother gave them each a sugar comfit from the tin she always carried in her pocket. *For being so good . . .*

Anne stood on the stoop, holding David by the hand, and watched the physician's cart bounce down the lane. The next day, she and David sickened and went on to survive very mild cases of the pox, as was expected.

"Being inoculated has saved both our lives," Anne mused aloud. "Had he not been inoculated, my brother would most likely have succumbed to the disease, during the Canada campaign—as so many of our soldiers did. And I most likely would have perished along with my husband and son . . ."

"Yes," Enslin said. "Inoculation saves lives."

Anne stopped in her tracks. "Do you wonder, Lieutenant, why a woman, when saved by her mother from contracting a virulent disease, would not do the same for her own son?"

Enslin took Anne's arm and looped it through the crook of his elbow. "It is clear to me you loved your boy very much," he said, pulling her along.

Anne was grateful for the man's arm, and for the regular crunch of their footfalls in the snow moving her forward. She was of a sudden so weary—encumbered by the drag of days gone by.

"You know, Mr. Enslin, there are those for whom inoculation proves fatal." *Crunch, crunch, crunch.* "My mother was one. She contracted a terrible case, and a week after we were all inoculated, she was dead."

"*Ach, ja—*" Enslin's slip into Dutch the first deviation from his otherwise perfect English. "A burned child dreads the fire . . . Of *course* you are wary of inoculation."

"I was not wary, Mr. Enslin. I was fearful. I was never brave enough to do for Jemmy what Mother did for me." Anne looked up at the Lieutenant. The compassion in his eyes—as blue and calm as lake water—allowed her to crack the door open on her sadness. "I paid an awful price for my cowardice, and I live every day knowing my fear of losing Jemmy is what caused me to lose him." Anne heaved a sigh, her breath puffing out on a cloud of vapor that vanished almost as soon as it was realized. When Enslin spoke, she startled.

"My old grandsire once told me regretting the past is like chasing the wind." Enslin offered Anne a handkerchief tugged from his pocket. "I say to you, Mrs. Merrick, you are not a coward. You did what all good mothers do—you protected your dearly beloved child as best you knew how. Live every day knowing that."

Anne used the hankie to blot the tears from her cheeks, and smiled. "My grandmother once told me the kindest men always have handkerchiefs at the ready."

As they reached the top of a hill, the Lieutenant pointed and announced, "There is the quarantine."

Near the stables, the Flying Hospital stood newly completed, smoke billowing from a pair of chimneys, one at either end. A building twice as long and half again as tall as a standard hut, Washington had ordered two such hospitals to be constructed for each brigade. The harsh winter impeded the progress of construction, and as yet, most of the severely ill soldiers were shipped off to hospitals outside the camp.

The Lieutenant took Anne by the hand and together they ran the rest of the way down the hill. Enslin pushed the door open to a long, narrow, and very crowded room. Lit with glass-paned lanterns hanging from the rafters, Anne could see there were bunk beds three berths high lined up along either end, but many were sitting or lying on straw pallets laid out on the dirt floor. Seeing an aggravated woman with bucket and copper dipper making her way about the room offering water, Anne was reminded when she and Sally worked the British hospital. The foul yet familiar smell permeated the woolen muffler she'd pulled up over her nose—a decoction of sweat, urine, and vomit overlaced with the strong smoke of burning sulfur.

"There is Mr. Barnabas Binny. You see? The man in the old-fashioned wig," Enslin said, pushing the door shut. "He is the surgeon in charge. Go to him. He will know what's become of your boys."

Wending a path between soldiers sitting and standing bundled in blankets and coats waiting their turn for inoculation, Anne untied her muffler and headed toward the man wearing an iron gray curly wig.

He'd set up shop with a table and stool beside the nearest hearth. A rib-thin soldier sat shivering on the tall stool, bare-chested, his shirt and blanket in a heap on his lap.

"Hold still, now . . ." With lancet in hand, Mr. Binny very carefully incised a half-inch-long opening into the soldier's upper arm, sopping up the trickle of blood with a rusty old rag.

Anne cleared her throat and said, "Beg pardon, Mr. Binny . . ."

He looked up, and Anne was surprised to see he was much younger than his style of wig indicated. As if reading her thoughts, he said, "Paid a shilling for it. Not the mode, I know, but it keeps my pate and ears warm. If you are looking to be inoculated, miss, you'll just have to wait your turn. If you've come to help, present yourself to Mrs. Snook, our matron. She puts every willing hand to some use."

Anne pulled off her mittens. "I'm looking for two drummer boys from Pennsylvania's Thirteenth, inoculated recently. Could you tell me where I might find them?"

Binny turned his attention back to his task. Using a snuff spoon, he scooped up a bit of the matter collected on a china plate, and carefully inserted a small dollop of pus into the soldier's open wound. "Quarantines reside at the other end. Look for your boys there."

Enslin led the way through the crowd. The west end of the hospital was occupied by soldiers in various stages of the disease, though it seemed—to Anne's great relief—no one was suffering from any kind of a serious case.

"Here they are!" Enslin called Anne over. Brian and Jim were sitting on an upper bunk in the far corner, huddled together under a pair of shabby blankets.

"Jim! Brian!" Anne waved her hat as she made her way over. "There you are!"

Jim hunched his shoulders and mumbled, "Hullo, Annie."

Brian asked, "What are you doing here?"

"That's a fine greeting—" Anne tugged on their blanket. "Come on down so I can have a good look at the two of you!" The boys came down slowly, and she at once understood their reluctance.

Pressing hand to foreheads, Anne was instantly relieved to find no fever, and see the few pox that had erupted on their faces were beginning to scab up. She pointed to their bare feet, and asked, "What's happened to your moccasins?"

When no answer was forthcoming, she jerked aside the shabby blankets they wore to reveal they were practically naked beneath, in nothing but thin undershirts and breeches.

"Where are your jackets? What's become of the shirts and weskits we made for you?"

Heads hung low, Brian said, "Stolen."

"Stolen?" Anne could feel the blood rising to her cheeks. "Who stole your things?"

Lieutenant Enslin said, "Name this thief, and I will have him arrested."

Jim looked to Brian, and Brian only shook his head, negative.

Anne glanced at Enslin, and the Lieutenant added, "Name the thief. That is an order."

"D' rather not say," Brian muttered.

"*Lieutenant Enslin . . .*" Anne and the Lieutenant both turned to find an armed soldier with snow collected on his hat and the shoulders of his caped overcoat. He added, "Colonel Malcolm wishes for you to report to headquarters, Lieutenant."

"Very good, Sergeant," Enslin said. "I will be on my way as soon as I finish here . . . You are dismissed."

"No, sir," the Sergeant said. "I've orders to escort you to the Colonel's headquarters, posthaste."

"I see." Enslin closed his eyes for a moment, and drew in a breath. To Anne he said, "It seems I am needed at brigade headquarters—I can arrange for a man to escort you back to your hut . . ."

"Oh, please don't bother. I'll be fine on my own." Anne dipped a slight curtsy. "Thank you, Lieutenant. You couldn't have been any more helpful or kind."

"My pleasure." Lieutenant Enslin bid adieu with a brief bow and followed after the Sergeant.

"My pleasure," Brian repeated with scorn, his narrowed eyes following Enslin out the door. "You best keep your distance from him."

Anne was aware many soldiers were very bigoted against the German deserters from the British lines who joined their ranks, and she said, "Don't worry. He's not a Hessian. Lieutenant Enslin is Dutch."

Jim piped in, "It ain't about him being Dutch."

Brian drew himself up tall and in a stern voice said, "You just stay away from him, Annie, you hear me?"

Anne snorted. "Has the pox addled your brain?"

"I'm tellin' you to stay away from him, Annie. He's . . . Well, he ain't regular; that's all."

"And what does that mean?"

Brian looked off at the corner of the ceiling. "He's a molly."

"What?"

"He don't fancy girls," Jim explained.

"I *know* what a molly is." Anne gave Brian a sharp poke to the shoulder. "And you both ought know better than to make up such a vile lie."

"'Tain't a lie," Jim said.

"I swear on the altar of the Almighty, it's true." Brian made the motion crossing his heart. "Why on earth would anyone make up sech a thing?"

"Ensign Maxwell told us so hisself." Jim folded his arms across his skinny chest. "He ordered all of us drummer boys to keep our distance—told us they caught Lieutenant Enslin in *flag-ron-tay* with John Monhort."

"Monhort's a molly, too," Brian added.

"Listen to me—both of you." Anne took them each by the shoulder and gave the boys a good shake. "This kind of talk is wicked and slanderous, and can get you into trouble. Lieutenant Enslin is an officer, and he has proven very kind to me. I'm so disappointed in you both. Enough of your vicious gossip," Anne said. "Tell me what's become of your shoes and clothing."

Jim shook his head, and Brian's brows wove into one angry line. Neither of them offered up a word.

"Alright, then." Anne grabbed the boys by the arm. Dragging them along, she pushed a way across the room and plunked them both down before the fire. She tugged the shawl out from under her coat and draped it over Brian's shoulders. Her woolly muffler was wound around Jim's thin neck. "Stay here, where it's warm—and don't scratch," she said, slapping Brian on the wrist. Anne pulled the package of shortbread from her pocket. "Here. Though you don't deserve them, Sally sent you both some petticoat tails to share. I'll be back tomorrow."

Brian kept his head down and muttered, "Thank you, Annie."

Jim hopped up and gave her a hug. "Don't be mad at us too long."

Stepping out the door, Anne recognized at once the wind had picked up. The light snow was flying in on a horizontal trajectory, and was mixed with little pellets of ice that bored into her skin like pieces of gravel thrown up from a wagon wheel. Stuffing hands up sleeves, she tucked chin to chest and cut a path uphill through a stand of chestnuts, the shortest route back to her cabin. Trudging through the snow, Anne couldn't stop thinking about the gossip the boys had repeated. *It can't be true . . . It must be a misunderstanding . . .*

Breaking through the trees, she trudged up to the crest of the hill, and saw a figure standing on a rise facing the artillery park. Through the snow, she recognized the wicker pack and red-brown coat of the peddler woman, but the greeting Anne called out was lost in the wind.

As she drew closer, the woman twisted around to avoid bearing the full brunt of a wicked blast of wind, and Anne could see the peddler was using a pencil to scratch tick marks onto a slip of paper cupped in her hand.

She's counting cannon!

Anne skirted sideways, stumbling and sliding the rest of the way down the hill, hoping she hadn't been seen.

❧ FOURTEEN ❧

*Our support and success depend on such a variety of men
and circumstances, that every one, who does but wish well,
is of some use.*

THOMAS PAINE, *The American Crisis*

"She's a pretty woman . . . carries a big wicker pack and goes about selling buttons and needles . . ." Anne thought for a minute, then added, "Her coat is British red, dyed brown with walnut—"

"We think the woman is a spy," David said.

"I for certain recollect the one you speak on. Hair and eyes as dark as Egypt—very friendly and interested in our works—" The duty Sergeant at the main gate stopped to worry the stubble on his chin. "A spy, you say?"

"A clever spy," Anne said.

"Very clever, she was, now that I think on it . . ." The Sergeant leaned in on his musket. "How she eyed the position of the guns—struck me as odd, until she said her husband was a gunner what died at Breed's Hill."

"Probably true," Anne said. "Except she neglected to mention he was a Redcoat gunner."

"That's where she got her coat . . ." The Sergeant snapped his fingers. "Oh, she knew her business, Cap'n—she had a signed pass and knew the proper countersign when challenged."

"Send a runner to alert the pickets at all points of entry," David said. "I want her apprehended and brought straight to headquarters—understand, Sergeant?"

"A-yup!" Squinting in the sunshine, the Sergeant brought a knuckle to his brow in salute. "My boys'll keep an eye to windward, Cap'n. The she-spy has but t' show her face, and we'll nab her lickety-click."

Anne followed after her brother, walking in one of the frozen wheel ruts leading up the Gulph Road. Anne pounded her bundled head with mittened fists. "It was niggling at my brain the day I met her . . . there was something so familiar . . . I'm sorry."

"You've nothing to be sorry for," David said over his shoulder. "You saw her counting the guns and reported directly."

"But her cheerful air, the instant camaraderie—all methods Sally and I used to cull information from our marks in Burgoyne's camp. I couldn't put my finger on it then, but I know now why she seemed so familiar. I saw myself in her." Anne crossed through the deep snow to walk in the opposite rut, on parallel course with her brother. "She owned a forged pass and managed the daily countersigns. Your sergeant's right. This woman knows her business."

David limped along, keeping up with his sister's pace. "I've been making inquiries all morning. It seems she covered every inch of our camp—from the entrenchments to headquarters—she even wheedled her way into the General's kitchen selling buttons to Cook. Who knows what she may have seen or overheard?"

"Yet she's vanished like a ghost at cockcrow." Anne huffed a sigh. "I believe counting cannon was her final task before heading back to Howe."

"She assessed our defenses, counted guns and manpower, observed our training and our weakened state," David said. "She even learned the numbers of infirm from one of the surgeon's mates. Howe will soon know he can swoop in and topple our entire army with not much more than a feather."

"You think he's planning an attack?"

"He'd be a fool not to," David asserted.

"Remember—Howe proved himself a great fool by not pressing his attack on Long Island. If there was ever a chance to crush us, that was it—and I heard many a British officer in the Cup and Quill opine likewise."

"I know Howe dotes on his winter comforts, but still . . ." David turned up the collar on his overcoat, and stuffed his hands back into his pockets. "I find it galling he's sent spies to crawl all over our camp, and we know naught of the works and doings in Philadelphia."

As they passed the parade ground, Steuben's big hound came at them, bounding through the snow, practically knocking Anne off her feet. "Azor!" She laughed, giving the hound a good scrub about the ears.

David tugged his tricorn down to shade his eyes, and watched the Model Company being put through their paces. Major Steuben's commands, barked in French, and echoed in English, had the troops executing not quite in clockwork, but better than when first drilled. "Our Prussian seems to be making some progress."

"They are still an army of ragamuffins," Anne said. "But I agree, there's a marked improvement in performance and bearing."

"At least something is improving." David bent to rub his bad leg.

Anne sent Azor galloping off to his master's whistle. "Is your old wound giving you trouble, David?"

"My barometer," he said, flashing a smile. "Lets me know when a storm is on the way."

They continued on toward headquarters, and when they reached the crossroads, Anne gave her beleaguered brother a hug. "We'll see you at supper?"

"I'll be late. There's a staff meeting this afternoon . . . Wait!" David tugged her by the sleeve. "Come with. I'm so behind, and could use another hand."

"Alright," Anne said. "But just for an hour or so. I plan to fetch the boys from hospital today."

To David's pleasure, the sentry posted at the stoop of Washington's headquarters went beyond a perfunctory exchange of parole and countersign, to vigorously question their identities and purpose before allowing them to enter. "Another marked improvement," he noted.

"Courtesy of Madame She-Spy!" Anne said, and David laughed, swinging the door open to the surprise of the ensign on the other side of it. In the entry hall, a tall officer was buttoning up his coat.

"Colonel Tupper—" David swept his hat off in salute. "May I present my sister, Mrs. Anne Merrick."

The Colonel gave Anne's hand a hearty shake. "The one who spied the spy?"

"The very same." David beamed.

Anne smiled at the Colonel's play on words. "Purely a happenstance."

"I hate to appear rude, Mrs. Merrick, Captain Peabody"—he offered each of them a slight bow—"but I'm en route to the Bakehouse for an important session."

"Court-martial?" David asked.

Tupper's pleasant smile straightened to a grim line as he fit his tricorn onto his head. "The Dutchman," he said, flipping a thumb toward the stairs.

Lieutenant Enslin stood at the top of the staircase, dressed in a dirty shirt with tails untucked and wrists bound before him. Gazing through wisps of unkempt hair, he and Anne locked eyes only for an instant, before he turned away.

"G'won . . ." The guard standing behind gave him a poke with the butt of his musket, and Enslin came down the stairway, the irons shackled to his ankles jangling loud with each step. He kept his gaze elsewhere, and as he passed, Anne could see his feet were bare of shoes and stockings.

Anne called out, "Lieutenant Enslin!" and in the brief moment before the door banged shut, Enslin glanced over his shoulder, his sad blue eyes filled with fear and desperation.

"You know him?" David asked.

Anne nodded, unwinding her muffler. "A good man. A real gentleman. What could he be charged with?"

David dropped his voice to a scant whisper. "It seems the Lieutenant employed his parts on male bums, not female hearts."

"No! That's . . . That's nothing but vile rumor," Anne said with a shake of her head. "I don't believe it . . ."

"Believe it, Annie," David said. "The Dutchman's fully admitted to it."

"Oh." It was as if the air'd been pinched from her lungs by a sharp blow to the belly. She wandered to the window to watch poor Lieutenant Enslin, without a cloak or blanket, stumbling along in his shackles, barefoot on the snowy path.

"Will they hang him?"

"I don't know," David said, joining her at the window. "Tupper's a fair man, but it's a bad business. I don't envy him this case."

Anne let out a little gasp seeing Lieutenant Enslin stumble and fall, and her heart broke watching for what seemed an eternity, as he tried without any success to rise, bound and shackled as he was. One of the guards at last showed some pity, and jerked Enslin up to his feet. When the entire cortege disappeared down the path to the covered bridge, she turned to her brother and asked, "Would it help him, David, if I were to testify as to his kindness?"

David put his arm around her shoulders. "I'm afraid nothing will help him, Annie. The Dutchman is a lost cause."

With Jim and Brian to her left, Anne took a step forward and asked, "What do you mean, they can't go?"

Four quarantined soldiers snapped eyes up from their card game, and Anne knew her voice had gone out loud and sharp.

"I meant what I said." Seated in a crouch on the surgeon's stool near the fire, Mrs. Snook took a tug on the clay pipestem clenched between gaping, yellowed teeth, and puffed out an unholy halo of evil-smelling smoke to wreath her narrow head. In a voice made gruff by tobacco she said, "They's unfit for duty."

It was warm near the hearth. Anne swiped her hood back, and pushed the cape of her cloak off one shoulder. "You misunderstand my intent, Mrs. Snook. They aren't being returned to duty of any sort. I mean to take them off your hands—to care for them in my hut."

The matron shifted in her seat, as if considering Anne's proposal. Deep purple crescents sagged beneath watery, ferret eyes blinking at the acrid smoke emanating from her pipe. Her ears poked out from thin hair pulled tight into a scrawny tail, and she was made most ridiculous by the man's velvet and tasseled nightcap she wore perched at a jaunty angle. "Eyah . . . I understand . . . but them two aren't fit for duty and they stay put."

Anne plunked fists to hips, her brow knit. "Are you deaf or daft?" She leaned forward, speaking loud and slow, as one would speak to an imbecile. "I'm taking these boys where they will receive better care— so they can be *returned* to duty—and not to their graves."

The soldier-patients were drawn from their humdrum routine by the rumpus, and the able-bodied crowded in to witness the exchange between the two women.

Unfolding like a jackknife, the tall, thin matron rose to her feet. Folding arms across her sunken chest, she restated her dictum. "You can go where you please, but these boys are in *my* charge, and I take my duties to heart, ye hear?"

"Heart! If you indeed own one, I'd wager it's no bigger than one of old Methuselah's shriveled bollocks." To the guffaws of the onlookers, Anne grabbed Jim and Brian by the hands and hustled them toward the door.

Mrs. Snook called out, "Bar the door, Sergeant McQuigg. If they take a step beyond the threshold, arrest the boys for desertion."

Anne spun on her heel and charged back to stand toe-to-toe with the hospital matron. "Tell me, Mrs. Snook, what manner of sotweed have you tamped into your pipe?"

The soldiers gathered around burst out laughing. Anne grabbed Jim and Brian—wrapped in their shabby blankets, faces dotted with scabby pox, hair matted, and barefoot to boot—and she pushed the boys to stand front and center.

"Look at them, Mrs. Snook, these fine specimens in your charge— practically naked and as thin as ramrods. These boys under your care

are no better off than a beggar is in a stinking gutter in New York town."

"The beggar in the gutter's better off than we are," one of the soldiers chimed in.

"Aye," another agreed. "Any beggar worth his salt'll beg enough for a pint now and then."

Mrs. Snook was not budged by sentiment or satire. "These are soldiers under quarantine, treated no better or worse than any other."

"They're boys—and they are helpless in this place. I can give them proper care."

"They're soldiers in my charge," Mrs. Snook said with a nod, "and they stay put."

"Your charge." Anne reached out and snatched the ridiculous nightcap from the matron's head, shaking it in her face. "I'd wager the corpse from which you pilfered this cap was in your charge as well." Anne flung the nightcap into the fire.

Mrs. Snook gasped and watched the nightcap burst into flames, then she turned and gave Anne a hard shove, sending her back a step.

"I'm warning you, Mrs. Snook, I'm in a thin skin today." Hands curled into fists, Anne could feel the bite of fingernails digging into palms. "I'm taking these boys with me . . ."

"Give her what for, Annie!" Jim shouted.

Mr. Binny came barging through the crowd, and, like wind on water, a disappointed groan rippled across the hospital as the surgeon grabbed Anne by the shoulders.

"Mrs. Merrick! Mrs. Snook!"

Anne heaved a heavy breath, and relaxed the muscles bunched in her shoulders.

"I apologize, Mr. Binny, for this disruption, but I find I have no tolerance these days for idiots of any kind." Anne shot the matron a look that would turn sweet wine to vinegar. "As I explained to deaf ears, I will see these two boys cared for. If you require, Mr. Binny, I'll swear an oath to keeping them quarantined from the rest of the population."

"No oath required, Mrs. Merrick, and any relief you might give to

our effort is much appreciated. Mrs. Snook seems to have forgotten it
is a hospital we are running, not a prison."

"Thank you, sir, and good day."

Anne pushed the boys out the door, where Sally and Pink were
waiting, waving their arms and stamping their feet beside bundles of
clothing.

"What took ye so long?" Sally asked.

"You should have seen, Sal." Jim bounced around, punching the
air. "Annie was at loggerheads with pinch-faced Snooky."

"Enough of yer blether. Hurry and put these on, so we can be on
our way." Sally handed Jim and Brian stockings and shoes and teased
Anne with a smirk, "Fisticuffs with the matron, Mrs. Merrick?"

"We exchanged a few words between us." Anne shrugged.

"Hey!" Jim complained. "You gave me girl's shoes!"

"And girl stockings," Brian added, holding up the pair of hose Sally
had given him.

"Aye, and be glad for 'em." Sally pulled a yarn cap over Jim's head.
"Unless yid rather cross the valley barefoot, this is what we have to
spare."

The boys sat down and scrambled to pull on socks and shoes in the
cold. Anne helped Brian into her Hessian coat, and Pink draped Sally's
red cloak over Jim's shoulders. Fastening the clasp under his throat,
she drew the hood up.

"What a pretty little girl," Brian teased, patting Jim on the head.

Jim gave Brian a shove. "Shut your hole!"

"Let's go!" Anne waved everyone onward, and together they set off
to the cabin on the other side of the valley.

Jim took the point position and urged, "At the quickstep, please—
I don't care to have any of my mates t' see me wearing lady clothes."

Anne said, "Maybe you should have thought of that before you
sold your nice clothes away."

Brian's eyes narrowed. "Why don't you believe us? I ain't never had
a shirt as fine or warm as the one you made for me. Why in heaven's
name would I ever sell it?"

Jim added, "We tolt you true, Annie. Our things was stolt from our backs, and there ain't nothin' to be done about it."

"Mmmmph!" Sally snorted. "If yer shirts were truly stolen from your backs, ye must have seen the thief. Why will ye no' name him?"

"We can bear being cold and shivery," Brian said. "But we'd not bear being cold and shivery and beat to a pulp."

"And ratting on this fellow will garner us a bad beating for sure," Jim said.

"Ratting on what fellow?" Anne pressed.

Brian groaned. "Can't say, Annie. It'll go hard on us if we do. Truth is, we oughta known better, and harbored our goods more careful-like. Without Jack and Titus and Cap'n Peabody at our backs, there was no way for us to keep our nice things. Not in this camp."

Brian trudged along with his big feet stuffed into her old buckled walking shoes. Anne noticed the wisp of a mustache just beginning to form on his upper lip. *And Jim could pass for a girl . . . a very thin and ornery girl. Both of them, so young . . .*

These boys had been swept up in this war—engulfed by it—first on the battlefield, then in prison, and now in camp. Yet, no matter the depth of the water, or the strength of the current, they somehow always managed to kick up to the surface, take big gulps of air, and keep on swimming forward.

They know how to survive.

Jim fell back to flank Anne, and he slipped his thin, cold hand into hers, squeezing it tight. "Don't be angry, Annie."

"I'm not angry with either of you . . . I'm just . . . just feeling out of sorts. Some days this war gets me down, and I wonder whether all our tribulation is worth the price paid." Anne forced a smile. "I'll feel better once we get the two of you well and squared away with some proper gear. We can't have your mates see you walking about in lady clothes, can we?"

Sally threw her arm around Brian. "There's a kettle of pease porridge on the grate, and Pink says she's going to make some Southron biscuits to go with it."

Brian's eyes lit up. "Beaten biscuits?"

Pink nodded. "Beat for an hour at least with the flat of an ax."

"I can help," Brian offered. "My ma taught me how."

"Stop!" Sally raised her hand and they all pulled to a halt, listening. "D'ye hear that?"

A spate of gunshots rang out and echoed through the valley, making it hard to discern the direction of the fire. Pink near leapt from her skin when a cannon boomed, and flocks of birds roosting in the woodlands went fluttering up into the air.

"Redcoats?" Jim asked.

"Wheesht!" Sally cocked her head. "The shouting—it's coming from the main gate."

They struggled up to the hilltop to see a company of horsemen riding as advance and rear guard to a string of eight covered wagons drawn by mule and ox.

"They're back!" Anne yelled, and took off in a run, tumbling and sliding down the steep hillside shouting, "Jack! JACK!"

Standing in the bandbox of the fourth wagon, Jack waved both arms over his head. "Annie!"

Covered in snow, Anne clambered up into the slow-moving wagon and threw herself, laughing, into his arms. Jack drew her down to sit on his lap, and she covered him with kisses—kissed his beard caked with ice, his skin burned red with the wind, and lips chapped and cracked with the cold. "I'm so glad you're back . . ." she said, laughing and crying at once. "So glad . . ."

"My sweet Annie, I missed you so." Jack touched her cheek and caught a tear on his gloved fingertip. "Don't cry. It's too damn cold for tears."

"Jack! Woo-hoo! Woo-*hoooo!*" Brian and Jim whooped, galloping in a cloud of snow coming down the hill.

Arm in arm, Sally and Pink came downhill using a more careful step, and Sally called, "Welcome back, ye rascal pirates!"

Jack waved and asked, "Is that Pink with Sally?"

Anne nodded. "Captain Dunaway passed on, and she's been staying with us."

"No disrespect for the dead meant, but Titus will be glad to hear it—he's been like a bear with a sore head ever since laying eyes on that woman." Jack squinted in the sunlight. "Is Jim wearing Sally's cloak?"

"It's a long story . . ." Anne slipped from Jack's lap to sit beside him. "It seems everything went awry when you shipped off."

Jack took up the reins and, wrapping his arm about Anne's shoulder, pulled her close. "Well, darling girl, I'm back in the boat now, and together we will get it aright."

Anne worked her needle quickly, adding a durable whipstitch to finish the seams on the uniform coats Jack procured as a portion of his pay for the use of wagons and beasts. She tied off with a knot and bit the thread. "Sally, can I bother you for the seam ripper?"

"Mm-hmm . . ."

Sitting beside Anne on a bench drawn close to the fire for good light, Sally set aside the shirt she was stitching for Brian, and delved into the mending basket at her feet. The petticoat sacrificed for the boy's new shirts was donated by Pink, very fine quilted flannel in a soft shade of sky blue.

"Here ye go . . ." Sally tossed the ripper onto Anne's lap.

Anne set to work cutting the shiny pewter buttons off the coat. *A real shame* . . . She thought the buttons rather pretty—embossed with a stylized sunburst and the tiniest "3G" in the center—but as the boys refused to even consider wearing them, she added them to the pile on the hearth, where Brian and Jim were melting them down in the ladle Jack used for making lead ball.

"This coat is ready for the blue!" Anne eased the fabric into the dye pot. She'd paid General Washington's cook two pennies for eight pieces of the dark blue paper that loaves of shop sugar come wrapped in, and Pink used the paper to cook up a rich indigo color. The coats Jack salvaged were meant for drummer boys in the British 3rd Regiment of Foot, and were made of white wool with blue facings and cuffs. She was optimistic the fabric would take the dye well.

"Those shirts will be a nice match," Anne said as she used a piece

of kindling to poke away air pockets floating the fabric up to the surface.

Sally reached out with her foot and gave Brian a little nudge in the
ribs. "Hear that? We'll bring out the blue in yer eyes, lads, and ye'll
have t' beat th' young lassies off with yer drumsticks."

The boys were taking turns pouring molten pewter into the but-
tonmold David lent them. "Have a look . . ." Brian went to show Anne
one of the finished buttons, cast complete with a shank and the entwined letters "USA" embossed on the face.

"How nice!" Anne said, holding the button to light. "Make enough
so we can stitch a few inside your facings, for spares."

The door bar banged up, and Jack, Titus, and Pink swooped in
with a blast of cold air. Jack held a rolled-up piece of leather over his
head, a rare commodity in a camp of shoeless soldiers, and announced,
"We got a whole half hide!"

"From the Oneidans?" Sally asked.

"Yep." Jack unfurled the leather and tossed it down onto the floor.
"I knew one of 'em had to have some tucked away—and he couldn't
resist Titus's offer."

"I drove a good bargain," Titus said, setting a corked earthenware
jug on the tabletop. "Traded for the hide, this jug of maple syrup, and
a trifle for Miss Pink."

"It's no trifle!" Pink shed her cloak and showed Anne and Sally the
silver brooch she had pinned to the top edge of her stays. "See? Two
hearts twined together."

"Gweeshtie! A luckenbooth brooch!" Sally wagged her brows.

Pink traced the two silver hearts with the tip of her finger. "I never
had anything so pretty."

"It's a beautiful brooch." Anne caught Titus's eye. He flashed a grin
and shrugged.

Jack hung up his coat and plunked down on the bench beside
Anne. "Not a bad trade for an old hat picked up on the battlefield."

"Your Hessian hat?" Jim looked worried.

Titus pulled the other bench closer to the fire and he reached over to scrub Jim's noggin with his knuckles. "Don't fret, little brother. I never cared much for that hat. Too many geegaws and fiddle-dee-dums on it to suit my taste."

Anne contained her laugh. For all the years she'd known him, Titus's penchant for ostentatious hats had never wavered. *Until these boys needed shoes . . .*

"Make way . . . I need t' tend t' my stew." Pink shooed the boys and the button-making operation to the end of the hearth, and put her spoon to work stirring the pot of rabbit stew she had bubbling on the grate.

"Smells real good," Titus said, as he fished his moccasin-making tools from his pack.

"Have a taste . . ." With hand cupped under the bowl of the spoon, Pink delicately fed Titus a mouthful, dabbing at a slight dribble on his chin with the corner of her apron.

Sally leaned in and whispered, "Our Titus is fair smitten."

Anne nudged Jack and muttered, "I'd say Pink has Titus on her line."

"Him?" Jack snorted. "He's hooked, and flopping around in the boat."

Anne threaded her needle, watching Brian stand on the hide with feet an inch apart as Titus traced the outlines with a chunk of charcoal. He stood and studied the leather for a moment, then declared, "I will just barely squeeze four moccasins out of this elk skin."

Pink sidled up and rested a hand on Titus's broad shoulder. "I've been thinking about makin' some cornmeal dumplin's for the stew."

"Dumplin's!" Titus slipped his arm about Pink's waist and gave her a squeeze. "I haven't had cornmeal dumplin's since I was a barefoot boy running the hills in Virginia."

"How sweet are they?" Anne gave Jack a nudge. "Happy's the wooing that's not long a-doing."

Titus Gilmore was her oldest friend, and, together with Sally, they shared the memory of life under Peter Merrick's harsh rule. Titus was there to welcome her to her new home on her wedding day. Titus congratulated her the day her baby was born. He sat vigil with her the night her son died, and was at her side when Jemmy was buried. Titus's hand ran her press when she was too grief-stricken to even swing legs from bed, and Titus never hesitated to put his own life at risk to help save Jack from the gallows.

"You see?" Anne whispered in Jack's ear. "They can't keep their hands off each other . . ."

Taking Anne by the hand, Jack said, "You know, my coat has a hole in the pocket . . . Come on, I'll show you."

"Why do I have to go to the coat?" Anne complained, trotting along with him to the far corner where his coat hung on a peg. "I can't see anything in this light, much less a hole in a pocket . . ."

Gripping her hand tight, Jack pulled her behind the blanket hung to provide a modicum of privacy for the chamber pot, and pressed her up against the wall.

"I can't keep my hands from *you*," he whispered gruffly in her ear.

And Anne was swept into a kiss—the set-her-heart-racing sort of kiss so absent since they'd arrived at the encampment—the deep, hungry kind of kiss that made her leg rise up, and pull him close.

Jack groaned, pushing aside her shawl, nuzzling her neck, the two-day stubble on his cheeks scratching the soft mounds spilling up over her stays. He reached down and his hand found the way through layers of wool and flannel petticoats to the place between her legs.

A soft "Ohhh!" puffed out from her lips. Eyes squeezed tight, Anne clung to Jack's shoulders, and struggled to stifle her moan.

"I need the piss pot."

Eyes popped open, Anne could see young Jim, peeking around the edge of the curtain he'd pulled slightly aside.

Jack barked over his shoulder, "What?"

Jim blinked. "I *really* need the piss pot."

Anne pushed Jack away, breathing hard, and, with downcast eyes, she straightened her skirts.

"No." Jack tugged the curtain closed, and added, "Go find a tree."

Jim's stockinged feet were dancing beneath the bottom edge of the curtain. "Annie tolt us we catch the devil if we set foot out the door while under quarantine—"

"I did." Anne nodded. "I did tell him that."

Jim whined, "Would you have me piss my only pair of britches?"

"All right, use the piss pot." Jack thrust the curtain aside, and stomped away. Anne slipped out behind him, and Jim scampered behind the curtain, unbuttoning his britches. A moment later his stream was singing its way into the tin bucket.

Anne followed after Jack, hurrying across the room, suffering the smirks and giggles of their fellows at the fire.

"Goddamn it . . ." Jack flopped down to sit on Anne's bunk, chin in hands, his face a dark storm cloud. "A man can't even find a moment alone in the privy around here."

"You wouldn't be as rankled if Jim busted in on you *alone*," Titus pointed out.

"Set the piss pot outside the curtain next time," Brian chided. "That's how Titus does when he and Pink cuddle behind the curtain."

Dark brows met in two angry furrows, Jack announced with a wild wave of his arm, "This is why I'll never join the regular army!"

"You're not the only one who suffers, Jack Hampton," Sally said. "And all yer whining doesna change a thing."

Sitting beside Jack, Anne brushed the loose hair from his face, saying, "It's hard for me, too . . ."

"Not anymore it isn't," Sally called over her shoulder. Titus, Pink, and Brian all burst out laughing. Though the color rushed to her cheeks, Anne was happy to see Sally's ribaldry had eased Jack's clenched-jaw anger, and he, too, laughed along.

Swinging his legs up to lie flat on his back, Jack pulled Anne to lie beside him. He kissed the top of her hand and whispered, "We had more privacy living among the enemy than we find here in this camp. I miss those nights when I would scale the wall to your garret room . . . I want for us to have a night like that."

A sharp blast of wind whistled in through a gap between the logs, knocking a dried chunk of mud and moss chinking onto the bed. "That's a bad draft." Jack turned to rise up on his elbow, and began fiddling with the loose pieces to puzzle the chinking back into place.

Anne whispered to his back, "You know what I want? I want a home and hearth of our own . . ."

"You already have a home."

"This isn't a home."

Jack looked over his shoulder. "I meant the Cup and Quill—once we drive the British out, we can get married, move back to New York, set up shop, and get to work making a host of new Hamptons."

"Drive the British out!" Anne snorted. "You're measuring the cloth when the web isn't even on the loom."

"Ah, now, Annie . . ." Successful in plugging the draft, Jack laid back, lacing an arm around her shoulders. "You know there's talk of the French joining in the fight, and as bleak as it's been, there's still good hope for our cause."

"I don't care about the French. I'm tired of living no better than a tinker. I want a proper home with a husband in my bed, and children of our own to care for." Anne stared at the bed boards overhead, and whispered aloud the question so heavy on her mind the past weeks. "Haven't we done enough for the cause?"

"It's not something I can measure for you, Annie, but I'm in this thing whole heart to the end, no matter how bitter or sweet." Jack pulled her hand and pressed it to his chest. "I'd have you by my side, for it . . . but if you want, I suppose you could go back to Peekskill . . ."

"To my father?" Anne shuddered. "I'd rather make the collections for Mr. Binny's pus plate."

"Then have a little patience. Everyone is heartily sick of this war, including the British. We routed Burgoyne, and this summer's campaign will break the Crown's back. I know it . . . *Goddamn* this worthless chinking!"

The dried mud fell out once again, and the rumble of drums blew in with the icy air. Jack called to Titus, "Hear that? Sounds like they're beating the call to assemble."

Anne and Jack hopped onto their feet, and Titus was already donning his coat and running out the open door.

Sally stood wide-eyed, the shirt she'd been stitching in a tumble on the floor. "Could it be a call t' battle?"

The drums were getting louder and louder. Pink ran out after Titus, and, throwing on her cloak, she yelled over her shoulder, "Everyone's runnin' toward the parade ground."

Brian and Jim joined Anne and Jack at the open door. "Sounds like the whole drum line is out in force."

In no time, Pink and Titus were running back to the cabin. Waving her arms over her head, Pink shouted, "No attack!" Flying in through the doorway, she said, "I need a hat . . ."

"The army's assembling on the parade ground," Titus said, shutting the door. "They're drummin' some officer out of the camp."

"An officer!" Jim and Brian were practically jumping out of their pockmarked skins. Transgressing officers were rarely punished so publicly. "Which one?"

"I don't know," Titus said, tying his plain felt hat down with a woolly muffler. "But if anyone plans on going to watch, best bundle up. Don't let that sunshine fool you—it is jeezly cold out. The wind is a razor."

Brian turned to Anne. "Can I borrow your old shoes and coat?"

Jim jumped up. "I need to use your cloak, Sally."

"Are yiz both daft?" Sally shrugged into her Hessian coat. "Ye canna go prancing about all pocky-faced on the parade ground."

Anne swirled into her cloak. "Sally's right. You two have to stay put."

"No!" Jim stamped his stockinged foot.

Pink handed dumbfounded Brian a spoon. "Mind the stew."

Jack donned his overcoat and tricorn, and scrubbed the top of Jim's head. "We'll tell you all about it when we get back."

They joined the masses streaming to the call of the drums like farmhands to the dinner bell. Positioning themselves on a slight rise, as close as they could for a good view, they huddled together—Pink clung to Titus, Anne looped her arm through Jack's, and Sally nestled in between the two couples.

"I think we'll be within earshot," Jack shouted over the drums.

The scene on the parade ground was a combination of chaos and order. Drummers from every regiment were gathered into one massive band, and their music was so resounding, the sound seemed to penetrate up through the soles of Anne's feet to thrum in her breast. Thousands of soldiers scrambled into position, pushing and shuffling to form even ranks on the snow-packed field.

The effects of the recent supply train were evident. Many of the officers straightening the lines and several companies were sporting red coats and clean white breeches salvaged from the British supply ship. But seeing the entire army turned out made it clear the overall need far outweighed whatever was carried in from the ship, as most of the enlisted men were still lacking decent clothing and footwear.

The center of the field was the heart of order. General Washington and his brigade commanders sat in a row mounted on horseback, as still as statues, engulfed in vapor clouds snorted up from horse nostrils. Standing to the left of the commander in chief, with colors in full array, were the ranks of officers and soldiers serving with Washington's Life Guard, David among them.

"My David sparkles on parade," Sally boasted. "I'm glad I saw to polishing his buttons."

With one swoop of the drum major's sword the drumming ceased. The drum major turned and in a loud, clear voice read out the charges.

"At a General Court Martial whereof Colonel Tupper was President, Lieutenant Frederick Gotthold Enslin of Colonel Malcolm's Regiment was tried for attempting to commit . . ." The drum major hesitated. "For attempting to commit *sodomy*, with John Monhort, a soldier."

Though armed with foreknowledge of the Lieutenant's court-martial and admitted crime, hearing the charge read aloud, Anne could not help but join in the crowd's collective indrawn breath. But for the noise of the regimental colors snapping on the breeze, the parade ground was as quiet as a graveyard.

"Secondly," the drum major read, "for perjury in swearing to false accounts, the accused is found guilty of the charges exhibited against him, being breaches of Fifth Article, Eighteenth Section of the Articles of War, and do sentence him to be dismissed from the service with infamy. His Excellency, the Commander in Chief George Washington, approves the sentence and with abhorrence and detestation of such infamous crimes, orders Lieutenant Enslin to be drummed out of camp by all the drummers in the Army, never to return."

"I'm glad he's not sentenced to hanging," Anne said.

Jack said, "Many would prefer hanging than suffer being drummed out."

The drum major gave a signal, and, coming from behind the ranks of the Life Guard, Lieutenant Enslin was paraded out and presented to the High Command. Unbound, and dressed in a complete uniform with hat and shoes, the condemned Lieutenant presented a much better figure than when she'd seen him last.

The Lieutenant's regimental commander, Colonel Malcolm, marched forward to stand before him. "On your knees, sir," he ordered.

Malcolm began the drumming out by knocking Enslin's tricorn to the ground. Very methodically, using his short sword, the Colonel started at the shoulders, ripping and cutting away all signs of rank and regimental honor. Every single epaulet, decoration, and button taken from the Lieutenant's coat was thrown with utter disdain to the snow.

"Your sword, sir."

Enslin drew his weapon from its scabbard and the very quiet crowd gasped when Colonel Malcolm held it in gloved hands, and snapped the blade in two over his knee. "See to his dress," Malcolm ordered, tossing the broken halves away.

The drum major jerked Enslin's uniform coat off and, after turning it wrong side out, handed it back to the Lieutenant to don.

A pair of very young drummer boys, no older than Jim, stepped out from ranks and spun their drums to rest on their backs. The first boy slipped a halter over Enslin's head, and the second pinned a fluttering sheet of foolscap to his back.

Pink asked, "What does it say?"

"Hard to make it out," Titus answered. "But it can't be nothing good."

The drum corps began beating a slow, ominous tattoo, and the little drummer boy jerked Enslin's halter, and tugged him up to his feet.

."A funeral dirge," Jack noted.

To the sad music, the little drummer led the disgraced man before all the ranks, as if he were a rare beast on display, first from right to left—then left to right. Enslin bore this indignity with shoulders back, head high, and eyes forward, focused on some distant horizon. The wind plastered the paper sign to his back, and the message was clear for all who knew how to read the big black letters—SODOMITE.

The drum major signaled again and the drum corps struck up the "Rogue's March." The little drummer boy turned to lead the Lieutenant off the parade ground, followed by the drums. The ranks were dismissed, and entire crowd followed along, many of the soldiers running ahead to fling snowballs and insults Enslin's way.

Jack shook his head. "The last time I heard this tune was when the mob knocked down the statue of King George down on the Bowling Green. This pitiful fellow doesn't appear to be in the same league, does he?"

Anne said, "My heart aches for him. He's a very nice man."

"He is?" Jack asked.

Anne nodded. "He's the officer who helped me to find the boys in quarantine. I was so upset—in tears—and he was more than kind to me."

"What's become of the other fellow—the one he dallied with?" Titus asked.

Sally said, "Run off afore he could be arrested."

Jack watched Enslin. "The punishment seems out of balance. His partner in this crime was a willing participant. This fellow didn't desert, or thieve, or plunder . . . and from what I've heard, if he hadn't forgotten to pull the latchstring in, all would still consider him a model officer."

Marching to the solemn dirge, the little drummer led Enslin all the way to Sullivan's Bridge crossing over the Schuylkill. Cutting the man from his halter, the drummer boy issued one last indignity, sending the banished Lieutenant from camp with a hard kick in the backside and with orders to never return.

The crowd cheered, and let fly a barrage of snowballs to rain down as Enslin ran full speed across the bridge without a backward glance.

"Flog the bloody bugger."

"Bugger the bloody bugger!"

"Hang him!"

A gang of jeering soldiers ran up on the bridge, shouting and throwing snowballs, and when their target disappeared out of range, they began flinging them at one another.

Sally grabbed Anne by the forearm and pointed. "Look there— th' tall soldier—th' one wearin' a Third Yorkers coat—I swear he's sportin' the shirt you made for Brian."

Anne studied the fellow Sally pointed out, and as he swung around to pitch a snowball, she caught sight of the familiar green-striped flannel petticoat she'd sacrificed, peeking up above the edge of his weskit.

"The thief!" Anne said.

Jack asked, "Are you certain?"

"I'm positive."

"What do you want to do?" Titus eyed the soldier. "He got his mates around him."

"I don't care." Jack handed Anne his hat. "I'll knock him down, Titus. You keep the others at bay."

Titus put his hat and muffler in Pink's care. "Let's go!"

They ran full speed, straight for the thief. Jack plowed into the fellow, knocking him flat to the snow. Titus didn't have to do much more than look fierce with fists clenched, and announce, "This man's a clothes thief!" to deter any interference from the gathering crowd as Jack sat with his knee dug into the man's gut, and tugged a fistful of green-striped flannel tight at his throat.

Anne came running up with Pink and Sally. "That's it—that's my petticoat!"

Titus said, "This rascal's also wearing the gaiters I made for Brian."

"Give over—the shirt, the gaiters . . ." Jack jumped up and delivered a swift kick to the ribs. "Along with anything else you stole, you fucking thief."

Curled in a ball, the soldier coughed and sputtered, "I din't steal nothin', mister—God strike me blind if I'm not tellin' the truth." With difficulty, he sat up to remove the gaiters, his fingers trembling with cold or fear, fumbling on the buttons. "I paid in hard silver for both this shirt and these gaiters. Ask Theo there; he'll tell ye—I paid an officer two shillings for 'em—I never thieved."

"I tell you what," Jack said, snatching the gaiters from his hand. "Give me the name and regiment of the man who sold these thieved goods to you, and you can keep the shirt."

"I'll gladly take that deal, mister." The soldier rose up to his feet. "Lieutenant William Williams, Thirteenth Virginia—he be the scoundrel yer looking for. My word on it." The soldier offered Jack his hand. "I hope you wallop the bejesus out o' the bastard."

Anne hiked her skirts and took the stairs two at a time. She marched right into the first door on the left without knocking and said, "David Peabody, tell me it isn't true."

David looked up from a table scattered with papers and ledgers, shaking his head. "Oh no . . . You're not allowed up here without authorization . . ."

Anne folded her arms. "Just tell me it isn't true, and I'll be on my merry way."

Footsteps pounded up the staircase and the breathless old sentry poked his head in the doorway. "Paid me no mind, Cap'n. I tried to stop her, but she squittered right past."

"My apologies, sentry. Rest assured, nothing short of a round from your musket could stop my sister when she has her mind set on plaguing me. You can return to your post." David leaned back in his chair. "I told you, Annie—I have no control over these matters."

Anne slapped her hands down on his desk. "You have to do something! A most vile thief—an officer, no less—preying on young soldiers in such a vicious way is charged with ungentlemanly conduct? This cannot stand."

"What does the charge matter? Williams has been tried and cashiered from service. Justice is served."

"By what wicked design is this considered justice? Williams has walked out of this camp, la-di-da, the silver realized from the sale of his thievery jingling in his pocket, while poor Lieutenant Enslin was humiliated and vilified before thousands for a crime that harmed no one. Where's the justice in that?"

David leaned to his left, looking beyond his sister, and said, "Yes, Billy?"

A stocky black man dressed in powdered wig, feathered tricorn, and Continental blue and buff stepped into David's office. "The General kindly asks to see you and yo' sistuh in the dining hall, presently."

"My sister?" David repeated, pushing up to a stand.

Billy nodded. "Yessuh. General's order."

"Wonderful." David limped around the table donning hat and muffler, staring daggers at Anne, and gave her a little shove toward the door. "G'won. Now we're in for it."

Anne shoved him back. "I didn't do anything!"

"You came up here and caused a rumpus, didn't you?"

Billy chuckled, and led them down the stairs and out the back door to the new annex cabin everyone had taken to calling the "dining hall." Bigger than the standard cabin, the dining hall boasted two windows cut into the log walls on either side of the doorway, fitted with leaded panes of crown glass. It was hard to make out anything through the blurry, frosted panes but the fuzzy bright spots of light from lanterns and candles.

Mounted on brass hinges, the door swung open easily, and Anne stepped onto a plank floor to find Sally sitting on a chair beside the door. She looked up from twisting her mittens in a knot. Her face was as white as a floured piecrust and she answered the unasked question, "We dinna ken why we were summoned."

Jack and Titus stood beside Sally, and Jack whispered, "What's this about, David?"

David shrugged, shaking his head. "I don't know."

"I expect we'll find out soon enough." Titus waggled his brow in the direction of General Washington sitting at the end of a long dining table in a pool of light, methodically adding his signature to sheet after sheet of paper. Without glancing up from his task the General said, "I'll be with you and your party in a moment, Captain Peabody."

"Yes, sir." David stepped forward, doffing his tricorn with a sweep and, tucking it under his arm, he stood at ease with hands clasped behind his back.

The fire snapped and hissed, burning in a huge fireplace backed with cast-iron plates. Anne shuffled over to stand beside Jack, and unwound her muffler.

The General was positioned close to the fire, the varnished table he worked at surrounded with ten padded chairs. A large matching sideboard took up the wall to the left of the hearth, where Billy was busy ladling hot cider spiced with cloves and cinnamon from a steaming kettle into a crockery pitcher.

Washington set down his quill and stood up, gesturing for them all to come forward. Anne was surprised to see he was taller than Jack and Titus, who were always among the tallest in a crowd. Though she'd seen the General before on horseback and about the camp, his stature was even more imposing within the confines of four walls, and a bit intimidating.

The General came out from behind the table to greet them, shaking hands first with Jack and Titus. "Mr. Hampton, Mr. Gilmore—good to see you both well and working hard for our cause. The shipment from Wilmington was much appreciated." Washington turned and greeted Anne and Sally with a bow. "Mrs. Merrick, Miss Tucker, your facility so aptly demonstrated when entrenched amongst the enemy has proven most beneficial to your country."

Washington moved to the free end of the table, calling David to sit with him on one side, and indicating for the rest to take seats opposite. Lacing the fingers of his large hands, he announced, "I will go straight to the heart of the matter. I must call upon you all to once again enter into dangerous service."

Sally groaned, and Anne felt as if a toad had landed in her belly. Beneath the table, Jack took her by the hand.

"We are at a decided disadvantage, operating with so little intelligence, our army is not best prepared to face the British in campaign. Your country needs you, and I ask you all to go and ply your considerable skills in Philadelphia—setting up an operation similar to the one that served so well in New York."

Anne kept her eyes focused on the beautifully beveled edge of the table, afraid to speak the answer that leapt to her lips. *No. No, no, no . . .*

For what seemed the longest time, not a one of them uttered a word, until Sally very softly said, "I've never been to Philadelphia."

Anne looked up. "I don't know if we would realize any success, General. Philadelphia is much bigger than New York—and New York was home." Anne looked to Jack, shaking her head. "We don't know a soul there . . ."

"The Quaker's in Philadelphia." Jack shrugged. "He could help us."

"Mrs. Loring is there, Anne," David added. "You could reestablish your ties with Howe's mistress . . ."

"And running a coffeehouse, you'll be making social connections," Washington said.

Anne blinked, overwhelmed by the whole proposition. "You mean for us to open a coffeehouse?"

The General nodded. "I will be making funds available to set up the entire operation."

Sally worried, "B-but what's to become of our young lads?"

"And Pink?" Anne added. "You don't want to leave Pink behind, do you, Titus?"

"I don't see why she shouldn't come with." Titus folded his arms. "She'd be a help."

"Captain Peabody will be in charge, and I'm sure all accommodations can be made to satisfy the operation needs." Sensing her resistance, Washington added, "I expect the assignment will be a short one, Mrs. Merrick, three or four months at most, until we retake the city."

Jack squeezed her hand. "That's not so bad . . ."

"Like old times, Annie, na?" Sally leaned in to bump shoulders.
Anne nodded, fighting back her tears.

Billy set down a tray bearing the pitcher of hot cider, eight punch cups, and a cut crystal decanter half-full of amber-hued liquid. Washington poured a good amount of spirits into the pitcher. "Whiskey from my plantation at Mount Vernon—warms the belly and the brain," he said, flashing a rare smile. "We have a fine distillery there, do we not, Billy?"

"Very fine," Billy agreed, taking the pitcher to pour out eight cupfuls of hot punch.

The General held up his cup. "Can we drink on our new venture?"

Jack, Titus, and David were quick to take up their cups and stand. Sally joined them

Anne heaved a sigh and rose to her feet. Reaching across the table to tap Washington's cup, she said, "I expect to see you, very soon, General, in Philadelphia."

Part Three

PHILADELPHIA

On our brow while we laurel-crowned liberty wear,
What Englishmen ought, we Americans dare!
Though tempests and terrors around us we see
Bribes nor fears can prevail o'er hearts that are
FREE.
Hearts of oak we are still;
For we're sons of those men
Who always are ready—
Steady, boys, steady—
To fight for their freedom again and again.

HEARTS OF OAK, Author Unknown

Sasafras or Race Street

Mulberry or Arch Street

Seventh Street
Sixth Street
Fifth Street
Fourth Street
Third Street
Second Street
Front Street

B

G

D

High or Market Street

E

N

Chestnut Street

A

Walnut Street

H

C

**British Occupied
Philadelphia 1778**

A The Cup and Book
B Hadley's Engraving
C The Darragh House
D The White Swan
E The Penn Mansion
F Southwark Theatre
G Dressmaker's Shop
H Edw. Shippen Mansion

Spruce Street

Pine Street

F

South or Cedar Street

❧ FIFTEEN ❧

The larger we make the circle, the more we shall harmonize,
and the stronger we shall be.

THOMAS PAINE, *The American Crisis*

IN BRITISH-OCCUPIED PHILADELPHIA
NO. 177, ON THE EAST SIDE OF SECOND STREET

Walter Darragh followed the golden arc cast by the beeswax taper in the candle dish he carried, wandering down the hallway in nightshirt and cap, his felt slippers *whoosh*ing along on the waxed floorboards. He called out quietly, "Lydia?"

With no answer forthcoming he moved on, turning the doorknob to his eldest son Daniel's empty bedchamber. In mobcap, chemise, and woolen night jacket, his wife sat on the floor in the moonlit room, crouched like a tree toad, scratching away with a graphite pencil on a loose sheet of paper.

Walter whispered, "Wife . . ."

Lydia looked up, her pretty face framed by the ruffled edge of her mobcap. With blue eyes wide, she pressed the tip of her index finger to her lips. "Shhh . . ."

"Enough." Walter took a step into the room. "I'd have thee come to bed."

Whispering, "Will thee hush?" the tiny woman tugged off her

mobcap and curled down to lie with ear pressed to the floorboards. Lydia's hair, plaited in a single braid for sleep, slithered over her shoulder like a viper on the hunt.

From the floor below Walter could hear the squawk and scrape of chairs being pushed back from their family dining table, and the accompanying deep rumble of male voices. He near leapt from his skin, and Lydia bolted upright at the sudden loud knock on their door.

Folding her page, she stuffed it and the pencil under the mobcap pulled back onto her head, and waved her husband off. "Go! See what they want."

Walter unbolted the lock and swung the door open to a British officer standing on the landing.

"We're finished for the night, Mr. Darragh . . ." The Captain fit his tricorn on his head. "It seems Lieutenant Croker's taken off with my keys—would it be too much of a bother for you to douse the lights, and lock the door behind us?"

"No bother, Captain Lockhart." Walter could feel his wife's little hand rest light between his shoulder blades as she drew beside him, yawning and rubbing feigned sleep from her eyes.

The Captain swept his hat off. "Sorry to have disturbed you, Mrs. Darragh. I know the hour is very late."

"Not to worry, Captain—I was meaning to have a word with thee by and by . . ." Lydia Darragh clutched her night jacket closed with the flat of her fist pressed over heart. "I was thinking about having Polly wax the floors . . . The boots are taking a toll. Do you think thee'll be using our room again on the morrow?"

"We will." Lockhart nodded his head in the affirmative. "I'm afraid General Howe has called a council meeting for the afternoon."

"Very well." Lydia smiled. "The waxing will wait for another day, then."

Walter bid Captain Lockhart good night. He waited in the doorway until he heard the downstairs door click shut before turning to his wife.

"Lydia, I find thy eavesdropping unsavory, and now I hear thy tongue speaking words unplain."

"Walter ..." Lydia Darragh smiled. Rising up on tiptoes, she pulled him down to meet her soft kiss, and she whispered in his ear, "Go lock the door, husband, then hurry thee back to warm my bed . . . Are these words plain enough?"

THE WHITE SWAN INN ON FRONT STREET NEAR THE FERRY SLIP

With a laundry basket full of clean linen propped on her hip, Bede Seaborn was just about to give a customary tap before resorting to her keys, when the chamber door flew open on its own accord. With his tricorn slapped haphazard on the back of his head, waistcoat unbuttoned, buckling on his cross belt, Major Nicholas Sutherland came near to bowling Mrs. Seaborn over. Barking, "See to the muddle in my chamber," over his shoulder, he thundered down the stairs.

Of the six Redcoat officers quartered at her inn, Major Sutherland was not only the most callous of the lot, but also the one most prone to having a lie-in and leaving his chamber in an awful mess.

"And a good day t' you, Major Sutherland . . ." the innkeeper cheerfully called, then added a muttered, ". . . you lazy-arsed bastard." Stepping over the threshold to find her chambermaid slipping into her chemise and frantically gathering up the rest of her clothes from the mess on the floor, Bede sighed. "Oh, Nell . . ."

The girl stood upright. Doe eyes wide and blinking, she stuttered, "I—I was just about bringing in the water jug, Mrs. Seaborn, but the Major . . ."

"Have you not a bit of mother's wit?" Bede shook her head. "The man's a rogue through and through. He'll leave you with naught but a babe in your belly and a broken heart . . ."

"He's not like that." Nell plucked at a pinchbeck locket pinned to the blue ribbon tied around her neck. "See? He gave me this. He cares for me. I know he does."

Bede set her basket down beside the bed and said, "Very nice, but you know the devil always baits his hook with all manner of pretties when he goes fishing."

Defiance straightened Nell's spine and colored her cheeks a bright pink. With complete conviction she said, "I love him." Snatching up her things, the girl rushed out into the hall, bare feet pounding up the stairs to the garret.

Bede heaved a sad sigh, and muttered, "There are none so deaf as those who will not hear."

Swinging the door shut, the innkeeper whisked the heavy draperies from the window and took in the clear blue sky over the shimmering Delaware. *Winter is getting ready to turn the corner to spring.* On a day like this her husband would have cajoled her into a walk along the river, or a picnic on the wharf, and it was on days like this she missed her Rob the most. *A great one for spring, he was.*

Humming a cheery tune, Bede stripped the bedclothes from the bed. She rolled the mattress up, and gave the bedcords a good tightening. After plumping the pillows, she stuffed them into starched pillow slips, and snapped crisp, clean sheets over the mattress.

Sweeping the ashes from the stove, she set the ash bin outside the door for Nell to collect. After tossing the contents of the washbasin out onto the street, Bede stood for a moment and considered the mess left on the washstand.

"Careless . . ." Bede grumbled. "Heedless, they are, these Redcoats."

The Major's shaving kit was left to flounder in a sudsy mess. Bede hung the leather strop on the hook provided, fit the lid onto the silver lather bowl, and rescued the ivory-handled razor from a puddle, folding it shut. Whipping out the scrap of old flannel she had tucked under her apron strings, she wiped up the washstand and the puddle on the floor, then turned with arms akimbo to contemplate the chaos of the Major's campaign chest.

"You'd think a whirlwind'd come through here . . ."

The doors of the chest hung open. All manner of contents spilled forth from the extended and near-empty drawers, as the majority of the Major's clothing lay on the floorboards in a jumble. Bede dove in, humming along to the tune playing in her head as she set about pairing up stockings and gaiters. She folded shirts, neck stocks, and monogrammed handkerchiefs, all the while intently eyeing the papers the Major had left scattered on top of his chest.

Once the gear was all properly stowed, Bede gathered the Major's papers, methodically reviewing and piling all but one of the pages into a single stack centered on the polished mahogany. She dropped this segregated page to the very bottom of her laundry basket, and plopped the soiled bedclothes on top. All smiles, Mrs. Seaborn scooped up her basket and bustled out the door, almost trampling young Nell, who'd come to collect the ash bin.

"My soul and senses, Nell! You're like to give me apoplexy, sneaking up on a body thataway." She hoisted her basket onto her hip. "I'm off to run errands. Once you finish the rest of the rooms, see to putting a shine on Major Sutherland's windows."

"Yes'm," Nell agreed with a smile and a slight curtsy.

"Good girl." Bede was glad to see there was to be no bad blood between them. Trotting down the stairs, she heard Nell singing the words to the catchy little tune Bede'd been humming all morning—

> *A fox may steal your hens, sir,*
> *A whore your health and pence, sir,*
> *Your daughter may rob your chest, sir,*
> *Your wife may steal your rest, sir,*
> *A thief your goods and plate.*

THE CUP AND BOOK COFFEEHOUSE ON CHESTNUT NEAR THIRD

Anne drew the key ring from the pocket of her new day dress, calling out, "I'm opening up!"

"We're ready!" Sally answered, bustling through the open back door burdened with two steaming coffee urns. Pink scurried from the kitchen house as well, carrying a tray piled high with scones, sweet biscuits, and loaves of gingerbread baked fresh that morning.

Sally set the heavy urns on the grate in the huge fireplace centered on the long wall. Pink arranged her tray on one of the sideboards at the back of the room, and went out to fetch the rest.

The doorbell jangled continuously, and chairs scraped on the floor-boards as the breakfast crowd came in to take their seats, the tables closest to the hearth being the first to fill. Wearing matching blue tur-bans and striped aprons, Sally and Pink bounced from table to table, serving hot drinks and the sweet bites to go with. Anne noted with much satisfaction the numerous Redcoats filling the chairs in her es-tablishment. Open for business for less than a month, the Cup and Book was a great success.

She snatched up a few newspapers and went to collect a plate of cookies from the sideboard, where she and Sally met in a whisper.

"These Redcoats swarm to your sweets like bees unhived."

"Aye." Sally grinned. "And where there're bees, there's honey."

Armed with a pretty plate of cookies, Anne reconnoitered the room, touching a shoulder here, giving a nod there. "Good morning, Captain Avery—Lieutenant Silk. Please try one of Pink's mackeroons, gratis," she said, placing a cookie on each officer's plate. "Baked fresh this morning and light as a feather . . ." She tapped a shoulder adorned with fringed gold epaulet, offering the copy of the *London Gazette* tucked under her arm. "I was saving this for you, Colonel. The latest news come in on the packet docked yestereve."

Anne paid a higher rent for the narrow two-story building on Chestnut Street, the location so perfect for their requirements, she deemed it was worth the extra cost. In the heart of the city, the store-front had belonged to a Patriot silversmith, who'd quit the city when the British occupied. There were only three tiny bedchambers and a small parlor up the stairs, but Anne saw this as a bonus, eliminating all possibility of being forced to quarter any of the twenty-three thou-sand Redcoat soldiers and sundry wives and children occupying the city—something she was desperate to avoid at all cost. The kitchen-house came with a fully equipped cook hearth and an oven where Sally and Pink could work their magic. Best of all, there was a deep well in the garden providing excellent clean water, fewer than ten paces from the kitchen door.

Once the lease was secured, Anne saw to furnishing and supplying the business. What seemed such an obstacle amid the privation at the encampment in Valley Forge proved not to pose a problem in the occupied city. Philadelphian docks and warehouses burgeoned with trade goods, and she was able to procure with ease the finest coffee and cocoa berries. Black bohea and sugar of all types were plentiful. Establishing good relationships with reliable miller, milkman, egg man, and butter woman at market stalls on High Street was made simple when orders were paid for in advance with Spanish silver supplied by General Washington.

To draw the desired military clientele, the Cup and Book offered a convenient, friendly, warm shop serving quality fare, at reasonable cost—not cheap enough to attract riffraff regulars, but not so dear as to put too big a pinch on an officer's pocket. As an additional lure, Anne paid a premium for the latest newspapers and magazines arriving weekly from London—news from home made available to her customers free of charge.

Anne also devoted a good portion of their funds to developing a lending library, stocked with novels and other books of interest. When she set about painting the shingle to hang out on the lane, she added a flourish to curry the custom of literary gentlemen in the officer ranks. Under the image of a steaming cup centered over an open volume, she'd written the Latin motto *Liber amicus*: A book is a friend.

In the lull after the morning rush, Anne poured herself a cup of chocolate, and took a seat on a stool behind the counter she kept in front of the pair of shelves housing the lending library at the back of the shop. She exhumed a stack of receipts and her ledger, pen, and inkwell to work on the accounts. Anne added to the various columns, still somewhat amazed by the speed with which they had fallen into the routine of running a coffeehouse and a spy ring.

The Redcoats trained us well, Anne thought. *Made us experts at striking one tent, and pitching another on new ground . . .*

With the coffeehouse on firm footing, she decided it was time to take the next step, and delve deeper into Philadelphian military society. Today was the day she planned to pay a teatime call on Mrs. Betsy Loring, General Howe's mistress, and an acquaintance from the days she and Sally worked for the tailor's ring in New York.

Pink came over to the counter and mentioned, "There's an ugly fella over at the window with his eye on you."

"Where?" Anne looked up, scanning the room.

Pink turned. "Oh . . ." She shrugged. "He's gone now."

Anne gathered up her receipts. "When you have a moment, can you make up a pretty package of your mackeroons for me to bring along on my call this afternoon? Betsy Loring has a terrible sweet tooth."

Pink smiled. "Be happy to, Annie."

Adding Pink to the mix proved a boon beyond Anne's expectations. Not only did she lend an extra pair of able and hardworking hands in cleaning, cooking, and shopping, but Anne came to realize those who've suffered in bound servitude made for the most accomplished spies. The ability to hover inconspicuous and eavesdrop was ingrained in Pink from childhood. Favored with sharp ears and eyes, and an agile mind, she possessed a keen instinct for gleaning important fragments of information from ongoing conversations. Not being able to read or write was her only shortfall, and together, Anne and Sally would work to see it rectified.

The doorbell rang, and Anne glanced up from her accounts. A smile flashed across her face to see the small woman in plain dress with book in hand step briskly to her counter. Anne hopped from her stool. "Good morning, Mrs. Darragh! Did you enjoy the book?"

"Good morning, Anne Merrick—I did."

Anne noted the Quakeress's greeting and remembered how Friends did not use titles of any sort. Lydia Darragh set the volume titled *She Stoops to Conquer* on the countertop, the irony of the gilt letters vivid on the green polished calf not lost on either of them the week before, when Anne recommended the book.

"Not anything like my usual reading, but in truth, I enjoyed thy book immensely." Lydia smiled within her starched white bonnet, her eyes as bright as blue glass buttons. "Does thee have another, along similar lines?"

Anne slipped the little green book into her pocket, and turned to search her shelves, amused by the Quaker woman's budding penchant for bawdy comedy. "I know just the thing . . ." She tugged a thin book bound in blue morocco from the top shelf, and handed it to Lydia. "*The Rivals*—a play added recently to the library. I haven't read it, but the bookseller tells me the story is quite humorous."

Lydia signed the lending ledger in a precise round hand to check out *The Rivals*. "This is light reading. I expect I'll return thy book to thee on Sixth Day."

Anne questioned, "Sixth Day?"

"In plain speech," Lydia explained, "today is Third Day, Anne Merrick."

"Oh! I see." Anne nodded, calculating to Friday from the offered reference point. "I'll see you then, Lydia Darragh, on Sixth Day."

"Good day, Friend Anne."

Putting her ledger away, Anne went to find Sally in the kitchen house. "I'm going upstairs," she said, and, using a brand to light a candle, she patted her pocket. "A delivery from Mrs. Darragh."

Sally smiled. "Regular as clockwork, our Quakeress."

Anne carried the candle up the stairs. Shutting the door behind her, she set the candle on her desk, and flung herself down onto the bed to take a breath and a moment to enjoy the curious pattern cast by sunlight playing through the lace curtains.

After months of living either under canvas or in a dirt-floor log hut, she relished every minute in her little room. Despite the initial resistance given to the General's request that they set up shop in Philadelphia, she no longer regretted the move—especially on the nights when Jack let himself in through the back door with the extra key she'd given him.

Enough woolgathering . . . Anne sat up and pulled the book from her pocket. She flipped through to the folded sheet of foolscap in the center. Listed on it, in Lydia's neat round hand, were the highlights from the most recent council meeting held in the dining room the British Army appropriated from the Darragh family.

As usual, Anne thought, laying out her writing supplies, *the least likely make for the best spies.*

She was struck dumb the day the tiny Quaker woman came into the Cup and Book the first week they were in operation, wanting to borrow a copy of *Gulliver's Travels*—the prearranged signal David devised for use by the loose network of Patriot spies already operating in the occupied city. The Quakers were renowned for their strict adherence to pacifism and neutral stance in the war against the Crown, and Anne found it very odd indeed for Friend Lydia to be part of their spying operation.

To her right, Anne set the bottle of new invisible ink General Washington had supplied for their mission. Unlike the hartshorn ink, which was brought to the eye when put to the heat of a candle, the words written in the new ink could be made visible only with the use of a secret, counterpart chemical agent. Anne appreciated the added security provided for their dangerous correspondence, and she liked to imagine Billy, in his white wig and persnick uniform, brushing the "sympathetic stain," as the General had called it, onto her messages, bringing the hidden secrets to light.

Anne slipped the page she'd transcribed in invisible ink into a slim leather wallet, and put Lydia's original notes to the candle flame, dropping the burning page into a tin bucket she kept for the purpose. A soft tap on the door was followed by Sally's voice calling, "It's me."

"Come in," Anne replied, watching the damning page go to ashes.

"A busy day today, na?" Sally dropped a copy of the *Royal Gazette* on the desk. "The innkeeper's widow came through th' garden gate, asking me to bring this Tory rag up to ye."

Anne flipped to the center of the newspaper and found the sheet Bede Seaborn had inserted, a letter written in a loose and careless hand, rife with scratched-out words and dappled with ink blots.

"This Major Sutherland has the penmanship of a six-year-old . . ." Anne took the page to the window to decipher the mundane letter the

Major wrote to his father in England. Coming to the last paragraph, she looked up and asked Sally, "Is Bede waiting in the shop?"

"Where she might be forced to part with coin? Na . . ." Sally shook her head. "Pink set her up in the kitchen with a mug of chocolate and full plate of mackeroons." Hovering at Anne's elbow, she asked, "What is it, Annie?"

"Important news. Sutherland says General Howe plans on resigning his post, and returning to England. Clinton is slated to take over as commander in chief." Anne reinserted the page. "Information worth a dozen mackeroons at least."

Sally said, "Th' sort of news best not put to paper, Annie."

"Agreed." Anne nodded and handed the newspaper to Sally. "Return this to Mrs. Seaborn—she must be anxious to put the letter back in its place—then send Pink up. She's for this errand."

THE WORKSHOP OF ELBERT HADLEY, MASTER ENGRAVER, ON THE CORNER OF EIGHTH AND SASSAFRAS

Examining the space between the rollers, Jack gave the screw the slightest twist. "Give the wheel a half-turn," he said, watching the action of the works as Titus turned the big wheel on the engraving press.

"I think it's good," Jack declared. "Let's pull a sheet and see how it prints."

At the front of the workshop, with burins in hand, seated on tall stools, Jim and Brian bent over their work, glancing now and then to the illustration of a long-eared owl in the open volume lying between them, incising copies of the image onto eight-inch-square copper plates.

"Remember to maintain control over the depth of your line . . ." Strolling slowly around the long table with a little black-and-white mongrel carried in the crook of his arm, Elbert Hadley rubbed the dog's bony topknot, his voice as calm as blue water. "The deeper the line, the deeper the tone. Lighter line—lighter hand."

Seeing the boys apply their drawing skill to a trade pleased Jack to no end. Clean, well fed, and well clothed, both Jim and Brian flourished under Elbert's patient tutelage, and were dedicated to learning an honest and valuable trade from a master in the art of engraving.

Elbert dropped the thick-lens spectacles resting on the top of his bald pate to perch at the bulbous end of his nose, and bent down to inspect the boys' progress. "You've got it, Jim. Perhaps a little more detail about the tail feathers?" the engraver encouraged, selecting a tool from his kit. "Very good, Brian. Very good—but use the proper tool for the proper task—don't forget to make use of the Florentine liner for your fill work."

It's a good thing Elbert was able to make a place for us here . . . Jack was happy to be immersed once again in the smell of ink and wet paper, working with his hands at something more than cleaning the lock on his rifle, or manufacturing bullets. In exchange for the roof over their heads, and the boys' informal apprenticeship, he and Titus were glad to pitch in and help however they could, from presswork to chopping firewood. Elbert Hadley welcomed them into his home and business with open arms, happy for the help and company, and thrilled to be once again in good service to the cause of Liberty.

They first met the odd little engraver in British-occupied New York, where he joined the well-oiled machine of spies and smugglers organized by tailor Hercules Mulligan. Elbert had provided the expertly engraved plates for the failed counterfeiting scheme that ended with Patsy Quinn dead, Jack near hanged, and their escape from New York.

It was Mulligan who dubbed the little engraver "the Quaker"—the nickname based on his hailing from Philadelphia. No matter how often the gentle little man protested, "I'm not a Quaker; I'm a Deist," they all continued to call him the Quaker. He bore this mis-moniker in good humor, but now that they were in the land of true Quakers, the nickname seemed silly.

Elbert suits him better.

Jack called to Titus, "Toss over the small mallet . . ."

Copperplate engraving and printing was a specialty business. Elbert was employed directly by Philadelphia's book and news printers to provide the copperplate-engraved pages to be included in larger works, and his considerable skill was in high demand.

The engraver's location on the edge of town and the cover of legitimate employment proved perfect for relaying the gathered intelligence to David and Alan McLane, whose duties kept them on horseback in the countryside beyond the outskirts of the city.

Good thing Annie agreed to come to Philadelphia . . . The assignment in Philadelphia suited everyone better than the rough existence in the winter camp, and gave them opportunity to gather the intelligence Washington needed, and maybe help bring about the end to the war sooner than later.

The doorbell rang, and the engraver scurried out of the workroom to the small storefront area at the front of the house. The door barely clicked shut behind him before Elbert came bustling back into the workshop with Pink in tow.

Jack jumped up. "What's happened to Anne?"

"Don't fret. She's fine," Pink said, throwing back her hood. "She's paying a call on that Loring lady, and the news I come with can't wait." She set her heavy basket on the table, and other than flashing a beautiful smile Titus's way, Pink was all business. Clasping her hands together, she recited, "An important message from a reliable source. General Howe is to resign his post and return to England in May. General Clinton will be assigned as the new Commander-in-Chief in America."

"Clinton!" Jack was not pleased with this news. He encountered this particular general back when he infiltrated the British attack force on Long Island, and Sir Henry Clinton was one of few British officers who would recognize him for a rebel spy on sight. He rolled his sleeves down, buttoning the cuffs. "Who's the source?"

"A letter writ by Major Sutherland, brought in by Bede Seaborn, the innkeeper's widow from the White Swan. There's more . . ." From her basket, Pink produced a ream of writing paper wrapped and tied with blue grosgrain ribbon. "Page fifty-four is news from the Quaker woman, written in the most secret ink."

"We'll go." Brian popped up from his seat; as much as he enjoyed his lessons, he was always keen for adventure of any sort.

"No. You two will stay with Elbert. Me and Titus can handle this delivery."

Titus asked, "Farmers?"

Jack nodded. "Let's get the pushcart ready."

THE PENN MANSION, ON SIXTH AND MARKET

"Anne Merrick! My stars and body!" Merry blue eyes a-sparkle, Betsy Loring skipped down the stairs to the entry hall, greeting Anne with a beautiful smile and a kiss on each cheek. "Come. You *must* join us for tea."

"It is so good to see you, Betsy, but I don't want to intrude. I only thought to leave my card . . ."

"Don't be a noodle!" Looping an arm through hers, Betsy led Anne up the stairway. "You cannot imagine how happy I am to see you here in Philadelphia. I was very worried about you, my dear, after that awful incident at your shop in New York . . ."

"Please . . ." Anne squeezed Betsy's hand, and heaved a little trembling sigh. "So terrible—the threat to my safety sent me flying to live with my father in Peekskill."

"William and I were so concerned. But living with your father . . ." Betsy cringed. "Almost as bad as having to cohabitate with Mr. Loring!"

Anne did not pretend her sympathetic shudder. Joshua Loring was an odious Loyalist opportunist who willingly traded his wife's favors to General Howe in exchange for a lucrative post. As Commissary of Prisons in New York, he was responsible, together with the Provost, for the inhumane treatment of the Patriot prisoners of war. Betsy never bothered to disguise the disdain she bore her husband.

"Let's talk of pleasant things." Anne turned the conversation to Mrs. Loring's favorite subject. "How are you? Are you enjoying your stay in Philadelphia?"

"No, I miss New York . . . I cannot abide all of these plain folk lurking about all brown and gray—so morose." Anything but plain, Betsy Loring wore a perfectly fitted gown of rose-colored Italian wool. Her golden blond hair was gathered with a matching ribbon in a soft chignon at the back of her neck. The soles of her blue silk slippers tapped lightly on the marbled treads as they moved toward the second floor. "I am required to dance in attendance on these local Loyalists and their simpering, simpleton daughters. Ugh!" Betsy continued, "Only this morning I said to the General—I said, Billy, between you, me, and the bedpost, I frankly prefer it when society names me whore, and leaves me to my Faro table."

"You are incorrigible!" Anne laughed. She admired Betsy's forthright manner, a desirable trait in the person who was her direct link to the most powerful Englishman on the Continent. A self-centered, ambitious woman, Elizabeth Loring never allowed wagging tongues or provincial sensibilities to prevent her from fully enjoying her position as consort to the commander in chief of the British forces.

Betsy stopped at the top of the stairs and whispered, "The daughter of the Chief Justice, and the daughter of a member of the Provincial Council." Anne followed behind as she swept into the drawing room.

It was a bright and cheerful room, with immense double-hung windows facing Market Street. The plaster walls were painted a pleasant shade of marigold, trimmed with crown and skirting boards enameled bright white. Two young women sat together on a blue brocade settee, thick as a pair of inkle weavers, whispering and giggling. A beautiful silver tea service was arranged on a low table between the settee and a pair of chairs upholstered in a deeper blue.

"I see our tea has arrived!" Betsy made the introductions: "Miss Peggy Shippen and Miss Peggy Chew of Philadelphia proper— Mistress Anne Merrick, a dear friend of mine from New York."

No more than eighteen years old, the girls were dressed in almost identical floral chintz gowns, overfestooned with lace and furbelows, and they wore their hair puffed very high in the latest French fashion. Though dressed alike, these Peggies could not have been more different. Miss Shippen's cherubic peaches-and-cream prettiness was the complete opposite to Miss Chew's brunette and angular beauty.

Fair Shippen, and Dark Chew . . . Anne decided with a smile. Like many of the young Loyalist women in New York, it seemed Philadelphia's daughters were also on the hunt for quality husbands among Howe's officer elite.

Anne removed her cloak, and before taking one of two chairs, she handed Betsy the pressed paper box of sweet biscuits Pink had prepared. "Mackeroons—a specialty at the Cup and Book."

"J'adore les macarons!" Betsy exclaimed with a tolerable French accent. Peeling off the ribbon, she popped one in her mouth. "You must have angels working in your kitchen—these are *heavenly!*"

"The Cup and Book," Dark Peggy asked, reaching for one of the mackeroons Betsy offered. "Isn't that the new coffeehouse on Chestnut everyone's talking about?"

Anne beamed. "The Cup and Book is my shop."

Fair Peggy let out a high-pitched *squee* and clapped her hands, and Dark Peggy explained, "We've been meaning to frequent your very shop, Mrs. Merrick . . . John's been raving about it."

"John?"

"Major John André," Betsy said. Shifting her chair forward, she began to pour the tea. "He's the darling of the Twenty-sixth Foot, and has set every female heart from the Delaware to the Schuylkill aflutter."

"How can you not know who he is? Johnny frequents your coffee-shop daily!" Fair Peggy was fair perplexed by Anne's unfamiliarity with Major John André.

Anne gave a little shrug. "So many British officers frequent the Cup and Book . . ."

"You *must* know him. He is very well-favored," Dark Peggy said.

"The Twenty-sixth Foot?" Anne thought for a minute. "Does he sketch? There is a handsome young officer from the Twenty-sixth I've noticed—very solitary. Sits alone near the window with his chocolate, sketching street scenes . . ."

"That is him." Dark Peggy accepted the cup and saucer Betsy passed her way. "Major André is a gentleman of many talents."

"He cuts silhouettes, and he paints the backdrops for the theater company," Fair Peggy said with a nod.

"You should come with us to the theater, Anne," Betsy said.

"Oh, I couldn't . . ." Anne heaved a sigh to mask her excitement at the invitation. She was certain to make good connections mixing with the theater crowd. "I'm so very busy, getting the shop in order . . ."

Fair Peggy said, "They are staging a comedy this Friday evening— *No One's Enemy but His Own* . . ."

"All proceeds go to the benefit of army widows and orphans," Dark Peggy added.

Betsy plunked a lump of sugar into her teacup. "All work and no play makes Anne a very dull girl. You'll be a guest in our box," she insisted. "William will be most pleased to see you again."

BEYOND THE BRITISH OUTPOST LINES—WITHIN THE ROOFLESS
WALLS OF A DILAPIDATED CABIN

Jack looked up at the thick gray clouds and announced, "I am sick to death of snow."

"That makes two of us, brother." Titus sat beside him on the log they'd pulled up onto the old stone hearth, monitoring a dozen eggs clattering in a tin pot of water boiling away on the gridiron. Judging them ready, he fished each out with a wooden spoon, setting the steaming eggs one by one inside the crown of his hat. Titus tapped Jack on the head with the spoon. "Get the bread and tea fixin's."

Yawning, hands stuffed into pockets, Jack shuffled over to their pushcart and pulled back the canvas cover. He tucked one of the loaves they'd purchased from the baker's stall on Market Street under his arm and found the sacks of bohea and maple sugar. "How about some cheese?"

A turkey answered from a thick stand of pine trees to their left.

Titus stood, and snatching up his rifle, he cocked the hammer back. Jack cupped hand to mouth and gobbled out a response. After a moment, David and Alan McLane came out of the trees, leading their mounts. Titus waved and shouted, "Just in time for breakfast!"

Jack got the horses situated with their steaming noses buried in oat-filled feed bags. David and Alan took seats close to the fire, and Titus served the saddle-haggard officers eggs, crusty bread, and mugs of sweet, hot tea.

Alan tore off a bite of bread and used it to scoop up the soft-boiled egg from its shell. "Mmm . . . good eggs, these," he said between mouthfuls.

Jack dropped a woolen blanket over David's shoulders, relaying the verbal message concerning Howe's retirement, and handed him a letter from Sally. "There's a package of paper with something from the Quaker woman as well—page fifty-four."

"Already? Mrs. Darragh is as rich a vein as we've ever mined . . . Her son's an ensign in Wayne's Brigade, you know." Unfolding the page, David huddled into his blanket to read the letter from Sally.

"You don't say? A Quaker officer . . ." Jack dipped up a cup of tea and sat down beside David. "I was wondering what it was that got Friend Lydia to working for our war effort."

"Women are all alike." Titus sliced a wedge of cheese from a waxed round and passed it to Alan. "A pup in distress turns a Quaker ewe into a she-wolf."

David's head snapped up. "Sally says here that you and Titus are spending nights at the coffeehouse?"

"So?" Jack took a gulp from his cup. "What of it?"

"What of it!" David threw back the blanket. "It's true?"

"It's true Sally has a big mouth," Jack said.

David gave Jack a shove. "Are you sleeping with my sister at the Cup and Book?"

Dark brows met in a knot at the bridge of his nose, and Jack resisted shoving him back. "That's none of your business."

"Such an *idiot* . . ." David turned to Alan. "He's intent on dancing from the gallows once again, and taking my sister along with him this time."

"Unpinch your arse, David," Jack bristled. "We only go at the dark of the moon, and we leave well before daybreak."

"Don't you understand? The two of you are the link between us all, Jack. If you or Titus were to be apprehended," David said, "and if anyone could connect you to the Cup and Book, then Anne and Sally and Pink would all be in terrible jeopardy."

"We've only gone twice, David, and I swear no one's seen us," Titus asserted. "We're always very careful."

"We *have* to check in on them once in a while," Jack said. "They need some guarding—they need some regular connection to the rest of us."

Alan McLane stood up. "I'm afraid David's got the right of this one, fellows. The rule is minimize contact and minimize risk." He waved a finger. "Keep little Jack and little Titus buttoned inside your breeches from now on—no more nighttime trysts. If I catch wind you're even strolling past the Cup and Book, you'll be dismissed from the operation. Understand?"

"Put an end to it—both of you—you hear?" David added.

Jack threw up his hands. "Enough already . . . I heard."

"We understand," Titus said.

Alan and David loaded their saddlebags with fresh supplies. After Jack and Titus waved them off, they packed gear into pushcart, topped it off with as much cordwood as they could fit, and headed back to Elbert's.

A westerly wind came in to blow the early-morning cloud cover away, and they pulled their load back to town on muddy roads under sunny skies. The British pickets barely glanced at the passes Elbert had forged for them, and Jack and Titus were turning onto Market Street in no time. Pushing their heavy load of firewood along, they found the main artery void of foot and wheeled traffic, and the sound of pipes and drums echoing over the noise of their cart wheels on the cobblestones.

"You hear that?" Titus noted. "They're playing the 'Dead March.'"

A gang of boys came tearing pell-mell out of an alley.

"Hey!" Jack called. "What's going on?"

One boy flashed a big grin over his shoulder. "A hanging!"

Jack and Titus parked their cart between two empty stalls and ran toward the skirl and rattle of pipes and drums. As they neared the waterfront, the pipe's drone ceded to a continuous drum rattle. Gasping for breath, they reached the large crowd gathered on Front Street just after the drumming abruptly ceased and the crowd's collective gasp yet hovered in the air.

From the fringe, Jack could see a company of gold-jacketed drummer boys and a group of red-coated British soldiers in the center before a gallows tree erected of fresh-milled beams. Thousands of Philadelphians had gathered, and all eyes were captivated by the hooded figure suspended from the gallows, her skirts and petticoats ruffling on the stiff breeze blowing off the river.

The crowd was still, and Jack could swear he could hear the gallows groaning as the woman's body spun to and fro like a plumb-bob at the end of a carpenter's line. Catching his breath, he felt oddly lightheaded, as if he might cast up his breakfast on the spot. Grasping Titus by the shoulder, they pushed forward into the crowd.

"Too big," Titus whispered into Jack's ear.

Jack sucked in a deep breath and nodded. *She's too big around to be one of ours . . .*

They squeezed through the tight crowd, inching forward, and Jack could see the woman's bare feet were calloused with coarse bunions. Her work-worn hands were bound behind her back. Someone had pinned a piece of paper to the woman's breast, and as the corpse slowly spun around, he could now make out the words printed in very neat block letters—REBEL SPY.

He tapped a plain-dressed older gentleman on the shoulder. "Do you know who it is they've hung?"

"Obedience Seaborn," the man replied. "The innkeeper's widow from the White Swan."

"I, for one, am not surprised to see Bede Seaborn hung for a spy."

The woman standing beside him sniffed. "Her man was a rebel through and through—fought and died at Breed's Hill."

The news was like a rifle butt to the chest, stopping his heart for a moment. Jack nodded and managed a, "Thanks, friend."

Titus tugged on Jack's sleeve. "I can see Pink," he said, pointing to the opposite side of the circle gathered around the gallows, and the bright blue turban Pink wore, standing together with Anne and Sally.

Titus said, "Looks like you're not the only one gone gray about the gills . . ."

Tall men, Jack and Titus tended to stick out in a crowd, and Anne spotted them when Titus waved. She started to wend her way through the dissipating crowd, and as much as Jack wanted nothing more than to hold her in his arms, he looked over to the Redcoats massed in the center, scrutinizing the crowd for any signs of unrest, and he shook his head. Anne pulled up short, but he could see the tears sprung to her doleful blue eyes.

"Goddamn it . . ." Jack growled, ripping at the buttons on his coat and digging down into his shirtfront, pulling forth the little half crown he wore hanging on a leather thong for her to see. He clutched his fist around the token, and forced a smile.

Anne nodded. Her attempt at a smile was weak, and her breast rose and fell with the deep breath she heaved before she turned away to take Sally and Pink by the hand.

Jack and Titus watched the women head back toward Chestnut Street, and Titus asked, "How are we supposed to protect 'em if we can't go near 'em?"

"I don't like it, either, Titus," Jack said, his eye on the Redcoat soldiers. "We are committing our lambs to the custody of the wolves."

✎ SIXTEEN ✎

What are salt, sugar and finery to the inestimable blessings of "Liberty and Safety"? Or what are the inconveniences of a few months to the tributary bondage of ages?

THOMAS PAINE, *The American Crisis*

A GATHERING OF SPIES

Church bells bonged the seventh hour, announcing Friday morning market, and Pink stood by the front door ready to go, basket in hand. "The butter bell's a-ringin'," she said.

Throwing a shawl over her shoulders, Sally's befreckled scowl was fierce. "Show a leg, Annie," she shouted up the stairs, "afore all th' goods are gone!"

Anne came scurrying down the stairs, tying hat ribbons under her chin in a sturdy bow. "The wind just banged the shutters closed," she said, handing pins to Sally and Pink, and the three of them used the pins to secure their straw hats.

Sally made sure the placard hanging in the window was turned to "closed" before she and Pink stepped out to wait while Anne locked up. They headed to Market Street, baskets in hand, and Anne trailed behind, going over the list she'd scratched out on the stitched pad of paper she always carried in her pocket.

"We need cinnamon bark, vanilla beans, blade mace, raisins and currants . . ."

"Eggs and butter," Pink said over her shoulder.

Anne stopped to dig for a pencil in her pocket and added the items to her list. "I forgot to put down eggs and butter . . ."

"Och! Will ye come on, ninny." Sally grabbed Anne by the sleeve and tugged her along. "We willna be forgetting th' butter and eggs."

They strolled past the big butcher's stall with sides of beef and pork hanging from the rafters on hooks and chains, skirting around the crowd of German *hausfraus* haggling over the price of hog heads and trotters. Anne pulled to a stop in front of the poulterer's stall and a sign that read, *50 pigeons / 1s*.

"Fifty for a shilling—that's a bargain."

"A lot of plucking feathers and birdshot for scant meat," Sally cautioned.

The poulterer stepped out from behind his stall. "Purchase a hundred birds, Mrs. Merrick, and I'll see them plucked and breasted for you—an excellent value."

"Pigeon pies, Annie," Pink suggested. "My hand for the paste, and Sally's for the gravy."

"Sold for a penny a pie, we might turn a tidy profit." Anne paid the two shillings, and made arrangements to have the birds delivered to the Cup and Book.

They moved down the street, from stall to stall—spice merchant, to egg man, to butter woman, to greengrocer—Anne doling out silver from her pocketbook, Sally and Pink filling their baskets along the way.

"*Gweeshtie!*" Sally gasped as if she'd seen a ghost. Grabbing Anne by the arm, she pointed up the street to a crowd of women gathered at one of the last of the stalls. "Lookie there! I think it's a lemon-trader!"

They ran to the stall burgeoning with the first fresh citrus fruit Anne'd seen since living in New York. The wonderful smell of oranges, lemons, and limes overtook all sense and reason. She ordered a full bushel of each to be delivered to the shop, and purchased three bottles of orangeade, justifying the expense with, "The Redcoats are mad for punch."

"Compliments, ladies!" Pleased with the size of the order, the happy lemontrader placed three oranges into Sally's basket. The women scooted over to the side to peel and share one on the spot.

"Mmmm . . ." Sally moaned with pleasure, and cracked the real first smile Anne had seen in days and days. "So good . . ."

Pink giggled, wiping the sweet juice from her chin. "Like eating a little bit of heaven, in't it?"

Good to see them truly happy for a change . . .

In the afterclap of Bede Seaborn's execution, Anne did not know what else to do but carry on, and they kept the Cup and Book open, putting on cheerful countenances as if nothing was amiss. The charade, difficult in the best of circumstances, was very wearing under these worst of circumstances. Isolated from the company of their men and surrounded by an enemy proven fearsome, they'd spent the past two weeks moving between sadness, worry, and plain anger, without direction or word from any quarter.

Anne pulled an orange from the basket. "Let's peel another . . ."

Of a sudden, something came flying through the air, striking Sally square in the chest to land with a plop in the basket hooked over her arm. For a brief moment Anne thought it was a bird, until she heard a boy's laughter and saw Jim Griffin run up, grinning and pointing.

"Beg pardon, miss, but that's my ball . . ."

Anne, Sally, and Pink were speechless when quick as a wink Jim reached in with both hands to rifle through Sally's goods.

"Here 'tis!" he said, producing a small ball made of stitched brown leather and stuffed tight with cork shavings and feathers. With a wink, and a smile, he ran to rejoin his mates and their game of rounders.

Sally looked down into her basket and said, "Th' wee blackguard made off with the last orange!"

"But look—he left a note." Anne plucked out a dirty, folded piece of paper, no bigger than the palm of a young boy's hand. They strolled away nonchalant and rounded the corner before crowding together to unfold the slip and read the message.

"That's David's hand," Sally said. "I'd know it anywhere!"

"What's it say? What's it say?" Pink asked, bouncing on the balls of her feet.

"It's a list." Anne read it aloud, " 'Hat, Quakers, sixth day, forty.' "

Sally puffed out a breath. "Well, I'm fair puggled—what's it all mean?"

Anne shrugged, repeating, "Hat . . . Quakers . . . sixth day . . . forty . . ."

Pink ventured, "I think maybe it means we're invited at Mr. Hadley's today for tea."

"Sixth day!" Anne exclaimed. "Of course! At Quaker's Friday for tea!"

"Yer daft clever!" Sally laughed, and gave Pink a hug. "Do you think David will be there?"

Pink nodded. "He wrote the note, didn't he?"

Sally laughed and clapped her hands. "Let's go home. I want to bake some treats for our tea."

Ripping the message into tiny bits, Anne spun on her heel, sprinkling them on the breeze as if she were sowing seed. Looping arms with Sally and Pink, they skipped all the way back to Chestnut Street.

"Welcome, ladies, welcome!" The odd little engraver met them at the shop door wearing blue-glass spectacles. Elbert hurried to slide the bolt home and draw the curtains closed, all the while his little spotted terrier leaping and barking like mad.

"Here, Bandit!" Sally called to the engraver's dog and he leapt up into her arms, lapping at her face. She beamed. "See how the wee scoundrel remembers me!"

Anne reached over to give Bandit a scratch between the ears. "Of course he does. He remembers both of us."

"No time for dawdling, no time for dawdling." Elbert urged them forward, swinging the door to the workroom open. "My impatient fellows await the pleasure of your company . . ."

The engraver's workroom was a pleasant space. To the left walking in, a steep oak staircase led up to the second story. On the wall opposite, three large, south-facing windows looked out onto an open field, letting in great swaths of sunshine. The long table, usually pushed up to the windows to take advantage of the daylight, had been pulled out to the center and surrounded by a collection of mismatched chairs and stools.

"They're here!" David called, jumping up from his seat at the head of the table; he moved from window to window pulling the canvas curtains closed, casting a bit of a pall on the room.

"Davy lad!" Sally skirted around the table and skipped into his arms. "I hardly kent it was you without yer uniform."

Dressed in the plain clothes of a Quaker, David laughed. "Well, I wouldn't get very far in this city wearing Continental blue, would I?"

Pink and Anne made a beeline to the back of the room, where Jack and Titus stood in shirtsleeves and leather aprons at a washbasin on the counter, wiping their hands dry. Tossing the towel aside, Jack met Anne with arms wide. Pulling her into a hug, his whisper tickled her ear. "I've been missing you so, so much . . ."

Anne wrapped her arms about his waist, pressed her cheek to his chest, and simply took in the smell of him—the familiar compound of ink, soap, leather a soothing calmative—a tonic that at once remedied the ills of her troubled heart. "The very best place in the world," she murmured, "in your arms . . ."

"You are the darling of my heart." Jack rested his chin on the top of her head and held her tight. "I could carry you away right now and never look back . . ."

Elbert held the back door open and Brian came bustling through carrying a steaming pot of coffee, with Jim right behind bearing a tray piled with cups and saucers and spoons. David called out, "Gather round, everyone!"

Hand in hand, Pink and Titus left their whispered huddle in the corner, and came to join the rest, taking seats opposite Anne and Jack. Handsome in a plain brown weskit and bright white shirt and cravat, David sat at the head of the table with paper and pencil, and Sally was at his right.

Looking very young and cavalier with his wavy hair falling about his shoulders, Quaker-style, Sally was clearly enamored with David's choice of disguise. Leaning over she said to Anne, "Yer brother looks just like a schoolmaster, does he na?"

*"Pfttt!"*Anne teased. "More like a schoolboy with his pretty curls!"

"I'm supposed to be plain, not pretty!" David wadded a sheet of paper and hurled it at his sister, hitting her on the head.

Sally set out some scones and sliced her loaf of soft gingerbread. Pink whisked aside the napkin from her plate of mackeroons. The boys set the table with blue and white delftware cups and saucers, and Elbert made the rounds, pouring coffee from a matching teapot, boasting, "Not a drop of tea has flowed from this spout since 'seventy-three . . ."

Reveling in the company, the room was filled with the chatter of loving friends. Elbert had Brian and Jim display the recent products of their apprenticeship—hand-colored, engraved illustrations of birds, lizards, frogs, and plants—and the boys were duly praised and encouraged. They all cheered and clapped when Elbert showed off Bandit's latest trick—balancing a bite of ship's biscuit on his nose, before flicking it neatly into his mouth.

David told about the doings back at the encampment. "Since Congress signed the alliance with the French, there's been regular shipments of food and clothing," he said. "Coupled with the success of Major Steuben's training practices, you wouldn't recognize the troops. They actually look and move like a proper army."

Playing the gracious host, Elbert broke out a bottle of Armagnac. "More good cheer for our good company." Bustling around the table, he splashed a dose in every cup. Raising his own cup high, he offered a toast: *"Ubi libertas, ibi patria!"*

The boys groaned, obviously suffering from overexposure to Latin, and Jim said, "In English, Elbert!"

"Oh!" With a blink and a shake of his bald head, the engraver translated. "Where liberty is, there is my country!"

Arms stretched with teacups held high, they all responded with a happy, "Cheers!"

David stood, rapping his teaspoon to the table. "Time for us to set our boat aright . . ."

"I can tell you this about our 'boat' . . ." Jack tilted his chair back, rocking it back and forth on the two hind legs. "Since the Redcoats sent Bede Seaborn to the gallows tree, we've all been heads down, David, lying on our oars, just trying to gauge the wind . . ."

"And hoping to not be hanged for it," Titus added.

"I know. What happened to Mrs. Seaborn was a shock to us all," David said. "Good intelligence is very valuable but, in this case, purchased at too dear a rate."

"Are we going to shut it down, then, Cap'n?" Brian asked.

"That's what we're here to decide." David sat down. "Tell me, how do the winds blow?"

"Lydia Darragh is undeterred." Anne was the first to speak up. "She is still listening in on the British council meetings and bringing report. It seems all is at a standstill with word of Howe's retirement—more discussion of horse races, cockfights, and theater plays than wartime strategy. I expect this will change once Clinton arrives to assume command. The good news . . ." Anne looked around the table, smiling. "As far as *our* operation, I think we can all rest easier. From what Lydia's overheard, it is very clear Bede never divulged a word about any of us. They were certain she'd break when faced with the noose, and because she did not, the British are convinced she was working alone."

"The butcher's boy tolt us 'twas the chambermaid at the White Swan who pointed Bede out to the lobsterbacks," Brian said.

Jim said, "The chambermaid spied the innkeeper's widow goin' through some officer's papers, and then she went and squealed like the Tory pig she is."

"Major Sutherland's papers?" Sally asked.

"That's him," Jim said. "They say the chambermaid's being rogered by the Major . . ."

Brian gave Jim a hard shove. "Will you mind your damn tongue?"

Jim shrugged. "That's what *they* say . . ."

"Poor Bede. One day she's in our kitchen having a chocolate and eating mackeroons, and the next . . ." Pink shook her head, and left her sentence to trail off.

"The lobsterbacks willna be after hanging a woman again anytime soon," Sally said. "The talk in the market, even among the Tories, is much against it. Over harsh, they say."

"Most Redcoats don't like it, either," Pink added. "At least the kind that come to our shop. Uncivilized, I heard one say. Another said hanging women makes the rabble uneasy."

"Bastards didn't hesitate to send a message, though, did they?" Titus shook his head.

"We all dodged a cannonball," Jack said. "That's for certain, and after listening to what Anne had to say, there doesn't seem to be any value in our staying on. I say we pack it in."

Anne turned to Jack. "Really?"

Titus folded his arms across his chest. "I'm with Jack. The gain is small, the risk—too high."

"How do we gauge value?" David poured himself another cup of coffee. "Though Anne says it is quiet now, I think there is value in having an agent fully entrenched by the time Clinton takes over. The Cup and Book is becoming a magnet for Redcoats. When the wind does begin to blow, the sails on our mill are then ready to turn."

Brian slid a mackeroon off the plate being passed around. "In't there some value to General Washington in learning that there ain't nothin' to learn?"

Sally said, "It would be a crying shame to abandon all th' hard work gone into opening our shop. There's value in tha, no?"

Anne said, "And there is great value in exploiting Betsy Loring while she still holds some influence. Through her I've made friends with Peggy Shippen and Peggy Chew, who've already introduced me to a Major André and others in the upper echelons."

"That's true," Elbert said, balancing his teacup very gingerly on one knee. "When nothing is ventured, no laurels are won."

"I'm more worried about our hides than any laurels," Titus said.

Matching Titus's stern posture, Jack folded his arms across his chest. "Agreed."

"You agree? I'm absolutely baffled." Anne shook her head. "You're the man who once told me you were in this thing whole heart. Blood has been shed, you said, and you would not have your fellows die in vain. But now Bede's been hanged, and you want us to pack it in?"

Jack groaned. "That was different. I was talking about men dying at Concord and Lexington . . ."

"Why is it different? Because Bede was a woman?" Anne gave Jack a little shove. "Bede Seaborn sacrificed her life so that we could live and continue our work here . . ."

"I will not have you sacrifice your life for the cause, Annie . . ."

"And I will not have Bede's sacrifice be in vain."

The room went still, and Anne could tell no one wanted to be the first to step between them. At last, Jack heaved a great sigh, and took Anne by the hand. "You've got the right of it . . ." he said. "We should carry on for Bede's sake, and for the sake of our cause."

David stood up. "Is everyone agreed that we continue?"

All heads were nodding, except for Titus, who sat stone-faced, big arms still crossed over his chest. "I'm not as yet feeling all smiles and cookies. If we're t' carry on, we all need to be more careful. I won't be able to take seeing one of us swinging from a gallows tree. I swear t' Christ, I won't."

"Titus has a point," David said. "Minimizing risk necessitates some change. We need to tighten our operation, so I've devised a new system using signals and drops."

"Like we did with Burgoyne?" Titus asked.

"In a way. . . ." David sat down. "Elbert will become a regular borrower at the Cup and Book library."

"That's good." Elbert nodded. "I'm one for enjoying a good book."

"On the days when Sally wears a striped apron," David continued, "Elbert will borrow the book Anne suggests from the library, containing missives written in secret ink in the margins of certain pages."

"Striped apron," the engraver very seriously repeated.

"Elbert is the least likely spy," Sally said with an approving nod, "and those are th' best kind."

"The boys will then deliver the book to a place I've readied under the hearthstone at the old cabin. I will pick it up from there."

Jack inched forward in his chair. "The boys deliver?"

David nodded. "Armed with fishing poles and creels, they are far less likely to arouse suspicion from any Redcoat outliers."

Titus asked, "What do we do? Jack and me?"

David squared his shoulders. "You're both going back to Valley Forge with me . . ."

"What!?" Jack pushed his empty cup away, sending it in a skitter across the table where Titus managed, quick as a cat, to catch it before it hit the floor.

Jack threw himself back in his chair, his mouth a snarl and brow dark. "This is about the night visits, isn't it? Well, you can kiss my back cheeks, David. There's no way I'm leaving here."

"This has nothing to do with the night visits . . ."

"What a load of cock and bull!" Jack pounded the table with his fist. "You're a vengeful taskmaster, Captain Peabody, but you forget, Titus and me are no regulars to be ordered about at your whim. We're staying put, and that's that."

Anne tried to calm Jack with a hand on his arm, but he shrugged her off.

"Be sensible, Jack," David said. "I'm not your taskmaster— necessity is *our* taskmaster. Washington needs experienced scouts . . ."

Titus interrupted, "We don't go to the Cup and Book anymore— tell him, Sally."

Sally nodded. "It's truth, David. They've stayed away."

"We all know better now," Pink said.

David threw his arms up. "I'm telling you all, this has nothing to do with the night visits to the Cup and Book. You spoke of value, Jack—well, the General's devised a new mission and Morgan himself recommended the two of you, as did Alan."

Jack asked, "What mission?"

"Small, swift groups of irregular scouts and Oneidans employed in the country between the Delaware and the Schuylkill under Alan's direction. You're to observe enemy movements, making mischief as you can, inciting terror among the Redcoats with well-placed rifle shots, disrupting their communication—very similar to your mission up the Hudson. You won't be far away, and once the city's retaken in the summer, the mission is over."

"Sounds like your cup of tea . . ." Anne put her hand on Jack's knee.

Jim chimed in, "Use the proper tools for the proper task—that's what Elbert says."

"I don't know, David . . ." Jack said with a shake of his head. "I don't like leaving them here all on their own—a tribe of petticoats, two un-licked cubs, and Elbert—no offense, Elbert."

"None taken." Elbert smiled.

David added, "I can tell you Ned and Isaac have already signed on as scouts."

Titus asked, "Tell me, who's to take action here if aught goes amiss?"

"What's to go wrong?" Pink piped up. "We work the Cup and Book with eyes and ears open . . ."

Anne said, "I go to a few card parties and plays—if we learn any-thing of value, we pass it to Elbert."

"I dinna ken why yer both bein' such pains in the arse. It's much less risky for us here in th' city than when we were in amongst Burgoyne's lot," Sally said. "Bede Seaborn—God rest her soul—was caught be-cause she was careless. We know what we are about, ye ken?"

Anne massaged the bunch between Jack's shoulders. "It's only for a few weeks. We'll be fine. Once Washington retakes the city, we've done our duty."

"Nonetheless, as a precaution," David said, "I want you to put a plan in place, if needs must, to fly the city at a moment's notice."

The women all nodded at the sense of David's suggestion. Titus and Jack exchanged a look, and Jack heaved a sigh. "Alright, then."

Titus shrugged and said, "We'll join the General's mission."

David slapped hands to the tabletop. "Good!" He went over to the windows and peeked out the curtain. "Gather your gear. We'll leave at nightfall—about an hour, I'd say."

Sally came up behind David and wrapped her arms around his waist, her voice sad. "I guess there's naught to do but kiss and part once again."

"Kiss and part . . ." Jack puffed out a breath and scraped his chair back. "I'd better go and pack . . ."

Anne grabbed him by the hand and tugged him down to whisper in his ear, "I think a kinder kiss could be had up in your room . . ."

Jack's grimness turned into a grin. "Why, Widow Merrick . . . how you talk!"

Hand in hand, they ran up the stairs.

❦ SEVENTEEN ❦

*Some secret defect or other is interwoven in the character of
all those, be they men or women, who can look with patience
on the brutality, luxury and debauchery of the British court,
and the violations of their army here.*

THOMAS PAINE, *The American Crisis*

MIXING AND MINGLING

"Beg pardon, madam, but I think you dropped your fan?"

"How kind . . . Thank you." Anne smiled, and accepted the fan offered by a fair-haired Redcoat captain, who seemed to be in her orbit since she'd entered the theater.

"May I?" he asked, indicating the empty seat beside her.

She nodded and opened her fan, beating the air with a very controlled tremble of the wrist. *Young for a captain . . . He's either very rich or very brave.*

The Captain leaned in and asked, "Are you looking forward to the production, Mrs. Merrick?"

Anne stilled her fan. "You play familiar with my name, sir, yet I don't recall our being introduced . . ."

"You've caught me out," he admitted with a boyish smile, genuine and quite charming. "I've been admiring you these days from afar, Mrs. Merrick, and I strong-armed Mrs. Loring for an invitation to her box tonight."

"Hmmmph . . ." Anne resumed fanning. "You are a deceiver, sir."

"A rascal of your devise, madam," the handsome Redcoat acknowledged. " 'Most dangerous is that temptation that doth goad us on to sin in loving virtue.'"

Impressed with the young man's dash, Anne raised an eyebrow and murmured, *"Measure for Measure . . ."* The slightest Scottish lilt in the Captain's voice quoting Shakespeare sent Anne straight back to Burgoyne's lamp-lit woodland dinner under the trees, and Simon Fraser's recitation from *Henry V.* Her brain hopped in a twinkling from one memory to the next, and she found tears sprung to her eyes recollecting Geoffrey Pepperell's smile the moment before he died.

Extending his hand, the Redcoat added, "Captain William Schaw Cathcart, at your service."

Grateful for the dimness of the light in Howe's box at the Southwark Theater, Anne blinked away her sudden tears. She reached out to recognize the introduction with a momentary grasp of the man's fingers, and in catching a glimpse of the number embossed on the silver buttons on his cuff, she actually winced, touched by yet another specter from her past.

17th Dragoons.

Edward Blankenship, the Redcoat she shot dead in her shop in New York, had been a captain in the very same dragoon regiment.

An ill omen . . .

Mrs. Loring and William Howe were the last to be seated in the theater box, and in a noisy rustle of pink taffeta, they took the chairs directly behind Anne. Tapping Anne on the shoulder, Betsy leaned forward and said quietly in her ear, "I see you have a new admirer!"

Anne leaned back and muttered, "Too young."

"Don't be a fool," Betsy whispered. "Lord Cathcart is very smitten with you."

Anne leaned back, using her fan to mask her lips. *"Lord?"*

"Scottish peerage—son of the ninth Baron. The boy's a favorite of General Clinton."

Anne snapped her fan shut. Letting it dangle from the silken cord on her wrist, she turned to the young Captain and said, "From your quoting Shakespeare, Mr. Cathcart, I take it you are a regular patron of the theater?"

"A patron and a sponsor, Mrs. Merrick."

"Please . . ." Anne reached over and rested her hand on the young man's knee for just a moment. "You must call me Anne, and I shall call you William, for I can tell already we're going to be fast friends."

"Dear Anne . . ." Her simple touch had Lord Cathcart flushed and grinning like a cat what'd licked the cream from the milk jug.

Betsy leaned forward and muttered, "Reel him in . . ."

"William . . ." Laying her hand on the Captain's forearm, Anne asked, "Would you happen to know the title of tonight's performance?"

"A comedy . . ." Lord Cathcart dug into his breast pocket. Producing a playbill, he read the title. *"A Wonder! A Woman Keeps a Secret.* I've seen a production in London—very humorous."

Another omen . . . Anne snapped open her fan to cover her smile.

The theater boys came around, dimming the houselights and turning up the wicks to brighten the oil lamps at the foot of the stage. One of the violinists waved his bow, and the musicians in the pit struck up the overture. It was amusing to watch from up high the scramble for seats in the gallery. The audience at last quieted when the curtain was drawn, and two actors stepped out onto the stage, entering into a lively dialog:

"My lord, Don Lopez."

"How d'ye do, Frederick?"

"At your lordship's service. I'm glad to see you look so well, my lord. I hope Antonio's out of danger?"

"Quite the contrary; his fever increases, they tell me, and the surgeons are of opinion his wound is mortal . . ."

Of all British military social whirl, Anne did love going to the playhouse. She accepted all invitations to join Betsy Loring and company in the Royal Box—the best seats in the house at the Southwark Theater. It was the only guilty pleasure she derived from her assignment in Philadelphia. Just as she settled back to enjoy the play, she was jerked around in her seat by the call of her name.

"Anne."

In the row behind, Betsy was leaning against the General's shoulder, watching the play through a squat monocular opera glass. The two Peggies, sitting beside Betsy, were spellbound by the stage—not a one of them indicating the least interest in speaking with her.

Odd. Anne turned back to the play. *Something's out of square here . . .* Shifting in her seat, an uneasy feeling crept up her spine like a deliberate spider. *It's what Cathcart said—admiring from afar . . .* She glanced to her right, but the young captain was completely engaged by the antics on the stage. *He seems harmless enough . . .* Anne suppressed a shudder. She was not keen on being the one who was watched unawares. The audience burst into laughter and Anne almost leapt from her skin.

Cathcart leaned over and whispered, "My friend Delancey is an outstanding actor, is he not? An unnatural talent."

"Unnatural . . ." Anne nodded, taking in a breath to steady her racing heart. She was the one always accusing Sally of being over fearful, of always seeing an Indian behind every tree and a snake beneath every bush. *I'm suffering the same affliction . . .* Fanning her face, Anne set her eyes, ears, and mind to the diversion offered onstage. *Stop making a mountain out of a mouse.*

After the play, Anne took William Cathcart's proffered arm and they strolled along with a jovial crowd to Howe's mansion on Sixth and Market for after-theater drinks. Betsy and the General gathered a foursome in the dining room for a game of Euchre. Anne followed a small group to the punch bowl in the upstairs drawing room, and squeezed in between the two Peggies and their polonaise puffs of pastel silk, to share the settee.

"I tell you, my dears, I verily *dread* the departure of our General!" John André threw himself onto a brocaded chair, tugging at his neck stock. "Say farewell to theater plays and dancing assemblies, and anything else that makes this dreary colonial backwater tolerable."

"You've got the right of it . . ." Fresh from the stage, Captain Delancey plopped down into the second chair. "Lord Howe understands how to compensate for the roughs and smooths of a soldier's life. Henry Clinton, on the other hand, is a by-the-book soldier."

André added, "And he's no patron of the arts."

"We'll be campaigning soon, and Sir Henry is a superb tactician and strategist—" With punch glass in hand, Cathcart struck an elegant pose near the mantel. "I, for one, am not dreading his command at all."

"Of course you've nothing to dread, Your *Lordship*," André scoffed. "There'll most undoubtedly be a colonelcy in the switch for you, but this fellow . . ." He waggled his fingers. "This fellow will now need to embark on yet another campaign of arse-kissing and shoe-licking."

The Peggies giggled, and Anne suggested, "If that's the case, Captain André, you ought take advantage of the present clime, and have one last, grand party before General Howe returns to England . . ."

"What a fantastic notion! A phenomenal idea!" André sat bolt upright in his chair. "We can hold a gala with drink and music—a ball—no! *A masquerade!*"

The Peggies bounced up and down, clapping hands, and Fair Peggy exclaimed, "In fancy dress! In fancy dress!"

"*Pffft!*" Delancey scoffed. "And how are we going to pay for such a thing? My pockets are dark."

"We'll call it 'A Last Farewell to our General, Lord Howe' and take up a collection among the wealthiest officers. The sluggards will be falling all over themselves to donate to that, won't they?" André slapped his knee. "By God! We can do it!"

Just before opening time, Anne came to the kitchen house door, pad and pencil in hand. "Is there anything you two need from the market?"

Hearth and oven on one side of the small room, counter and cupboards on the other, Pink and Sally prepared for the morning rush maneuvering the narrow aisle, dipping and weaving like a pair of dancers doing a *gavotte*.

Sally said, "Stop by the dairyman, Annie, and have him deliver two more big jugs of milk."

"Dairyman." Anne jotted the note onto her pad. "Milk. Two jugs."

Pink came at her wielding trays of baked goods. "More eggs," she said, darting out to the shop.

"Eggs . . ." Anne scribbled. She snatched up the cup of tea she'd fixed about an hour before and took a sip.

Back into the kitchen for a stack of clean plates, Pink pulled to a stop and brushed the backs of her fingers to Anne's cheek. "You're lookin' a little poorly, honey . . ."

Anne shrugged, and took another sip of her cold tea. "I'm fine."

Pink bumped Sally with a hip. "In't she looking peaked, Sal?"

Sally looked up from sliding a batch of scones off a hot iron into a basket. "Aye . . . she does look a bit peelie-wally . . ."

"Is it your bad time of the month?" Pink asked. "I'll make you a cup of raspberry leaf tea . . ."

"No . . ." Anne thought for a moment. "I'm just a little tired, I suppose—the comings and goings for the party . . ."

"With all yer runnin' about for this Redcoat Messy-anza business, I wager ye havna eaten a proper breakfast in weeks," Sally said, offering a scone from the basket.

Anne grimaced, and refused with a shake of her head. "I'm worried about the two of you. There's only three days left to get the baking done. The Redcoats are paying us a pretty penny for the order . . ."

"Aye, dinna fash—mackeroons and cupcakes—we can do tha' in our sleep, na, Pink?"

"No worries, Annie." Pink hoisted the two big coffee urns from the grate. "At least this here Messy-anza is good for puttin' silver in folks' pockets."

"It's 'Meschianza,'" Anne corrected, and gulped down the rest of her tea.

"Oo-ooh! Mesh-ee-yaan-za!" Sally spread skirts with both hands and accomplished a florid deep-kneed curtsy.

"I swan." Pink laughed. "If that ain't the stupidest name I ever heard for a good time . . ."

"I know, I know . . ." Anne tucked pad and pencil into pocket. "Some Italian nonsense Captain André concocted about mixing and mingling . . ." She traded apron and mobcap for shawl and straw hat. "I'm off to the mantua-maker. I'll open shop on the way out."

After letting in the first customers, Anne set out, French heels *click-click-click*ing on the cobblestones as she crossed over Market Street on her way to the dressmaker's shop in the alleyway off Mulberry and Second.

The Meschianza . . . Anne thought it ridiculous, but to her surprise, the idea of a party presented as a farewell celebration for their beloved General Howe proved so popular, André and his cohorts were able to raise more than twelve thousand pounds to fund the gala event.

An obscene amount of money . . . Anne hopped over the gutter and skirted around a knife grinder who'd stopped to secure the string on his shoe.

Intent on spending every single silver penny raised, André's initial plan for a ball had ballooned into a full-day extravaganza that included a riverboat regatta, a stylized jousting tournament, and a lavish banquet culminating with a masquerade ball and fireworks. Engraved and hand-inscribed invitations were sent out to the elite of military and Philadelphian society, and Anne Merrick was one of four hundred invited guests.

Both a blessing and a curse . . .

Along with the two Peggies, she volunteered to help with the planning and organizing—spending every spare moment with the likes of John André, William Cathcart, and Oliver Delancey—planning menus, designing invitations and programs, and devising decorations.

With only three days remaining to the big event, the town brewers, bakers, tailors, and dressmakers were working day and night preparing drink, food, and dress. The large, level lawn of the Wharton riverside mansion was selected as the party site, where carpenters had been toiling to build immense temporary pavilions for dining and dancing. Philadelphians were at once abuzz and aghast. Never had anyone seen so much money spent on such a frivolity.

Hundreds of pounds wasted on swathes and festoons—as if they'd already won this war . . .

It made her stomach turn to consider the privation the Continental

Army endured in comparison to this latest British excess. On the bright side, the Meschianza was just the avenue she required to court and solidify the connections she would use to cull information once Sir Henry Clinton gained position.

The doorbell rang out as she stepped into Mrs. Downey's small shop, conveniently wedged between a milliner and a cordwainer. "Good morning! I'm here for my fitting."

Like her name, Thea Downey was plump and round and soft as a pillow. She hopped up from sitting on a low stool positioned to take advantage of the daylight coming in from the shop window, her ruddy face framed with a curly fringe of dark hair escaping from beneath her cap. With a tape measure for a necklace, and a pincushion tied to her wrist like a bracelet, the seamstress wore her pocket outside her skirt—seam ripper, bodkins, spools of thread, and snips always at the ready. Thea Downey set aside her work and waved Anne to the back of the shop. "Come! Let's see how your dress suits . . ."

Anne darted behind the drape hung for modesty, and stripped down to stays, chemise, and stockings. "Your shop is quiet with the ball but three days away."

"You're an early bird, Mrs. Merrick." Mrs. Downey sorted through a pile of half-finished frocks, most of them in fashionable pastel pinks, yellows, and blues. "This Meschianza has my business in an uproar. Never fear; the shop will be aflap with the tittering of discontented magpies soon enough. Here it is—" Mrs. Downey draped a dress of deep purple blue over her arm.

Anne so disliked wearing bolsters and whalebone panniers, she challenged the dressmaker to design a gown for the masquerade that would not require any of those fashionable contrivances. Given nothing more than that direction and an allegorical theme of Night, Mrs. Downey created a costume beyond expectations.

"It's *lovely!*" Very pleased, Anne brushed her fingertips over the midnight blue lutestring silk. The formfitting bodice was sprinkled with silver sequins of graduated size, the tiniest near the square-cut neckline, graduating to the size of a penny near the pointed waistline. The lustrous silk skirt was topped by a sheer layer of matching blue silk gauze, scattered with five-pointed stars embroidered with silver thread.

"Careful, now, there're yet a few pins in it . . . Arms up . . ."

Open down the back, Mrs. Downey held the garment out, and Anne slipped her arms into belled medieval sleeves that were fashioned from the sheer silk gauze, and spangled with tiny sequins. The seamstress spun her by the shoulders to face the full-length looking glass mounted on the wall.

"Very striking!" Mrs. Downey admired as she pinned the gown closed. "This deep blue suits your coloring, and will set you off from the gaggle of shepardesses, milkmaids, and fairies," she said, jerking a disdainful thumb to the pastel pile of work in progress. "Worn with the proper mask, in this gown you will be Night personified, floating on the dance floor." The dressmaker murmured, "Hmmmm . . ." and came around, pulling at the fabric drawn tight across Anne's chest. "You've gained weight since we last measured . . . I could add a bit to the plackets in the back . . ."

Anne set her hands at her waist and studied her reflection. "Perhaps you mismeasured. If anything, I've lost some weight . . ."

"I never mismeasure." Mrs. Downey whipped the pins out. "You're slim as a wafer, that's true, but the gain's all up top," she said, "in the bubbies."

"I was rushing this morning . . ." Anne suggested. "Maybe my stay strings are too loose?"

Mrs. Downey produced a stay hook from her pocket. "Let's give 'em a good tug and try again."

Anne took in a deep breath and focused on keeping a firm stance to offer resistance as Mrs. Downey worked her way up from the bottom eyelets, pulling up the slack. Suddenly, her image in the mirror began to waver, and little silver lights, like sequins catching the light, blinked in the periphery of this distorted vision, sending the room into a spin.

"Gracious!" The seamstress caught Anne before she crumpled completely and helped her the few steps to a chair. Quick as a wink,

Mrs. Downey cut the stay strings with a pair of snips, and forced Anne to bend forward. "Breathe in through the nose, out through the mouth. Head down between your knees. I'll be right back."

Anne blinked and, with elbows propped to knees, clutched her head with both hands, and did as told. The dressmaker hastened back to wave a small glass of wine under her nose.

"Drink . . ."

Groaning, Anne turned to the side, gagging.

Belying her size, with the speed of a lynx, Thea Downey swept up an armload of gowns, clearing the area just before Anne vomited, retching up bitter bile onto the floorboards.

"Oh, dear!" The seamstress sighed and scurried off to return with a damp rag to mop up the sick. "A close call, that."

"I'm so sorry, Mrs. Downey." Anne pulled the hankie from her sleeve and wiped her mouth and tearful eyes. "I woke up with a sour stomach. There must have been a bad oyster in those Captain André served last night . . ."

"Oysters in May! Did your mother not tell you to *never* eat oysters in months without the letter R?" Mrs. Downey pressed a hand to Anne's forehead. "You're not fevered; that's good. Tuck into some bread and butter when you get home, and have a nice cup of tea. That will sort you out."

"I'm feeling much better now that I've gotten rid of it." Anne rose slowly to her feet. "I think we can finish with the fitting . . ."

On the way back to the shop, Anne stopped to do the marketing, and purchased a well-fired loaf of bread from the baker. Her empty stomach was grumbling, and she looked forward to taking Mrs. Downey's good advice, but no sooner did she step through the door of the Cup and Book than Sally and Pink ran up. "To the kitchen," Sally said. "There's trouble."

Anne groaned, untying her hat strings. "What's happened now?"

"Th' Peggy lassies have come to pay a call," Sally said. "But th' fair one got to skirlin' and birlin' like a stuck pig."

"What about?"

Sally and Pink both shrugged, and Sally said, "I couldna make head nor tail of it. Somethin' t' do with Quakers, I think."

"We put 'em in the kitchen so's not to disturb the customers," Pink said. "Chocolate and mackeroons seems to have quieted the girl."

Through the kitchen house door, Anne could see Dark Peggy and Fair Peggy sitting on the raised hearth, a plate of sweets and two cups between them. She heaved a sigh and went in, with Pink and Sally on her heels.

"Sally tells me you have some trouble . . ."

"Oh, Anne!" was all Fair Peggy could manage before bursting into tears.

"A terrible calamity!" Dark Peggy declared. "Mr. Shippen has forbid her from attending the Meschianza."

"Forbid?" Anne hung her hat and shawl on a hook by the door.

Fair Peggy nodded, swiping her tears with a wadded wet handkerchief. "Damn, damn Quakers!"

Anne dropped down to sit beside Peggy Shippen. "What have the Quakers to do with it?"

Dark Peggy explained, "It's the Quakers who are saying it isn't fitting to celebrate in time of war. The Quakers say a masquerade is licentious and lewd, and now her papa has forbid her from going to the Meschianza."

Anne asked, "Did you try to reason with him?"

Peggy sobbed. "I begged and pleaded, but Papa said we Shippens need to start straddling both sides of the fence. He said the British intend to soon abandon the city to the rebels."

"Abandon the city?" Anne gave Peggy Shippen a little shake. "He said those words?"

"I don't believe it, either, but that's what he said," Dark Peggy asserted.

Fair Peggy grabbed Anne by the hand and clutched it to her breast. "It is so unfair! I was to be one of the Ladies of the Blended Rose!"

"I—I don't know what to tell you . . ." Anne said.

"Tell her to mind her da," Sally said, folding her arms across her chest.

"Mm-hmm . . ." Pink agreed. "He sounds like a sensible man."

Fair Peggy shot Sally a look that would slice through granite, and Dark Peggy said, "Is it possible to continue our discourse without the ready ears and loose tongues of servants lurking about?"

"Lurking!" Sally looked ready to reach out and give each girl a good slap across the face, but Pink stepped between, and pulled her out to the shop.

Satisfied, Peggy Chew began, "We've come up with a scheme, and we desperately need your help."

"I'm resigned to the fact that I won't be there for the regatta or the tournament," Fair Peggy said with a sigh. "Papa will be keeping an eagle eye on me, and if I were to go missing, knowing exactly where to find me, he'd not hesitate to come and make a scene."

"A huge scene," Dark Peggy agreed.

"But Papa and Mama retire early. I can easily sneak off to attend the masquerade." Peggy took Anne by the hand. "I need your help—a haven where I can dress, and some kind of transport to the Wharton mansion."

Dark Peggy hedged. "It's a terrible sacrifice, we know . . . asking you to miss out on all the festivities. Peggy is my dearest friend, and I would do it in a heartbeat, but we agreed it would be too cruel to Captain André to deprive him of two Ladies of the Blended Rose at this late date . . ."

"Say no more." Anne smiled, and took Peggy Shippen by the hand. "Of course I'll do what I can. I'll wait for you here. Pink and Sally can help you dress, and we'll go to the masquerade together."

Both girls squealed and threw their arms about Anne, squeezing her so hard, she was like to start seeing stars again.

Anne untangled from the tearful, giggling mass and led the Peggies to the front door. "Come for chocolate tomorrow. We'll sort out the details then."

Church bells began ringing the hour as she stood beneath her shop sign and watched the happy girls skip up Chestnut Street and turn the corner onto Fourth. Sally and Pink came out to stand beside her.

Sally asked, "D'ye think there's any truth t' their stupid bletherings?"

Pink said, "I surely hope so."

"So do I." The church bells ceased, and the echo of the quivering brass hung in the air. Anne glanced up at the steeple of Christ Church. "Ten bells already! Elbert will be by in an hour. Best put on your striped apron, Sally. I'll ready the book."

✹ EIGHTEEN ✹

Yet panics, in some cases, have their uses; they produce as much good as hurt. Their duration is always short; the mind soon grows thro' them, and acquires a firmer habit than before.

THOMAS PAINE, *The American Crisis*

MASQUERADE

As promised, at half seven, Peggy Shippen came knocking at the coffee shop door, breathless, a bundle of striped silk clutched in her arms. She scooted inside, and Anne looked up the street to see if anyone was following.

"I climbed out the drawing room window," Peggy said, with a giggle. "Such an adventure!"

"Dress quickly, now." Anne bustled the girl up the stairs. "I ordered the coach for eight o'clock."

Leaving Peggy in Pink's patient and capable hands, Anne went to her room to dress. Sally helped to lace up the blue gown. In keeping with the simplicity of her costume, Anne decided to wear her waist-length hair in loose, natural curls, completely unadorned, and opted for a mere touch of rouge on her cheeks and a bit of lip pomade. Horse hooves echoed on the cobbles below, and Sally glanced out the window. "Th' coach's here."

Anne sat to secure the silver ribbons on her new blue brocade slippers. "Tell Peggy, then have him wait—I'll fix my pocket and be down in a tic."

Hopping to her feet, she checked the content of her coin purse before slipping it into her pocket. She added the door key, a clean handkerchief, and, as was her habit whenever she went out alone among the enemy, her half of the crown token from the fence at the Bowling Green. Patting her pocket, she muttered, "Money, door key, hankie, and Jack . . ." and ran down the stairs. "Where's Peggy?"

Sally shrugged. "Trying Pink's patience, no doubt."

"Peggy!" Anne called up the stairs. "Time to go! The liveryman's here!"

Pink was the first to come down the stairs, shaking her head, rolling her eyes. "I only did as she tolt me. That girl's run amok."

Swinging her mask by the ribbons with one hand, Peggy Shippen came to stand at the top of the stairs, announcing with a flourish of her shepherd's crook, "Behold, an Arcadian Shepherdess."

Peggy's face and chest were sponged with a base of white face paint, making the rouge smudged on cheeks and lips especially garish. Piled up high, her blond curls were cluttered with a chaos of bows and silk flowers. She wore a frilly white blouse with ribbon-laced stays pressing her breasts up to the verge of embarrassing calamity. Blue-striped skirt and lacy petticoats were kilted up to the knee, giving a daring view of legs encased in white silk stockings drawn tight to ankle and calf, and dainty slippers made of crimson red prunellos.

"You make for a lovely shepherdess," Anne cajoled the girl down the stairs. "Come along, now . . . Let's be off."

Peggy cried, "I forgot my lamb!" and disappeared.

"Shepherdess, mine arse!" Sally burst out laughing. "More like a bordello whore!"

"No wonder her father forbid her from going," Anne said.

"I can't get over how pretty your dress is, Annie," Pink said, fussing with the drape of Anne's skirts. "As sheer as a dragonfly's wing, this here gauze, and the dressmaker used just the right touch of sparkle."

Sally agreed. "Yer th' image of a starry night. I only wish I could be there t' see ye dancing . . ."

Anne huffed a sigh. "I only wish it were all over."

Peggy came tearing down the stairs with a little stuffed sheepskin complete with black button eyes draped over one arm. "I'm ready now!"

Giving Pink and Sally a farewell hug, Anne reminded, "Leave a candle burning for me . . ."

They climbed up into the carriage, and with a *"Los! Los!"* their German liveryman urged the horses up Chestnut Street.

"We're on our way! Can you believe it?" Peggy clapped her hands. "Oh, I know I've missed the regatta and the tournament, but the masquerade is bound to be the best part, don't you think?" The girl chattered on like an organ grinder's monkey. "Frivolous and lewd—Papa is so provincial. He doesn't know what he speaks of. He simply has to be absolutely wrong about the army leaving the city. Why on earth would they leave? I'm sure Johnny André would tell me if he was leaving—he is definitely sweet on me, though Peggy Chew would not have it so . . ."

The giddy girl's nonstop chatter devolved to nothing more than a buzz in Anne's ear—a steady drone to the *clip-clop, clip-clop* of the horses' hooves as they rode to the Wharton estate at the bend in the Delaware.

It was a fine, clear evening—warm enough to keep the canvas roof on their landau carriage pushed open. The view of the stars improved the farther they rode from the city lights. Anne leaned her head back and pressed her hand to the love token in her pocket, comforted by the view of the open night sky. A very bright star twinkled with a golden light, just above the horizon to the west, and Anne wondered if it might be Capella. She tried to remember the names of the brightest stars, and imagined Jack somewhere in the Pennsylvanian hills, stepping away from a campfire with Titus, Ned, and Isaac, to study the sky and identify the stars.

"I hear music!" Peggy exclaimed. "We must be close. Can you hear it? Do you think they're already dancing?"

"Probably . . ."

Peggy leaned forward, slapping the driver's seat back. "Hurry! *Schnell—schnell!*"

The liveryman snapped the reins, and the carriage jolted forward at a faster pace.

Anne handed her mask to Peggy. "Help me tie the ribbons on mine, and I'll tie yours."

In keeping with her dress, Anne's Venetian eye mask was fashioned of lightweight papier-mâché, and covered with matching blue silk and a sprinkling of silver crystals. Peggy's white mask was adorned with gold sequins and multicolored jewels, and had a short tuft of ostrich feathers jutting up at the center of the brow.

The carriage turned through the gates of the Wharton estate, and the robust music of a full orchestra sent Peggy bouncing in her seat. The vast lawn between the mansion and the river was taken up with the two huge pavilions erected for dining and dancing. Simply built of sailcloth fastened to a timber structure, the pavilions glowed golden from within, like immense isinglass lanterns.

"So many lights!" Peggy cooed. "Like some kind of a fairyland . . ."

On a rise beyond the pavilions, the manor house stood ablaze with candlelight shining from every window. A brigantine and three schooners were moored on the Delaware, their ship's lights twinkling bright reflections on the water. Hundreds of glass-paned lanterns were hung from the tree branches, casting soft pools of light on wooded pathways leading from the lawn to the river. The carriage rode up the long drive to the mansion steps, and the German driver helped the women debark.

"Let's go!" Peggy whined, and tugged Anne along as she kept an eye on their carriage, making certain the driver understood her direction to park and wait with the others.

The music came to an abrupt halt, followed by the applause, whoops, and whistles of the happy dancers. As the women approached the doorway of the pavilion, some breathless masqueraders spilled out to take the air between dances, and Anne and Peggy laughed at the ironic pairings.

Peggy pointed out a red-caped cardinal strolling arm in arm with a horned and tailed devil. At the doorway they bumped into a six-foot rabbit leading a cowled nun by the hand to scamper off behind the trees. Anne pulled to a stop at the doorway.

"Oh my word! How *beautiful!*"

During their committee meetings, she'd heard the British officers bandying about the dimensions of the pavilions, and listened to their lavish plans for decorating the interiors, but the final result went far and beyond her most wild imaginings. This Meschianza was more extravagant than any ball or *fête* she'd ever attended in New York.

More than two hundred feet long and forty feet wide, the pavilion walls rose to at least twenty feet tall. Utilizing his talent at designing stage scenery, André painted the canvas ground of pale blue with *trompe l'oeil* gold moldings and faux festoons of dark blue draperies. Structural beams and columns were painted a matching pale blue and decorated with pastel-colored fabric buntings, bunches of silk flowers, and trailing green ivy.

A series of twenty brass chandeliers hung from the rafter peak, ablaze with at least thirty candles each. The fifty-six pier glass mirrors André "borrowed" from local mansions and estates were mounted along the sidewalls, reflecting the light to illuminate the dreamlike scene of masqueraders making merry.

"Johnny outdid himself setting this stage," Peggy said, squeezing Anne's hand.

"I see Betsy!" Anne pointed to the raised gallery at the far end of the pavilion. Masked with a sheer veil drawn over the bottom half of her face, Betsy Loring was unmistakable standing at the gallery railing, looking down upon the crowd. Dressed in bejeweled pink satin and silk gauze, the turban on her head was strung with strands of gold beads and plumed with an explosion of ostrich feathers.

The Sultana . . . Anne admired how Betsy Loring managed to cock a snook at the snide nickname Howe's officers bestowed upon her.

The orchestra was seated in the ivy-wreathed bower beneath the gallery, and the refreshed musicians began tuning up. Couples whooped and skipped out to line up for the next dance, and the plank floor beneath their feet trembled with the rhythmic thrum of foot stomps as the musicians launched into a rousing *gigue*.

Anne could not help but bounce along to the rhythm and laugh at the sight of masqueraders crowding the dance floor in costumes ranging from the sweet and humorous to the macabre and fantastic. Anne accepted a glass of champagne offered by one of many black waiters dressed in flowing white silk shirts, trousers, and turbans.

"Oh . . ." Peggy issued a sad sigh. "It seems I'm not the only Shepherdess . . ."

There did seem to be an inordinate amount of shepherdesses and milkmaids hopping about on the dance floor. Anne noted more than several of them were very large, and one sported Hessian mustachios.

A Harlequin in a black eye mask came up and gave them each a tap on the shoulder with the slapstick he carried. After taunting them with the traditional, "I know you—do you know me?" he executed a perfect backflip.

Anne laughed and clapped. Dressed in tight trousers and a jacket made of diamond-patterned silk in bright red, green, gold, and blue, William Cathcart was perfectly suited to play the athletic Harlequin.

A masked brunette milkmaid in kilted red-striped skirts, complete with pail in hand, ran up and screamed at Peggy, "I know you! Do you know me?" Grabbing each other at the shoulders, the Peggies danced around in a squealing circle.

Another masquerader came off the dance floor to join their group. He wore a formfitting black velvet suit to show off a manly build, and a clever full-face mask, half-white, half-black—the white side the smiling face of comedy, the dark, frowning in tragedy. His disguise was topped off with a wide-brimmed hat cocked on one side to accommodate flowing ostrich feathers of red and white. Anne turned to the man she guessed was Oliver Delancey and said, "I know you—do you know me?"

Delancey swept off his magnificent hat in a cavalier's salute, and lingered over the kiss he placed on the back of her hand. "You, madam, are an *Enchantress* . . ."

"She's nothing of the sort," Peggy Shippen said. "She's Night, and I'm an Acadian Shepherdess."

"Fair Night . . ." Pulling Anne so close, she could smell the Armagnac on his breath, Delancey's whisper was provocative. *"All the world will be in love with Night and pay no worship to the garish sun."*

"Make way, Theater." A half-masked Greek god wedged between the pair, dressed in a white toga leaving one muscular shoulder and arm bare; he was otherwise adorned with nothing more than a crown and belt of silk grape leaves and bunches of purple papier-mâché grapes. The god offered a toast with the enormous golden chalice he carried. "At long last, the coming of Night. I welcome her and claim, I know you—do you know me?"

Anne dipped a curtsy and answered, "You are Bacchus, of course."

"I'm afraid you mistake me for my father." John André raised a haughty chin, and rested fist to hip. "You see before you Comus, God of Excess!"

"Nothing but appropriate!" Anne noted, tapping her wineglass to his.

Leaning in, André whispered in her ear, "It will be a pleasure to dance with something other than a dreary shepherdess or milkmaid." Taking Anne by the hand, he led her out to the dance floor.

Unfamiliar with the dance figures, Anne usually avoided the dance floor, but with face obscured, she was able to let such misgivings fly to the wind, and she hopped and skipped along with the free and easy crowd of merrymakers.

As the evening wore on, it was clear young Harlequin had laid claim on Night's attentions, but even so, Anne never found herself at a loss for dance partners. She linked elbows with a winged Cupid, did *chassé* with a Quaker, and danced a staid *minuet* with a very roguish Scaramouche. When the orchestra broke for a drink, Anne followed suit, making her way to one of the alcoves where refreshments and sweets were offered. A Plague Doctor with a long beaked nose and spectacle eyes handed her a glass of punch, saying, "Strong port for beaux, weak punch for belles. In a turnabout, I bring *you* a drink."

Full-face masks made identification difficult, but with a knowing wag of the finger, Anne said, "I know you . . ." recognizing the voice of a Cup and Book regular, Lieutenant Silk.

"The Sultana beckons . . ." Lieutenant Silk said, pointing across the dance floor where Betsy Loring stood waving a feathered fan over her head. Anne made her way through the crowd to greet her with a hug and an, "I know *you* . . ."

Betsy held Anne at arm's length. "Clever girl! Contriving a costume to show your lovely make and beautiful dishabille. You've caught many an eye, and one in particular. He hasn't taken it from you since you've walked through the door."

Anne smiled and nodded. "My Harlequin."

"Not that panting puppy . . ." Turning to glance up over her shoulder, Betsy said, "The mysterious Domino in the gallery."

Anne looked up to see the Domino Betsy spoke of, standing with one hand resting light on the rail. There were a great many Dominos at the masquerade, but this one was the most austere she'd seen. Attired in black from head to toe—plain tricorn, silken cloak, leather gloves and boots—the only dash to his costume was the unexpressive full-face mask, painted a metallic gold. From a distance his eyes seemed like gaping, black, malicious holes, forcing Anne to turn away.

"He's not watching me at all," Anne said. "I dislike Dominos, anyway. An uninspired costume suggesting a lazy, boring character."

"Really? I find the Domino most mysterious." The Sultana glanced back up at the gallery. "This one in particular is a cipher. Strong or timid? Friend or fiend? Saint or monster?" She beat her fan and with a sly laugh said, "I know this—tall and broad-shouldered—your Domino's a man who would fill a woman's bed." Betsy leaned in to give Anne a kiss on the cheek. "I'm off to the gaming tables next door— they tell me the Faro dealer is using gold coins for checks. A most splendid party!"

The musicians found their seats and began tuning their instruments. Anne watched Cathcart and Delancey pushing through the crowd in a race to claim Anne's hand for the next dance. Harlequin was the winner who led Night onto the dance floor.

In promenade toward the gallery, Anne looked up to see the Domino leaning on the balustrade, black-gloved fingers like talons gripping the wooden rail with both hands. She asked her partner, "Do you know the Domino up there? In the gallery?"

Cathcart glanced up and shook his head. "Why?"

"I feel his eye upon me."

Her Harlequin took her by the hands and they skipped back to their position. "I'd say most of the men here have their eye on Night."

Whether dancing, having a drink, or sharing a sweet, every time Anne looked up, she found the Domino watching her from on high like a black hawk, as if he were waiting for the right moment to spread his wings, swoop down, and snatch up his prey. None of the other officers seemed to know who he was, but after several hours passed with the Domino never once leaving his perch, Anne tried to shrug off her unease. *Probably a local Loyalist. Most likely timid and shy . . . inept with women . . .*

"Ladies and gentlemen!" the violinist announced. "This last dance of the evening is followed by a *feu de joie* at riverside."

The words brought about an instant scramble for just the right partner. Anne spun around to the tap on her shoulder, expecting Harlequin and his slapstick, but instead meeting Domino, looming. With a brief bow, and in a low, graveled voice he asked, "May I have the pleasure of this dance?"

"I think not . . ." Anne shook her head, turning on her heel, searching the crowd for Cathcart, or Delancey, or anyone other than this Domino to share the last dance with. "I'm afraid this dance is spoken for . . ."

"It's taken me hours to work up the courage to ask . . ." The thick golden mask kept the man's eyes in shadow, but his gruff voice, though odd, seemed to carry a smile with it. "Fair Night could not be so cruel as to refuse me now?"

Anne rose up on tiptoes, scanning the crowd for a more likely partner. "I am sorry, sir, but I did make a promise . . . Another time, perhaps—"

"Alas, I doubt I'll have another opportunity anytime soon—my company leaves on campaign at first light."

Anne dropped down to her heels. "None of the other officers have made mention of any campaign . . ."

"Not common knowledge amongst the lower orders." The Domino leaned in, whispering in her ear, "I'm with Clinton's advance corps—at the vanguard of a new offensive."

"You are correct, sir." Anne smiled, and dipped a curtsy. "I cannot be so cruel as to refuse you this dance."

They moved to take positions opposite each other, and the Domino's silken cape fluttered open long enough for Anne to catch the briefest glimpse of his crimson red jacket.

Ripe fruit . . .

As they spun and skipped and twirled, Anne kept her eye on the movement of her partner's loose cloak, hoping to spy a gorget, or catch sight of buttons or lacing—anything that might indicate the Redcoat's rank or regiment.

He must be among Clinton's High Command . . .

The music of the last dance ended all too soon to a chorus of groans and complaints, as many masqueraders crowded forward to beg the orchestra for one more song.

"The masquerade is over . . ." Anne reached up, as others did, to loosen the ribbons of her mask, but the Domino stayed her hand, grasping her softly by the wrist.

Head bent to hers, his raspy voice tickled her ear. "Like a covered dish, a woman masked increases a man's appetite. Let us take the air."

Nodding, Anne left her mask tied. For a man claiming to lack the courage to ask for a simple dance, there was suddenly little timidity in his manner, and something familiar in the way he pressed his hand to the small of her back, guiding her out the doorway.

Anne looped her arm through his and they strolled slowly, following along with other couples heading to the riverfront along a lantern-lit path. As they walked in silence she cast sidelong glances, studying the set of his shoulders, the tilt of his head, and the color of his hair in the lamplight, wondering how she might know this particular Redcoat.

"It's a shame we did not meet earlier," Anne ventured. "Will you be back to Philadelphia soon?"

His laugh was gruff and he shrugged. "One of the many unknowns of this soldier's life . . ."

"I don't envy your day in the saddle after a night of frolic," Anne said. "Will you be traveling far?"

"Far enough. My turn for a question." The tall Domino leaned to the side and in a playful whisper asked, "I know you . . . Do you know me?"

With a shake of her head Anne admitted, "You are too clever—the Golden Cipher I cannot figure."

Stopping in his tracks, the Domino reached out to stroke her cheek with the back of his gloved fingers. "Yet you are clear as glass to me."

Anne took a step back. "Were you with Burgoyne on the Hudson?"

The Domino chuckled. "Were you?"

Anne wagged her finger. "Then you must be a customer at the Cup and Book . . ."

In a voice suddenly less raspy he said, "She's pretty—the half-caste you have working for you now . . ."

Now? The word—the tone—froze Anne to the spot. Multiple rockets whistled up into the moonless night, shattering the star-strewn sky in fractured bursts of gold and silver.

"*Feu de joie!*" The Domino tossed his tricorn to the side and reached to loosen the ribbon at the back of his head. "I know you . . ." he said, in a clear voice, sweeping the mask from his face. "Do you know me?"

Anne went cold, as if an icicle had been drawn down from the nape of her neck to the base of her spine. Dancing at the outer edges of her awareness since she'd first glanced up to the gallery, his name escaped from her lips like a puff of frosted air.

"Edward."

The fierce saber slash Jack Hampton dealt Edward Blankenship had left a thick pink scar, beginning just above his left brow. It wormed over his eye, coursed across his nose, and cut the corner of his mouth, giving his smile a downward twist. His left eye was sewn shut, and there was a gaping dent at the bridge of his nose, where sharp steel had ravaged bone and cartilage.

"You must recall," he said, touching the tip of his middle finger to the circular scar centered on his forehead, "the tender remembrance you left behind."

Anne grabbed up her skirts and ran as fast as she could. She checked over her shoulder, and though Edward Blankenship did not give chase, she continued with all the speed she could muster, to reach the hired carriage.

The liveryman sat on the driver's seat, eyes to the sky, watching the fireworks as Anne threw herself against the side of the carriage. "Go now! Go! Go! *GO!*" she shouted, climbing up onto the driver's seat.

Surprised, the German fumbled for the reins and slapped the horses into movement. Anne turned to see Edward Blankenship standing in a beam of lantern light, tying the golden mask back onto his face.

"*Schnell! Schnell!*" Anne screamed, pounding on the driver's back with her fist. She looked again to see the caped silhouette with arm raised, waving good-bye.

"*My God . . .*" Heaving a sigh, she squeezed her eyes shut and held tight to the edge of her seat as the carriage sped through the gates and careened out onto the road back to the city.

Slamming the shop door shut, Anne grabbed the candle dish, hiked her skirts, and went tearing up the stairs screaming, "*Sallyyy! Piiiiink! Wake up! Get up!*"

Sally and Pink shuffled into the hallway in shifts and braids, blinking at the sudden light.

"Get dressed. Time to fly!" Anne breezed past them to her room, setting the candle on her desk. The bleary-eyed women followed in after, and Anne waved them off. "Go! Pack your necessary pockets . . . I'll ready the guns." She kicked off her slippers and turned her back to Sally. "Can you loosen these laces?"

Pink scrubbed her eyes. "Guns?"

"Yes. Guns. Hurry!" Anne gave Pink a little shove to the door. "We have to move fast . . ."

"Why are ye in such a swivet?" Sally asked, yanking Anne's laces loose. "Where're we goin'?"

"Back to Valley Forge—I sent the liveryman for fresh horses and a wagon." Anne spun around, shrugging out of her gown, and, seeing the two of them still standing there, she threw up the lid on the chest at the foot of her bed and shouted, "Do as I say! *Go!*"

"Stop and take a breath," Sally scolded. "Yer not makin' any sense."

"There's no time!" Anne tore through the bed chest, tossing items onto her bed. "He knows we're here . . . He's alive and he's coming . . ."

Sally grabbed Anne by the arm. "Who's comin'?"

"Edward Blankenship!"

"*God almighty!*" Sally ripped off her nightcap, and went running to her room.

Pink threw up her arms. "And who's Edward Blankenship?"

Anne stepped into her skirt. "The Redcoat I thought I killed in New York."

"Lord in heaven!" The answer sent Pink flying off.

In a matter of minutes they gathered back in Anne's room, dressed in common skirts, stays, and blouses, wearing sensible shoes and woolen shawls. After Bede's hanging, they worked together to devise a plan to slip away quickly if the need arose, taking only bare essentials with them. Sally carried a small gunnysack with her letters from David. A purse with all the money she'd earned as a free woman was tucked into Pink's cleavage, and she pinned her lucken-booth brooch to the inside of her stays. Anne added to her pocket a heavy bag of coin, the bottle of sympathetic stain, the mourning brooch containing a lock of her son's hair, and the wooden heart Jack had given her.

The case of dueling pistols lay open on the bed. Anne struggled to keep a steady hand, tapping the right amount of priming powder into the pan on the flintlock. After loading both guns, she buckled on a leather belt, stuffing one pistol at her waist and handing the other to Sally, who did the same.

They ran down the stairs and out the door to find the German liveryman waiting under the streetlight with a pair of fresh horses hitched to a light wagon. He smiled in relief to see Anne, and, point-ing to the wagon, he asked, *"Ist das gut, madam?"*

"Very good!" Anne said, relieved he'd understood her panicked instructions. The driver was a brawny young man, and she clapped him by one shoulder and pointed to the west. "You take us west—to the American camp. Valley Forge, *ja? Schnell, ja?"* She pulled the sack of coin from her pocket, shaking it in front of his eyes before pressing the money into his hand. "There's twenty Spanish dollars for you . . ." Before he could refuse, Anne stepped up into the wagon bed. The German stared to the west, his face impassive, weighing the purse in his big palm.

Sally and Pink climbed in behind Anne, and Sally said, "D'ye un-derstand, ye huge cabbage-eater? *Amerikaner* camp, *ja?"*

"Ja," the German said with a nod as he hopped up to take the driver's seat. *"Ich verstehe . . ."*

"Th' jingle o' silver is a universal language, na?" Sally said, as they settled into their seats with backs against the wagon wall and legs out-stretched.

"You—" The driver swung around in his seat, pointing to each of them in turn. *"Amerikaner, Amerikaner, Amerikaner—"* Slapping his chest, he added, *"Me—Amerikanisch!"* With a chipped-tooth grin he tossed the bag of coin into Anne's lap, snapped the reins, and the wagon lurched up Chestnut Street.

"Fancy that." Sally laughed. "He's a lad o' parts, our German—a rebel!"

Once they turned onto Market Street, the German broke out his whip, building quickly to a steady gallop, the ironshod hooves and wheels rumbling loud on the cobblestones. Anne settled back be-tween Sally and Pink, and they all held hands.

"We are a-fleetin' and a-flyin' now!" Pink said. "We'll be there in no time."

Sally added, "Fresh horses, a good driver, and less than twenty miles betwixt us and safe haven in Valley Forge."

With a bone-rattling thump they crossed the city limit and the place where stone paving abruptly transitioned to a rutted dirt road.

The pace slowed, but they left the telltale rumble of wheels on stone behind.

"Day's breaking," Anne muttered, and, sitting up she stared at the eastern sky brightening with the rise of the sun. "Do you hear that?"

"Hear what?" Pink asked.

"Horses."

"Yer overwrought," Sally insisted. "Naught but wagon clangor yet ringin' in yer ears."

Anne rose up on her knees, tugging the pistol from her belt. "We're being followed . . ."

Sally pulled Anne to a sit. "Frettin' yer guts t' fiddle strings does ye no good."

"He's toying with me, like a cat with a mouse," Anne said, her eyes riveted to the east.

Pink moved forward, squinting. "There *is* somethin' out there . . . You can see 'em now."

Along with the clatter of many horse hooves echoing in the quiet of the dawning, a string of tiny specks danced on the horizon. The German cast a glance over his shoulder, and shot up to his feet, cracking the whip over the horses' heads. *"Gott verdammt! Britische dragoner!"*

"There's at least a dozen horsemen . . ." Pink said. "They're gaining on us."

"There's no way horses pulling a load can outrace a company of British dragoons . . ." Anne clacked her pistol to half cock. Sally drew hers, and did the same. The German looked back and raised a brow. He sat down and pulled an ancient musketoon from beneath his seat, laying it across his lap.

The sun inched up in the sky as the wagon rumbled along the rutted road, the tiny dark specks grown to full silhouettes, riding two abreast. The dragoons came upon them, red horsehair tails streaming from the tops of their leather helmets, galloping along the roadside, staying just out of pistol range.

These light cavalry dragoons were expert horsemen. Armed with sabers, carbines, and the long-barrel pistols, dragoons were trained to fire and reload at full gallop. Another order was shouted and the horsemen turned, coming in at an angle to the road and the bounding wagon.

"They've come into range." Sally braced the barrel of her pistol on the wagon's edge. "Do ye see him, Annie?"

"He's the one masked," Anne said, "riding the bay charger."

Wearing a black kerchief tied over the left side of his face, saber raised, Edward Blankenship directed the charge from the rear of the oncoming attack.

Sally aimed and pulled the trigger. "Shite!" she cried, her shot jerked high by a bump in the road. "Wasted!"

The horsemen pushed their mounts to full-stretched gallops, now running parallel to the road and the wagon. The German leveled his weapon at them. In a flash of smoke, the blast of buckshot flying from the flared muzzle of the musketoon sent the attack force into a scatter, three riders dropping back, slowing to a canter.

"Huzzah!" Sally shouted.

Blankenship sheathed his sword, drew his pistol from the saddle-mounted holster, and spurred his mount. Anne took a shot at the fast-moving target to cover the German rushing to reload his musketoon, but the dragoon Captain charged forward unfazed. He came sweeping past, no more than five yards away, and discharged his weapon. The women ducked down at the flash, arms thrown around one another, but the driver was hit square in the chest, the blast from the high-caliber weapon throwing him from his seat. Anne shot up to see the German left behind, lying in a heap at the side of the road.

Terrified by the gunfire, the runaway horses careened off the road, and the women were thrown flat as the wagon veered precariously, wheels crashing and bouncing over the rough terrain. Anne struggled to keep her balance, trying to clamber over the driver's seat and gain hold of the reins snapping like satin ribbons in the air, just beyond her reach.

The wagon jolted over a tree stump, knocking Anne back with Pink and Sally being thrown from one side of the wagon bed to the other as the driverless, exhausted horses slowed, dragging the wagon to a complete stop.

The fecund steam of sweating horseflesh was suddenly over-whelming as the dragoon company circled the wagon, the horses all huffing great breaths of air. Lying in a dazed tumble, head pounding, Anne tried to catch her breath, but the menacing, dull note of hoof-beats closing in set her heart racing anew.

In a creak of leather, several dragoons dismounted, and one leaned over the edge of the wagon, the death's-head emblem painted on the frontpiece of his black leather helmet gleaming in the oncoming day-light. He issued a terse command. "Out!"

Dazed and shaken, the women helped one another over the wagon side. With the muzzle end of a carbine prodding her ribs, Pink was herded off to one side. Anne and Sally were grabbed gruffly by both the arms and pushed to stand before Edward Blankenship.

Prancing and curveting on a big bay stallion, Edward Blankenship cajoled his mount to stand beside Anne. Sally shrieked when he zinged saber from scabbard, swinging the blade as if to lop Anne's head clean off, stopping short to let the honed edge hover one scant inch from her neck. Knees buckling, Anne remained upright only with the rough support of the soldier holding her steady.

"This one," Blankenship said, lightly touching the saber tip to Anne's forehead, just above the right brow, tracing a diagonal line across her face, mirroring the scar on his own. "I'll have her bound, gagged, and placed on my horse."

One of the soldiers pulled a dirty rag from his pocket, stretching it tight to cut the corners of Anne's mouth. Another bound her wrists with a length of rough hemp rope.

"Cowards! Preying on helpless women!" Sally struggled against her captor's grip, kicking and wriggling. "Lickin' the arse of this devil . . ." she shouted. "Can ye no' see he's a mad, twisted devil?"

Leaping from his saddle, Blankenship tossed off his helmet and marched up to Sally. "I am a devil of your mistress's making," he shouted, ripping the kerchief aside for all to see his horribly scared and mangled face, "come to you straight from the maw of this hell." Pull-ing a fist, he punched Sally so hard in the stomach, she dropped to her knees, coughing and gasping for breath.

Pink pushed past her guard, and ran to crouch beside Sally. Blankenship brushed the dirt from his retrieved helmet and retied his kerchief to mask the worst of his injuries as his men hurried to hoist Anne onto his horse. Swinging up behind her, the Captain ordered his company to remount and re-form. Bound, gagged, and caught in the vise of Blankenship's arms and legs, Anne looked as sad and helpless as a rag doll caught in a mongrel's mouth.

Pink cried out, "Where're you taking her?"

His scarred mouth twisted into an odd half smile, half snarl, and Blankenship called, "You can tell him I've taken her to the Provost Marshall in New York. The traitor Anne Merrick will answer there for her crimes." Raising his hand in command, he led the company wheeling to the east and they galloped into the glare of the rising sun.

Sally clutched her middle, keening and sobbing. "There's no savin' our Annie . . . Blankenship will see that she swings . . ."

"Moans and wailings mend nothing . . ." Pink held out her hands. "Come on."

"The monster has Annie in his grip." Sally stumbled to her feet. "You can see it in his eye—his heart's turned black and bitter as gall . . . There's no hope."

"There's always hope." Pink pulled Sally to the wagon. "Th' man coulda kilt th' three of us with a snap of his fingers—but he din't, did he? No—he give us a message for Jack—and there's the hope." She hopped onto the driver's seat, and pulled Sally up to sit beside her. With a click of her tongue, Pink gave the reins a snap and a tug, turning the horses back toward the road.

"Hold tight—for we're goin' to fly like a feather on the wind."

✺ NINETEEN ✺

You have already equaled, and in many instances excelled,
the savages of either Indies; and if you have yet a cruelty in
store, you must have imported it, unmixed with every human
material, from the original ware-house of Hell.

THOMAS PAINE, *The American Crisis*

AS BLACK AS HELL

Anne lay flat on her back, centered inside the Captain's tent, staring up at the tin bottom of the lantern hanging from the ridgepole. Bound wrists resting on her stomach, she wiggled her bare toes to encourage circulation beyond her tightly bound ankles. With a groan, she rolled into a curl on her side, the movement of the items hidden in her pocket shifting to slide over her hip, giving her comfort.

Stretching her bound arms out, she inched forward, ever so slightly, toward the pair of saddlebags Edward Blankenship left behind. *There's a knife in there . . .*

She lifted her head and looked out the wide-open tent flaps at the company of dragoons gathered around a cheery campfire, having their supper. With half his face covered in a black kerchief, Edward Blankenship sat on a campstool precisely positioned for a clear view inside his brightly lit tent, his eye never wavering as, machinelike, he shoveled in his supper, hand to mouth, as if synchronized to the beat of a drum.

Anne flipped to lie on her back again, preferring the bottom of the

lantern to her captor's unceasing gaze. "Always watching," she muttered. "If I had a knife, I would cut his good eye out for relief."

Huffing a sigh, she stretched her arms toward the lantern, clench-
ing and unclenching fists. Her backside and legs ached from the full
day's hard ride astride in the saddle, wedged in the small space between
the upward slope of the cantle and Edward Blankenship's hard body.

He'd removed the awful gag when the company clambered aboard
the ferry to cross the Delaware, saying, "One peep from you, and I'll
cut your throat." Not wanting to do or say anything to trigger the
rage he'd exhibited with Sally, Anne kept her mouth shut. Other than
single-word, necessary directives, his threat was the extent of their
communication during the whole long ride.

Entrusting her care to no other, astride or dismounted, Edward
Blankenship was a constant at her side—to the point of giving only
the slightest, gentlemanly turn of the head when she needed to relieve
herself—and taking her along when he needed to do the same. There
was no opportunity to enlist the sympathy of a compassionate by-
stander. No slipping away unnoticed. No screaming for help. No
gnawing at the ropes keeping her hands immobile.

No chance to escape.

It was clear to Anne this man had spent the long months of his con-
valescence weaving and finessing a plan for wreaking vengeance, and
she was certain it did not include fair trial for treason. His allowing
Sally and Pink free was at once a relief and a worry—passing the news
of her capture to Jack became her only hope, and her fiercest dread.
Though she prayed Jack would not rise to the bait so carefully arranged, she knew he could do nothing else.

This Edward Blankenship is a monster of our creation.

The canvas trembled and Anne snapped her eyes open to see the
Redcoat captain coming through the doorway to rest on haunches,
setting down a tin bowl of stewed beans and a ship's biscuit at her side.
He produced a folding knife from his pocket, and flicked it open with
a click to cut her bindings.

Anne sat up, rubbing wrists and ankles where the rough rope had chafed her skin raw, and eyed the soldier's fare he brought with some suspicion. Blankenship settled in to sit tailor style beside her, and, tapping the bowl with the knife blade, he said, "Eat."

At a loss with no utensil to use, Anne slid the biscuit from the bowl, and nibbled on the rock-hard edge.

Blankenship snatched the biscuit away. Crushing it in his fist, he sprinkled the crumbs onto the beans and said as if reading her mind, "I daren't give you fork or knife, lest you put out my other eye." His face twisted into his odd half smile, and he produced a horn spoon from his pocket.

Like a gentleman scientist studying the eating habits of the African ape, Blankenship sat watching her every move. Spoon in hand, Anne was sorely tempted to wolf down the meal—her first in more than twenty-four hours. She concentrated on feeding herself slow, dainty bites, determined this man would not turn her into a groveling beast.

"You must be thirsty." Blankenship broke out a tin canteen from his pile of gear and handed it to Anne, saying, "This is like a picnic, isn't it? Just like the ones we used to have."

Anne gulped down the water, nodded, and whispered, "Yes."

Blankenship threw his head back and announced to the peaked canvas, "She speaks!" He pulled the seemingly bottomless flask she'd seen him sipping from throughout the day from his breast pocket, proclaiming, "This calls for a celebration! Scots whiskey?"

With a slight shake of the head, Anne said, "No, thank you."

"Ahhh . . . I recall now—you aren't one for strong spirits, are you? A woman who likes to keep her wits about her, aren't you?" Blankenship threw back a gulp. "I enjoy drink far more than I should these days. Medicinal. I find it helps to purge the melancholia." Lifting his flask in toast, in a voice growing overloud, he recited:

> For valour the stronger grows,
> The stronger the liquor we're drinking.
> And how can we feel all our woes,
> When we've lost all the power of thinking?

He drained the flask dry, set it aside, and dug another exactly like it from his saddlebag. Flipping up the lid, he sniffed, and informed Anne, "Rum."

Anne reached for the water canteen, asking, "May I?"

"Of course. I only wish I had something more suited to your taste—Champagne, or the citrus punch you are so fond of . . ."

"I'm fine with water." Anne took a drink, and plugged the cork back in.

"That fop André's Meschianza business was quite the spectacle, was it not? The masquerade added a certain dramatic dash to my purpose, don't you think? I have to admit, it was most amusing, playing you with your own game. The look on your face . . ." Blankenship inched closer. "You must tell me—were you really there? On the Hudson with Burgoyne?"

Anne kept her eyes on her bowl, scraping up the last few beans without answering his question.

Blankenship slapped his knee. "You *were* there!" He laughed and took a drink of rum. "You are a clever one, and Washington is nobody's fool for putting you in service. It makes me feel better, knowing I am in good company within the web you spin."

Anne set her bowl aside. "Thank you for the supper."

"Oh, fye!" Blankenship sighed. "No need for thanks—we're old friends, are we not?" He shifted over to sit with an arm thrown around her shoulders. "I'm glad we have this time together. You've been so often in my thoughts, dear Anne."

Anne drew her knees up, hugging them to her chest, and whispered, "I didn't want to shoot—I wish . . ."

"*Pfft!* If wishes were horses, beggars might ride . . ." he said, with a wave. "Put it out of your mind. The bullet didn't do much more than dent this hard skull of mine—too weak a charge in your pistol, I'm afraid, much to my good fortune. The saber slash did give me some trouble. It festered badly. Cost me the eye . . ." His arm dropped from her shoulder, and he began toying with the hinged cap on his flask. His voice grew quiet. "It was the unseen wound to my heart that almost killed me. A wound most grievous . . . more difficult to cure, I'm afraid."

Anne resisted a sudden urge to touch him, and whispered, "I'm not that woman, Edward. I might not look like one, but I'm a soldier, like you, fighting for my cause . . ."

Blankenship nodded. He sat sipping his rum, draining the flask dry, staring beyond the tent flaps into the darkness beyond the campfire. After some time he spoke.

"I was out of my senses for that woman. I loved her so much . . ." He smiled. "I even recited poetry to you—do you remember?"

Anne nodded. There was a marked change in his voice. No longer filled with bitter bravado, it was the voice of the handsome, caring man she had betrayed so terribly.

For liberty, for freedom . . .

"You filled my dreams," he said, slipping his arm about her waist. "I dreamed of having you in my bed—of taking you home to Devonshire to marry—to raise a family . . . But you're right—you aren't really the woman of my dreams . . . are you?" Pulling the kerchief from his head, his scars grew vivid in the lantern light, and his voice suddenly harsh. "But look at me. I'm surely the stuff of your nightmares."

He slammed his forearm across her throat, pushing her flat to her back. Keeping one arm crushed against her windpipe, Blankenship grabbed her flailing wrist, and twisted to lie on top of her. Pinning her to the ground, he began to recite:

> *My love is as a fever longing still,*
> *For that which longer nurseth the disease;*
> *Feeding on that which doth preserve the ill,*
> *The uncertain sickly appetite to please . . .*

Gasping for breath, Anne struggled against his weight, feeling the arrhythmic pulse of him growing hard against her leg.

> *My reason, the physician to my love,*
> *Angry that his prescriptions are not kept,*
> *Hath left me, and I desperate now approve*
> *Desire is death, which physic did except . . .*

Struggling for air, her lips unable to even form the word "please" as Blankenship pressed his face so close to hers, she could see faint hash marks beneath a thin layer of scar tissue grown over the black stitches holding the sunken hollow of his left eye shut.

> Past cure I am, now Reason is past care,
> And frantic-mad with evermore unrest;
> My thoughts and my discourse as madmen's are,
> At random from the truth vainly expressed . . .

Blankenship's knife clicked open and the blade flashed in the lantern light. With his forearm jammed against her chin, her screams were muffled, and her arms flailed. He sliced a diagonal gash from the inside corner of her right eye across to her jawbone, and ended his poem:

> For I have sworn thee fair, and thought thee bright,
> Who art as black as hell, as dark as night.

With those words, Blankenship released her, and, rolling off to sit up, he heaved a breath in and out. Clicking the folding knife shut, he tugged the kerchief back over his head to mask his scars.

Anne sat up, sobbing, trying to stanch the bleeding with her hands, tears mixed with blood to seep through her fingers, dripping down onto her chest, staining her hands and shift crimson.

With mask in place, Edward Blankenship reached for his saddle-bags. "We need to see to your wound," he said, his face twisting into a friendly smile. "I am a deft hand at dressing wounds, but I'm afraid a cut like that is bound to leave a scar."

"*Stop!* Are you insane?"

"I'll tell you what's insane, David—" Jack swung his saddle onto the sheepskin he'd laid over the gelding's back. "It was insane for me to leave them there alone." He bent down to reach under the horse's belly and grasp the girth strapping.

"You think I wanted this to happen? She's *my* sister . . ." David grabbed Jack by the arm. *"Goddamn it,* will you just wait and let us think this through . . ."

Jack jerked away. "The bastard has two days on me. There's no time to waste. This is a now-or-never business."

The scouting party had been at their supper when David and Alan galloped up. The ill news of Anne's arrest at the hands of the risen-from-the-dead Blankenship sent them all moving to help Jack ready for the long ride to New York. David was alone in questioning his sanity.

"I filled your canteen," Ned said, securing Jack's bedroll and pillion bag with the leather straps at the back of the saddle. "There's three days' rations—pemmican, jerky, johnnycakes, some coffee and sugar."

"Keep the coffee," Jack said. "I won't be taking the time for it."

Alan McLane dipped up a cup of the coffee bubbling on the campfire. "You may not need the rest, Jack, but your horse will."

"He can always get another horse," Isaac said, slinging two full feed bags connected with a single length of rope over the gelding's rump. "It's not so easy to find a good woman."

Titus slapped a sheathed knife into Jack's hand. "I just put a sharp edge on it. Nothing as quiet as a knife in a pinch." Jack slipped the weapon into his boot.

David shook his head. "Why is everyone encouraging this madness?"

"Because Jack's got the right of it," Titus said. "This here's a one-man job."

"Alan, will you tell them?" David implored. "If we just take a minute, we can come up with a better plan."

"There's no planning a mission like this, David." McLane set his mug down. "The chances are slim, but I agree that a single man moving quick and light has the better chance in this situation. Once Jack gets in the city, he can figure the best plan to suit the circumstances."

David sank down on a log, head in hands. "This is all my fault. I should have never put Annie in this kind of danger . . ."

"Stop talking nonsense." Jack sat beside David. "It was Anne who led Blankenship in a merry dance. Then I came along to rub his nose in it and near cleaved his face in two—she put the bullet in his head—and we left the man facedown in a pool of blood. This is not your fault." He threw an arm over David's shoulders. "Listen to me. I know we don't always see eye to eye, and I know you're worried to death, but I love your sister more than I can say in words. I'm going to bring her home, or I will die in the trying."

"Here . . ." David swiped at his eyes, and fumbled under his jacket, pulling forth his pistol. "I think small arms are better suited for this mission. Your long rifle cries 'Yankee.'"

"You're right." Jack stood and shoved the pistol in his belt. "Thanks."

McLane handed over his pistol as well. "Always good to have a spare string for your bow."

Jack drew the strap of his pouch over his head, and found his hat. "That's it. I'm ready."

"Keep your mind on the main chance," Ned said, shaking his hand. "Worry tends to blunt the edge of your blade."

Isaac grabbed Jack by both shoulders and looked him straight in the eye. "Use what you've learned here. Approach like a fox. Fight like a lion. Disappear like a bird."

"You might need this." Titus came up and dropped a small sack of coin down Jack's shirtfront. "Remember this Redcoat bastard is lying in wait—best go through the back door, even if it costs you some time."

"It feels odd leaving without you, brother." Jack pulled Titus in for a hug.

"You'll do this, Jack," Titus said into his ear. "I know you'll bring Annie home."

Swinging up into the saddle, Jack fit hat to head and, with a wave, headed toward the darker sky.

* * *

At every bend in the road, at every stop to water the horses, or feed the troops, she expected—prayed—wished Jack would come swooping down like Perseus with his winged sandals, and rescue her from the monster's grip.

Every one of the four days she shared a saddle with Edward Blankenship, Anne watched the sun moving lower on the horizon, willing it to stay put with all her might. The sun paid her no heed.

Every night Anne shared a tent with Edward Blankenship, and watched as he dosed his madness with liquor, and she endured his drunken attempt at a lover's spoon, curling to press up against her back. Though she could feel the tickle of his breath moving the small hairs on the back of her neck, and his ardor grow and ebb, never once did he attempt to force himself upon her.

Yet.

Come morning, her captor would bring breakfast and tea, and shades of the Edward Blankenship she knew in New York would rise to the surface. He was very kind and tender cleaning and applying a soothing salve to the wound he first inflicted, then stitched, all the while telling the same story about a seaman named Abner, who cared for him when everyone else had called his cause a lost one.

Then he would bind her wrists and hoist her up into his saddle, and she would spend the long hours pondering what day she would change if given the opportunity to spin back time.

The day I met Edward? The day I agreed to quarter him in at the Cup and Quill? The day I first encouraged his kind affections? The day I shot him? Anne glanced down at the arm wrapped round her waist. *If I went back to that day, I'd be certain to load my pistol with plenty of powder.*

When the dragoon company approached the fort at Paulus Hook and readied to board the ferry to Manhattan Island, she couldn't help but voice her surprise. "We're really going to New York?"

"To the Provost as promised," Blankenship said. "To set the bait."

The company was dismissed when they reached the city limits.

Blankenship turned his horse into the yard behind the Provost Prison, and helped Anne dismount. Pointing to the prison gallows, he asked, "Fond memories?"

The gallows was much weathered since the night Jack earned his hanged man's scar. Turning on her heel, the sounds of cart wheels on Broad Way and peddlers hawking their wares on the streets came familiar to her ear. A half mile down the thoroughfare was the Trinity churchyard, and the grave of her only child. She stared out at the green of the Commons, and she looked up to the familiar steeples of St. Paul's and the Presbyterian Church, feeling like a cat in a strange garret. Anne'd walked these streets for ten years, and now it was all tainted with the bad smell of British occupation.

Hand pressed to the small of her back as if he were leading her out to the dance floor, Edward escorted Anne up the stairs, their footfalls resonating in the desolate hallway leading to the quarters of New York's Provost Marshall.

Hundreds of prisoners were confined in the Provost Prison, among them Britain's most notorious rebels. A damp, malignant odor like the smell of rotten cabbage seeped into the brick and mortar of the building, permeating the stark order of William Cunningham's office.

Centered before two windows barred with iron, the Provost Marshall was seated behind a big desk, scribbling away in a ledger with a quill pen. To allay the evil stink, a thick bayberry candle burned in a dish beside an elegant silver tray equipped with crystal decanter filled with amber spirits, and a pair of stemmed glasses.

The only other furniture in the room were two ladder-back chairs in the corner occupied by Cunningham's minions, who were all too familiar to Anne's eye. Sergeant O'Keefe was fatter than ever, stuffed into his regimental red coat. Near strangled by the black leather neck stock, his veiny, carbuncled nose seemed on the verge of explosion.

Anne was surprised to see Richmond, Cunningham's mouth-breathing mulatto slave and hangman. The night Jack was near hanged, Richmond was felled by a shot from Tully's pistol. The hangman was even more menacing with the thick-matted snakes of hair he once sported shorn off, and his pate shaved clean and greased. Anne noted he still took to wearing a knotted noose slung over his thick neck.

Tall and lank as a starved weasel, dressed like a Puritan preacher, William Cunningham, New York's Provost Marshall, came out from behind his desk to greet them.

"Captain Blankenship! What a pleasure . . ."

By misappropriation of funds, outright theft, and sheer inhumanity, William Cunningham had lined his pockets with silver and gold by allowing hundreds of American prisoners of war in his charge to die of starvation and horrific mistreatment unsanctioned by any convention.

Overshadowed by a beak of a nose, the Provost's gaunt face was riddled with pockmarks and suffered under the round weight of a cauliflower wig. Cunningham leaned in and peered at Anne. "What have we here, Captain?"

"I'm delivering on my promise." Blankenship set his heavy dragoon's helmet on the desk, and pulled Anne front and center. "Dressed in whore's clothes, this is one of the gang of rogues who plucked Jack Hampton from your gallows the night I was near murdered."

Anne snapped her head up.

"You promised to bring me Jack Hampton . . ." Cunningham lifted the stopper from the crystal decanter sitting on his desk and poured two glasses. "There were three treacherous whores that night. One was left for dead in the churchyard; the other two—" He shrugged his sharp shoulders. Coming around the desk, sipping his whiskey, Cunningham leaned forward to study Anne's features in profile. "Hard to tell now—almost a year ago . . . and we were deep in our cups that night. She could be one of them, I suppose . . ."

"Don't be fooled. She was there. She's a chameleonlike serpent, capable of changing her hue to the nearest object." Blankenship took up his glass and tossed down his drink.

Cunningham poured two more drinks. "But for the gash on her face, she's sweet and tasty to the eye. I'll gladly take a piece of that . . ."

Blankenship tore off his mask with a guttural growl, and whipped out his sword, catching it just under the tip of Cunningham's hooked nose. "Touch her, and I'll carve you a smile to rival my own."

"You said she was a whore . . ." Writhing and wincing like a frog on a skewer, Cunningham croaked, "Apologies, sir. I was confused."

"She's mine." Blankenship whipped his sword in Anne's direction, and her flinch provoked a menacing smile. "Can you not see she bears my mark?"

"Of course, sir." Cunningham nodded. "I understand now."

Anne shifted her gaze from one man to the other, caught like a sparrow between a hawk and a buzzard—one ready to eat her alive, the other waiting to pick at her bones.

"Beware, Mr. Cunningham, the woman is an arch deceptress. There is no correspondence between her fair face and her foul heart." Blankenship swung his sword to tap its tip to the skin sewn shut where an eye should be. "She and her rebel lover have cost me dearly."

"Then we are kindred spirits, sir. The rogue has caused me a few scars as well." The Provost lifted his wig slightly to display a bumpy white scar curling over his ear. Cunningham scooted out of sword's reach, backing around to sit behind the relative safety of his desk. "I hope Jack Hampton rises to the bait as you say he will. He's a crafty fellow to have escaped my gallows."

"Every man has his *tendo Achilles*, and this woman is Hampton's." Blankenship sheathed his sword, and took up his glass. "Before Jack Hampton dances on your noose, he will watch me fuck this whore just before I slit her throat." He tossed back the shot of whiskey. "You, sir, are charged with keeping our bait contained while I pursue the quarry." Dropping a bag of coin on the table, he said, "Fifty guineas for the service, Cunningham."

"I'll see to it personally, Captain."

"Farewell, my pretty little bird." Blankenship grasped Anne rough by the chin and pressed a kiss to her forehead. "Try not to beat and flutter against the wires of your cage—I don't want your feathers too damaged." Pulling the kerchief back to mask his scars, he fit helmet to head and left.

Waiting until the boot falls faded down the hall, Cunningham flopped into his chair and blew out a whistle. "Mad as a hatter, isn't he?"

Anne's nod was vigorous. "The madman abducted me from my home in Philadelphia. I swear to you, I do not know this Jack Hampton." She held her hands in supplication, no need to pretend the tears streaming from her eyes. "Please, sir. I am an innocent. I beg you, free me from this monster!"

"And turn his wrathful eye on me? I don't think so." Cunningham gave the heavy leather purse a shake, the silver singing, *shink, shink, shink.* "There is method in his madness, and I will abide by the madman's judgment."

"I have money!" Anne said. "I've friends who will pay in gold for my release . . ."

"O'Keefe. Richmond . . ." Cunningham called his hirelings forward.

"I swear to you, sir," Anne pleaded, "you are making a grave mistake. I can pay in gold . . . more than he . . . a hundred guineas!"

"Better gag her," Cunningham advised. Dipping his pen in the inkwell, he scribbled across a page. "Here is an order for her imprisonment."

"NO!" Anne shouted. "Please . . ."

O'Keefe came from behind to hold her by the arms, and for all that she pursed her lips and flailed her head about, Richmond managed to stuff a greasy rag in her mouth. Anne tugged free and swung around, first smashing her bound fists into O'Keefe's jaw. Landing a solid knee to the fat Irishman's bollocks, she sent the Sergeant into a moaning squat.

Anne spit out the vile gag, and glared at Cunningham. Richmond flung his noose over her head—pulling the knot tight—jerking her down to her knees.

"You fucking witlings—g'won, now—take the bitch away!" Cunningham reached for the whiskey. "And have her properly shackled."

O'Keefe straightened up, his face as red as a beet. "Where ought we take her?"

"To the *Whitby.*" Cunningham dropped the sack of guineas into a desk drawer. "No one can get to her there."

*   *   *

The East River was calm and gray as the dusk sky, and the little dory moved slow against the current as they rounded a highland on the Brooklyn shore. With hands manacled behind her, Anne shifted in her seat facing aft, unable to find any position to allay the piercing pains at the small of her back, watching the last vestiges of New York City disappear from her view.

"*Unhh.*" Anne's breath puffed out in a bitter grunt. With every dip and tug of Richmond's oars, she felt little bits of hope peeling away, lost to the wind, like the chips of faded paint from the dory's hull.

"There she is—" At the back of the boat O'Keefe pointed and added with a sneer, "Your new cage, little bird."

The *Whitby* was moored in Wallabout Bay, centered in a shallow channel between the rising shoreline and an oozing mudflat, secured with a heavy anchor chain the thickness of a man's arm stretching out at fore and aft. No longer seaworthy, cannon, colors, sails, masts—anything that ever once made the warship proud or beautiful—had been stripped away. The gunports were fastened over with rusted iron bars, and here and there Anne could spy what seemed to be faces lurking, observing their approach.

As they drew closer to the dark hulk, Anne could make out figures lining the rails on the gangways, and many more moving around on the deck. With a shake of her head she said, "I didn't know it would be so crowded . . ."

"Don't worry, darlin'; there's plenty room for you. Death daily makes a place for fresh comers." O'Keefe pointed to a gondola pulled up alongside the *Whitby*, and bodies wrapped in wool blankets being passed down from the ship's deck and stacked four high, like so many meal bags at the miller. At the other end of the hulk, stevedores on a single-masted shallop were off-loading eight heavy hogsheads of freshwater with the aid of a derrick.

O'Keefe shouted, "Ahoy!" as they pulled up to the gangway ladder mounted to the larboard side of the hulk. Richmond wrestled with a heavy key ring to unlock Anne's shackles, and he held on to the ladder to steady the rowboat, waving her up. It was slow going, as she struggled to negotiate skirts while climbing the rungs. Following behind, O'Keefe gripped her bottom with a squeeze, saying, "Up-a-daisy, darlin'!"

Anne turned and glared down at him. "I'll be certain to tell Captain Blankenship of your liberties, Sergeant."

O'Keefe snatched his hand back, grumbling, "No call to make threats . . . Only tryin' to give you a boost . . ."

They ascended the gangway at the top of the ladder, and the crowd of ragged, emaciated prisoners parted to make a path as a pair of Hessian guards came to escort Anne and O'Keefe. She tucked the loose tendrils back behind her ears, and kept her eyes downcast as they passed through the murmuring crowd up the stairs to the quarterdeck.

Sergeant O'Keefe completed the transaction, relinquishing the authorization signed by Cunningham and the prisoner to the duty officer in charge. The hard-looking Hessian with stiff-waxed mustachios sat on a stool at a small desk, dipped his pen in the inkwell, and enrolled her name on the roster: *Anne Merrick, widow, rebel, spy.*

With a "Pardon, madam . . . but we must . . ." the Duty Officer ordered one of the guards to search her body for weapons. A blush came upon her, and Anne held out her arms and squeezed her eyes shut, enduring the humiliation as best she could.

O'Keefe leaned back against the railing and smirked, watching the guard rub his hands over Anne's breasts, hips, and down her legs. "Doesn't he have the best duty aboard this tub?" he sneered. "Relax and enjoy it, little bird."

The guard snapped to attention. Pointing to Anne's right hip, he said, *"Es ist etwas da . . ."*

"My pocket," Anne explained. "Only a few silly things . . . a woman's necessaries."

The Duty Officer held out his hand. "Your pocket, please, madam."

Anne untied the ribbon around her waist and pulled the pouch up through the waistband of her skirt. The officer emptied it out onto his desk and sorted through the items—coin purse, hankie, half-crown token, wooden heart, and mourning brooch. He counted the eight shillings in her coin purse. The Hessian lingered on the brooch, studying the single blond curl lying beneath a convex crystal. The brooch was a quality-piece with a fine gold case, encircled with a frame of seed pearls. He asked, "From your husband, madam?"

"No. My son."

The Hessian nodded, swept everything into the pocket, and handed it back. Before Anne could utter a thanks, O'Keefe snatched the pocket from her hand.

"I'll have a go at that . . ." He first reached in for the coin purse, emptying the eight shillings into his pocket. When he pulled out the brooch, Anne lunged out to grab the Irishman by the arm.

"You thieving bastard!"

The Hessian officer was on his feet in a thrice with sidearm drawn and cocked, shouting, *"Halt!"*

Anne backed away, palms up, chest heaving, tears streaming down her face. The Hessian stepped toward them with eyes narrowed, and jammed his pistol into O'Keefe's fat gut. "Return ze pocket, Sergeant."

O'Keefe tossed the pocket onto the floor and Anne scooped it up.

"Und ze rest . . ." the Hessian said. "Vat you stole."

"Stole!" O'Keefe sputtered. "She's a bleedin' rebel spy!"

The two guards had swung their muskets from shoulders and clacked back the hammers.

O'Keefe fumbled in his pocket, and snapped eight shillings onto the officer's desk. "One, two, three, four . . ."

"Und ze brooch." The Hessian smiled, holding out his hand.

"I'll be making a report of this to the Provost," O'Keefe said, slapping the brooch into his palm.

As if O'Keefe were nothing more than an annoying fly, the Hessian waved him off the quarterdeck. "You are dismissed, Sergeant."

O'Keefe went running down the stairs. He stopped at the gangway ladder, and thrust his arm up in a two-fingered salute. "Take that, German twats!"

One of the guards leaned over the rail and shouted, *"Irish arschficker!"*

Anne took the brooch from the Captain, and dropped it into her pocket. "Thank you, Captain. Please keep the coin for your trouble. I don't have the words to explain how much this brooch means to me."

"*Nein.*" The Hessian officer swept the coins from his desk and held them out to her. "I'm afraid you vill need more zan I, madam."

The guards escorted her down to the main deck. Night was falling and a blue-jacketed soldier made the rounds lighting the ship's lamps. Anne could see the lantern swinging on the little dory Richmond rowed around the bend back to the ferry landing.

The prisoners had all been herded below, and the guard who'd cursed at O'Keefe became grim-faced, and pointed to the hatchway with an apologetic shrug. "*Los, madam.*"

Clutching her pocket in her hand, Anne looked down into the hatchway at the steep stairway disappearing into utter black darkness. A foul-smelling updraft pushed her back a step.

"*Los . . . los . . .*" the guard urged.

Taking in a deep breath, Anne took four steps down before finding the handrail. The noxious effluvia of sick stomachs, loose bowels, and unwashed flesh grew more pungent at every step, and she slapped a hand over her mouth to keep from retching. Stomach roiling with nausea, legs going limp, Anne sank down to sit on the stair tread. She glanced up at the guard still standing over the hatchway, and said, "I can't . . ."

The guard said, "*Das ist gut, madam, das ist gut,*" dropping the hinged metal grate over the opening and locking it in place.

The grate cast a faint checkerboard shadow on her new world. Anne leaned her head against the handrail and pressed the back of her hand to her forehead. *Feverish.*

To the right and left of the stairway, the lower deck was bereft of any light. Anne could hear the moans, groans, snores, and coughs of a multitude, but all she could see was the faint movement of shadows shifting and writhing.

Skinny gray shadows crept up from this all-enveloping darkness, joining her on the stairway. Thinking they were coming to take her down into the dark pit, she whispered, "I'm sorry. This is as far as I can go . . ."

"'Pon my word, missus," a dull voice responded. "You've found the spot what serves as heaven aboard the *Whitby*."

Heaven . . . The stench was overpowering, and Anne raised her nose to the grate to harvest a breath of fresh air, trying hard not to think about what generated the awful smell. *Worse than the sewers of New York* . . . Reminded of volunteering at the hospital in King's College, she dug into her pocket for her handkerchief, and brought it to her nose. *Lavender*. Folding the linen into a triangle, she tied it over her face, like a highwayman's mask. *That's better.*

Anne pulled out her brooch, and swiped her thumb across the crystal. "Jemmy," she whispered. Making a silent vow to never speak ill or unkindly of Hessians ever again, she pinned the brooch to the inside of her stays.

The Hessian said I'll need my silver . . . Anne ripped a few of the stitches holding up the hem of her wool skirt, and one by one slipped the eight coins inside the wool casing.

Next, she drew out the bit of broken cast iron. *No one would steal this.* Closing her fist around it, she let the rough edge of the ragged metal bite into her palm. *Jack wore his around his neck . . .* Anne slipped the ribbon string from her pocket, and tied it onto the token, making a half-crown necklet to hang over her heart.

Heart . . . She delved into her pocket for the last valuable needing safeguarding. She set the wooden heart on the first stair tread, centering it in a faint square of light beaming in through the grating. She traced her fingertip over the smooth curved wood, and the words Jack had etched into it.

Love Never Fails.

It seemed forever ago she and Jack lay entwined together on a bed of sweet balsam, staring up at the same stars. Anne yawned, and heaved a smiling sigh, remembering how she'd first scoffed at the bed Jack manufactured for their woodland tryst.

What I would give for a sweet balsam bed right now . . .

Anne tucked the wooden heart between her breasts and tried to make the best bed she could of the stairs. Legs curling to the side, hip propped on the fourth stair, head cradled on arms braced on the first stair, she peered up through the grate and could see the swath of stars Jack called the Milky Way. *So many stars, they appear as a mist to our eyes* . . . She could almost feel his warm breath in her ear, whispering, *I'll rescue you from any monster—land or sea* . . .

Keeping her eyes focused on a tiny patch of sky, trying very hard not to blink, it didn't seem to take long for the heavens to oblige and send a shooting star streaking through the sky.

"Rescue me, Jack." The moment the wish escaped her lips, she imagined the whisper slipping through an opening in the grate, flying through the night sky, across earth and water to land dancing in his ear.

Plying through water as black and smooth as a good Irish stout— oarlocks and oars muffled with rags—Jack maneuvered between the British war and merchant ships moored at Peck's Slip on the East River.

Heeding Titus's good advice, Jack came to New York by the round-about way of King's Bridge, taking the back roads to the village of Haarlem. There, he traded his gelding and the purse for a weather-beaten skiff and worn fisherman's gear. Riding the outgoing tide by the dark of the moon, Jack had reached the city in no time.

A ship's bell chimed nine, and the tide was just beginning to rise. Jack drew in his oars to coast under the pier and tie his skiff up to a barnacle-crusted piling. He hurried to pull on soft sealskin boots, tucking the loose trousers into the cuffed tops. Stuffing two pistols and a knife into the sash tied around his waist, Jack donned a dark fisherman's jacket and slouchy knit cap. He hoisted himself onto the pier, sending a pack of wharf rats scurrying to the dark end.

The streets seemed much livelier in the occupied city than the year before, when British martial law was first declared. Jack hurried down Water Street, collar turned up, cap pulled down to eyes, hands stuffed into pockets. It was Friday night, and the dockside taverns and trulls were doing a brisk business. Jack ducked into a deep doorway to avoid confrontation with a jovial group of drunken Redcoats coming out of the Three Cups, and found he shared the dark corner with a couple in amorous congress.

Before reaching Queen Street, he turned to cut through an alleyway and, counting from the left, pulled himself up over the garden gate of the fifth gabled house, landing in a soft thump.

The blossoms were blooming on the tailor's peach trees, and Jack hove in a noseful of the pleasant perfume that served to calm his racing heart. Skirting around the privy, past the kitchen house, he headed straight to a pair of shutters keeking yellow light around the edges. He rapped three double taps in quick succession, and waited.

Jack could hear shuffling and muttering, but no one came to unlatch the shutters. He knocked the signal once again, this time whispering, "C'mon, Stitch—it's me—Jack—"

The shutters swung open accompanied with the clack of flintlock weapons. Stocky Hercules Mulligan stood in a brilliant burst of lamplight, a pistol in each hand. Jack spun to see Tully coming up from behind, armed with a mean-looking stevedore hook, ready to do some damage.

Jack swiped off his hat, and threw up his arms. "For chrissakes, Stitch—I used the fucking signal, didn't I?"

"I'll be *bumswizzled!*" Hercules Mulligan lowered his weapons, and leaned out the window, a huge smile cracking his ruddy face. "If it isn't Jack Hampton himself!"

"You used the old signal—" Squinty-eyed Tully hung his hook onto his belt, and in a voice graveled by years of smoke and rough drink, the old smuggler said, "I near gutted your arse, you stupid bastard." Swinging a leg over the windowsill, Tully asked, "Where's Titus?"

"He's back in Pennsylvania, scouting for Washington." Jack followed Tully in through the window, and latched the shutters closed. "He's got a woman now."

"Rascal, you!" The tailor pulled Jack into a bear hug, then held him at arm's length. "You could use a shave, boyo . . ."

Jack worried the whiskers on his chin. "I've been on the move."

"There's a lean, hard look about you, lad." Hercules pointed to the scar on Jack's cheek. "Very menacing, that one. I'd head the other way, if I saw you coming at me."

Jack smiled and hooked a finger on the scarf at his neck, pulling it aside to show the hangman's scar. "You haven't seen this one yet . . ."

"A badge of honor, that scar. You bear it, but we all had a hand in earning it." Mulligan went to the cupboard where he kept his liquor, and poured out three glasses of whiskey.

"I've earned a few more badges since then," Jack said, plopping down into the desk chair.

"If we're showin' scars," Tully said, taking up a glass of whiskey, "I've got a dandy on me hairy old arse . . ."

Jack laughed, and the tailor proposed, "A toast—" Raising his glass, he said, "The dew may kiss the morning grass. The clock may kiss the hours past. A lad may kiss a maiden lass. And you, my friends, may . . . drink hearty!"

They tossed back their whiskey, and had a good laugh. Jack heaved a sigh, and raked his fingers through his hair. "It's good to see you both . . ."

Hercules Mulligan, tailor turned spy, refilled the glasses. "As glad as I am to see you, Jack, it's not the safest place for you here— minching about New York. Our Provost has a long memory, especially for a gallows thief like you. What are you about?"

Jack tried to smile. "Thought we'd share one drink afore begging a favor."

"Ah, now . . ." Hercules pulled up a chair. "There's no begging amongst true friends."

Tully straddled his chair. "Out with it . . ."

"They've taken Anne"—Jack's voice cracked—"and I need your help getting her back."

❧ TWENTY ❧

Heaven knows how to set a proper price upon its goods; and it would be strange indeed, if so celestial an article as FREE-DOM *should not be highly rated.*

THOMAS PAINE, *The American Crisis*

DARK AS NIGHT

"Raus!"

The abrupt shout was followed by a jangle of keys, the shriek of rusty hinges, and a reverberant clang as the iron grate was swung open. Head cradled on arms, Anne yawned, tugging at the handkerchief tied over her nose. Pulling the linen past her chin, she greeted both the daylight and the guard leaning over the hatchway with bleary-eyed blinking. Entranced by the fuzzy balls of gold wool quavering at each point of the guard's tricorn, her sleepy brain worked to connect the morning's sights and sounds. *Hessian. Keys. Locks. Prison . . . prisoner.*

The Hessian leaned in and gave her a poke with the business end of his musket. *"Raus!"*

Sitting up, very stiff, Anne wiped sand from her eyes, noting, with a bit of a chuckle, that she'd found a better night's sleep on the stinking stairway of a rotting prison hulk than in the arms of Edward Blankenship. She reached back to knuckle-rub a cramping pain at the base of her spine, and noticed the gray congregation of emaciated, bedraggled men gathered at the bottom of the steps, all waiting patiently while she so blithely stretched and preened.

"Oh, dear!" Anne grasped the rail and pulled up to a stand, her empty pocket fluttering down the steps. A tangle of skeletal arms reached forward to snatch it up.

"My apologies, gentlemen," she stammered. "I—I had no . . . I'm not accustomed . . ."

"Don't fret, missus," a voice declared. "You're wakin' was a pretty sight to behold. Isn't that right, fellas?"

Nodding heads all affirmed agreement, and Anne could feel a blush rise to her cheeks. One of the prisoners ventured up the stairs, offering the pocket she'd dropped.

"Yours, miss . . ."

"Thank you . . ."

He'd stepped into the beam of daylight illuminating the hatch-way, and Anne could see the man's few wisps of thinning hair were bespeckled with nits, and his scalp was crawling with vermin. She turned and ran up the few stairs—stomach heaving—barely making it to the railing on the landward side in time to lean over and retch up a viscous, yellow sputum.

Throat burning with the rancorous bile, she shivered, and let the pocket flutter down to the water. Anne used the hem of her petticoat to wipe vomit from her chin, and dab away the salty tears stinging the cut on her cheek. Light-headed, she leaned against the rail, studying the bright red blossom staining the edge of her shift, and fingered the cut on her cheek.

Bleeding . . .

The violence of her stomach caused the wound to tear. Inflamed and tender, the skin immediate to the cut felt hot to the touch. The salve Edward applied the day before was dried and crusted, brown flakes of it sticking to her bloodstained fingers.

Thump, thump, thump, thump . . .

Anne looked up to see a frail-looking man pulling a heavy, blanket-wrapped parcel up through the hatchway. Another followed after, and another, and another— *The dead . . .*

Thump, thump, thump, thump . . . Bony heels striking the wooden stair treads thudded a rhythmic dirge as ten corpses were dragged up the hatchway stairs and laid side by side beneath the stairs to the quarterdeck. Someone had taken the time to sew three of the deceased into their blankets; the rest had no shroud other than the filthy, feculent rags they had died in. Anne untied the handkerchief from her neck and crushed it to her nose, grateful for the vestige of lavender clinging to the threads.

It was clear two of the dead had perished from the pox, every square inch of exposed skin erupted in sores caked with dried pus and blood. The other dead men were unlike any corpse she'd ever seen—their bodies gray, desiccated hulls—reminding Anne of the empty cicada shells one might find scattered beneath the trees in the fall.

Jail fever. She could only guess these had died from hunger, dysentery, and sheer misery. Anne pressed a hand to her forehead. *A little warm?*

A never-ending multitude continued to shuffle up from belowdecks—all sorts of men—white, black, and brown—sailors, soldiers, and citizens—all mingling together with no apparent distinction given to rank or race. Some of the prisoners collected to sit in small groups where worn playing cards were dealt, or lead dice made from musket balls were thrown from cupped hands. One ambitious man received customers at his impromptu barbershop, equipped with a crate and a small pair of sewing shears.

A handful of the prisoners stood out clearly better off than the majority—relatively heartier, more fit, and less ragged.

Fresh comers, no doubt . . . like me.

Anne flinched to see a fresh comer breach the hatchway. He wore the uniform of her brother David's old regiment, the Third Yorkers. Oozing pustules had broken out on the young soldier's face, neck, and hands, and his eyes were glazed with fever. It was odd to see a man with such a rampant case of smallpox wandering free, but on a ship so crowded and confined, there was no point in enforcing quarantine.

Stomach still a bit wambly, Anne turned her back to the forlorn scene. Leaning elbows on the rail, she gazed across a short stretch of water to the shore, no more than a hundred yards away.

It was a pleasant sight—like a painting—neat and ordered. A hill rose up from the sandy beach, where a small gristmill straddled a millstream, the waterwheel turning slow. The peach trees in the orchard were just past blossoming with a scattering of pale pink petals still clinging to the branches. An iron weathercock mounted on the peak of the mill was directed by an easterly breeze, and a woman wearing a bright white sunbonnet and apron worked a hoe in the garden.

A fellow prisoner standing off to Anne's right said, "The miller's daughter keeps a nice kitchen garden. She even has a bed of sparrow-grass."

Barefoot, and equal to Anne in height, he was dressed in a faded, checkered frock shirt, and sailor's baggy striped trousers. The silk kerchief tied at his neck was grimy and veered to ragged, but Anne could imagine it was once a nice bright shade of yellow. He had a head as round as an orange, and the ginger hair sprouted on noggin and chin was cropped to an uneven curly fuzz by an uncaring barber with haphazard shears.

Anne asked him, "How do you know—about the sparrowgrass?"

He inched a little closer. "I'm among them what pass for fit, and lucky to be chosen for burial duty." He jerked a thumb to the row of dead bodies. "We haul the corpses past the mill, and bury 'em on the beach over yonder."

"Poor souls." Anne squinted at the sandy beach the sailor pointed to.

"Aye, that." He scowled. "They don't even make fit food for worms, do they?"

"A difficult duty, seeing to the mortal remains of your brother prisoners," Anne said. "Very Christian of you, sir."

"Not difficult at all," he said. "Dig a trench till the guard says deep enough. Roll 'em in, and toss a bit of sand over 'em." The sailor reached back to scratch between his shoulder blades. "Nothing Christian in it, either. Do it mainly to get away from this stink and set my feet upon hard land. Getting a whiff of sweet earth and grass now and then helps to keep me from being sewn into my blanket."

Anne sighed. "From here, the little mill seems almost a dream, doesn't it, Mister . . . ?"

"Jones. Trueworthy Jones." The man introduced himself, bowing slight at the waist. "Once with Glover's Marblehead Mariners, of late a seaman on the captured privateer sloop *Deane*, out of Boston."

"Anne Merrick." She managed a grin and dipped a slight curtsy, taking the line from the Hessian's roster. "Widow, rebel, and spy."

"Spy! Always somethin' of consequence to land a woman in this hellhole." Trueworthy smiled and revealed a set of tobacco-stained, rotted teeth.

"There are other women aboard?"

"None now, save yourself," Jones said. "Women are a rarity here." Before Anne could ask what had become of the other women, the sailor offered, "Some among us remembers you from the Cup and Quill."

Anne perked up. "You know the Cup and Quill?"

"The best coffee in New York town, as I recollect." The sailor scratched inside his shirt. "And Miss Sally's scones . . . a wonder!"

Anne heaved a sigh, relieved by the thought of Sally and Pink safe with David and Titus. *They must have gotten word to Jack by now . . .* Quiet for a moment, she asked, "Has anyone ever jumped ship? The shoreline is so close and the water seems calm . . ."

"Put it from your thoughts." Jones lowered his tone, wagging his bushy brows toward the Hessians armed with rifles posted up on the quarterdeck. "They'll sink you afore you're two strokes out."

Anne stiffened. A sharp pain knifed her in the belly, as if someone had wrapped a wire around her innards and pulled it tight. She sucked in a gasp, and let her breath out slow as the pain subsided.

Trueworthy's blue eyes popped in alarm. "Are you all right, missus?"

"It's nothing. A crick in my spine." Anne rolled her shoulders, grinding both fists into the gnawing pain at the small of her back. "That's what I get for making a bed of stairs."

"I don't know . . . You've gone wan as a milk-washed fence . . ."

"I am feeling a bit . . . off." A shrill, high-pitched tone began squealing in her right ear.

"A-fevered?"

"I don't think so . . . a little dizzy."

"Have you been pox-proofed?"

Anne nodded. "As a child."

"That's good." Trueworthy Jones studied Anne's face. "Let's get you a drink," he said, guiding Anne forward with a push on her elbow. "The scuttlebutt's at the bow."

"Water would be good," Anne said. "Maybe something to eat?"

"We won't be getting our rations until later in the day, and fresh comers aren't accounted for in the shipment, so you won't get a share till 'morrow," he said.

"I see . . ."

"Don't be downgone; you're not missin' much—rancid salt pork and weevilly biscuit, if we're lucky. I've a spare ship's biscuit put by . . . hard enough to break a rat's tooth, but better than naught. I can give you a piece to nibble on."

"That is most generous, Mr. Jo . . ." A wrenching cramp stopped Anne in her tracks and pulled the wind from her lungs. Drawn into a hunch, she tried to choke back her cry. Tiny silver explosions erupted around the spinning periphery of her vision, and she wavered trying to maintain her balance.

Murmuring, *Feu de joie . . .*" Anne tottered sideways as if felled by an ax, last aware of the sickening crack of her skull hitting the deck.

"Jack—wake up."

Jack snapped his eyes open and bolted upright from the rough pallet he'd made for himself under the potted lemon tree in the corner of the tailor's office. Sweeping his hair from his forehead, he asked, "What time is it?"

"Time to wake . . ." Hercules sat in his desk chair, tape measure strung around his neck, shirtsleeves rolled to elbows, his brawny forearms braced to knees. "Tully's brought news."

Jack followed the tailor's troubled eyes to Tully standing in the doorway, and felt his heart slip to his stomach. Afraid to say the words too loud, he whispered, "Is she . . . ?"

"No . . ." Tully came into the room and pulled over a ladder-back chair to straddle. "She's not dead. The word's been put out loud and clear—the Widow Merrick's been arrested by the Provost for treason and assault and will be tried and hanged."

"That's fantastic news!" Jack brightened. "Where she's being held? The sugar house?"

"Well . . ." Tully shifted in his seat. "Hard to say . . ."

"I'll go out and see what I can learn . . ." Jack tugged on his hat.

Hercules shook his head. "You best not show your face, Jack. Tell him, Tully."

"Dragoons are out in force, patrolling the highways in and out of the city. They are crawling over the waterfront—questioning every man working the docks, the fishboats, or ferrying over from Paulus Hook and Brooklyn." The old smuggler took a deep breath and turned to the tailor. "How about pourin' us all a little scoof o' your rye whiskey, Stitch?"

Hercules folded his arms across his chest. "Quit scrubbing around it, Tully. He needs to know . . ."

Jack looked up. "Know what? What is it?"

"No one could tell me a peep about where Anne is being held. I tapped all my sources and came up dry as an old nun's twat. I was on my way back when I bumped into an old mate—" Tully rubbed the stubbly, steel gray hair on his head. "You remember Dobbsy?"

Jack nodded. "I do."

"Aye, well, we got to palaverin', ol' Dobbsy and me, and he tells me he's been making solid silver a-stevedorin' for this boatman who hauls water . . ." Tully's squinty eye twisted tight in grimace. "Out of the clear blue, he tells me he saw that fat bastard O'Keefe, pushing the Widow Merrick up the larboard ladder on the *Whitby* yestereve."

"The *Whitby*?"

Hercules said, "The prison hulk the bloodybacks have moored out in Wallabout Bay."

"A prison hulk?" Jack fell back against the wall. "Was Dobbs drunk?"

"Dobbsy's always drunk." Tully shrugged. "I didn't want to question him too deep and risk tipping our hand. The man can't be trusted when his pocket's dark and he needs a drink."

"He's a drunk. He might be mistaken : . ." Jack pulled the hat from his head.

"It's too much of a coincidence, Jack." The tailor's voice was soft.

"Fuck me!" Jack dropped his head back to bump against the wall, and stared at the ceiling. "A hulk."

"There might be a way in," Hercules said.

Tully cautioned, "With Hessian guards on duty day and night, I don't see how he can get in."

"A hulk," Jack repeated to the ceiling. "I need a way in *and* out. It's impossible."

"What did you think?" Hercules gave Jack's foot a kick. "Did you think they'd set Anne out on the Commons so you could stroll up la-di-da and whisk her away? Put your mind to it, lad. Once more to the breach . . ."

"I can't think. I'm put to wit's end." Jack gave his head a shake. "I thought she'd await a hanging at the sugar house, like I did. I know the lay of it . . . I already figured a disguise—one of those sergeants who comes around trying to recruit rebel prisoners. I'd get in the yard when there was a crowd—like when they parcel out the day's rations. Then I'd create a diversion—a fire, maybe—start a panic, grab Annie, and get out in the confusion."

"Hmmmph!" Hercules nodded. "That's actually quite a good plan."

"But she's not at the sugar house." Jack stared at his open palms. "A prison hulk . . . Fucking Blankenship."

"There's a lesson learned." Hercules shrugged.

Jack nodded. "Make certain your enemy's dead once you kill him."

"Dash me timbers!!" Tully slapped his knee and rasped, "I think I know a way!"

"How?"

Plucking the tape from the tailor's neck, Tully pulled it tight to measure the breadth of Jack's shoulders. "A-yup!" He smiled, and gave

Jack a shove. "You'll fit, alright." Fumbling in measuring Jack's height from seat to the top of his head, he grinned and affirmed, "Aye, a tight squeeze, though . . . but you'll fit just fine . . ."

Hercules snatched the tape away. "Tell us what you're bletherin' on about!"

Tully fell to his knees and grabbed Jack by the shoulders, his squinty eye almost open. "The water barrels, Jack! The water barrels!"

Jack blinked for a moment, then grabbed Tully by the side-whiskers. "Why, you gnarly old son of a sailor's whore!" he cried, planting a kiss right on the top of Tully's stubbly head.

Hercules laughed and pounded both Tully and Jack on the back. "The fuckin' water barrels, lads!"

Water. She tried to swallow, but her throat was sore and parched. *The scuttlebutt's at the bow . . .*

Anne's eyes fluttered open. Dim light and a breeze off the river was coming through a small barred opening. A gull sailed through one of the patches of blue sky. It was very quiet but for the creak of ship's timbers and a droning hum in her head. Heavy wooden knees curved off the ship's skeleton just to her right, supporting the beams and planking of the deck above.

The prison hulk . . .

"Hullo there!"

Anne turned her gaze to the right. The sailor she was just talking to at the railing was now sitting at her side with two tin basins—one filled with water, the other with fresh butchered beef.

She rasped, "Trueworthy Jones."

"That's right! That's my name," he said, dipping a handkerchief into the water. "You gave us all quite a scare, Mrs. Merrick." Jones smiled and looked over his shoulder. "Didn't she, lads?"

Trueworthy sat before a low wall made of four sea chests stacked two high. Three scruffy heads peered over this partition, smiling and nodding; one man waggled his fingers in greeting. Anne tried to wave back, struggling to find her hand under an itchy blanket pulled up to her chin. Crinkling her nose at the bad smell puffing up from under the wool, she asked, "Where are we?"

"The gun room—belowdecks." Trueworthy draped the wet handkerchief over her forehead. "The officers allowed a place for you here. A woman needs a bit of privacy."

Anne attempted to elbow up to sit, but her head began to throb, and she fell back to finger a large knob risen under the hair on the side of her head.

"You have to rest, Mrs. Merrick . . ." Trueworthy scolded, rearranging the compress that had slipped from her head. "You've lost a lot of blood."

"Blood?" she squeaked.

Jones turned to his mates and snapped, "Shove off, you lubbers. Mrs. Merrick needs her rest."

Anne shifted her shoulders, suddenly aware of the lumpy strawfilled pallet she was lying on. Under the blanket, her skirts were all bunched around her hips, and the rough osnaburg canvas was like pumice stone on the bare skin of her bottom and legs. She could now see that what she mistook for raw beef in the basin, was in fact a mound of bloody rags. "What . . . ?"

Grasping her gently by the shoulder, Trueworthy leaned in and whispered, "I'm afraid you lost the babe."

"Babe?"

"Not more'n a mite. Two months gone, were you?" he asked, scooping up a cup of water from a small pail. "Hard on a woman's soul, losing a youngling at any stage." Trueworthy slipped an arm under her shoulders, and held the cup to her lips. "You're fevering. You should drink."

Anne gulped down the water, brack and bitter as it was. "A baby . . ." she murmured, lying back. *Two months gone. The farewell at Elbert's . . .*

"I cleaned you up as best I could," Trueworthy said, replacing the compress with one fresh and cool. "I'm no stranger to the way of it—

eight sprouts, we have, Mrs. Jones and me. I helped in birthing three, and was by her side when she lost a youngling or two as well."

"A baby . . . lost before I even knew it was there . . ." Anne began to sob. "What kind of woman am I not to know? The signs were there. I should have known, Mr. Jones. I could've . . ."

"Now, now. No use in that kind of talk. Probably for the best, at any rate," he said, stroking her head. "Lord knows this hulk's no fit place for human beings of any sort, much less a woman alone with a babe in arms."

"I didn't have to be alone, don't you see?" Anne whispered. "He's a good man, my Jack. He would have taken care of us."

Trueworthy's face took on a hard look. "Aye . . . well where is he now, this Jack?"

"Scouting for Washington. Sally will get word to him and he'll come for me . . . I know he will—" Anne grabbed the seaman by the arm. "You can come with us, Mr. Jones, when we escape."

"I suppose he give you this, your Jack." Trueworthy slipped the little wooden heart into Anne's hand. "Found it when I loosened your stay strings."

It had grown too dark to read the words, but she clutched it in one hand, and reached for the half crown strung round her neck with the other. "Jack said he'd rescue me, on land or sea . . ."

"Best not to dwell on such fancies . . ." Trueworthy said. "There's no rescue from this hellhole we're in—you hear me? None. Put your mind t' getting strong—put your mind to surviving. This war can't last forever."

"No rescue . . ." she repeated, turning her head to stare at the darkening sky out the window.

Anne could feel them leave her—hope—faith—confidence—courage—twining up to disappear into the atmosphere like the tendrils of steam from a cup of tea. It wouldn't be long now before she was completely empty, like the cadavers up on deck.

She that dances must pay the fiddler . . . Anne rolled toward the sound of water trickling into the tin basin and the copper-tinged smell of the blood-soaked rags. *Yet another child of mine, lost—dead—* She reached out and grasped Trueworthy by the wrist and said in a heart-aching whisper, "I wish I were dead, too."

"Aye . . . don't we all . . ." he murmured, and pressed the cool cloth to her head.

❧ TWENTY-ONE ❧

The cunning of the fox is as murderous as the violence of the wolfe.

THOMAS PAINE, *The American Crisis*

THE PRICE OF FREEDOM

Jack peered into the looking glass Hercules held out, set the razor aside, and used a towel to wipe away the dregs of lather from his fresh-shaven face and neck.

"Not really long enough for a proper Hessian mustache, is it?"

"It's good enough," Hercules said, twisting in a bit of beeswax to curl up the ends.

"What you lack in mustache, you gain in hair," Tully said, tugging the long braid trailing down Jack's back. "Any Hessian would be proud to sport this here rattail."

The tailor coached, "Let's hear your German once again— *Fire! All hands abandon ship!*"

Jack barked, *"Alarm! Feuer! Alle mann von bord!"*

"Aye, aye, Captain."

Jack snapped his heels in attention. *"Jawohl, Herr Hauptmann!"*

Tully grinned. "Sounds like a proper cabbage-eater to me."

"Excellent," Mulligan agreed.

"I better get a move on." Jack buttoned up his weskit made of golden yellow wool, and brushed away a smudge from the white breeches he wore. "The waterboat leaves for the *Whitby* at five o'clock . . ."

"Don't you fret. The boatman'll wait for his silver." Hercules helped Jack into a regimental jacket of Prussian blue with facings to match his weskit. "The last hundred pieces cross the bastard's greasy palm *after* Tully sees your barrel loaded onto the *Whitby*."

"That's an awful lot of money, Stitch, and I'm grateful to you for it—for everything. I would never have managed any of this without you . . ." Jack pulled Hercules into a hug. "Both of you." Throwing his arm around Tully's shoulders, he said, "I swear on all I hold dear, no man could want for better friends."

Hercules pulled away, swiping a tear from his eye. "Enough folde-rol. Let's get this barrel packed." He snatched up a full gunnysack and dropped it into the empty hogshead centered in his office. "There—that will also serve as a bit of a cushion for your backside. You're next. Scoodle down in."

The big water cask was just a little more than four feet tall. Tully held it steady while Jack hopped up to sit on the edge, swing his legs around, and slip inside the barrel. Curling his shoulders inward, he managed to clear the narrow barrelhead to sit with knees bent, back supported by the bellying slope of the barrel staves.

"Anne's clothes are in the gunny you're sitting on." Hercules began to tick off the list he had scribbled on a scrap of paper pulled from his pocket. "Pry bar?"

Tully handed down a short, iron bar. "Secure this somehow—you don't want it banging about in there—"

Jack slipped the pry bar inside his weskit.

"Tinderbox?" Hercules read from the list.

Jack patted his chest. "In my pocket."

"Good. The diversions?" Hercules asked.

"This here's the whale oil." Tully handed down a corked tin bottle, which Jack situated near his feet. "And here's your bomb and match." Tully gave Jack a heavy corked grenade, and a coil of cotton cord soaked in salt peter and coated with gum spirits.

Looking very much like the pomegranate the French named the little bomb for, Jack weighed the iron ball in his palm before buttoning it into his coat pocket. "Packed tight with powder?"

"Filled to the brim," Tully assured. "And that there's a quick match, so light it and get out of the way."

"Hat!" Hercules grabbed the tricorn decorated with fuzzy yellow balls of wool at each tip. "Try to keep it from being crushed. And last but not least . . ." The tailor passed down a fungus-covered chunk of rotting tree bark. "This is a good idea. I hope it works."

"So do I," Jack said, tucking the chunk of foxfire between the gunnysack and the barrel wall. "It's bound to be as dark as a coffin in the hold of that ship."

Hercules reviewed his list. "That's the lot. Close her up, Tully."

"Once I fit this lid on, you latch it on the inside." Tully pointed to the hooks mounted around the inside edge of the false barrelhead he'd devised. "I only drilled three small holes to give you some air— anything more might attract notice—so it'll be close in there."

"I'll be fine." Jack looked up at both heads peering over the barrel edge, one ruddy and ginger, the other grizzled and gray. "I'll get word to you somehow, once we get settled."

Hercules reached in and squeezed Jack's shoulder. "You're using one of your nine lives doing this thing."

Jack grinned. "That still leaves me with four, by my reckoning."

"Good luck to you, lad."

"I'll need it." Jack knuckled his brow in salute, then to Tully said, "I'll be seeing you soon, my brother."

Tully grasped Jack by the hand. "Look for the signal. I'll be there." He slid the lid into place.

The barrel went dark, and the foxfire glowed eerie green. Jack moved his fingers methodically from one hook to the next, making certain each was firmly affixed. Once finished, he settled in, rapped his knuckles to the barrelhead, and shouted, "Let's go!"

* * *

Edward Blankenship produced a watch from his weskit pocket and flicked the gold casing open. "I mean to have my company aboard the six-o'clock ferry, Provost."

Narrow shoulders hunched, William Cunningham dipped his pen in the inkwell, and continued to scribble as fast as he could, his ferret eyes darting from his hand to the officer waiting impatiently on the other side of the desk. "Tedious, I know, Captain, but the Hessian in charge will never release her without the paperwork in order."

The Provost dipped his pen one last time to scrawl his signature and, without looking up, said, "I know the widow once risked her neck for her rebel lover, but it doesn't necessarily mean Hampton'll be returning the favor. He may value his own hide overmuch to walk willingly into your snare. You haven't been able to find him—for all your effort—and he might not even be in town."

"Hampton is like the dove, ever constant to his mate." Glaring one-eyed out the barred window, mouth turned down in perpetual snarl, Blankenship muttered, "He's here. I can feel it." Snapping his watch closed, he returned it to his pocket, and fit his dragoon's helmet over the black silk scarf masking his scars—the death's head emblazoned on it stark in the light of the oil lamp.

Cunningham hurried to sprinkle the document with sand from the pounce pot and waved the paper about to dry the ink. "I hope you're right. I, for one, will revel to see the bastard twist in the wind."

Blankenship leaned over and snatched the page from the Provost's fingers, giving it a brief glance before folding it twice and stuffing it into his breast pocket. "Prepare a hanging party. Send out your invitations, Mr. Cunningham, and have your henchmen spread the word— guilty of treason, Anne Merrick will be dancing on the gallows tonight. The news will be sure to flush our quarry from the weeds."

Anne lay curled on her side, staring at the little square patches of blue sky exposed between the crisscross of rusty iron bars. Rough fingers pressed her cheek for a moment, and then the back of her neck. Trueworthy Jones dropped to a sit, gently tugging her by the shoulder until she relented, and rolled onto her back.

"You're still fevering . . ." he said, eyeing the full cup of broth he'd left that morning, untouched and gone cold. "And you haven't swallowed a drop of the beef tea the fellows made for you."

"Give it to another, Mr. Jones," Anne said. "I've no appetite."

Leaning in, Trueworthy smiled and said, "I worked the burial crew today, and I brought you some presents—bound t' give you some cheer." Digging down into his shirt, he pulled out a small clump of green grass no bigger than his fist. "Plucked this up when the guards weren't lookin'." He held the grass to Anne's nose. "In't it grand?"

Anne gave a little shrug, eyes drawn back to the blue sky beyond the bars of her prison.

The sailor reached into his shirt again, and brushed a bit of white fluff against her cheek. "Believe it or not, this was just rolling along the beach—soft as a feather from a cherub's wing—swansdown, I think."

Anne rolled back onto her side to gaze up at the window.

Jones gave her a nudge. "What say you come up on deck and take some air? Might spark your appetite . . . You have to eat something."

Anne sighed, her voice sounding as small as she felt. "Not today, Mr. Jones."

"The day's a-wasting, and the fresh air will do you some good . . ."

Anne didn't respond.

"Come, now." Trueworthy tugged at her sleeve. "I won't be taking no for an answer . . ."

Anne pulled her arm away and curled her legs up.

"Stop this nonsense!" Trueworthy leaned over, his face inches from hers. "You can't just give up!"

"Why not?" Anne rolled onto her back. "You were the one who said there was no hope. None."

"I said there's no hope for rescue, but that doesn't mean there's no hope at all! Once the war's over we'll all be . . ."

Anne heaved a breath. "Please, Mr. Jones—leave me be."

"No." Trueworthy stood. Straddling her prone body, he grabbed

Anne by the wrists, and levered her up to a sit. "I won't let you lie here and rot in the stink with the goners and the rats. Up, up!" he urged. "The bloody Hessian bastards yet allow us a bit of fresh air and sunshine, and by God, you are going to take some in."

Sapped of all energy to resist, Anne found herself pulled up to a stand. With bare toes grasping at the rough canvas pallet, her stomach lurched and her head spun, and she felt as if she were caught in a cyclone of liquid spinning down toward a great drain. Anne snapped her eyes wide-open and braced a hand to the seaman's bony shoulder to keep from dropping to her knees. If there'd been anything in her stomach, she would have lost it on the spot. She gasped. "This isn't a good idea, Mr. Jones—"

"Call me True," he said, wrapping an arm about her waist for support. "We're ol' mates, you and me, are we no'?"

She steadied her mien, took a deep breath, and blinked away the onslaught of dizziness. Ahead, a bright beam of daylight sliced in from the hatchway, beckoning, like a magical arrow pointing the way up from hell to heaven. Even her smile was weak. "All right, True—but only if you call me Anne."

"Easy goes it, Annie. That's the way . . ." True cautioned. "You'll have your sea legs under you in no time."

Anne shuffled forward step by step, True charting a mazelike course around the inhabited pallets of the men too sick and far gone for anyone to bother with. Anne turned her eyes from the gaunt faces and scabrous heads crawling with vermin, fearful of seeing her own end in their suffering.

Once they breached the hatchway at the top of the stairs, a strong voice called, *"Guten abend, madam."* The Hessian Captain and his grand mustache peered down over the quarterdeck railing, smiling.

Fevering and as filthy as she'd ever been in her life, Anne traversed the crowded gangway, leaning heavily on True's arm, greeted by her fellow prisoners doffing ragged caps, and wishing her good day, as if she were out taking the air on the Commons on a Sunday morning after church. Trueworthy led her to a halt amidships.

"This will do."

Anne shifted to lean on the railing, letting the fresh spring breeze wash the awful smell of the lower deck from her nostrils. "It must be Monday," she said, watching the miller's daughter moving along a clothesline taking in the wash. Anne imagined herself standing amid the snapping sun-bleached linen, folding clean bedclothes into neat, crisp-cornered packets.

"Good, isn't it?" True patted her on the back.

Anne nodded. "You can almost smell the lye soap."

"Ahoy, *Whitby!*"

A shallop knocked up to tie alongside and deliver the drinking water. Three of its crew scrambled up the larboard ladder and began working the derrick near the bow end of the *Whitby*, while the others secured chain and line to the first barrel being unloaded.

A single boatman began singing, and soon the rest joined in—including many of the sailor-prisoners watching the goings-on from the railings. The shanty provided the perfect rhythm for the men turning the windlass on the derrick to hoist the heavy barrel up out of the shallop:

> *I wrote me love a letter, I was on the* Jenny Lind
> *Heave away, me jollies, heave away!*
> *I wrote me love a letter and I signed it with a ring*
> *Heave away me jolly boys, we're all bound away!*

A very distinctive, gravelly voice rose loud above all others, and caught Anne's attention.

> *So it's farewell Nancy darlin', 'cause it's now I'm gonna leave ya*
> *Heave away, me jollies, heave away*
> *You promised that you'd marry me, but how you did deceive me*
> *Heave away me jolly boys we're all bound away*

After listening for a moment, Anne muttered, "It can't be him . . ." She moved toward the bow of the hulk for a better view of the operation, with True padding along, right on her heels. Her breath caught in her throat.

"It *is* . . ." she whispered.

Stamping boots to the deck in time with the song he sung, Tully marched in a tight circle with his mates, singing at the top of his lungs, putting his back into pushing on the arm of the windlass. The old smuggler looked up at Anne, and, his one eye asquashed in squint, he pounded a fist to his chest, and sang even louder.

> *Come get your duds in order 'cuz we're bound to cross the water*
> *Heave away, me jollies, heave away!*
> *Come get your duds in order 'cuz we're bound to leave tomorrow*
> *Heave away me jolly boys, we're all bound away!*

Tully wore his checkered shirt loose and open, sleeves rolled to elbows, arm muscles flexed as he pushing against the weight of the one-hundred-forty-gallon hogshead being lifted up from the shallop. Anne could clearly see Jack's little half-crown token swinging by a leather thong from Tully's neck.

Of a sudden, Anne felt them rush back inside—hope—faith—confidence—courage—filling her heart and mind like a gale wind whooshing into the sagging canvas of a ship floating free of the Doldrums. She grabbed hold of True to keep from being swept away.

"Would you look a-there!" True exclaimed. "Why, that jobber's wearin' a necklet just like yourn . . ."

It was an odd feeling, lying with back pressed against the concave curve of the barrel, legs tucked up. *Like a baby in a cradle . . .*

The barrel swayed on its chains as it was first hoisted up from the shallop, then swung over and lowered down with a bump into the cargo hold. Jack braced himself as best he could when the stevedores rolled his cask up into the big rack used for keeping barrel stores stationary when at sea.

The air he was breathing went from fresh to dank while Jack waited until all twelve barrels were rolled into place. Soon the jingling chains and the singing and shouting of the crew faded away, and the big cargo hatch banged shut.

"I'm in," Jack whispered to himself. Unlatching all the hooks, he pounded the meat of his fist against the barrelhead to pop the lid off.

Like a moth from its cocoon, he wriggled out of the hogshead, and took a moment to stretch his limbs. He rubbed the knuckles of his spine, and stamped circulation back into a left foot tingling as if a colony of ants were crawling over it.

Black as Pluto's chimney in here . . .

But for some faint slivers of light filtered around the frame of the hatch high above, the cargo hold was even darker than he'd expected. With a dearth of light, the foxfire seemed to shine even brighter, and Jack was glad he'd thought to bring it.

As Jack moved forward he caught the glint of animal eyes, and could hear the tiny claws on wood as the ship's rats scurried ahead of his footfalls. As his eyes grew accustomed, he could discern the humping shadow of the swarm moving away from his scent and his light, like a gray wave retreating back into an ocean of darkness.

What a stink!

Jack walked slow, with hand cupping his nose. The farther he moved from the water storage, the worse the smell grew. If someone were to cook up a soup made of soured cabbage, spoiled meat, and rotten eggs, it would be a sweet perfume by comparison. He turned toward a looming shadow on his right.

Stairs . . . and the source of the awful putrid stench. Jack shone his light up to the iron grate blocking the hatchway to the deck above, and mounted the stairs. All was dark on the deck above, but there he could hear the pathetic sound of human misery—coughing and moaning.

Jack went back to his barrel and fished out the whale oil, tricorn, and gunnysack he'd left behind. Plopping tricorn onto head, he dropped the oil bottle into the gunny, flung the sack over his shoulder, and put the false barrelhead back into place.

Can't be too careful.

Foxfire lighting the way, with quicker, more certain steps, Jack mounted the stairs and jimmied the flat end of his pry bar under the hasp on the lock. Whispering, "One, two . . ." he jerked down on the pry bar to pop the lock from its seat with a crack loud enough to make him wince. The grate opened with an ear-jarring squeal. Jack scrambled up to the between deck, surprised that he had not yet brought down the wrath of the Hessian guard.

Guided by his foxfire, Jack made his way toward the dim shaft of light just barely illuminating the stairs to the upper deck.

"Christ almighty!" he muttered, cupping one hand over nose and mouth. "The smell of this place could lift a scalp . . ."

It was no wonder the Hessians did not wander down to the tween deck. The floor was littered with a tumble of ragged blankets, rough pallets made of old sailcloth, and random piss and shit pails. Some of the sleeping places were occupied by human skeletons, whose miserable plight was made even more gruesome in the eerie green light. The thought of his Annie spending one second on this ship of horror was enough to make Jack want to keck up his insides.

Shouts and sharp whistles were sounded above deck, and the whole ship creaked with annoyance as the prisoners were herded down the stairs. Jack hunkered down, tucking his foxfire under his jacket. A weak voice to his left wheezed, "Cabbage-eating butcher . . ."

"No. I'm not a real Hessian," Jack whispered. "My name's Hampton. I've come for my woman—Anne Merrick—do you know her?"

"Ain't . . ." The voice halted to hack up a globule of phlegm. "Ain't no women on this here ship."

A sea of moving shadows clogged the stairway and hundreds of prisoners stumbled about in the dank dark as the tween was repopulated by the fitter prisoners who'd wisely spent the day above deck. Jack unsheathed his foxfire and moved forward through the crowd, whispering, "I'm looking for Anne Merrick. Do any of you know where she is?"

These men all stared, or turned away. No one answered his questions. A hand clawed at his leg, and fingers wound about to grasp his ankle as a voice rasped, "Any grub in that there poke sack?"

Jack pulled his leg free, panic rising from his gut and souring his mouth. *Dobbsy's a fucking drunk. Everything . . . the whole stupid plan based on the ramblings of a drunk . . .* He raised his voice. "I'm searching for a woman called Anne Merrick. Has anyone seen her? Does anyone know where I can find Anne Merrick?"

"She's in the gun room."

Jack spun around, his light shining on a man wearing a regimental jacket, sitting with his back braced to a column, his face an eruption of oozing pustules.

"Can you take me to her, friend?"

The soldier jerked in a halfhearted chuckle. "I'm spent, mister—lucky to make it up and down those stairs today."

"Where's the gun room?" Jack asked.

"Aft, ye lubber." The voice coming from behind bore a Scottish brogue. "They put her there when she miscarried her wean."

"Miscarried?"

"Aye. Keep moving toward the stern." A large hand landed on his shoulder, and pushed him forward.

Another shadow sidled up to him, and pulled him along by the arm. A young voice squeaked, "I'll take you."

Shining his light on a thin freckled face, Jack stumbled behind the boy, who was adept at slithering through the moving sea of human beings. A muttering and movement grew in their wake, and Jack could see others were following along. The boy pulled to a stop and pointed.

"Back behind those sea chests, you'll find her there. She's sick, mister."

Jack approached the makeshift wall, sweeping the foxfire across the area behind the chests.

Anne was propped up against the bulkhead, her hands limp on a woolen blanket covering her lap. Sitting tailor style, a small man with close-cropped hair and bushy brows pressed a cool cloth to the hollow of her neck. He glanced up at the light.

"Here I thought she was daft with fever, but there you come, just as she said you would."

Jack skirted around the chests, set his gunny aside, and dropped to his knees.

Anne smiled. "Perseus."

"You're so ill . . ."

The sailor rose to his feet, allowing Jack to sit beside Anne. "Weak and helpless as a cotton sack, she is. Miscarried a babe yestreen . . ."

Jack groaned. "A baby—oh, Annie . . ."

"I'm sorry," Anne whispered. "I didn't know . . . I would have . . . I could . . ."

"Shhh, shhh, shhh . . ." Jack leaned forward and grasped Anne by the hand. "Put it behind for now. I'm going to take you from this place and we'll go far away—begin anew. We'll make lots of babies. I promise." Jack pressed fingertips to the swelling welt slashed across her cheek, the skin hot to the touch, and clenched his teeth to combat the rage that whirled in his chest like a firestorm.

"The bastard cut her." The sailor leaned down and rasped in Jack's ear. "I fear it's festered bad . . ."

"Blankenship . . ." Anne winced, brushing Jack's hand away. "His mind's twisted with the thirst for revenge. He'll come for us. He'll never give up . . ."

"No . . ." Jack took Anne firmly by the hand. "We're together now. He won't ever harm you again—I swear it."

Anne relaxed and looked up at the sailor. "I told you, True. Land or sea . . ."

"That's right," Jack said. "Any monster, land or sea."

"You have a plan, Jack?" Trueworthy asked. "How do you mean to get her away?"

Jack turned and scanned the huddle of figures crowded around the aft corner of the tween deck, and he announced, "I'm going to fire this ship."

It was dead quiet for the longest time, until someone with a thick brogue said, "This fella's a madman."

Jack centered the foxfire and proceeded to empty the gunnysack and his pockets. "I've fuel, bomb, and quick match. I'm going to douse this end of the ship in oil and set the fuse alight. We'll all storm the deck after the explosion, my fellows, and make a great splash."

"We'll all be roasted to death, you eidgit," the brogue growled. "There's a padlock on tha' hatch."

Jack grinned and tugged the pry bar up from his weskit. "I need a strong man at the fore to spring open the hatch."

"Good lad! I'll take tha' duty." The Scotsman snatched the bar from Jack's hand.

"What about the guards and their muskets?" someone asked.

Anne's sailor said, "If the ship's afire, everyone will be jumping the rail—Hessians included."

"I won't lie. There's no guarantee," Jack added. "Some will perish. Some will be captured—but I think many stand a chance to break free."

"What about the goners?" a voice queried. "We can't just leave them to roast."

"No, we can't," Jack said. "Strong men will partner up with our weaker brothers. Get them to the beach, at least. Those lending a hand to the infirm are the first up the stairs."

"I don't know about the rest of you fellas," Trueworthy said. "But I'd ruther drown or die in flames than end up starved, wallowin' in my own piss and shit like them goners. I say we do it. I say we fire the ship."

"Aye. We've made ourselves sheep, and the wolves have been making a meal of us here," the Scotsman declared. "I'm for taking my chances. I'm for firing the ship."

Grunts of assent swept through the tween.

Trueworthy called out, "Any opposed? Speak up now . . ."

Jack sat holding his breath and Anne's hand. But for the shuffling of feet, and a random cough here and there, no one said a word. He stood up.

"We're agreed. This hell will end in smoke." He slapped Anne's sailor on the back. "Hold the light, friend, while I set the bomb?"

"Trueworthy Jones." The sailor offered a hand. "Rebel, mariner, and privateer."

"Jack Hampton." Jack clasped his new friend in a firm handshake. "American, scout, and spy—pleased to make your acquaintance."

After wedging the iron ball between beam and rafter, Jack uncorked the grenade and tucked one end of the six-foot match cord down into the powder. "This bomb'll blow the horns from the devil," he said.

"What happens, Jack, once you and Annie pull free?"

"I've a friend waiting with a boat . . . You can come with us . . . There's room."

Trueworthy shook his head. "My family's here on Long Island. I'm going home to my wife. Where'll you go?"

"Somewhere far away from this war," Jack said. "South, I think."

True nodded. "It's a nice warm winter down south."

Jack handed True his tinderbox. "There's a candle in there with the flint and steel. Kindle a light for us while I help Annie into her new duds."

Anne donned the disguise Stitch had provided in the gunny—a sailor's frock shirt, baggy trousers, and a snug yarn cap. "Can you get your hair up into it?" Jack asked, trying and failing to tuck the heavy strands under the little cap.

"It's too long," Anne said. "Do you have a knife?"

Jack nodded, digging his folding blade from his pocket.

Anne pulled her waist-length hair into a thick tail at the back of her neck. "Cut it off . . ." Jack groaned a little as he chopped it off just beneath her fist.

"It will grow back," she said, pulling on the cap. "It's better this way."

The dark deck was writhing with prisoners gathering belongings, struggling with the infirm, and shifting to crowd around the one staircase leading to the upper deck. Jack helped Anne over to the stairs, and the crowd parted to allow her a prime position holding on to the handrail. Trueworthy handed Jack the stump of candle he'd lit.

"Pass the word—get ready." Jack held the candle aloft and rasped, "I'm going to light the fuse—are you set with the pry bar, Scotsman?"

Crouched at the top of the stairs, the brogue called, "Aye!"

"There's six feet of quick match between flame and powder. Once the bomb blows, I want everyone to raise a ruckus—you can bellow like a bull with its pizzle caught in the garden gate, but we'll be orderly up the stairs. Agreed?"

There was a laugh and a muttered assent. Jack kissed Anne on the top of her woolly head. "Wait for me here. I'll be right back."

Jack splashed the oil on the decking just beneath the bomb. Taking in a deep breath, he touched the candle flame to the end of the fuse, ran back to the stairs, and wrapped his arm around Annie's waist. "Stick to me like a tick, you hear?"

Anne nodded.

The fuse fizzled and popped, and everyone watched the sparkling bright light climb up the length of the match cord and disappear for a blink of an eye, before exploding in a blinding, thunderous explosion and crack of splintered wood. The Scotsman pried open the grate, and, shouting like madmen, the prisoners moved up the stairs.

Flames crackled and crawled, licking at the tween deck ceiling, and smoke billowed out the gaping hole blown through the bulkhead. Jack pulled Anne up the stairs, her bare feet just skimming the treads. They tumbled out onto the confusion of the ship's deck. Everyone was making for the bow end, away from the fire. Hessian guards on duty spun in confusion, and more ran out of their quarters under the quarterdeck. Jack saw one soldier toss his weapon, strip his jacket, and fly over the rail.

Shouting, *"Alarm! Feuer! Alle mann von bord! Alle mann von bord!"* Jack dragged Annie toward the stern, to the accommodation ladder—the egress reserved for officers' use. He scooped her up into his arms and carried her down the stairway that sloped down to a landing three feet above the waterline.

One after another, men were leaping from the gangways like lemmings into the sea, the dark water dotted with bobbing heads swimming to shore. There was another explosion, and a ball of fire burst up through the upper quarterdeck, brightening the sky.

The fire roaring inside the hulk muffled the screams and shouts of the men leaping from the decks, and flames shot out from the barred window openings, and licked up the tarred planking on the hull.

"We're almost free . . ." Jack shouted, setting Anne back on her feet. She wavered and sagged against his chest, the heat of her fever penetrating the thin linen shirt she wore.

Jack stood and watched the commotion on the beach as the first of the survivors staggered out of the water. The scene was confused with shouts and shadows of horsemen riding to and fro with torches and lanterns bobbing about.

"Horses?" He scanned the dark coastline and whispered, "Come on, Tully . . . where *are* you?"

A bright pinpoint of light flashed three times in the trees to the left of the bay in answer to his question. Jack caught his breath and watched the spot, wanting to make certain his eyes weren't playing tricks when the signal flashed anew.

"There it is, darling girl! Good ol' Tully's waiting for us." Jack lifted Anne once again into his arms. Saying, "Here we go!" he stepped off the platform.

The weight of Anne's almost-unconscious form, and the heavy Hessian jacket, dragged them all the way down. Jack gave a mighty kick off the sandy bottom, and they rushed back up to break the surface. Jack pulled in a deep breath, and Anne floundered, coughing and sputtering.

The bay seemed calm in the dark, but the outrushing tide grabbed at their legs, pulling them both toward the chaos on the mill end of the beach, away from the calm regularity of Tully's blinking light.

Clutching Anne as best he could, it was impossible to make any headway swimming against the strong tide. The cold water had revived her some, and Anne kicked and flayed about, gasping, coughing, and choking all at once, taking in mouthfuls of salty water.

"Goddamn it!" Jack growled and just gave in to the current. He was able to keep Anne's head above water as they floated away from Tully's signal, to join the vast multitude bobbing toward the closest shore. Chest heaving, Jack helped Anne struggle up onto the beach.

Her cap was gone. His shoes were lost. He looked over his shoulder to see the tiny light blinking three times.

The scene on the beach reminded Jack of a time when a pack of weasels gained access to the hen yard on his family farm. Screaming chaos. The handful of armed dragoons and Hessians shouting, threatening, trying to gain control over the panicked and confused jumble of survivors—some barely alive, most struggling to catch a breath, very few getting their legs moving to break free and make a mad dash for the trees.

"Oh noooo!" Anne moaned. "He's coming for us."

Jack turned to see a mounted soldier wheel his horse and canter toward them, pointing with his saber. The dragoon shouted, "You, there!" The officer was wearing the death's-head helmet of the 17th· and his face was half-masked with a black scarf.

"It is him." Jack grabbed Anne and threw her over his shoulder like a sack of meal, and headed in, straight toward the worst confusion, but Blankenship moved his mount forward, blocking their path.

"You, there! *Soldat! Halt!*" Blankenship shouted, and Jack had no other recourse but to obey, as any good Hessian would.

"Have you seen the woman?" he asked, leaning down, staring with his one eye. *"Eine frau?* Have you seen her?"

Anne whimpered, and Jack looked the monster in the eye and saluted. *"Nein, Herr Hauptmann. Feuer. Alle mann von bord."*

Blankenship sat there, looming in the saddle, firelight flickering gold on the polished steel of his blade. Suddenly, he wheeled to the flash and bang of a musket shot, spurring his horse to give chase to a band of hearty souls making a break for the woodland.

Jack moved fast. Once he skirted around the mound of drowned bodies being gathered by a few lethargic and soggy Hessians, he ran as fast as he could with Anne bouncing on his shoulder, down a rocky shore, to where he thought he'd seen the blinking light.

"Tully!" Jack called as loud as he dared. *"Tully, where are you?"*

❧ TWENTY-TWO ❧

*I dwell not upon the vapours of imagination; I bring reason
to your ears; and in language, as plain as A, B, C, hold up
truth to your eyes.*

THOMAS PAINE, *The American Crisis*

THE DAWNING

Wallabout Bay was bright with the light cast from the ball of flame that
was once the *Whitby*. Bellowing huge gray clouds of smoke, the orange and yellow light flickered on a score of bodies bobbing facedown
in the shallows.

Hessians and dragoons with bayonets attached prodded the exhausted survivors into ranks, few of them able to stand on two feet.
Torch in hand, Blankenship maneuvered his stallion up and down the
rows of wet, shivering prisoners, examining each and every one.

Mustache drooping, in shirtsleeves and bare feet, the Hessian
Captain called, "I'm sorry, Captain, but ze voman is not among ze
survivors . . ."

Blankenship dismounted, his voice a low growl. "She was in your
keeping, sir . . ." From his pocket he jerked the document the Provost
had signed, poked it under the Hessian's nose, and screamed, "YOUR
KEEPING!"

The Hessian took a step back. "This voman vas very ill, sir. I do not think she could have survived. Burned—she is—perhaps drowned."

"Bloody stupid German cunt." Blankenship turned his back to the Hessian and marched over to where a pair of his dragoons oversaw the gathering of the dead. "Have you found her?"

"No, Captain, but we haven't sorted through them all. There're many yet floating out in the bay."

"Ahh, now . . . Give it up, fellows. You won't be finding Anne Merrick among the dead, Cap'n One-Eye, and you know it."

Blankenship spun to the voice. A short sailor with close-cropped hair dropped the corpse he was dragging, and padded off to fetch another. Blankenship called out to him, "You, there— Halt!"

The sailor froze in his tracks and turned about, sharp. With an oddly merry grin on his face, he knuckled his brow in salute. "Aye, Cap'n?"

"Where is she?"

"Anne Merrick? Why, she's disappeared in a puff of smoke!" Trueworthy laughed, and clapped his hands together. "Poof!"

Blankenship tossed off his helmet and rushed forward, saber zinging from scabbard. "Tell me where she is."

"Certainly, Cap'n. Happy to be of service." Trueworthy pulled back his shoulders. "Annie's with Jack, and he's taking her to a safe place—to a place where you'll never find 'em."

Blankenship made a guttural sound—as if he were choking. Tugging the silk scarf from his head, he turned to glare at the Whitby.

"Only one eye in yer head, but you see now, don't you, Cap'n?" The little sailor stood there grinning. "Aye, the fire was no simple happenstance, was it? It was all Jack's doing, aye? And we helped him—helped our brother rebel, yes we did."

Blankenship's fingers gripped the hilt of his sword, the scar tissue slashing across his face tight as his mouth, twisted in a rictus of anger and pain. An animal growl rumbled deep in his chest.

"Oh yes . . . They're off together into the happy ever after, Anne and her Jack. Far from this war . . ." The sailor laughed. "Leaving you with naught but a face uglier than any baboon's arse . . ."

Blankenship's saber flashed once in the flickering firelight, and he brought the furious edge down on the sailor's neck.

Dropping to his knees, the little man pressed a palm to the blood oozing down over his chest, and, still smiling, he muttered, "Thank you, Cap'n . . ." and toppled over onto the sand.

With Anne over his shoulder, Jack stumbled along the riverbank, searching the dark vista for the signal light. He began to fret that the blinking light he saw from the deck of the *Whitby* was but a figment of his imagination, when he heard a rowboat thumping against the rocks, and he called out softly, *"Is that you, Tully?"*

A small dory floated out from the shadows into view, with Tully at the prow. "Arrah, Jack! I *knew* you'd make it!"

"A welcome sight, you are." Jack splashed into the river. "What happened to your light?"

"Had to toss it in the drink when a pair of dragoons came nosin' about the shoreline." Tully jumped out to help Jack hoist Anne into the boat.

Anne's eyes fluttered open. "Hello, Tully."

Tully heaved a sigh. "Thank God, she's alive."

"We got her in the nick of time. Blankenship's on the beach looking for her as we speak." Jack pulled himself into the forward end of the dory to sit with legs sprawled and back braced against the seat plank. He tugged Anne's wet, shivering form into his arms and commenced to rubbing her briskly. "We did it, Tully—approached like foxes, fought like lions . . ."

"And now we disappear like birds." Tully tossed over a pair of woolen blankets, took a seat, aft, and put his back to the oars, turning the boat toward the Manhattan coast.

Jack bundled Anne into the warm dry wool, and as the hue and cry of Wallabout Bay gave way to the serene dip and trickle of Tully's muffled oars, he watched the fiery ball of flame diminish to no more than a spark in the distance.

"That's it." Jack whispered in Anne's ear. "We've done our duty,

Annie. We're going far from this war—you and me—south—where the sun shines brighter, and it's always warm."

Anne laid her fevered cheek to his chest and sighed. "I don't care where we go, as long as I'm with you."

"You've the right of it, darling girl. We're a pair, you and I." Jack pulled her close. "Inseparable."

❧ EPILOGUE ❧

They have refined upon villainy till it wants a name. To the fiercer vices of former ages they have added the dregs and scummings of the most finished rascality, and are so completely sunk in serpentine deceit, that there is not left among them one generous enemy.

THOMAS PAINE, *The American Crisis*

AUGUST, 1778
BRITISH COMMAND HEADQUARTERS, NEW YORK CITY

"I must say, Legion green suits you, Edward!" Young William Cathcart welcomed Blankenship to his office with a firm handshake. "You cut a fine figure in your new togs. Whiskey?"

Edward Blankenship nodded and took a seat in front of a desk nearly covered over with a large map of the American colonies. Doffing his new leather helmet, he fluffed the green plume before setting it aside, unbuttoned his smart green coattee, and said, "After so many years wearing regimental red, I find I rather favor this green, Colonel."

"I am so pleased we were able to woo you away from the Seventeenth." Cathcart took a seat behind the desk and poured two glasses of Scots whiskey. "I never thought it possible."

Blankenship adjusted the black scarf he wore tied over one eye. "A promotion and the promise of waging a real war against these rebels was all the wooing I required, sir."

Lord Cathcart slid a full glass of whiskey over the polished walnut, and raised his own in toast. "To green jackets and the newest addition to our new British Legion—*Major* Edward Blankenship."

Edward downed his drink, and hitched his chair forward to focus on the map. "Tell me, where is our Legion bound?"

"South." Cathcart leaned in and dragged a finger down along the coastline from New York to Georgia. "Be ready to live in your saddle, Major. Ours is to be a hard company of raiders. We'll be on the move—swift and light—for these are no conventional battles we'll be waging."

"Excellent!" Blankenship slipped off his mask. His scarred mouth twisted into a smile, and he bent close to study the map with his single eye. "This is a happy turn of fortune's wheel for me for—as you know—I'm not one for convention."

All countries have sooner or later been called to their reckoning; the proudest empires have sunk when the balance was struck; and Britain, like an individual penitent, must undergo her day of sorrow, and the sooner it happens to her, the better.

THOMAS PAINE, *The American Crisis*

HISTORICAL NOTES

The following characters and terms appearing in this novel were drawn from the historical record. All other characters evolved in the gray matter between my ears.

In order of appearance:

Jane MacCrae—on her way to marry a British officer, she was murdered and scalped by Burgoyne's raiding Indians. Her killing was successfully exploited by the Patriot propaganda machine, and turned sentiment away from the Loyalist cause.

Lieutenant General John Burgoyne—Commander of the "Canada Army" and armed with a plan to end the war, Gentleman Johnny surrendered his five-thousand-man army after a series of battles that are regarded as a major turning point in the American War for Independence and in world history.

Mrs. Fanny Loescher—the mistress General Burgoyne brought along to keep him company during the Saratoga Campaign.

Brigadier General Simon Fraser—mortally wounded at Bemis Heights, he perished on the Baroness's dining table and was buried on a redoubt overlooking the battlefield.

Baroness Frederika von Riedesel—with children in tow, the Baroness braved the wilds of Canada and America to follow her husband on campaign, and authored a detailed memoir of her experiences.

Major General Baron Friedrich von Riedesel—survived the Saratoga campaign to surrender his sword.

Colonel Friedrich Baum—suffered a mortal wound at the Battle of Bennington and died soon thereafter.

Brigadier General John Stark—a member of Rogers Rangers during the French and Indian War, the daring strategies he employed led to victory at Bennington.

Colonel Daniel Morgan—confounded the enemy by taking advantage of American skill with the rifle and using guerilla and targeting tactics considered dishonorable at the time.

General Benedict Arnold—there is an unnamed monument at the Saratoga battlefield paying tribute to the injured leg of this American hero, whose name is now listed as a synonym for the word "traitor."

Tim Murphy—the diminutive Irish marksman reputed, among other things, to have fired the shot that killed Simon Fraser at Bemis Heights.

Harriet Acland—pregnant Lady Acland traveled through enemy territory to her wounded husband being held prisoner of the Continental Army. She nursed him back to health and they returned to England.

Thomas Paine—radical author of *Common Sense* and *The Crisis* pamphlet series used to incite revolution and inspire the citizen-soldiers at Valley Forge.

Major General Friedrich Wilhelm von Steuben—this Prussian volunteer authored America's first manual on military regulations without being able to speak English, and transformed common rabble into a proper army.

Azor—Steuben's beloved hound.

Lieutenant Friedrich Gotthold Enslin—the first American soldier to be court-martialed and subsequently drummed out of the military for engaging in homosexual behavior.

Colonel Tupper and Colonel Malcolm—the officers presiding at Enslin's court-martial and drumming out.

General George Washington—Commander-in-Chief of the Continental Army, he established a network of spies to gather the intelligence vital to the cause of Liberty.

Billy Lee—the manservant at Washington's side throughout the Revolution. Citing Billy's "faithful services," Washington freed his slave in his will in 1799.

Lydia Darragh—when the British military in occupied Philadelphia commandeered a room in her home, the clever Quakeress eavesdropped and smuggled the intelligence learned to General Washington in Valley Forge.

Betsy Loring—General Howe's Faro-loving, champagne-swilling, blond bombshell of a mistress.

Peggy Shippen and Peggy Chew—Philadelphia belles who vied for the attention of Major John André. After the British withdrew, Peggy

Shippen courted and married the new American officer in command, General Benedict Arnold.

Lord William Schaw Cathcart—promoted twice on the field of battle, he earned an appointment to command the British Legion.

Major John André—the driving force behind the Meschianza was hung for a spy in 1780.

The Meschianza—the extravagant gala event to commemorate General Howe's return to England at a cost of over £12,000—a huge number for the time, in a country at war.

William Cunningham—occupied New York's Provost Marshall and all-round nasty fellow.

Hercules Mulligan—tailor to the British officer corps in Occupied New York City and leader of the Mulligan Spy Ring.

Richmond—the Provost's hangman.

The *Whitby* —the first of several notorious prison ships parked out on Brooklyn's Wallabout Bay (present-day Naval Yard) burned in the night in February of 1778. It is estimated more than 11,000 American Patriots died from hunger, disease, and privation imprisoned aboard these British hulks.

Notes

Some of the dates for the actual events depicted have been manipulated, compressed, or expedited to suit the pace of this fictional account.

The number of lashes dealt the Redcoat soldiers court-martialed for desertion was adjusted from a thousand lashes (according to the record) to five hundred lashes. I feared the former, though accurate, would seem unbelievable to the modern reader.

The parole words and countersigns used in the telling of this story are taken directly from historical record.

The Meschianza included a regatta, a medieval jousting tournament, a grand banquet and ball, but most of the guests were neither costumed nor masked.

READERS GUIDE FOR

The Turning of Anne Merrick

by Christine Blevins

DISCUSSION QUESTIONS

1. "It's the least likely who make the best of spies." What are some of the differences in skills, social standing, religion, and character that aided the various spies in this story in their pursuit of intelligence?

2. "Aye, Annie—make yourself pleasant, and I'll commence baking," Sally said. "Time for us t' go a-soldiering." Discuss the frustrations Anne felt in serving her country. Compare Anne's situation to issues faced by modern-day women in service.

3. How do you think Anne and Sally's attitudes might have been affected by their proximity to and relationships with the enemy while following Burgoyne's army?

4. "Beware, Mr. Cunningham, the woman is an arch deceptress. There is no correspondence between her fair face and her foul heart." Anne wrestles with the sins she has committed and continues to commit in the name of her cause. Can deceit ever be good? Name the consequences—good and bad—for the deceivers in this story.

5. The slave woman, Pink Dunaway, grieves the death of her master and balks when given her freedom. Was this a rational reaction? How would you react to such a sudden change in status?

6. Anne and Sally are often parted from their men over the course of the war. In the eighteenth century, British and German soldier wives and children routinely followed husbands and fathers from garrison to battlefield. What are some of the benefits inherent in having women travel with the army? The detriments?

7. Can imaginative storytelling enhance the understanding of history? Discuss the differences between reading a work of historical fiction based on American history and the history one learns in school.

8. "Our army is outmatched and outgunned at every turn and sorely lacks supply and matériel. Our soldiers are daily deserting by the drove. The only way we can ever hope to defeat the British Empire is by our wits . . ." The Patriots resorted to unconventional methods in their fight against the British, such as the use of snipers to target officers, guerrilla warfare, and scorched-earth tactics considered immoral and akin to modern-day terrorism. The British were equally brutal in their use of Indian raiders and the horrific mistreatment of prisoners of war. Have the notions of civilized warfare and rules of war changed from the eighteenth to twenty-first centuries? How?

9. Edward Blankenship is a monster of Anne's making, his rage fueled by his thirst for revenge. Do you think she deserves the consequences for action taken for a higher cause?

10. What do you think is the meaning behind the title of this book?